PLAN TO STAY™

Funding Provided By:

The Peachtree City Library
Expansion & Renovation Project
Voter Approved Bond Referendum

November 4, 2003

He Drown She in the Sea

Also by Shani Mootoo

Cereus Blooms at Night

Out on Main Street

The Predicament of or

He Drown She in the  Sea

SHANI MOOTOO

Grove Press
New York

Published simultaneously in Canada
Printed in the United States of America

FIRST EDITION

Library of Congress Cataloging-in-Publication Data
Mootoo, Shani.
 He drown she in the sea / Shanti Mootoo.
  p. cm.
 ISBN 0-8021-1798-8
  1. West Indians—Canada—Fiction. 2. World War, 1939–1945—Caribbean
Area—Fiction. 3. Caribbean Area—Fiction. 4. Friendship—Fiction.
5. Immigrants—Fiction. 6. Islands—Fiction. I. Title.
PR9199.3.M6353H4 2005
813'.54—dc22   2004065653

Grove Press
an imprint of Grove/Atlantic, Inc.
841 Broadway
New York, NY 10003

05 06 07 08 09 10 9 8 7 6 5 4 3 2 1

For Dhanwatee and Deoraj Samaroo,
and Essie Boodoosingh—

everywhere you are

He Drown She in the Sea

The Dream

Almost a decade after he left Guanagaspar, a dream he used to have recurs. Though he lives by the sea now, the sea in this dream is invariably the other one, that of his earliest childhood. In the dream he first notices that there are no frigate birds in the sky and that the sea has suddenly and strangely retreated. Then, there are no waves but the ocean undulates, and the level of the water on the horizon rises rapidly. On the exposed floor of the ocean gasping fish slap themselves until, exhausted, they give up and are still. The sea begins to swell, swelling until its surface is smooth and shiny, like a taut plastic bag on the verge of bursting. And he realizes that the reason there are no frigates in the sky is that from there they already saw the magnitude of the ocean's bulge, and, predicting the outcome of its inevitable and imminent belch, they took off to seek refuge.

For several minutes he watches to make sure he is not mistaken. The ocean is heaving now, sighing with its unusual weight, inhaling and exhaling painfully. There are many people on the beach. People whom he previously saw through the windows when the taxi he rode in on mornings with his mother passed through villages on the way to the city. Although all the people have noticed the swelling and are pointing at the sea, they settle themselves on the beach as if to stay and watch. He is the only one concerned. He begins to analyze and strategize. He can see that if the sea continues to grow like that, it is bound to split its plastic-like surface, emptying it of its intestines and all that it has swallowed.

He runs up and down the beach screaming to people. They see only a little boy, too young to know anything, too young to pay him attention.

When they ignore him, he begins forcibly pushing them off the beach, trying to sound like a reasonable adult, a big man begging them to get back inside and board up their houses, to shut their windows and doors and stuff blankets, newspapers, anything in the cracks. But he is too small, too young, for them to take seriously. One or two groups of people do get up and leave, but not because of his warnings; they have just had enough of a day at the beach. He rushes over to stray dogs and shoos them up the beach. He lurches at corbeaux that are too engrossed in the carcasses of dead fish and other animals to notice what the frigates saw from higher up.

He thinks of his mother and that if no one else will listen, he must save at least his mother and himself. He races up to his own house and explains to her what he has seen. He tells her that in order to protect themselves they must quickly and carefully prepare their house. His mother listens. She believes him. She goes outside and fetches all the chickens, brings them inside, and they begin to prepare ... he shuts and locks the front door, and she and he diligently seal every space between the door and the rough jamb, finally shoving a table up hard against it. Anywhere light from outside enters their house they shove a piece of paper, a piece of cloth, or nail boards over it. They mostly keep silent, uttering only quick orders. Their ears are trained on the ocean, listening to it as it continues to groan and creak under the strain of its swelling. When they are sure that the house is sealed tight, that no water, light, or air can enter, they sit down next to each other and await its thunderous cracking apart.

Then the quiet descends. The birds and the dogs are silent. Everything is still. Neither coconut, mango, nor lime trees rustle. The breeze that is a constant seems suddenly to have gasped in awe of what is progressing, as if holding its breath in terror. There are no sounds of the other people. The boy and his mother realize they will lose many people they know.

In the dream he knows that everyone else will be swept away by the sea, but it is more a feeling of regret that this will happen than one of panic.

And then the creaking of the ocean begins. As it gets louder, the dogs go mad, and they yelp in helplessness. The corbeaux begin to squeal and shriek and fight each other for space in the topmost branches of the trees. The wind starts up again, and in no time whips around the houses and trees and through the bushes. Then the humans cry out as they at last see what is about to happen, and he holds his breath and wraps his arms around his mother's waist. She clutches the chickens. He draws her to stand against the farthest wall of the tiny house, fairly certain, but not entirely, that they will be spared. There they wait. Anytime now. But no crash is audible above the din of the wind and the shrieking. The sole indication that the ocean has indeed burst open is the sound of water creeping swiftly up the beach, up over the sea grape vines, into the crocus patch, drowning all the orange flowers, and then up, way up the clay yard. They hear the thirsty clay ground suck at the first taste of water, but suddenly there is so much water rising that the ground chokes and spits and then succumbs in silence. They feel water rising under the house, lapping at the boards. And he knows that he has done the right thing by stuffing the cracks, because the secret to not being swept away is that no water, not the tiniest drop, must enter the house, otherwise it can pry open the boards like a crowbar and rip the house apart. There is one final surge, coming at them so high now that it crashes at half height of the house. But the house is like a rock in the ocean. The sea rises around it and then passes by. The water rolls on up the land a bit, and then they hear its retreat, and when the ground around them crackles dry again, they know it is safe to look out. He opens the door to find that the house is entirely intact, in its place, not budged an inch. It has been washed clean by the salty water. However, all around, the shattered remains of houses

*are strewn, and in the ocean, now settled back in its place, are floating
bodies and wood chips the size of matchsticks: the remains of boats, houses,
and furniture. He and his mother make their way to the water's edge and
see the bodies of people they know. Uncle Mako in his red marino and blue
swimming trunks floats by, and the boy and his mother sigh and shrug and
say to each other, "If only, if only."*

I

How Madam's Mouth Runneth Over

The Caribbean island of Guanagaspar. Present day.

It was not yet the end of the rainy season, and the air in the house bristled with all manner of trouble. Even though Piyari had already cleaned everything that same day, Madam took up the dust cloth and wiped counters, pictures, ornaments, and furniture as she spoke. Perspiration glistened on Madam's forehead and upper lip. Rivulets of it escaped from under her uncoiffed hair, slipped down her graying temples, and pooled about her neck, causing the plain gold-plate chain she wore to shimmer.

"Who would have thought, Piyari, that so late in life a person could get another chance? Look: I have two adult children, and with no warning whatsoever, in what should be the downward slope of life, a light light up, brighter than the sun, to point me in a whole new direction."

Madam crumpled the dust cloth into a ball, took a quick and deep breath, and pressed the dirty rag to her face. Piyari, startled, leaped forward and as quickly withdrew, realizing at once that it wasn't really possible for Madam to suffocate herself in this manner. She grimaced. How could Madam talk of happiness in one breath, she wondered, and in the next bury her face in that dirty rag full of dust and that white powdery mold that covered everything in the muggy months? But she was becoming used to the unusual behavior. Madam dragged the cloth across her face and, in so doing, erased the thick application of reddish-brown color from her lips. A dark wetness blossomed about the armpits of the yellow silk blouse Piyari had ironed for her just that morning.

"Let me say once and for all: from the day I left my mother's house and got married, nobody has bothered to ask me what I think or what I feel. Nobody in this country can imagine that I might have feelings. Not all those people who like to take pictures of Boss and me and put them in their papers, not even Boss, and certainly not the children. I pass my whole life in the service of those two children, and now look: I wouldn't see Jeevan unless I hand out formal invitation to him and his wife. And Cassie? You could understand why my only daughter had to go so far away, on the other side of Canada, to live? Well, if I didn't know better before, better and me have at long last become acquaintances. Everything change, Piyari. I am not stepping backward—I cannot go back to the way it used to be. Is time for a fresh start, in truth."

Piyari had learned to spot a story coming. She slid one of the caned high-back chairs away from the dining table and plopped herself down. An hour or two could pass like this: Piyari sitting, turning her whole body sometimes, sometimes just her head, to face Madam as Madam hustled, cleaned, and talked. And the more Madam provoked her future with stories of the summer past, the harder, the faster she swept, dusted, and polished furniture, cleaned cupboards, threw out old and long-unused household items. Madam's confidences bestowed much importance upon Piyari, but she knew well that such a privilege had the potential to one day prove burdensome. Still, this revolt brewing in her employer's house, right before her very eyes, she relished. And besides, the house, Piyari noticed, had never—at least not before that summer of which Madam babbled—been so spotless.

Madam put down the cloth and picked up a ceramic vase rendered in the shape of a fish that had leaped out of the sea high into the air and was captured by the artist just as it hit the water on its arched back. She lifted her head to the ceiling, closed her eyes, and ran a finger along the pale, curved belly line of the fish, and a fingernail into the deep blue iridescent grooves of its well-wrought tail fin. The high-pitched squeal of fingernail against glazed ceramic broke her reverie. She squeezed the unyielding fish with both her hands, then shook the vase. There was a slug-gish, guttural swish of old water. It had been almost a month since there were fresh flowers in the house. The water was at least that old, and surely, bitter with the odor of rotted chrysanthemum remains. Madam put her nose to the gaping mouth of the fish and sniffed. Piyari straightened herself, ready to answer to the accusation, ready to get back to her business of housecleaning, of doing chores like washing out that vase. But Madam did not even wrinkle her nose. Instead, with sudden swiftness, as if she had smelled a revelation in the belly of the fish, she gathered up and twisted her shoulder-length hair into a bun. With pins fetched erratically from the pocket of her skirt, she secured the bun, whipped the cloth off the table again, and began wiping, wiping, wiping every ornament in sight. Piyari made a mental note to wash out the fish vase.

Madam executed a sharp about-face and marched into the kitchen. Piyari jumped up and followed. Madam opened the door of the freezer compartment and stared for a long time at its contents. Piyari knew if she stayed still long enough, Madam would begin to reveal more about that holiday on the west coast of Canada and that the refrigerator/freezer would be as clean as the day it was bought, without her having to lift a finger. When Madam started pulling out frozen packages of meat and plastic containers of leftovers and piling them up on the kitchen table, Piyari leaned up against the counter and relaxed.

"What we keeping leftovers for? Throw them out. Look at this fridge. Throw everything out. Don't keep a damn thing. I have to say it yet again? Is time for a fresh start."

When the freezer was emptied, Madam looked around. Piyari anticipated her need and quickly fetched a bowl of soapy water and a sponge. Madam dipped the sponge in the water.

"Christmas round the corner, Piyari, but summer—like it was only yesterday—that summer just past was the candle burning bright on my future. And today, today-self, the future is unfolding." She turned back to the freezer.

"But let not one-man-Jack have cause to say I spoil their Christmas. I, exemplary wife, will make no waves before then. We will put up the tree—tell the yard boy to climb on top the cupboard in the storeroom and to bring down the white plastic tree, not the green one, but the one that nice and white and look like it have snow on the branches, and we will put out some ornaments. We will set the table for Christmas, usual as usual: turkey, ham, pastels, sorrel. But, mark my word, come New Year's, it will be a different story, because I am finished with 'exemplary.'"

Piyari perked up and, for the sake of the possibility, as slim as it was, of taking a little holiday time off, risked interrupting the flow of Madam's thoughts.

"You planning something for New Year's, Madam? Is best if I know all now so, so I will know what days off you giving me. But all what so will be happening, Madam?"

"All what so is happening? All now so, you see me standing here in front of this fridge, things happening. You asking? I not fraid to say, you know— not fraid, that is, to say to *you,* but what I have to say is not any and everybody business and is not to travel, eh. You hearing me good?"

Madam looked in Piyari's direction, but Piyari knew that she did not really see her. Madam inhaled and breathed out long and hard, then slowly shook her head as if regretfully resigned to the weight of what she was about to say. "Now, you must know, and you must know good, that until I was sitting right there in Cassie's living room in her apartment in Vancouver, with the telephone on the side table next to me, until the moment that I did it, I had had no plan to see the Eggman again. You know who I talking about? Ent you remember the Eggman?"

Piyari frowned. She did remember him. She was eager to hear why her Madam would telephone a man like him. She had heard that he had done well for himself up there, but still, it was strange that Madam would look him up.

"It was the same day that Boss left. You could well say that I waited for Boss to leave and then I ring the Eggman, and you would be right. But to this day the Eggman has not made any judgment whatsoever about me ringing him so. He say to me that if I need to go anywhere, if I want to shop, to see sights, to visit anybody, he was ready anytime to take me. He wanted to come that same day. But, I say, I busy. I wasn't being truthful. After all, what I would be busy doing up there? Life up there was quiet-quiet, and I liked the change from this place. I wasn't busy one bit. Still, I didn't think it right to behave too-too eager."

The main body of the refrigerator took longer to empty and sponge clean. Piyari, not too surprised that she hadn't received an answer to her sideways plea for time off, helped with this only so much as to give the impression of keeping busy, but reserved her movements to a minimum so as not to distract Madam's chatter. She thought of the Eggman coming to the house before he emigrated, in his rusted-out and rattling car to bring a basin of eggs, or a side of a goat, or a fowl plucked clean. If, when he came to the gate, the children were in the yard playing, they would run inside to call their mother, and well enough away from his seeing or hearing, they giggled and teased her about him.

Madam rested a bowl of rice on the table. Piyari picked it up. She removed the plate that covered it, smelled the contents, covered it again, and then, with the cloth she continuously

clutched for good effect, she wiped the condensation that had
formed about the bowl. She set it back down exactly where
Madam had put it. Madam examined a little piece of lime in
cellophane that had gotten lost at the back of the second shelf.
She handled various vegetables as if making a decision, and then,
her decision seemingly made, put aside a celery stalk, a sweet
pepper, and two hot peppers.

Piyari thought of Boss. He had laughed at the Eggman, too,
for coming around so often and getting no more, naturally, than
a five-minute conversation with Madam, and even so with the
gate drawn between them. Boss used to make good play of
being jealous, but of course this never amounted to anything. And
Madam herself used to laugh at the Eggman. Still, she always
seemed pleased by the teasing his visits engendered.

"I didn't ring him again. I didn't want to appear overly forward. Then two days pass, and thank blessed God I didn't ring
him again, because just as I was opening my phone book, it was
he who ring. He ask if Cassie and I had already made plans for
dinner that night. I tell him I would have to wait and ask her
when she return from her work. Like he didn't hear me, he asked
if *I* had plans. But I realize now that he well hear me. I say again
I had to wait until Cassie come home before I could really answer. He laugh—he has that way of laughing, you know? He say
he would ring back later.

"When Cassie came back, I didn't say a thing about his phone
call. Time pass, and since he didn't ring again, I start to prepare
dinner, and she and I eat. To tell the truth, I was disappointed.
But as I was cleaning up the kitchen, the doorbell ring. It was
his voice on the intercom. Well, Piyari-girl, I get confused. Cassie
raise her eyes, she put her hands on her hips and say, 'It's the
Eggman, Mummy. I didn't know you were expecting him.'

"She let him up, and before he arrive at the door, she went
straight to her room. Well, I get vexed with her for leaving me

like that. I went and tell her to come back outside and sit down. She talk back at me, that child, grinning like a grouper, 'He didn't bring any eggs with him?'

"She reckless too bad. I had to put my finger on my lips to hush her up. Sometimes she has no sense, that child.

"'I don't think he came to see me,' she answer me back, and she turn to face the computer screen. Well, she rile me up for so, but she is not a child. When they living abroad so, by themselves, they change plenty-plenty, you know. You can't make them do anything anymore.

"I standing up here in front of this refrigerator in my kitchen telling you this, and I can remember exactly how it was when I see him. All these years pass, and he didn't live an easy life like the kind of life people we know does live—his life wasn't all that easy—and still he never turned into a hard man, you know. He remain kind. And he was always good-looking, in a soft way. His skin lighten in the cold weather. He used to be dark-dark here. But he got a little fairer, and it suits him."

Madam sucked her teeth as if in resignation and added, "He would have made nice children, but he never had any. Not one. He would have made a good father, yes. I used to like the harder look in a man, but suddenly I see Harry St. George as a kind man, strong in a quiet kind of way. Not mousy, but not full of himself, either, and not bad-looking one bit. I offer him a sandwich, but he say he wasn't hungry. In any case, I still make the tea and a cheese sandwich and put it on the table in front of him.

"When Cassie finally make an appearance, he ask if she wanted to take a drive through the city and then up a mountainside road to a place they call Cypress Park. He wanted to go there so she and he could show me the city, all light up, from there. She say she had work to do but that it was definitely something I should not miss. It was like she eat hot pepper and her mouth wouldn't stay shut. She say she needed to concentrate on her work, but

the weather was just right for that kind of sightseeing, and so I
should take the chance to leave the house and get a bit of fresh
air. She didn't wait for an answer from me; she take a set of keys
off a hook on the wall and give them to me, saying not to worry
about time, that I should just come and go as I please. Well, I
can't tell you how vexed I get with her. I follow her back to her
room to ask her if she gone mad. I tell her that her father would
kill me, and I ask her what would people say back home if they
knew Shem Bihar wife had gone sightseeing with a man at night.
She say, 'And how would anybody know? Who knows you up
here? Guanagaspar is not exactly a place that people are too concerned about up here. Go and enjoy yourself. For once, at least!'

"So, I change my clothes. I put on a nice-enough dress and
a little color on my lips. I daub cologne behind my ears. I wrap a
cardigan around my shoulders, and out I went. You know, it was
the first time since I married that I went anywhere with a man
other than Boss.

"And he know the city well. After almost twenty years of living up there, I suppose it is to be expected. He give up some of
his Guanagasparian ways, though, you know. He used to be so
quiet here—almost frighten-frighten to come in our neighborhood—but he is a man of his own making now, you know. He
has his own business, and he employs people. He really come
up good, and with not one bit of help from anybody. If you see
where he was born, where he and his mother used to live when
he was a child. Well, the evening I speaking about, we drive—
we drive so much that if we had done that over here, we would
have circled the island a good few times in that one day-self. And
you know, nine, ten o'clock in the night it is still light—nobody
in their house sleeping—everybody outside—the streets full of
people walking, eating ice cream, window-shopping—and your
head turning this way and that, nonstop, because the place pretty-
pretty—you can't help but watch everything! We pass through a

park that was bigger than Marion. Stanley Park, I believe they call it? And we cross bridge after bridge after bridge, to all knd of different neighborhoods, one area they name Chinatown and another they call Gastown, to a market where, in the daytime, they sell fish and meat and yet the market clean-clean-clean and it don't have no bad smell whatsoever, and as I telling you, everywhere we went, he had some story to tell. He tell me the history of this and a story about that—but this history business is of no interest to me, in truth, yes. So I wasn't really listening to what he was saying. I mean, what is the point in knowing so much detail about a place you are not from?

"In any case, I thought Mr. Harry was just showing off how much he know. I say to myself he only interested in hearing himself speak, so stay quiet and let him speak. But a few times he ask me a question. And when I nod instead of answering his question, he realize I wasn't really listening. It was then I come to know that he was talking to me in truth, and not just to hear himself.

"So I try my best to listen. But is like you have to learn how to pay attention. It takes energy to pay so much attention, in truth. You know what I mean, Piyari? It make me uncomfortable for so to know he really addressing me when he speaking.

"For all the talk he talk, suddenly, driving up the mountain, he get quiet. I get the feeling his mind was on me, me sitting there in the car with him. It was a strange feeling. I was uncomfortable, yes.

"At a pullout halfway up the mountain road, he stop the car and we get out. It was so high up, Piyari. It was like looking down at a city from an airplane window, a city shimmering with lights."

Piyari, not having been in an airplane, couldn't imagine it at all.

"Even with the cardigan I was wearing, it was too cold to be outside so. But he don't miss a thing. He noticed me gripping the neck of the cardigan, so he went back to the car and he re-turn with a small blanket, a piece of flannel they call a throw. He open it out and throw it around my shoulders. It was nice and soft. And the minute it touch my skin, I stop trembling, it was so warm. It was then I realize I wanted him to keep his arm right there. Around me, I mean. But he didn't keep it there longer than it took to wrap the blanket-throw around me. Look how much time pass since then, and I can still smell the blanket. It smell just like him. The aftershave he wear. Like lime. I didn't want him to move away."

A sweat broke on the back of Piyari's neck and her upper lip. What she was hearing was, on one hand, better than any-thing she had ever seen on one of those late-late-night movies on Guanagaspar's only television station. She couldn't help being curious; she wanted, in truth, to hear if Mr. Harry had kissed her Madam, and how they had kissed. But it worried and fright-ened her, too. Something about Madam revealing all of this to her wasn't right, wasn't fair.

"On the way back to Cassie's apartment, he ask if I wanted to stop and get a hot chocolate and dessert. I say, 'You're hun-gry, eh? You didn't eat much for dinner.'

"He say, no, don't worry about him, he is fine. He talks nice, you know. Like Boss. You could still hear that a little bit of this place remain in him, but he sound Canadian. Is a good thing Cassie is up there. She speaks nice, too. Well, you have heard me—you know I can speak like them, too, if I want or if an oc-casion calls for it. But is different over here. We more relaxed over here, and besides, what you going to speak like that for on an everyday basis to people who don't know any better, and all you end up doing is making them feel uncomfortable and like you are plenty higher than them?

"As I was saying. He say, 'I thought you might like a hot drink to warm you up.' My mind went to Cassie. She might be worrying about me, I say to myself. And what, pray tell, she would be thinking of her mother taking off like that, staying out so long and so late, I wondered. So, we find a phone booth, and I ring her. You know, she wasn't there! She had work to do, my foot! She left a message on the machine saying 'we'—boldface so, you know! *We.* I knew immediately it was that woman she spending so much time with—'We went to the movies.' The message finish up with that casual way she pick up over there, 'Take it easy, now!' She bother to worry herself about me? But one good thing about that message: if her father had called looking for me, he would think that same *we* meant she and me.

"So I take hot chocolate and he take a soft drink. He ask what dessert I want, and I ask him back which he liked. He laugh, that same laugh again, like if he know something you don't know, and he say, 'Which do *you* want?' Piyari-girl, I come so accustomed to accommodating everyone else's wishes that I didn't even know I myself had desire. A simple thing like a dessert and I didn't know which one I wanted, but still, I say the first thing that jump in my mind—cheesecake. And is that we had."

By this time the refrigerator was cleaned and everything put back in an orderly manner. Madam wasn't finished, so she walked over to the oven. Piyari opened the cupboard under the sink where the oven cleaners and the mitts were kept. She took them out and handed these to Madam.

"After, he drop me home. He is a decent man, so he ride the elevator up with me. I push open the door, but I telling you, in all sincerity, he didn't even put a foot in the doorway. He waited right there while I turned on lights. My good-for-nothing daughter wasn't back yet. I was worried he might want to come in. If he asked, how I could say no? He had come such a distance to take me out, so kindly. But he had the car keys in his hand dangling, ready to leave. How long you think he stayed? Only so long as to say I should call him, that it still had plenty place he want to take me. But, he say, he didn't want to make a nuisance of himself, so it I was who was to call. I was sorry after all, yes, that he was so quick to leave. But I couldn't bring myself to invite him to come in. I was worried he might think bad of me. But that is another thing—if he had come in, I wouldn't even have known how to behave with him. That is young-people kind of thing. I remind myself I am a married woman. Married with two full-grown children. Imagine me thinking this way, and in my own daughter's house?

"I say to myself I will just step forward, give him a hug, quick, nothing too meaningful, you must understand, just to say thank you and goodbye, but he was halfway down the hallway heading for the elevator. Well, Piyari, I went inside the apartment and I was like a high school girl. I only hearing his voice in my head, and remembering how he asking me questions about myself and waiting for answers, and how when he look at me in my eyes I could hardly look back at him, fraid he see how I watching him. And I couldn't get over how his hair was black and soft. When he used to live here, he used to grease it up. Ent you know how fellows like to slick down their hair with grease? Well, he stop that, and I was surprised to see how thick and soft his hair get. And in a little breeze, the front part lift up nice-nice. And is a full head of black-black hair, you know, not a bit of gray in it. Oh Lord, that man confuse me for so that night. Piyari, you know what I like about that place? Nobody minding nobody business. I could sit down in a public place with a man like him and eat a piece of chesecake and enjoy myself and there was nobody watching my every move, ready to run their mouth off."

Suddenly Piyari straightened herself and looked toward the back door. She had heard the car. It hadn't yet pulled into the driveway, but she knew the particular hum of its engine as it rolled in front of the neighbors' houses toward the back gate. There was a time when Madam would have heard it, too, from well away, even as it entered the residential area from the highway. But not these days. Piyari lurched toward Madam, pushing her away from the oven and taking the cleaners from her. "Madam, that can't be Boss come for lunch? I didn't know you was expecting him."

The car horn sounded—three sharp hoots.

Piyari's hands flew to her hips, akimbo. "That Dass. Who he think he is, blowing horn like that? He is the only one of the court drivers who does blow up the horn when he come here. He too important for himself. And today, just because he driving the attorney general, he will be so full of himself. I have to give him lunch, too? But Madam, lunch not make yet. What to do so?"

Madam pensively fingered the gold-plate cross on the chain around her neck and calmly ordered Piyari, as if there were no urgency, to take out a can of beans and a can of sausages and to heat them up. Piyari cupped her face with her hands. With her eyes wide in disbelief, she contradicted her employer.

"Sausage and beans, Madam? Can food you want to give Boss? I hope you forgive me, Madam, but is best I fry up some salt fish and edoes, and it have a coconut bake in the freezer. Or you throw it out? Five-six minutes in the microwave, and the bake will thaw out. Otherwise I could lose my job this day self. Why you didn't tell me Boss was coming home for lunch, Madam?"

Madam walked away from the kitchen calmly, smoothing her hair. "Lord, in truth. What I was thinking? Is a good thing you here with me, yes. Don't worry yourself. Your job safe. He can't fire you but over my dead body. Who else I would talk to if not you? Who else would listen? Relax yourself.

"Don't forget to give Dass a plate of food. He have attitude, is true, but is lunchtime; he will be hungry. And you eat, too. I am going to take a little dip. If Boss ask for me, tell him I was feeling hot. That I in the swimming pool."

A House by the Sea

A coastal hamlet in southwestern British Columbia, Canada. Present day.

Harry heads to the retaining wall wearing his waterproof work jacket and rubber boots. Only a narrow strip of Howe Sound's ivory-colored water in front of his house is visible. A curtain of mist and clouds, hanging in the fjord for weeks now, blots out the shore on the far side.

In the past week he has left his property in Elderberry Bay only once. That was some days before Christmas. Kay had telephoned him several times, insisting that he spend Christmas Day with her, have lunch with her family, but he declined.

He wears heavy work gloves and carries a long rod and a steel pick for swinging into and catching the logs. The odor of the sea, its floor churned and spat up by winter storms, saturates the air. At the side of the house, pine needles and twigs and small boughs brought down in the storms threaten to bury the truck. It has been almost two weeks since he and his men stopped work for the season. He should have scrubbed and put away the lawn mowers, shovels, wheelbarrows, but they remain mud- and sap-encrusted in the back of the truck.

It is supposed to be eagle season, a time when one expects to see them by the hundreds, perched in the highest bare-topped trees along the shore or cruising the length of the Sound as they scan for salmon carcasses. They should be easily spotted on the water, poised on spinning deadheads, a whole fish squirming between a beak or flapping in the talon of a raised foot. But, with this rain one minute, wet snow the next, the fog and the mist, not one eagle is to be seen.

In spite of blowing rain, Harry has propped the front door and left a few windows slightly open; should the telephone ring, he wants to be sure to hear it. He is tired, but the clump of dead-heads banging against the retaining wall needs to be pried apart.

The New Year is just around the corner. Surely, he thinks, she wouldn't make him wait until then. If only she would tele-phone and they could speak, even briefly, he would be freed, better able to celebrate the New Year. Otherwise, likely, he would spend that holiday waiting and alone, too.

But he wasn't entirely alone on Christmas Day. Anil, his first friend in Canada, had made the hour-long drive from Vancouver to Elderberry Bay in the wet dark morning, his two grandchil-dren in tow, to pay the Christmas Day visit, a tradition now.

They sat on the enclosed verandah and watched wet snow fall. Harry warmed milk for the boys. They had brought him Indian sweets, which he put out on a plate and offered back to them. The children had expected that Harry, whom they knew to be a landscape designer, might have set up the yard with col-orful prancing plastic reindeer, and the roof with a gift-laden Santa, one foot already down the chimney, but he hadn't. They pestered him with questions about what decorations he had in his shed, about why he hadn't put out any, about the neighbor's decorations, about those of his clients, and more. Their disap-pointment was eventually diverted by the competing prattling of the lovebirds he had received as a present that summer past. Harry had become so used to the birds and their mess that straightening the living room where they were kept, any more than piling an array of landscaping and garden magazines and seed and equipment catalogs neatly beside the couch, hadn't occurred to him. The boys were intrigued by the sour, salty odor of birds inside the house, by their scatter of seed hulls and flecks of paper the female used in nesting. They lost interest, however, when one of them opened the cage and, attempting to coax a puffed-up reluctant bird onto a finger, was nipped so hard that an inverted purple-colored V-line blossomed instantly just under the surface of his skin. They left within an hour of arriving. That is how he spent Christmas Day. That and waiting. He had expected, hoped, that Rose would call, but she didn't. The last time Harry had taken it upon himself to ring, they spoke less than five minutes—she, whispering, nervous, from her bedroom, until Shem picked up the receiver in the den. Rose in an instant said, "You have the wrong number," and hung up on her end. He heard Shem say, "Is someone there? Hello?" and Harry, without saying another word, awkwardly put down the phone. She had asked him not to call again, promising to ring every other Friday evening when Shem was away playing poker with friends. And now several Fridays have passed with no word from her. He tries to understand, tries not to resent that he is not free to be in touch with her when he wants, but rather, must wait on her.

Whatever made him think he could, by himself, fish out the logs, he wonders. If he were to fall into that frigid salt water crammed with mountain-slide debris and logs escaped from booms, he would be beaten to a pulp so fine that he could be formed into the newsprint on which his obituary would be announced.

He turns back toward the house; he will wait until after the New Year, when he will call on one of his workers to help.

It would be good to see an eagle. Weeks into the season, and still not one is visible.

Pauses and Other Gestures

He lies on one side, his side, of the unmade bed, hands tucked behind his head. There is no food in his refrigerator. He has no choice but to drive into Squamish today, but he will lie here, wait, that is, just a little longer. He does not look at the phone on his side table, but is as aware of it as if it were a trailer parked at his bedside. He stares at a dolphin-shaped water stain on the ceiling and indulges in a particular remembering. He conjures up the same few moments time and again. While the several other occasions have blurred together, he keeps this one intact and clear. He had fetched her from her daughter's apartment in Vancouver's West End. They were to go to Shannon Falls and then beyond, to the art gallery in Brackendale to see paintings of eagles done by members of the Brackendale Society of Amateur Painters. But he knew, even before he had gone to pick her up in Vancouver, that when they reached Elderberry Bay, some distance still from Shannon Falls, he would stop at his house, the excuse made that he had forgotten his camera there.

Although he knew precisely where the camera was to be found, he told her as he pulled into the yard that he had to look for it, and invited her to come into the house with him. She hesitated, and he thought, with some surprise, that she was about to accept his invitation. She said, however, that she would remain in the car, quickly adding, as if needing to justify her decision, that she wanted to watch the high-tide waves form and roll in. He did not press her, but her hesitation loomed large in his mind.

He entered the house, his heart racing, his brain as if it were
on fire. He could barely think. He returned to the car without
the camera. He walked directly to her side of the car and opened
her door. She stared ahead at a wave forming. Neither spoke.
The swell erupted and splayed its foam far out on the surface of
the water well before it reached shore. She looked up at him.
He uttered a word: "Please?"

He allowed her to lead the way to the house, stepping ahead
to open the door only when they arrived at it. They walked quietly, he again behind her, down the hallway to the kitchen. He
walked toward the refrigerator. She had positioned herself against
a far counter.

"Will you drink something?" he asked. "Something light? Or,
I can make coffee."

She did not answer. He tried to read into her silence. Finally
she whispered, "No. I am all right. What do you want?" In the
quiet of her voice he had heard her composure, and his uncertainty vanished instantly.

These days he replays in his mind, over and over, the moments that followed.

He leaned against the refrigerator, his hands pressed behind
his back, and in the quiet save for the electrical humming, he
muttered, "This is strange, isn't it? Being alone with you, I mean.
It's good. Are you all right?"

She nodded, and so he stepped forward. But she raised her
hand and shook her head, gesturing *no* to his advance. He continued and she stepped sideways, raising both hands firmly in
front of her. She said, softly but sharply, "No, Harry. Don't.
Stop," but he mirrored her step and caught her hands in his. She
seemed weightless when he pulled her toward him. The heat of
her body and the form of her breasts, the unbelievable fact of
them against him, caused the light in the room to seem to dim,
and a quivering to climb his body, from his feet to his reddening

face. She had suddenly seemed to relax, and so, trembling un-abashedly, he loosened his hold. She remained there, lightly, against him, and this surprised him, as he knew she would have, through the thinness of her summer dress and the coarseness of his khaki trousers, felt his burning.

It was under the duvet of the same bed on which he lies alone, the full width of which he is still unable to reclaim for himself, that the two of them rocked their way into each other. But the point of his constant reliving of this time is always to arrive at the moment when, as if a decision had been made, Rose opened herself wide and, curling her body, drew him in.

Other occasions haunt him, too: the day she was in the water in front of his house, floating on her back, waving at him to join her. He had been watching her as he hosed down the path in front of the house. He had turned away long enough to shut off the hose and reel it onto its rack. When he returned, she had disappeared. Horrified, he ran into the house to fetch his binoculars. Through them he saw her walking on the gravel beach, with no towel to dry herself nor robe to wrap around her. When she reached him, she was tired but exhilarated. She had spotted a child in difficulty off in the distance and had swum to the child and taken her directly to the shore. She had been so at home in the water there, he imagined her content in Elderberry Bay.

His mind flits, too, to the time he had recounted for her his be-ginnings in Canada, the days when he drove for a taxi company so that he could put himself through school. He had wanted her to understand how he had risen out of adversity and with no fam-ily name or inheritance to ease him along, with no assistance from any arm of government—he had, as far as he was concerned, triumphed. He remembers her response: "I am married to a man who comes from the same background as myself, but it is a man who was once a taxi driver, and is now a gardener, who makes me happy."

He tries to understand why, on returning to Guanagaspar, she drove herself to the run-down village of Raleigh, where he was born. She looked up the old couple who were like his family. She was surprised that they had remembered her. How could they not have? When she was a child, she had visited the fish market with her mother. Uncle Mako had wrapped colorful footballer fish in newspaper for her.

On her return from that visit to his friends, Rose immediately telephoned Harry. She told him that the old people, wiry and a little age-bent, wanted to know if he was happy, how he was managing, if he had good friends, kind neighbors. Tante Eugenie, in her unchanged style, slid fresh carite slices into hot oil, and the three of them ate. They wanted to give Rose everything they had; Uncle Mako went to the back of the house and returned with a bundle of dasheen bush, milk dripping from its fresh knife cuts. He went down to the beach and returned dragging a crocus bag full of live conch. The bag was so heavy that it took him and Rose, both lifting it by its corners, to put it in the trunk of the car, which she had to have cleaned the instant she got back to her house. Before Rose left, the old lady took her hands in hers and said, "Child, we old now; we going to dead and gone soon. But until then, we here for you just like we was for him. If you need anything, you come to us. We don't have much, but whatever we can do for you, we will do." She removed a chain with a cross pendant from around her neck and handed it to Rose. "Take this. Is for you to hand to our Harry, but you wear it until, God willing, next you see him." It had been a gift from Harry's mother to Tante Eugenie, a piece of costume jewelry worth only the memory of an uneventful Mother's Day decades ago. Rose told Harry over the phone that she had not yet removed it, nor would she until she had the chance to give it to him herself.

All of this and then, so abruptly, no contact.

Was he no more than fuel to light a spark between her and her onerous husband? Was he, Harry, a good presence for them? In the silence that exists between them these days, such thoughts occur to him often.

Rain pellets flick hard at his window. He must go into Squamish before the shops close. He is bound to run into Kay in Squamish. After turning down the offer of Christmas lunch at her house, he dreads seeing her. But he does not have a drop of milk in the house, nor bread, nor eggs. He turns on his side and stares at the black piece of plastic that is his phone.

He picks up the receiver and listens. It works. In all of this rain, it still works. He replaces it quickly.

New Year's Eve is just around the corner.

The Spring Before That Summer

Last spring, during a visit to the Squamish liquor store, a woman he hadn't noticed before pushed a loaded dolly down an aisle toward him. She grinned so warmly that for a moment he thought they might have been acquainted, but he couldn't think from where.

"Nice day to be out and about. A little sun finally, eh? Not going to last, though—weatherman's prediction: thunderstorm tomorrow, of course!"

He couldn't place her. She swiftly slit open crates with a little pocketknife, whipped bottles out of the boxes and began shelving them. "So what can we do for you today?"

He realized that she was just being friendly. After that first time, whenever he went into the store, she seemed to go out of her way to chat with him, once even stepping away from her cashier's counter to offer him assistance. On one occasion, as he was leaving, she lifted her work badge toward him and said, "Kay. That's my name. And you?"

He clutched his paper bag of wine, twisted it at the bottles' neck, reached in the pocket of his jacket for his car keys, and said, all at once, "St. George. Harry St. George."

"St. George! Harry! Now, who would have guessed? Okay, St. George. Don't stay away too long, you hear? You come back and see me soon." But she was already taking a bottle from the next customer, so he couldn't tell if she was flirting, being friendly, or just spewing meaningless words. As he reached the door, he heard her shout out, "Don't get too burned in that sun." He turned to see her smile mischievously.

He found himself thinking of her now and then after that. He would walk in one day, he had thought, not buy anything, but go straight to her and invite her to go with him for a quick coffee in the mall. But he kept putting it off. Then summer came, and so did Rose, and Harry no longer had mind or heart for anyone but Rose.

It wasn't until Rose was back in Guanagaspar, and the days in Elderberry Bay were approaching autumn, getting shorter and cooler, that Kay and Harry were to run into each other again.

That Fall

It had been, for a good and pleasant while, that every other Friday evening, Rose from her home in Guanagaspar and Harry from his in Elderberry Bay would speak on the telephone. Harry would hurry from work so they might have a chance to chat well in advance of her husband Shem's return from his standing poker engagement with the boys.

However, one Friday evening in the late summer/early fall, knowing that Rose and Shem were scheduled to spend that weekend at their beach house, Harry, rather than return home to an end-of-week evening without Rose's scheduled voice in his ear, decided to eat his supper at the Squamish Hotel pub.

A mournful wail of country music from the jukebox clashed with laughter, excited chatter, the pings, whistles, and dings of pinball machines, the clack of pool balls, and an undecipherable buzz of commentary that accompanied car racing on a huge television screen in a corner. Two smaller screens hung from the ceiling near the bar, throwing irregular flashes of blue light throughout the room. One ran a sitcom with a black family. Their chatter was inaudible, yet every few seconds a burst of audience laughter erupted. The other screened music videos, though no sound was heard.

Harry had ordered the fisherman's catch and a local beer and sat at a table in an area he had determined to be the least noisy.

Along with two of his workers, he had spent most of that day, a cool but sunny one, crouched under rosebushes, tilling and turning powdered oyster shell and fresh compost into the soil around the plants' thick aged trunks where the toughest, largest thorns were. Long and unyielding spicules had gripped his clothing and etched his arms with inch-long blood-beaded slashes. His body burned and his scalp stung. He felt alive.

Under the dim yellow light of a torch-shaped wall sconce, he listed the following week's chores in a notebook, Rose always at the back of his mind, imagining that she, too, missed their week's end telephone engagement.

Copper fungicide on fruit trees, he wrote. *Spray can.*

Telephone Asha's Garden Center for grease bands. Call Dalton's.

He absently looked up. Among a handful of male patrons was a woman hugging the bar counter one minute, swinging around to lean her back against it the next. She wore a cropped blouse, one of those handkerchief-type tops that tie in a knot just below the breast area, and jeans that seemed to pinch her lower body into rigidity so that she swiveled on the pointed toes of her high-heeled shoes. Harry stared at the exposed belly and, when she swiveled, at the taut behind, of the flamboyant woman. Her roaming eyes caught his. She smiled quickly. He bent his head again.

Apply grease bands to apple trees MONDAY!

Mountain ash, strawberry flats for Osborne's.

Mildew spray/Dr. Chen's roses.

Suddenly his name was shouted by a woman's unfamiliar voice. Not expecting that any woman he knew would visit a place like this, he decided instantly that another patron named Harry was being addressed. The noise in the pub had certainly increased since his arrival half an hour earlier. He applied himself to the list again.

Birdseed.

Sharpen pruning shears.

Cultivator rental.

Shoelaces.

Unexpectedly his shoulders were grabbed, thumbs shoved into his back and released before there was time to react. He swung around and there was Kay. He pushed his chair back and stood.

She ignored his outstretched hand and wrapped her arms around him. He imagined he smelled of oyster ash, compost, and the sweat of a hard day's work. He looked to see from where she might have appeared: on the other side of the room was a congregation of women, some sitting at a long table, some milling about, all behaving rather raucously. Kay pulled back a chair and sat at his table. He lowered himself into his chair.

She was instantly full of chatter. She and her friends were celebrating the end of "summer camp for grown-up girls." She had won the prize for having the season's highest number of bogus golf shots. She carried on about not being much of a golfer; the only driving she really fancied was on logging roads that led to remote lakes and campsites. She laughed at herself, and he couldn't help but laugh along. He was happy to see her. It was good, to tell the truth, to have her come up to him and greet him so warmly in such a public place. It made him feel as if he belonged—nowhere in particular, yet everywhere. Sometimes, she was saying, she just got in her vehicle and headed to one of the lakes—she pointed vaguely behind her—to do a little canoeing.

And what about him, she perked up still more, startling him. He had no chance to consider the most meager of answers, for she continued: he was a wine drinker, that much she certainly knew. In fact, she rolled on, just the other day she had been thinking about his club and was curious about how it had come about. His club. He smiles at this notion.

"You don't too often see people from the islands—you know, people like yourself, darker-skinned I mean, if you don't mind me saying, is it kosher to say that? You don't see them paying close attention to the wines. Well, at least not as carefully as I've caught you doing. The ones you buy are always, and I mean *always,* winners."

He enjoyed the flattery.

She simply couldn't pass up this opportunity, she said, to hear about the club. "So, who else is in it?"

She was welcome relief from the isolation of his secret and enveloping liaison. And the topic of the club did concern her. It was she, after all, who, though still unknown to her, through an ill-conceived bit of deducing on her part, had planted the notion in his and his friends' heads that they were a wine-tasting club. When they called themselves that, it was in jest, mocking the eager clerk he had once mentioned to them.

As he turned in his mind what it was that this rather forward woman was wanting from him, and what he might offer her, his impulse was to provoke her. He told her that on arrival in Canada, to put himself through school—for he was a qualified gardener now, he injected—he had driven a taxi. He paused for a response, a show of surprise or some noticeable loss of interest, but she merely nodded to indicate her attentiveness. A few of the drivers in the company he had worked for became friends, and long after they had moved on from that line of work, they maintained their closeness.

Kay's attentiveness intrigued Harry. Happy now to be socializing, he expounded: at one of their regular rum-drinking gettogethers, one of the ex-taxi-driving friends, a man named Anil, waxed on with inebriated eloquence that fine-wine drinking was nothing but status-mongering; it served only to exclude immigrants and to imprison them—in particular those from the non-grape-growing equatorial climes, the darkies of the world—in what was supposed to be their rightful place: that of backwardness.

Unfazed, Kay asked, "And is this man still with you guys today?"

He nodded affirmatively.

"So his position has changed, then. Good. You're definitely a first. Carry on."

She was certainly a brassy woman. He noticed that the roots of her red-tinted hair were brown and that at the temples there were gray strands. He decided to relay what Anil had said, as if reciting a well-known piece of lore.

"'Fellows like we could smell curry a hundred miles away. We born with taste buds that mourning the scarceness up here of scents and flavors like hurdi, illaichi, dhania, the tandoor.' Do you know what those are?" he interrupted himself to ask her. "Turmeric, cardamom, Indian spices, and that sort of thing. So, to continue, Anil said to us, 'You ever hear of wine that have those flavors? Is a simple fact, man: people like us not born with a wine-tasting gene.'"

Alertness brightening her eyes, Kay opened her hands in a gesture of impatience, saying, "And so?"

And so, continued Harry, at the following gathering of the old friends, another ex-driver, Partap, deciding to prove Anil wrong, showed up with what had been determined for him— and Harry pointed to Kay as he said, "By someone exactly like yourself"—to be a so-called fine red wine.

Kay nodded as if accepting a compliment that had been slid to her across the table.

To the surprise of the old friends, they had indeed discerned the distinct aroma of oak and an unlikely tang of black pepper, exactly as the bottle's label had promised. Kay nodded aggressively, as if to say, "Of course!" With their curiosity piqued, the following week there was another bottle of fine wine, and the week after that, yet another. The jaded Anil proclaimed in good time that after one of their sessions, he had felt a tingling and a twitching deep inside of him, so deep he could hardly identify where, but he knew instinctively that it was the awakening of his latent wine-tasting gene.

And so the Once a Taxi Driver Wine-Tasting and General Tom-foolery Club, as they eventually dubbed themselves, was still un-corking. Kay clapped her hands as if she herself had triumphed. A mischievous impulse to rein in her too-eager enthusiasm prompted him to blurt out, "But tell me something, have you ever tasted the flavor of coconut in a wine? And lamb vindaloo? Because, I will tell you, we have tasted mango, curried crab, red fish, and chicken stew. We have even identified in certain South American reds a variety of styles of garlic—sliced, smashed, minced, roasted."

Kay showed no surprise but looked eager. She asked if he had a preference for a particular grape, or for the wines of a specific region. Before he could answer, she slipped in that she hardly ever drank anything but Italian, and mostly the heavier reds, the Barolos and Barberas, and she couldn't honestly say that she had ever tasted anything like curry or garlic in them. Harry was com-pelled to take advantage of how readily she indulged him.

He reveled, gilding fact and fiction, that he and his friends vowed to shun the Old World vintners—the wines of Europe. They, the dark-skinned island people, he said, squinting mischie-vously at her, had been too wounded by centuries of Old World greed and exploitation to unbegrudgingly partake of its stuffy fare, the result of which was that he and his ex-taxi-driver friends agreed to drink only the less expensive but lighthearted wines of Chile and Argentina, those of Australia, since it was, after all, a commonwealth country and, one way or the other, their con-sumption would benefit the aboriginal population. They con-ceded, Harry added, to support the British Columbia wine industry, and still drank Californian wines because they were all in agreement that much of the labor propping up that industry was immigrant, and it was the support of the immigrant—not the consideration of taste—that was of significance to them. Kay laughed raucously, blurting out that she thought he and his friends were wonderfully mad, and she drew out the word wonderfully.

Abruptly, she reached out, slid aside his beer mug, and cupped both her hands over the tiny blood-beaded dashes on one of his forearms. The fingertips of one hand, wet from the condensation on the mug, startled him.

"Animal or roses?" Her voice lowered in the noisy room; it was a few seconds before he realized what she had said.

He answered. She nodded knowingly, moved her cupped hand lower then higher, resting it lightly each time for a few seconds. Her forwardness was beguiling. On account of it, he had just revealed things about his life, made light of his insecurities, and suggested that there could be a frugal side to him. After being faced with Rose's discomfort of Harry's early Canadian work experiences, hardly any of this—even in jest—would he have dreamed of disclosing to her. But his friends, their club, their antics, and their delight in inventing off-color moral justification for their actions meant a great deal to him, and Kay's indulgence was a much appreciated validation.

Her hot hand, still on his arm, only made the rosebush wounds sting more.

"Well, I know a whack about you—still not enough—but fair is fair: let me tell you about myself," she said, causing him to realize that he knew hardly a thing about this person in front of whom he had so unreservedly revved himself up. She proceeded to impart that she had been married to a man from Iran. Peeved by this revelation, he slid his arm away from her; he mused inwardly that perhaps he was not special after all—it was merely that this woman liked foreign men, immigrant men. Perhaps his wine-club story wasn't all that interesting, he thought, and admonished himself to exercise more discretion with his babbling in the future.

After the second of two daughters was born, her husband left them and returned to his country, and ever since, she has been on her own, she said.

To break the awkwardness that immediately ensued, Kay, again gesturing to some undefined vicinity behind her, asked Harry if he had ever canoed on any of the lakes. He muttered that he hadn't. "Not very Canadian of you," she said in a tone of mock accusation. "We're just going to have to fix that, aren't we!"

Getting up as the waitress arrived with Harry's order of deep-fried seafood, Kay suggested that since fall was just around the corner, they take advantage of the good weather forecast for the weekend and head out the very next morning. Harry thought again of Rose; with Shem ever present, there was hardly a chance that she would try and contact Harry from their seaside home. Besides, he had no other pressing engagements. It was a well-timed opportunity, he reasoned, to do something out of the ordinary. From his notepad he tore a page and handed it and his pen to Kay.

Landscaping

Following the map Kay had drawn, the road curved sharply, and he was driving frighteningly close alongside the brisk Squamish River. Much of the valley—river on one side, low sprawling houses, fenced-in fields with grazing horses—was Native Indian land. He slowed to watch two deer on the road ahead, but the instant they spotted his vehicle, they bounded down a gully and were swallowed in the shrubbery.

At the gravel logging road, exactly as Kay had drawn, a posted sign read: Caution. road to carol lake deactivated. expect uneven sections/unstable areas and soft shoulders/ 4 × 4 only/ At your own risk. She had told him about that sign but added, "It's just letting you know the road is rough." He shifted into four-wheel drive and began the slow ascent. The path's surface coarsened. This woman is fearless, he mused. Her independence certainly intrigued him. The truck crunched loose shale, lurched over large rocks. Every part of the vehicle squeaked or rattled ferociously. A tool kit on the canopy-hooded bed slid about noisily. He had suggested they travel up together, but she said that she usually liked to get up there quite early and exercise a little on her own. The air bristled with diamondlike specks of dust. When he came to what seemed a relatively safe stretch in the winding road, he decided to stop and take another look at Kay's drawing. He switched off the engine. Dust raised by his vehicle swirled high upward before settling.

Where he had stopped, the land to his right plunged vertically. He congratulated himself on having had no more than two beers at the pub the night before, just enough to cause him to ramble on about the wine club, but not enough to have caused a hangover, dangerous on such a precipitous journey.

Ahead loomed range beyond range of ice-capped mountains. Here and there were bursts of lavender, clumps of mustard gold-enrod. Pride coursed through him; he had become an insider. By inviting him up, Kay was showing him something few people like him—he grinned at the thought—ever had the chance to glimpse. This was the Canada of postcards and tourism posters. In reality, it was his backyard. He wanted to get out of the truck and look around but had the sensation, terror really, that at any time the land and road could simply slip away. He thought about how Rose might be affected on learning that he'd had an accident or met his death while on a pleasure trip to go canoeing with a woman he hadn't mentioned. He wondered how far inland he was, how far from public roads, from a town, a gas station, a hospital, and decided it was better to remain inside. From there he took in the vista, a picture straight out of a calendar.

A vertical crevice in which a dollop of blue-edged ice was suspended triggered in his mind the phrase "hanging glaciers." A mountain-sized protrusion of rock, severely weather-sculpted to resemble a pyramid, provoked the term "Matterhorn." A knife-edged ridge produced "Arête." He couldn't recall the verbal definitions, but, from the high school geography texts in Guanagaspar, he instinctively knew the names of the formations around him.

He had just spent the better part of the summer leading, he mused, his Guanagasparian Rose around, showing her his version, a tamer one to be certain, of British Columbia. He hardly ever did anything he was unsure of. Yet here he was in unfamiliar terrain, about to have a boating adventure, initiated by a woman—cultures apart from his—whom he couldn't say he really knew. He wondered if Anil or Partap or any of the other men from the club had ever been up such a road, seen this kind of landscape, or known a woman—or even a man—as adventuresome as Kay.

He started the truck and continued somewhat less hesitantly. If the day turned out to be successful—that is, if Kay did indeed show, particularly after an evening of imbibing far more than he had; if the canoe didn't capsize; if he made it back to his house in Elderberry Bay in one piece—he would make at least one more trip of this kind. Then he could say he did this sort of thing, or used to, at any rate. Yes, it would be very Canadian of him to be able to say that he used to get up early on mornings, drive to a lake high up, awfully high up, in the mountains, and go canoeing.

Three dust-covered sport utility vehicles and a Volkswagen van were already in a parking clearing. His truck was no longer red but enveloped in gray dust. It made him proud.

Kay, already at the water's edge, waved when she heard the vehicle roll in. The owners of the vehicles in the lot were no-where to be seen. Neither was a canoe rental outfit visible. He wondered where Kay had gotten the one next to which she stood. Beside it, in a yellow life vest and wearing yellow rubber boots into which her faded blue jeans were tucked, she appeared tall and rather fit. Harry knew that in every sense he was in unfa-miliar waters. He stepped up his pace and headed down to her, ready to receive and return the friendly embrace that had sur-prised him the night before.

Instead, she handed him a cup of coffee poured from a ther-mos, and immediately opened her arms to the view, the icy green lake in the foreground, and backdropping it, a vivacious glacier-topped ridge, best seen to postcard-beauty standards only from this narrow angle of view. "Have you ever seen anything so mag-nificent? Have you?" She laughed as she added, "I feel like hell this morning, but I did get here an hour ago, and I've already been out for a little spin on the lake. It was damn cold. But it's warming up real quick, can you believe it! It's going to be a gorgeous day."

So early, so still the morning, and she was already chatting away. She handed him a bottle of mosquito repellent and a jacket like the one she wore. He muttered that even if he were to fall overboard and manage to remain afloat on account of the life vest, within seconds the iciness of the lake would numb him to death.

The sand around the boat was fine, shifty. With the slightest pressure, water oozed up out of it. When they were both ready, she set her feet firmly in the gravel, grasped the stern, rocked the boat, and gave it a little push so that its far end slid into the shallow waters. She treaded in behind it, steadying it by the stern. With her legs astride and firm, she grasped the sides. She directed him to reach across the boat with one hand and hold on to both gunwales as he stepped in. He was uncomfortable getting in before she did. He would have preferred to give her a hand in; she might have rested her hand on his, pressed with all of her weight, and his hand would have supported her like a rock. He followed her directions, stepped nervously in, and hobbled down the middle. He was about to sit on the bow seat facing inside the boat. He crossed over awkwardly at her instruction, gripping both gunwales with concentration. He lifted himself barely enough to angle his body so he might watch her, worried that she wouldn't be able to get in without toppling them both. The boat rocked from side to side. With a glance backward— at which she shouted, "Stay centered"—he saw that she had already seated herself and that a single paddle lay across her lap. It dawned on him that the canoe belonged to her. He wondered where she stored it. He didn't know which vehicle in the parking area was hers. On any of them, it would have to be strapped to the top. She must have brought it down herself. She wasn't in this moment physically appealing to him, yet such independence fascinated him.

By the time he looked back to the shore, they had already traveled a good distance from land. What had been the far shore when they started out was the nearer. The distant glacier, perfect as a picture from the vicinity of the picnic tables, was no longer visible. A thick cloud of mosquitoes appeared. Its hazy mass seemed to propel itself with a mesmerizing rotation as it hovered above the silken turquoise water, the surface of which the early-fall sun seemed unable to penetrate. Each fine grain of glacial silt, suspended on the surface, seemed to sparkle, but mere inches below was total opacity.

He had been quick to tell her stories last night at the pub, and she to listen, but now no words passed between them. The quiet on the lake was broken only by a rhythmic ripple, and an occasional hollow *thuck* as paddle shaft and gunwale made contact.

Kay stole into his thoughts. "Do you want to paddle?"

He had never learned to swim. "I am just fine here. You're doing a pretty good job."

"Oh, come on, try it!" she insisted. "What if I were unable to paddle? We're heading for that clearing over there. I will tell you exactly what to do."

The thought that he would have no idea what to do if she were indeed unable made him turn carefully and take the paddle she held out to him. He was not accustomed to following the lead of a woman. It seemed to him to be, however strange, a kind of intimacy. Unusual and compelling. He followed her precise, Spartan instruction, and it was he who paddled for the rest of the trip, gaining confidence and improving with each stroke.

Later, he helped her set the boat on top of the Volkswagen van. They drove down into Squamish together, he following her. She waved him over to the curb before the turnoff to her house, and invited him for a sandwich.

She left him in the living room, looking at her country CD collection, while she made tea and sandwiches. He put on a Jim Reeves disk and toured the room, peering at the numerous photographs on the walls, perched on tabletops. Most were of her and her two daughters at various stages of their lives: the girls square-dancing, canoeing, at various campsites, at a swim meet; one of the Volkswagen parked on the side of a country road; Kay and her daughters, young women by then, standing next to it. He wondered who that photographer might have been, and glanced around for other pictures that might have been taken on the same trip. He found nothing evidencing memories of anyone with whom she might more recently have shared intimacies. There were also numerous photographs of groups of women, her club, he guessed: one taken in front of a log cabin; one with several women at a train station; one with her and two others, all wearing baseball caps, hers with Mickey Mouse ears attached; and one of a woman about to swing an ax into a fire log. There was one that had not been framed, leaning against an ornament on the side table. In that one she looked much the way she did presently. She was standing on the front stairs of her house, the one he was in now, grasping the elbow of a woman who, from their strong resemblance, he guessed to be one of the daughters, a grown woman now. In all of them, Kay smiled broadly, and in some he could almost hear her laughter. He found himself wanting to laugh out loud with her. There is a woman, he mused, who knows how to have fun, and for the briefest moment he contemplated the possibility of a romantic liaison with her. It is I who would be introduced to entire new worlds, he considered, and I would not have to draw out of her every blessed feeling or desire.

She came out of the kitchen to find him looking at a small black and white of a man. "That's Ali."

She needn't have said; he had known immediately it was her husband, a tall, wiry man. Sitting next to him on a beach was Kay, as tall as he. She took the picture off the wall, blew a film of dust off it. She wiped the glass with the edge of her hand, the area of the man's face with a finger. "This here was two days before he left. At the time it was taken, I had no idea he was going to be leaving. He knew, but I didn't suspect it."

Harry wondered if she had taken Ali out on a lake in an attempt to Canadianize him. He asked if she missed him. She didn't answer that question but said instead, "I am able to look after myself. I get lonely. But my girlfriends, we keep each other company. And you know, I have that old van. Now, the van, that is my companion. But I admit I do miss having a man around."

He wondered if it was possible for one to look after these kinds of women as well as they would look after themselves.

She continued, "I manage. You know how you get used to things. Ali left when the children were very young. I haven't seen him since; they haven't, either."

They sat at the table and ate the sandwiches she had made. Kay wanted to uncork one of her Barolos, but what had compelled him before now unnerved him, and he thought better of sitting around and drinking wine with her. At the front door he observed that someone had been trying to build a trellis and had abandoned the project.

"It's a job for a gardener, don't you think? That's the sort of thing I do."

Two days later, he stopped at the liquor store to tell her he had enjoyed the day, particularly learning to paddle, and that he had arranged with his workers to build the trellis for her. She told him abruptly that after he had gone, she missed him. All he could say was "Yes, it was a good day. Really nice on the lake, wasn't it?"

Two months passed without contact. Then, just before Christmas, to his surprise, she telephoned him and asked him to have Christmas lunch at her house with her and her daughters, an invitation he declined.

Now, two days before the end of the year, Harry pries himself away from his home, and in a rain that is still coming down, although lightly now, he heads into the town of Squamish. Besides shopping for groceries, he must stop at the liquor store.

The Stawamus Chief

Harry ambles down an aisle to the British Columbia racks, distractedly glancing over the selection. He looks back at Kay. The line at her cashier's station is long. She has that unguarded look of concentration. He will join her queue, say a quick hello.

Not until he is next in line after the man whose purchases she is ringing up does she see him. Her solemn face brightens. She sets one hand akimbo. "Well! So what's this? You came to buy wine? Not to see me?"

Harry is relieved and at the same time made shy by her too-public attention. She operates the till again, self-consciously smoothing back her short shiny hair that needs no such fixing. She accepts money from and gives change to her customer, but her eyes are fixed on Harry. Kay places both palms flat on the counter and leans forward. "So why haven't I heard from you, St. George? What are you buying? I haven't tried this one. Are you in a hurry? I'm taking my break any minute now. Just wait. Let's go next door for a coffee."

She allows him no time to respond; she picks up her station's intercom phone. Her voice booms powerfully out of two corners of the ceiling. "Cashier to number four, please. Cashier to number four."

She doesn't dwell on his absence, offering only that on Christmas Day he was missed. She does say that her daughters were disappointed that they were not to meet the man from the islands whom she had taken canoeing and who had built the fancy trellis over her front gate.

Through the glass pane of the coffee shop, he watches the Stawamus Chief. The top half of that dark granite monolith had for weeks been hooded by a mass of heavy gray clouds. Revealed again, still streaked black along its cracks and crevices, but lightening and bluing where the magnificently sudden sun kissed it, it is an imposing wall. Since this past fall, he has come to think of this side of the big rock as Kay's country.

All at once there seems to be an abrupt increase in the number of cars jamming the entrance to the mall's parking lot. Throngs of pedestrians emerge, as if they had been awaiting the sun's cue. The coffee shop is crammed with customers, and the two cappuccino machines gurgle and spurt at full unceasing throttle. Harry wonders if he and Kay, so different from each other, look to the other customers and passersby like a couple, like lovers. She wears a collar pin of mistletoe that reads HAPPY NEW YEAR, and large shiny silver rings on three fingers of her right hand. If only he had heard from Rose this past holiday week, he thinks, he could relax and enjoy this moment with Kay.

She is saying something.

"Harry St. George, are you listening? I asked, do you have plans for New Year's Eve?

"Harry! Let's have dinner New Year's Eve together," she insists. "Oh, come on. It will be fun. Just dinner. Nothing fancy. I'll cook."

THE WEIGHT OF TOO MUCH–TOO MUCH

Guanagaspar.

Christmas came and went. The tree had been put up; there were Santa and reindeer ornaments and glass candle holders with deep red candles that were never lit. There were bunches of the white Christmas bush, cut from the yard and arranged in large copper vases, and gold-colored foil-covered pots of poinsettia. There was turkey and ham on the table Christmas Day, and Madam's son, Jeevan, his wife, and their children stayed for most of the day. But come Boxing Day, Madam had Piyari take down the tree and pack up the ornaments; the boxes were placed out of sight in front of the cupboard in the storeroom for the yard boy to put away the following day. Never had Piyari seen a Christmas disappear so swiftly.

And the house once more was as clean as if Madam were planning to show it to an inspector or a prospective buyer. She sat at the kitchen table, and by way of indicating to Piyari to sit down, too, she rapped the table with her knuckles. It had been some days before Christmas since Madam last spoke to Piyari of her summer on the west coast of Canada. But once she began, it was as if, to her mind, not a moment had slipped by.

"So, as I was saying, five days pass, and finally the Eggman ring. He tell me he wanted to show me, that same day self, a fishery where you could stand up and watch salmon try to climb up a wall in a river. And a canyon. He say to ask Cassie to come, too. I say all right, but if I speak the truth, I had wanted to be alone with him. But I didn't have to worry; before I could utter a word, she tell me, of her own accord, that she had plans for us: she and her friends were going to the beach for a day picnic. She treat me, for so, like dry bread she buttering, telling me that her friends always asking about me, and how they insist I go with them. And then, when I remain quiet, she add that they going kayaking. That mean they go out in the sea, each one in their own skimpy boat, and they paddle down the coast for an hour or so. Boldface so, she say I could take some magazines and read while I watch their things on the beach. I know her hour or so. She and her father may not get along, but no two people have ever been more alike. An hour or so, I knew very well, might turn out to be three hours or so, and I didn't want to be left minding other people's things as if I am their servant, you know what I mean? I tell her Harry invite us to go to a tourist site they call the Capilano Canyon. She didn't show any surprise, and it is a good thing that she didn't start up with any stupid teasing. She said that if I weren't going with her, she just might stay out with her friends for the evening, and that perhaps I could have dinner with Harry. So, you see how *everything* conspire to make this new step in my life possible? This is how I know I am not doing anything wrong.

"I had to wonder what exactly it was that she was intending, you know. It seemed like she was almost encouraging something between him and me.

"Anyway, up at the canyon, Harry never assume that I would be worried about walking on the suspension bridge. Now, suppose —just suppose—that when the children was young, Boss had brought us up here and taken us to a place like this. You supposing? Well, tell me if you can't imagine him saying, 'Let the children walk on it if they want. You stay here with me.' And you know, I would have stayed. And today I am aware of what I would have missed. The suspension ladder was as wide as three people standing shoulder to shoulder. Children was racing back and forth over it, making it bounce up and down, up and down. I went on it, but I hold on tight-tight with both hands, and I walk slow for so. Harry asked if I was all right, but he never make me feel like I wasn't capable or as if I was doing anything special. It had a group of women from India walking across the bridge. Maybe they were from Pakistan. Or maybe they were from Sri Lanka. I can't tell these things. They were much older than I. One of them might even have been my mother's age, if she were still alive today. Well, these ladies were wearing saris, not concerned one little bit about tripping on that swinging bridge, and not one of them was holding the railing. I take one hand off the railing, straighten myself, and walked along more briskly. Piyari, I tell you, I had never experienced anything like that before. In the middle of the swinging bridge, swinging from side to side, you know, I stop to look down. Below, far, far, far below, on the bottom of the canyon, it had a river and the water in that river was green, inky green, and it was flowing fast, fast, fast, over big boulders that was white like the cow's first milk. It had people down on the bottom; they look like ants, they were that far down, and they were hopping brave and stupid for so, from boulder to boulder. Harry ask if I liked what I was seeing, and I could only say, 'Is beautiful, is beautiful,' and I realize then that I didn't know how to describe what I was seeing or how I was feeling."

Madam suddenly stopped talking. She remained far away in thought, as if unaware of Piyari. Madam regularly had her hair set and combed, her nails shaped and painted. One would have thought that, it being the festive season and all, Madam would have had herself done up. But it had been over a month now since she had gone to the beauty salon. She distractedly picked remaining bits of color off her nails, amassing a collection of red enamel flakes on the kitchen table.

Assuming that today's reminiscing had come to an end, and mindful that dinner had yet to be prepared, Piyari stood up.

Madam rapped the table again with her knuckles, causing the nail-polish flakes to dance about.

"Where are you going? I'm not finished. I want you to hear me out, Piyari. I am not just running my mouth idle-idle, you know. I have to tell somebody, and you are the only person I can trust, not so?" Madam did not wait for an answer but added immediately, "So sit back down."

Piyari sat down instantly, feeling unusually trustworthy and at the same time fearful.

"So, that night we—Mr. Harry and I—didn't eat dinner together. He say he had to get back to his house early. I didn't want to ask him why. I get the impression he didn't want any-thing—you know what I mean—I mean that he didn't want any kind of freshness with me; he only want to show me the place, and to help out taking me here and there to buy this and that, so I was inclined to wonder if it had a woman in his life who was waiting somewhere for him. When I reach back at Cassie's house, I feel real lonely and I feel sad for so. That same evening I ring Guanagaspar. You remember? I ask you to speak with Boss. You tell me he was out, but you didn't know where he went. So I wait a good hour before I ring again. It would have been about midnight by then in Marion. And he answer the telephone. I could hear he was drinking. He didn't ask how I was, but he ask where his blue jacket was, that he had wanted to wear it and couldn't find it. Piyari, I tell you, girl, that was the first time in my life—in all my life, first time—I feel a hatred so strong. I didn't get vex, you know. I just feel this thing—like I was a deep-water well, and like nasty thick black-water was rising up in me. But I remain calm on the outside. I tell him the jacket at the dry cleaner's. I tell him where to find the receipt for it. I could hear him. He start fuming, breathing heavily, asking me why I didn't pick up the jacket before I went up to Canada. Well, the black water that had been boiling and rising up inside of me drop back down fast-fast in the well, and I start to get frightened. You know how Boss can be when his temper set loose. I start to tremble, and my body get weak. The phone could have fall out my hand. Out of the blue, I realize he was far enough away that he could huff and puff all he want but he couldn't lay a hand on me. My mind went on Harry—Mr. Harry. I was thinking about him putting the blanket-thing around my shoulder, and I start to smile. Boss didn't know how foolish he was sounding; he was telling me to ring the dry cleaner's—yes, telling me to ring them up from Canada—and tell them to deliver the jacket to his office.

"Well, shortening up the story, it turn out that Mr. Harry had no woman waiting anywhere for him. I went a good few times to his house. It has a verandah. It has a verandah running in front of his house, and all around the ledge of the verandah, he place milk cans—milk cans he had painted red. The cans had geraniums, and anthuriums, and the brown-leaf variety of bread and cheese in them, just like you see in front of houses in the countryside here. You must have like those in front of your house, not so?

"And I went to his work sites with him. In one place he had build a pond. I see it from the time it was nothing more than a hole in the ground. By the time I leave up there, it had fish in it, water lilies with buds on them, and insects, ones just like our battimamselles, flying and buzzing around. I never before realize what a nice noise insects make. The whole thing look natural-natural, as if it had existed forever. He strong and he has muscles for so, all that gardening work, you see, but he is not a gardener like Manilal, you understand. He is what they call up there a landscape designer. It means he has people working for him. He tells them what he wants, and they do the heavy work. Still, he does a lot himself. Boss would have caught heart attack and died doing even ten minutes of that kind of work—digging up the ground, dragging fertilizer, spreading manure, training hedges, planting big-big trees, pulling and pushing boulders here and there. When I went to the work site with him, while he did his business, I clipped old buds and old flowers from the rose trees—he puts rose trees in every garden he designs—and I weeded some beds. Yes, don't look at me so—I can weed and plant and water if I want to.

"We would go to the grocery together, and he and I would decide—together—what we want to eat for dinner. Then he might go in his office or go and work in the garden, and I would cook. Or he might stay right in the kitchen and cut up the onions for me, or mash garlic or peel potatoes and carrots. The first time I cook in his kitchen, he come and stand up behind me while I was stirring a pot of beef stew. I could feel his body close to mine. I turn around, and I put my hand on his chest to push him back—gentle, not aggressive—only so I could go to the refrigerator. He stay right there and stir my pot for me."

Piyari's face began to burn. Madam was giving too much information again, putting her in a dangerous position. She contemplated busying her mind elsewhere. But out of concern for Madam's welfare and fearful of the trouble she seemed to be courting, Piyari decided to pay close attention to all she was being told.

"The first night we eat together, he set the table. We eat together at his house many other times, and he always set the table. And he cleared it afterward, and he washed the dishes while I dried, and never once he made a comment about any of this. It was like it was natural for him. But you know he was an only child, and it was only him and his mother. So I suppose he used to help her, natural so. Well, standing up there, next to each other in the kitchen, he talk about any and everything, about the days when we were children. He could remember—better than me—how I was always trying to teach him to dance. He remember us playing teatime on my mother's front stairs. He remember how upset his mother would get when he and I start making noise. More than once, standing up there in the kitchen, he wanted to know if life had turned out the way I expected it would. He ask if I was happy. When I tell him yes, he wasn't satisfied, he ask again in a different way, as if he knew better, or as if he wanted me to say something I wasn't saying. He wanted to know what different I would do if I had a second chance. He force me to think. He make me speak. And it was in opening my mouth and speaking that I realize I did not live my life the way I would have liked. I ask if his life was turning out as he had hoped. He look straight at me and said, 'At this moment, I am the happiest I have ever been.'

"After dinner, before he take me back to the city, we might sit on a bench on the front lawn, with a little blanket-throw on our lap, and watch the water turn from orange to black. You know that water cold too bad! But still, I went in it. You know I can't pass up a dip in the sea. The only way to keep from freezing in that ice water is to keep moving. Now, if he and Boss have one thing in common, is that neither of them would too far go in the water, if even they go at all! And, too, both of them—no matter how much they wouldn't spend time in the water—both of them want to live near the sea. But Mr. Harry have reason; he was born by the sea, you see."

Piyari looked down at her hands clasped in her lap and muttered, "You can take the man out of the island, but you can't take the island out of the man."

Madam smiled, for that seemed like a good thing, and she continued.

"And there again, he would ask me questions—questions re-lating to something or the other I had said earlier, or even days before. He remembered everything I had said, and he had a question for everything. You could imagine that?

"One day we went to a place name Asha's Garden Supply. Is a woman who had emigrated from Lantanacamara who owns it. She was the reserved type, secretive for so. That was good, because I myself didn't want to be caught by anyone who might know Caribbean people—anyway, her business sold supplies for professional gardeners—all kinds of tools that we can't find in shops here. She had plants from down here, bromeliads, passionflower, pelican flower. She had a good few varieties of the Cereus plant, ent you know the night-blooming cactus? She had Caribbean broom and baliser. That sort of thing. I wanted to buy him a little present from that shop, so I pick a Norfolk pine. But she also had plenty birds. You know, he and his mother used to have chickens. As a child, he used to keep one for a pet. I told him that every respectable Eggman must have birds, so I buy two birds, two pretty birds that only staying chook-up-chook-up against each other. If one take two steps to the left, the other one doing the same, and they pressed up like they glued right next to each other. Yes, lovebirds. Well, we laugh about that a lot. He can really laugh, you know. He not serious-serious and stuffy at all."

Piyari wiped her mouth with her hand in an effort to hide a smile. Lovebirds. She noticed that for all the information Madam was willing to let loose, she still wouldn't say what else she and Mr. Harry might have given to each other. This side of her Madam excited her. She was keen to know more.

"Those are the happiest days I have ever known. How can I go back to my life as it was before, Piyari? Can you tell me? How can I? But you see how I let Christmas pass quiet so? Well, it is not going to be like that for long. You will help pack and get ready.

We will leave tomorrow, and all of us will spend the New Year, as we have done every year for the last twelve, by the sea. But because I have had a taste of life, Piyari. Whosoever so desires can say I get greedy, or they can say I get smart, but today I am not settling for anything less than the whole meal."

A Strange Complicity

The day before dinner with Kay, Harry is unsettled. He knows that if he were to speak with Rose, a quick exchange of season's greetings between them, he would be able to relax and enjoy a New Year's Eve celebration with Kay. He decides impetuously that he will not wait—he will not allow the enjoyment of the evening to be curtailed by waiting for Rose. He will call. If Shem answers, Harry will simply hang up, without a word. Seizing the moment, he composes the number. International code. Country code. Area code. And the number of her house.

After six rings he begins to doubt the wisdom of calling. He has the sensation of engaging in an act of breaking and entering. As he is about to take the receiver away from his ear someone is saying, "Morning, Bihar residence." He considers hanging up and the woman on the other end, clearly the maid, says in a questioning tone, "Hello?"

"Yes, hello. I am looking for Mrs. Bihar."

"They not here. Who is speaking, please?"

He ignores her question and above a faint static asks, "When will she be back?"

"They gone away for the holiday. Who speaking please?"

"I am just wondering when they will be back?" He realizes that he may be sounding rude.

There is silence. Then the woman says in a tone of strange complicity, at once a mixture of asking and confirming, "You calling from abroad?"

She must have guessed that it was an overseas call from the quality of the connection. He does not respond and she continues, "They at the beach house. They went up there day after Boxing Day. They bringing in the New Year there. I with them, too, but I just come back for a few hours to make sure everything here safe. You lucky you call now. Half hour again and you would of miss me. They coming back right after the New Year. You want her to call you?"

Her familiarity, the ease with which she has given up so much information, confuses him. Almost frightens him. Who, he wonders, does she imagine he might be.

He didn't answer. Nervous now, he ends the conversation with, "Don't bother her. It's nothing urgent. I will call next week."

How he wishes he had not called.

The New Year's Eve Dinner

British Columbia.

The bird in the cuckoo clock in the drawing room wobbles out of its house and begins to chirp just as the Volkswagen van comes to a wheezing halt. Harry, aware that he is being rather outdated, remains amused by the idea that a woman would drive such an unwieldy vehicle.

Once out of the van, Kay stretches tall, her nose to the sky. She closes her eyes, takes a deep breath.

"Winter in the Sound. Oh, Harry, I don't have to ask how you are! You look wonderful."

Her cologne, the scent of marigolds, overpowers the salty odor of the dried kelp and other flotsam on the low-tide beach.

"Well, I've finally made it to your house! The turnoff from the highway is not easy to find."

"They keep promising us a light. They're waiting for an accident, no doubt."

She hands him a tray with a foil-covered dish and fetches another and a straw basket from the passenger side of her vehicle. Harry asks about traffic. On the stairs of the house, she turns and looks at the garden.

"You can really tell that this here is done by a professional, can't you?"

Inside, she admires the red milk tins with the plants in them on the enclosed verandah, saying that they are more interesting than clay pots and plastic planters. On the way to the kitchen, she pauses at the entrance to the living room. He did remember this morning to clean out the birdcage and vacuum up the seeds, but more seeds already carpet the area.

Kay's marigold scent, concentrated in the warmth of the house, blots out the aroma of Harry's fish dish in the oven. She marches directly to the oven, opens the door, slides aside the sizzling fish, and places her dish next to it. She takes the straw basket from the counter and heads to the refrigerator, opens, and surveys. She makes room on a shelf for her salad and two bottles wrapped in brown paper. She pulls out yet another bottle and hands it to him.

"Now, listen. I know that you're some kind of activist when it comes to wine drinking," she teases, "but I took the liberty of bringing Italian. You'll like it!" She puts up her hands to halt the objection she anticipates. But Harry is amused.

"You know, I figure that whatever ills those Europeans have inflicted—and hey, I am a descendant, I can speak for them—I say do not, and I mean *do not* permit those ... those whatevers to keep from you the spoils they produce: I say, as long as you can afford it, you just put that whole damn continent—and descendants like me—to work for you. I say let them serve your taste buds. And now let me serve yours."

With that she holds out the bottle. One line of the label, reads *Marchesi di Morano,* the other *Colli Consola.* Was one the region and one the estate? He tries to guess which might be which. He has, in an instant of panic, forgotten how to read a label. It doesn't even seem to indicate a grape variety. He knows that if he utters a word, he could surely make a fool of himself. He nods approvingly.

"Open it, Harry. It's a pinot grigio."

Pinot grigio. Ah yes, of course. He takes the bottle and studies the label more carefully.

She has brought long tapered candles dipped in silver sparkles. She sets them on the kitchen counter and looks around for candleholders. "We could easily have eaten at my house tonight, but it's much nicer to be in a house by the sea."

A house by the sea. He has indeed accomplished so much in his life. He has come such a long way. He thinks this, pleased, sinks and turns the screw into the cork. He tells her she won't find candleholders in this house, to use saucers, or better yet, one of the tin cans he has stored under the sink.

"Why don't men ever have candleholders?" she says, feigning indignation. Harry explains that he—he himself, not able to speak for all men—has never understood the recreational use of candles, that he grew up in a country where, in some places, candles were the only source of electricity. Where there was electricity, candles were used only in the event of an outage. As if presented with a mission, she begins rummaging through the cupboards for something more suitable than a saucer or a tin can. The cork squeaks as he eases it up. It pops out in one piece, a pleasant sound. She comes across a stack of empty wine bottles in the recycling bucket under the sink, and examines some, remarking on those she recognizes. The wine makes its pleasant *glug glug glug* as it fills the glasses. He holds a glass out to her and prepares to make an early toast to the year ahead.

"No, not yet," Kay exclaims. She asks for foil and wraps two empty bottles in smoothed-out pieces he has found in a drawer that is crammed so tight with a mess of empty plastic bags, twist ties, a pair of pliers, masking tape, matches, and much more that it is difficult to open and then to close again. She flares the edges of the foil around the mouths of the bottles and shoves a candle in each. A residue of silver dust sparkles on the countertop.

"There you are. Silver candleholders. They will do, won't they? It's like being young and playing house, having to be inventive again, isn't it? Now, where is the table?"

The small table is clearly visible against a wall in the kitchen. He had thought they would pull it away from the wall and eat in the center of that room, with the stove and the refrigerator right there.

"Which table?" The question gives him time to adjust to the idea that he will have to clear the one on which months of paperwork, customer files, magazines, and gardening catalogs are stored, albeit neatly.

"The dining table."

He moves everything, trying to keep the piles intact, to the guest bedroom, the bed already overrun with papers and files.

After wiping the table, Kay sets down the candleholders and returns to the kitchen.

He leans against a counter, eyeing the forbidden wine, content to watch this woman in his kitchen open cupboard after cupboard, drawer after drawer. She pulls out plates and cutlery, two of everything, and sends him to set his table.

"What about the pinot grigio? It's getting warm, isn't it?" he blurts confidently.

"No patience, have you? That bottle is so well chilled that it could use a little cuddle." She has pulled the sleeves of her sweater up to her elbows. Her arms are severely freckled.

From her straw basket she pulls a plastic container with odd-shaped balls of a cheese that is unfamiliar to him. She cubes the cheese, chops basil and tomato, sprinkles salt and black pepper, and tosses the colorful dish with olive oil. Inspired by her busyness, Harry goes out the back door and clips cuttings from the *Cotoneaster horizontalis* that spreads fanlike, a fiery carpet running up the cliff. As he reenters the house, the aroma of fish with all its seasonings, and the sweetness of corn pie, greet him.

He places the fine-leafed dark sprigs with their brilliant orange berries in a chipped ceramic mug. From the verandah he brings a milk can with a red geranium, places it on the windowsill. There is seasonal color in the room. Kay nods approval.

She picks up both glasses, hands one to him, picks up the appetizer, and suggests they sit in the living room. She nestles into the corner of the couch, he in the other corner, the appetizer between them. They watch the birds hop in unison along a perch, to the left and then to the right and back again.

"So, you're a bird person," she says.

"I wouldn't exactly say that; these were given to me as a present in this last summer. Although, come to think of it, my mother and I kept chickens when I was a child. In fact, I had a—well, I had a cock for a pet."

Kay slaps her thigh and laughs generously. Should he tell her that the birds were a present from a childhood friend, a special lady friend from his homeland who visited him here in the summer? But before he can say anything, Kay rearranges herself, angling to face him. She crosses her legs and says, "Well, cheers to that, then!"

"To that, yes! And to the year that was!"

They lift their glasses to these, and to the light, the latter a formality, as in the yellow tungsten lighting in the living room, it is impossible to see this wine's true color. She brings the glass to her nose and sniffs. "Fruit," she says somberly.

"Ah, yes," he says, spotting an opportunity, "two distinctly different fruit."

She swirls it again and gravely announces, "Fleshy fruit."

He tilts the glass somberly. "Guava," he says. "Guava on a horizontal plane, and hovering just above, almost vertically, a note of seed of cashew. Rather, this has the smell of the taste of a cashew seed. If you know what I mean."

"I don't know the smell of guava, but if this smells of guava, then I must find myself a bottle of guava-scented cologne. And cashew seed? I don't even know what a cashew seed looks like. Would that be one or a handful?"

"More than one but not quite a handful."

He gathers from her acceptance of this New Year's Eve invitation that there is no man in her life. Swishing the liquid over and around and about his tongue, he swallows after his mouth has warmed it. Coconut. This is indeed what he tastes. Coconut in an Italian? He chews his mouthful, remaining quiet. A smudge of burnt-orange lip color rims Kay's glass. He does not mention the coconut.

He puts a forkful of her cheese-basil-tomato appetizer in his mouth. He sips the wine again—ocean wind, seaweed, oysters, crab, and at the back of his throat, more an odor than a taste, a low-tide mangrove swamp.

A tide of longing washes over him. Longing for Raleigh, a place he has not been to in years. For the faces of people he never really knew except as strangers he passed along the route from Raleigh to Marion. Of those congregated along the narrow and bustling streets of that town. Not wanting to talk about where he was born, about Raleigh nor Guanagaspar, he does not describe the experience of this other world in his mouth.

Kay has closed her eyes, her head to the ceiling, a hand laid palm-flat on her chest. She keeps her eyes closed, and in a low voice, almost a whisper, she says, "This is why I drink wine." After a pause, she looks directly at the birds in their cage and says, "You know, you have never really told me. You were married once, that much I know, but when? Was that here in Canada?"

He thinks of last summer and the two weeks Rose spent in his house. They behaved then as if they were married. Shall he simply tell her yes, but not to the woman he was in love with? The wine is going to his head. He looks at his watch and stands. She, too, gets up, and they make their way back to the kitchen.

Harry lowers the heat of the oven and tells her it is not much of a story, that it will take longer to tell her about it than it actually lasted.

They prepare to eat at the table. She finds the switch and turns off the dining room light. He goes to the table lamp in the far corner of the living room and turns it on. The room is softly illuminated, and the dining area by the light of her flickering candles only.

"I was about twenty-two or so. Most of my friends from school were either already married or engaged to be married. I hadn't shown any interest in girls—well, not suitable ones. Actually, there was a girl—"

"I see: an unsuitable one, then?" she mocks.

"Very unsuitable. Rather, I should say I was the one who was unsuitable. Actually, it is she who gave the birds to me."

Kay regards him quizzically. He says no more, and she, suddenly pensive, does not press.

She hands him the salad bowl. The sweater she wears tonight is tight. Perhaps it is the light of the candles that accentuates the shape of her breasts. He serves her before serving himself. Surprised, Kay sits back and places her hands on her lap. A woman from back home would have served him, he thinks.

It occurs to him that she is exactly the type of woman men from Guanagaspar—in general, of course—love to be with and at the same time fear. The type you don't have to worry over, as you know they are quite capable of taking care of themselves, and of you if it ever came to that. But the kind you don't dare fool with. Guanagasparian women tend to admire such women for what they would call brazenness, but in the next breath they would think these kinds mannish, harsh, too independent, too own-way.

As if attempting to move from too personal a conversation Kay asks about the house. "Such a lovely place you've got here, Harry. How did you ever find this house?"

The little piece of land with this house, part of a tight community nestled in a cranny at the foot of a mountain by the sea, is his. His piece of Canada. None of this would he have had in Guanagaspar.

How far back does one go? Finding this house began long before he came to this country, so shall he tell her about the little shack he lived in by the seaside in the islands with his mother? Shall he tell her how he dreamed as a child, as a youth, as a young man, of having a house and home that would have brought him and his mother a little recognition from the business community of Guanagaspar? Perhaps he ought to boycott the nature and lament of his longings and begin with when he first arrived in this country. Daytime, he studied landscape design at the technical institute, and nighttime, to pay for his studies, he drove a taxi. Long days, long nights, grabbing a little shuteye at Anil and his wife's house amid the screams and the full range of noises their young active children made.

Feigning levity, he tells her that in Guanagaspar, a gardener was a man who came to work barefoot on his bicycle that was held together by string and a prayer, who, before pulling out weeds and shoring up beds, washed his employer's car and after scrubbed the bathroom floor and tiles.

Kay is indulgent, arching her eyebrows, looking directly into his eyes. She interrupts, points to her empty glass. Before he can respond, still in the palm of his own reminiscence, she is up and away while telling him to continue, that she is listening. He hears the oven door opened, the foil pulled back, the door pushed shut again. The refrigerator door. A squeal of a cork from a bottle being pried up. He takes the opportunity to finish his salad. With this salad, wine goes back to being the taste of grasses and garden bugs. He must recommend to the membership of the Once a Taxi Driver Wine-Tasting and General Tomfoolery Club that they revise their politics. She is right. They must give the Europeans a second chance.

"This is indeed one heck of a salad," Harry shouts toward the kitchen. His words and voice are unfamiliar to him. With the last drop of wine in his glass thrown back, the flavor of garlic from the salad dressing stands erect, sweet, at the back of his tongue. She is here, bottle in hand, a smile of gratitude for the compliment. She is about to pour herself a glass but quickly recovers and sets the cold bottle, a different white, on a cork coaster. He obliges. Even in such light, one can easily discern that this one is brighter, yellower, than the last. He is eager to taste it. Seeing his empty plate, she clears the table of the half-full salad bowl and the salad plates. He could get up and bring in the fish and the corn pie, set out dinner plates. But his legs are heavy, and besides, he enjoys the sound of her, not Kay exactly, but a woman, the sound of a woman rummaging about his kitchen. He thinks of her in the Volkswagen van, and she is not a woman who has had lovers in the past, a woman looking for another lover, but a peaceful woman taking a long drive, a little holiday, by herself, and he wants to be in that van with her, she who would make his supper, put sugar in his tea and stir it, hang his pants, careful of the creases, and put slippers by the bed for him, so that in the morning when he awakens, he can be spared the rudeness of a cold floor.

Yet when she returns, places the fish and the corn pie on trivets, and sits in front of him, a sadness washes across him—if only it were Rose sitting across from him on this night. And as it comes, so it passes.

Kay sees the far-off look in his eyes. She puts the glass to her lips and swallows. Taps her tongue against the roof of her mouth. "Honey."

Harry feels a rush of wine, blood, and confusion.

"Taste it. Honey."

That old trick. He is surprised by his relief and by his disappointment.

"Where is this from?" He attempts a recovery from his confusion.

"Italy also. Different, though, eh? You were saying?" She speaks so innocently, but surely she meant to provoke him.

This time she scoops a serving of corn pie onto his plate, then onto hers. She serves him fish, then herself. She learns fast.

Taking a mouthful of fish, she clutches her chest with one hand and wrings the other. Harry pushes his chair back, ready to spring to some as yet undetermined action.

"Oh, Harry, Harry, Harry. This is heaven. It's so tender," she says, her mouth full of food. He relaxes and grins with pride. She prods with the tines of the fork at the fish, drawing out little shrimp and poking at cubes of cassava. "What is this? Potato?"

"Cassava," he says. She has never had cassava before. She marvels, and he is aware of the lightness of her voice, so different from the sturdiness of her actions. She asks what the strong taste is. "Cilantro, or it could be ginger," he tells her, not sure which she might be referring to. He takes a forkful of her corn pie. It is creamy and sweet. Like pudding. He tells her it is the kind of texture and soft taste one could reach for several times a day, just for its soothing. There is red bell pepper in it, not an ingredient he is used to.

They eat in silence. He sips the wine. Cilantro and red bell pepper, long since swallowed, seem to reemerge, to burst open fully, like blossoms.

They glance at each other, smiling.

"I was thinking. This beats being with my daughter's family and my grandchildren—much as I adore them all."

"Apples and oranges."

"Guavas and cashews. Handfuls of them."

This woman is good company, Harry admits to himself. She gives as easily as she takes. So ready to play, so eager to be played with. He glances at his watch. Quarter past nine. Quarter past midnight in Guanagaspar. He had not wanted to miss the moment of Guanagaspar's New Year celebration. But it has already passed. He has no clue as to what Rose and Shem might be doing. He wonders what the maid would have told Rose about his telephone call. He wishes again that he had not made that call. He imagines them passing the evening quietly, wind in the coconut trees and waves from the Caribbean Sea crashing on their beachfront property. Perhaps they went to their seaside neighbors for a celebration, or had friends up from town for the holiday, or their son and daughter-in-law and the grandchildren are passing the night in the beach house with them. No doubt they would sing "Auld Lang Syne." Even if they were by themselves, over the sound of waves and wind, they surely would have listened on the radio for the New Year countdown, or watched the TV with its snowy oceanside reception, and perhaps hummed along with the anthem. First the slow, nostalgic version, and then the same song, fast-paced, played by a pop and steel-pan band. Surely she must have hugged and kissed her husband, wished him a happy New Year. And he her. Would they have held each other in a long embrace? How many hopes for the future passed between them? He tells Kay that he feels a draft and excuses himself as if to check that the front door is shut tight. Kay prepares to rise.

"Don't get up," he says, pressing her shoulders as he passes. He goes to the darkened verandah and spends a handful of seconds watching the silver sea and night sky colored a brilliant orange by the lights of the distant city that is awaiting its midnight craziness. He sends wishes to Rose. He imagines he hears hers to him.

He returns to the dining table.

Kay asks if he is all right. He assures her he is, and quickly brushing her caring away as if it were one of those wool hairs come undone from her sweater, he begins to relate how he found his house.

"So, it was fall, late October. I was in Vancouver, nearing the end of a shift. There used to be a local radio show—*Bringin' Home the West Indies*—I was inside my idle cab on Eighth and Granville, listening to a prerecorded cricket test match. England and the West Indies."

He was never interested in the game of cricket, he tells her as he tries to shake the longing. Not even as an adult in Guanagaspar. When the cricket season began, the entire country caught cricket fever—the entire country, it seemed, but him.

"I find it to be a game that demands a great deal of patience, even from a spectator. Ali used to play." Seeing his look of confusion, she adds, "My husband."

"No, no. I know he was your husband. I am only surprised. I didn't know Iranians played cricket."

"Immigrants play cricket. He played with men from India, and from the islands—your islands. I went to matches with him, but no matter how many times he or anyone tried to explain the game to me, I remained baffled. It was such a slow game. I didn't mind the get-togethers and the parties after, though."

"There! We have something in common. I myself never received the calling to stand around in sweltering heat waiting for a ball to come my way. But the thing is, up here I was always yearning for anything from back home. So I used to listen to the commentary on the radio, and on that particular afternoon I was in my cab, waiting for a fare and listening."

He is relating an evening etched in his memory, an evening she wants to hear about, and he is aware of the thinness of her lambs'-wool sweater. He congratulates himself on having had the wisdom to not reveal that in his life, there is indeed a woman. However peripheral she has been lately. Thousands of little wisps of wool hairs rise out of the fabric, over the entire sweater. He imagines them against the palm of his hand. What would Anil say if he knew she—this white woman, the liquor-store lady that they tease him about—was having New Year's Eve dinner with him? Anil would be happy for him. That's the kind of friend Anil has been. Her sweater clings, showing the indentation of her brassiere where it cuts into her flesh. Glancing discreetly at the place where her bra straps would be, he imagines her flesh—solid, not flabby.

He attempts to draw a picture for her with his hands, spreading them on the table and in the air: the buildings of downtown, fewer then than now, the red sun gradually bathing the city in a fiery gold light. He is speaking, but he is distracted by the solidity of her body. He wants to tell her his story more than ever. He describes every detail, and she listens, her eyes fixed on his face, nodding, as she puts her fork, tipped with his fish, into her mouth, her eyes never leaving his. He talks and at the same time watches her breasts, her face, her hands, the knife in one, the fork in the other, cutting squares of corn pie. Such tenderness in her small gestures.

The red sun, he tells her, lit the panes of glass on the buildings, rendering each a little framed fire. On the far side of the water, the West Vancouver hills flared as if a spotlight had been thrown on them. The whites and pastels of buildings on that far shore jumped out against deep green trees.

Suddenly a man grabbed hold of the door of his cab and, without waiting for any indication from him, yanked the door open and pushed a woman in. The man slid in beside her and said, "Across the bridge. Elderberry Bay. It's up the Sound." That was a long drive. They would have racked up an enormous fare. The man wore a strong cologne, sandalwood and tobacco overpowering the stubborn scent of the thick plastic sheeting that covered the backseat. Traffic was heavy heading toward the bridge. If Harry could have turned them down, if it weren't illegal to refuse a fare, he would have; it was unlikely that he would pick up a return fare on that side of the bridge.

Kay has already helped herself a second time. She says that the meal is delicious, such a lovely evening and it isn't even midnight yet. Harry sniffs his wine: a Guanagasparian December's lash of seaside wind, the smell of oily sea salt.

"And?" Kay encourages, propping her chin on the back of one hand.

He decides to take a liberty. With a wink, as if imparting a confidence, he tells her that it used to be, in his taxi-driving days, a joke among cabbies that people from this side of the Lion's Gate Bridge weren't given to engaging in conversation with their drivers or being as familiar with them as passengers from the city's core. Those types would usually look out the windows absently or be hidden behind the daily paper for the entire trip.

"Now, not to interrupt your story, but don't you go thinking I am one of them," Kay says. "I live here because I work here. If I know anything about the high life, wine and that sort of thing, it's because I had to learn so I could serve this side's crowd." She feigns defensiveness. "Before I began working at the store, I knew nothing. When I was growing up, people didn't drink wine with meals. Wine was associated with wantonness. And by the way, Mr. Saint George, look at you, you've become one of *those* types yourself!" The teasing accusation flatters him, and a revelation unsteadies him: although this woman is from up here and, well, white-skinned is the best way he could put it, she is perhaps more like he is than he is like his Indo-Guanagasparian Rose.

He resumes his story, remembering precisely where he left off. The cricket-match commentary was still playing on the radio, quite low. The West Indies was batting and doing quite poorly. The man began whispering the instant the car pulled away from the curb. He soon dropped his guard against Harry's hearing, perhaps consoled by an idea that the game on the radio occupied Harry completely. But Harry couldn't have helped overhearing. They were in the midst of some unforeseen crisis. One could have told, in any case, that something was amiss from the instant the man opened the car door. You learn to spot these things when you drive for a living, if only as a matter of survival.

The woman was tall and thin. Although she hugged herself rather tightly, her face offered no story. The man wore a cream-colored suit. One could imagine that at calmer times, they might have made a handsome couple, except his face was unshaven and his suit crumpled, and the knot of his tie pulled down to his chest. His face was drawn, circles around his eyes.

The man was trying to reassure the woman that although they were on the verge of declaring bankruptcy, she should not worry; they could start life all over elsewhere. The woman was sullen.

Harry stopped listening to the radio and tuned his ears solely to the passengers. He heard the man whimper: "I'm sorry, I'm so sorry." He stole quick glances in the rearview mirror and saw that the man was shaking his head as though he couldn't believe what was happening.

In the mirror Harry saw that the woman's lips were pursed tight. She was staring out the window toward the distant sun-speckled mountains to the west, but Harry could tell she wasn't really paying them any attention.

Gritting his teeth, the man urged her to stop ignoring him. He was quiet for a minute as the car crawled down the decline of the bridge. Then he began repeating "I'm sorry" as though it were a mantra. He spoke loudly about their problems, admitting to a litany of sins. From the way he carried on, Harry imagined he might have thought Harry's English too poor for him to comprehend. Their house, the one he was driving them to, was about to be repossessed. Unless they made a quick sale, they would lose everything and have to declare bankruptcy. The man assured the woman that when he got home, he would get on the blower, he called it, call a few people and see if he could find someone with cash. Only then did the woman for the first time speak. "Who are you going to call? Who will take a call from you now?"

The man started breathing so hard that Harry surreptitiously glanced in the rearview mirror, afraid that at any moment the man might strike out at the woman. But the man was silent. Neither spoke again, except when the man mumbled to Harry to turn left off the highway.

Kay holds up her hands in the shape of a capital T. Harry stops.

"I'll make coffee," she states.

Harry jumps up, goes to a kitchen cupboard, and takes down a jar of instant coffee.

"Oh, instant. Is this all you have?"

He tells her, "Yes, don't worry, it's fresh, only been open for a couple of days." He reaches for the kettle, but Kay takes it from him. He leans against the counter as she searches and finds two mugs.

"Tell me the rest," she urges.

When they left the highway, they were winding their way on a dirt and rock road, lurching at times over small boulders. That year it had rained almost nonstop, and there were potholes so large that one could have fallen in and gotten lost.

The kettle reaches a boil. Kay lifts it off the stove and pours into two glass mugs.

"Honey."

This is the second time. She is doing it on purpose. She is flirting.

Harry opens a drawer and retrieves a packet of honey lifted from a restaurant.

"And you? Milk and honey?"

"Milk and sugar. Three teaspoons of sugar."

"Harry. Three teaspoons." She gasps.

"Well, just two. Two and a half, then."

"No, no, if three is what you usually take, I will put in three for you, but wow!"

Taking his mug from the counter, he ever so briefly places an open hand on her waist. She does not budge but keeps her back to him. He feels a residue, the ghost of her waist on the palm of his hand, the soft smoothness of the black wool sweater. The high protrusion of her hip. Having touched her once, he wants to do it again. She did not protest, but she did not react, either. She stays leaning against the counter, blows the surface of her coffee.

"We were approaching the house from above," Harry carries on, his voice thick.

Kay frowns, knowing that she entered his house from the back.

"The entrance used to be up there, on the road above. You couldn't tell from that there was a house below. It was only a dirt road up there that ended abruptly at the precipice. Let me show you."

She leans over the counter and peers through the window into darkness. He puts his hand on her back and points upward. That indentation, her brassiere strap. The wool soft against her firm flesh. The heat from her body tingles in the palm of his hand. Neither Kay nor Harry remarks on the fact that it is too dark to see what he is describing. But Kay nods as if she sees and understands. They lean their backs against the counter. He smells her cologne. He could put his arm around her and finish the story like that, or not finish it at all.

"There was a bit of red railing visible from up there, on the other side of the precipice," he says, cupping the steaming drink in both hands. "All one could see beyond was a hint of a roof, then the ocean a little farther beyond."

There is still time before the start of a New Year. He wonders if she will want to leave right after midnight. He walks to the far counter and puts the milk carton back in the refrigerator, then leans against that counter. There he remains. Kay looks from him to her coffee, no judgment, no clue to her desires, and she raises the mug to her lips.

"I heard water lapping at rocks, small waves breaking on the shore, felt the breeze through the trees. The words 'seaside house,' 'waterfront property,' formed in my mouth. I used to dream about living in a house by the sea. A real house in a nice neighborhood. I used to live by the sea with my mother when I was a child. But that house—with the two of us in it—could have fit in this kitchen. In that house, bedroom, kitchen, dining room, and living room were one and the same. And the bathroom and toilet were separate stalls outside in the yard. When I was a little older, we went to live in the town—my mother had married a petty businessman, and it was he who filled up my head with ideas and dreams about houses like this one. So it was as if my blood started racing when I saw this house.

"Well, the woman got out of the cab and disappeared down by the red railing, leaving the man rummaging through his pockets for the fare. Before I could think, I turned to face him in the backseat. 'How much do you want for it?' I asked."

Kay releases herself from the counter and covers her mouth with one hand. "Oh shit! You did not!"

Harry ignores her shock to good effect and continues.

"'What? Sorry, what did you say?' he asked. 'How much you want for your house?' I said again. The man collapsed in the seat and stared ahead. And then, words were tumbling out of my mouth. 'I couldn't help but hear. It is a small car. I am in the market. How much are you asking for it?'

"'You know, I was having a private conversation with my wife. I find this offensive. Do you make a practice of minding your customers' business?' 'Well, I am sorry, sir,' I replied, 'but it is a small car, you know.' The man began talking very softly, with a calculated hiss, you know, like this ..." and Harry did an imitation: "'Why don't you just mind your own friggin' business and get the hell out of here?' And I said back to him, in a really steady voice, 'I, sir, am not being idle. If your house is a good price, I will buy it from you this minute.'

"The man was slumped in the backseat, quiet for a long time. His wife reappeared to see what had kept him. He held up his hand to indicate that he would be along shortly. She waited a few seconds and dropped out of view again. 'For yourself?' the pathetic fellow whispered, becoming pensive. He muttered, 'But ...' and trailed off.

"I said, 'You're wondering *what*? I am making you a serious offer. You have a house to sell. I am in the market.'"

Suddenly the telephone rings on the kitchen counter behind Kay. Harry leaps forward but then halts, startled. Could it be Rose? He is surprised to find that he hopes it will not be Rose.

"Aren't you going to answer it?" Kay asks. He reluctantly picks up the receiver and hears not the expected voice but his good friend Anil shouting above a joyful noise—Indian music, chatter, reckless laughter, and the excited squeals of children. Anil is calling to wish him a Happy New Year. Kay turns to leave the room. Harry puts his hand over the receiver to conceal his voice from Anil and tells Kay there is no need, he will be only a minute. Anil realizes he has company and says he won't keep him long, but Partap is going to Fiji in a week for three months. He wants to get together before leaving. Partap comes on the phone. He is intoxicated and jovial. "Happy New Year. Happy New Year, man. Season's greetings." Why doesn't Harry come down to Anil's house right now. He hears Anil telling him that Harry has guests. Partap says, "Bring all the guests—leave now." Partap lets up only after Harry stops responding except for laughter. "All right, all right," but he insists on seeing Harry before leaving Canada. Wine tasting and general tomfoolery, how about it?

They decide on a date within the coming week.

Off the phone, Harry tells Kay the wine club is meeting soon. It sounds far more serious, the way he tells her, than it really is.

"'It's worth a hundred and sixty thousand,' the man said."

Kay interjects, "Whoa. In the early seventies, that was a lot of money for a house. As lovely as this is, that was a fair bit of money, Harry. What did you do?"

"A hundred and sixty thousand, a lot of money, in truth! Not the kind of money I stash under my mattress. I wanted to ask the man if he was quoting Canadian or Guanagasparian currency. I didn't have that kind of money. But I couldn't bear to look foolish in front of this fellow, even though I knew that I would probably never see him again. You know, being dark-skinned and all of that, I thought the joker would just think that every black person is a bluffer and an upstart, and I felt this responsibility to play my hand."

"And that would be the activist in you, I suppose?" says Kay slyly.

"You're right. Anyway, I had to tell myself it's a game, just a game. Take it easy and play the game. 'Well, I'm not sure it's worth a hundred and sixty,' I countered. 'Besides, do you think you'd get that today? I mean, you need a sale *today,* don't you?' to which he replied in a subdued way, 'You really were minding my business, weren't you.' I ignored him and continued, 'If you can get that much for it right away, all the best to you, man. All the best. I am in the market, but I am looking for a deal. One hundred and sixty thousand dollars ain't no deal.' And I turned to face the front of the car again. Now, where that kind of courage came from, I couldn't tell you. I never played any such game before, but I suppose that was the activist in me, eh! Anyway, I touched the meter, tapped it nervously. He still hadn't given me any money for the fare. 'I'll take seventy-five,' he said in a hushed voice."

"Seventy-five," squeals Kay. "Is that what you paid for this house?"

"Wait. Not so fast. How often would the likes of me hit upon such an opportunity, eh?"

Harry remembers the defining image that had flown into his head in the moment. He had imagined Rose descending the precipice, looking directly at him. He hadn't really believed then that she would ever have the chance to see that he, Harry St. George, was living in a fine seaside house in a respectable part of the world. He was ready to commit himself and all of his savings, which were well below seventy-five thousand dollars.

"'Cash?' I asked the man. 'Cash,' he said bluntly. 'When do you need it by?' I asked him. He said, 'The bank is supposed to call in everything in a day or two,' and was silent again. I waited and he breathed a low long sentence. 'In a day or two the effing bank will effing repossess my effing house—is that what you want to hear me say?' I didn't answer. He took out a pen and pad from the inside pocket of his jacket and scribbled. 'How soon can you come through with cash?' he asked. Realizing I had power in the situation, I became what even I would call perverse, so I said, 'Sixty-five, eh?'"

"Harry," Kay exclaims in mocking disapproval.

"I could feel his eyes pierce the back of my head. I wondered what he saw. I looked at him in the rearview mirror. 'I am not going below seventy-five. I would rather declare bankruptcy.' He was running his tongue around the inside of his mouth, distending his cheek and upper lips. He flung a twenty-dollar bill on the front seat and stormed out of the cab. 'Don't effing play with me. If you don't have that kind of money, what are you trying to—'

"'Cash,' I said firmly. 'Sixty-five thousand. Cash.'

"The man slammed a fist on the roof of the car. "'Take the damn thing for sixty-five, then. Sixty-five frigging thousand dollars.' I remember his words like it was yesterday. 'Sixty-five frigging thousand dollars.'"

"So, of course I asked if there was anything I should know about it. 'Is there a lien on it or anything? A body buried in the yard?' He said there was no lien on it. In fact, he said, 'There's not a damn thing wrong with this house or its title. And there is no body buried anywhere. I am no criminal, you jackass. I am just a man who takes risks, and usually they pay off, but I just took one too many— not for me but for my wife, who, if she is not careful, may not bear that distinction for much longer. I am going through a rough period. Is that a crime? Come. I suppose we have some things to figure out. I suppose you want to see it?'"

Harry remembers that he was thinking about all the people back home, how they would all be so impressed that Harry St. George was living in a seaside house that he himself owned— and in such a "good" neighborhood in Canada. He does not mention this, but he does tell Kay that his mother, long dead, would have loved this seaside home, and that he imagines his stepfather, if he were alive, taking walks down the roadway Harry and his workers would eventually construct, watching the neighbors' houses, and gloating.

"Harry, you were heartless." Kay grins mischievously. They watch each other, smiling. He marvels at how easy it is to speak with this woman. He remembers Rose asking him about the house in the summer, but he avoided imparting to her the circumstances under which he bought it.

Breaking the loaded silence that has ensued, Kay asks where the bathroom is. He leans back against the counter and points in its direction. For the first time, Harry notices that Kay is beautiful. He has the urge to follow her. Eleven thirty-five. He goes instead to the refrigerator, takes one of the champagne bottles from its paper bag, unties the wire net covering the cork. As he works the cork, he recalls that the man and he walked down the wet stairs to the side of the house. It was low tide. The man pointed to the bag in Harry's hand. Harry held the bag up. The man reached in and pulled out a ring of apple, popped it in his mouth.

"So, what was that you were listening to—or rather, not listening to—on the radio?" Harry remembers him changing the subject.

"Cricket."

"God. Are the commentators always so lethargic?"

Harry had the sense that the man had already moved out of the house and into some future he alone could see. He was probably accustomed to living on the edge of his pocket, to taking risks, losing some, gaining on others.

Harry had yet to look directly at the house. "It's a slow game," he told the man, feeling oddly defensive.

"Do you know hockey?"

He remembers rounding the side of the house on slabs of concrete embedded in the lawn grass. He got his first view of the garden: low retaining wall and tall unkempt grasses merging with a pebbly beach. Some boulders at the edges, an uprooted tree with cauterized roots facing the sky, rows of washed-ashore logs, then the sea. The man's wife stood on the lawn, facing the water, surrounded by beds of tall lime-green ferns. Hugging herself. She heard them and turned. Harry saw Rose again, imagined it was she standing there, and even without seeing the interior of the house, he knew that he definitely wanted it.

But this woman here with him tonight, listening to his every word and so ready to grin and laugh—he had the impression that she wouldn't care if he lived in a studio apartment. She didn't even seem to notice that he was rather incompetent in the recreational outdoor world that she so loved.

Freshly sprayed marigold scent announces her return. Her hair is neatened, fluffed up, her lipstick reapplied thickly. Harry hands her a glass of champagne. The bubbles rise swiftly to the top, jumping out of the glass, diving through the air like minute meteors. She sniffs the contents and, with the tips of her fingers, brushes her upper lip and her nose where bubbles have spat. Her preening flatters him.

She suggests going into the garden. Harry blows out the candles in the dining room and checks that the oven is turned off. They wrap themselves in coats, muffle their necks in scarves. He takes the open bottle swathed in a towel, closes the door behind them, and they carry their glasses of champagne across the front lawn to the water's edge.

From somewhere in the distance, over the water, comes music, and here and there the excitement of a high-pitched stray voice is dispersed by the whims of the night's brisk breezes. The air is dry. Clean and crisp, as if in readiness for a New Year that is just minutes away.

The tide is as far out as it ever gets. Harry extends his hand and helps Kay down the steps that lead from his property to the sliver of pebbled shore. The pebbles glimmer in the light of the bright sky. They step over a row of dead logs and amble, side by side. A black shape, a silhouette against the silver-black water, moves on a rock. It turns toward them. Closer, they see that it is a bald eagle. It remains firmly on the rock, not unduly perturbed by their presence. Kay raises her glass. He raises his, tips it toward hers.

She says in a quiet voice, "If there is one thing you could do all over again, what would that be, Harry? Do you have any regrets?"

He ponders having left Guanagaspar. He doesn't regret that. But it has been made clear tonight, by the light of this woman with whom he is spending this New Year's Eve, that he has spent a lifetime haunted by the desire to be a part of a particular Guanagasparian world in which he would, more than likely, never have achieved the status of insider, and this is the fuel under any fire that might have burned in him. He says only, "My mother. I might wish that I had left Guanagaspar sooner than I did, while my mother was alive. I would have brought her here with me. She would have come. She wasn't afraid of change. Yes, she would have liked living in this house. She and me, by the sea, just as we once had." Harry's halfhearted chuckle does little to belie the emotion washing over him. "But she died before it even crossed my mind to leave the island. She had a way of saying exactly what was on her mind, but she was never unkind." He feels certain that his mother would have been comfortable in Kay's presence.

A whizzing sound arches across the sky, though they see nothing. Ahead, far in the distance, coming from the direction of the city, flares shoot into the sky and quietly explode. Faint sounds of whistles, rattles, shouts of "Happy New Year" float across the water. Kay slips her hand under his arm and takes his elbow. He unhooks his arm, pulls her to him, and whispers in her hair, "Happy New Year." She returns the wish solemnly: "Happy New Year, Harry." She closes her eyes and lifts her face to kiss his lips. In the fleeting half second it takes for him to catch his breath, she has touched his lips with hers and already stepped back from him. She looks overhead at the sky as a wanton firecracker explodes.

"Everything and anything always seems so possible in these first few hours of a New Year. Don't you think so, Harry?"

He pulls her to him and kisses her again. A squeal of laughter and an isolated, drunken shriek sail across the water.

Riptide

How long the telephone has been ringing he cannot tell. Harry tries to sit up, but his head is heavy. The bedside clock's red digital numbers glow: 5:00. Who would call so early on a holiday morning? In an instant he bolts into wakefulness: he should not have let Kay drive home. They had certainly consumed a great deal of wine. He did want her to stay, but once they reentered the house, her mood seemed to change. She gathered up and shoved her dishes, dirty, from the sink, counter, and refrigerator into the bags she had brought. When Harry urged her to stay, citing for his case drunk drivers on the highway, moving toward the spare room to clear the bed there for her, she held him back, announcing, "I'm not ready, Harry. I'll stay when I'm sure."

Unprepared to handle bad news, he grabs the receiver, hesitates before putting it to his ear. "Harry? Is that you?" the caller tentatively utters. He sits upright and squeezes the telephone as he blurts, "Yes. This is Harry. Who is this?"

"It's Cassie, Harry. Cassie Bihar." The pitch of her voice is exactly that of her mother's. He is perplexed: why is Cassie calling him at five o'clock in the morning?

"I know it's early. I am sorry to wake you."

Kay's cologne, still permeating his house, has made its way into his bedroom. He can see little in the darkness of the room. Had Cassie called half a day ago, he would have been delighted to hear from her, from anyone with connections to Rose. He closes his eyes. "What's up, Cassie?"

"Harry, I should have called you yesterday." She hesitates before continuing. "I wasn't sure what to do. I am at the airport."

In the few words she has spoken, he hears not Cassie but Rose. Even Rose's daughter's voice can cause him to feel skinless and raw. He notices that they have not exchanged New Year's greetings.

"I am going home, Harry. Something has happened."

His head spins. He rubs the open palm of his free hand against his cheek and lethargically moves his feet off the bed. He shuffles about in an effort to find his bedroom slippers. "What is it?"

"I don't know. My father telephoned last night. Something about my mother. He won't say, exactly. Except that I need to come home."

Harry switches on the reading lamp beside his bed and stands unsteadily. A fleece shirt hangs on one post of the bed's footboard. He pulls it on, the motion seeming overblown and weighted down.

"I called Jeevan. But he, too, says don't ask questions, that they all need me, and that I must return, and everything will be clear then. I don't really know why I am calling you. I'm sorry. But I'm kind of scared."

Harry's heart races. During the summer Cassie wordlessly acknowledged her mother's and his affair; she had lied to her father several times when he telephoned wanting to speak with Rose, saying on one occasion that she had gone to the library, on another to a quilt-making session at the community center.

He thinks of the night just passed, of Kay. In the instant of a Bihar's voice in his ear, that evening's contentment, his closeness to Kay, is diminished. The entire evening suddenly seems irresponsible, an act of disloyalty.

In response to Harry's silence, she mutters, "Well, I just thought I should let you know." In the background he hears the public-address system announcing the boarding of a flight. Feeling a little stunned, he tells her to call him when she arrives, and feebly wishes her a good flight before she hangs up.

Unsettled, he is fully awake, his head feeling one minute like a lump of lead, and then the next weightless. He walks to the window and parts the curtain. Elderberry Bay is asleep in darkness. He makes his way down the dark hallway to the kitchen. By the light of the opened refrigerator door, he whisks a raw egg into a glass of tomato juice. He sips the reviver and contemplates.

New Year's Day, full of unanswered questions, seems interminable. Restless in the living room, he cradles the telephone in his lap, all but prepared to ring the Bihars' house and risk being answered by Shem. But he holds back. It is, too, with some difficulty that he resists contacting Kay.

The following morning he is awakened, again early, from a fretful sleep. It is Cassie. She is calling from Guanagaspar. There is much static on the phone. He can barely hear her. She seems reluctant to speak loudly, her words guarded.

"I wanted to catch you before you headed off to work. Have you heard from my mother?"

He is perplexed. "I haven't, Cassie. Aren't you there with her now? What's going on?"

"I don't know. I can't talk long. Can you come? Just say you will."

A surge of rage engulfs him, and as quickly as it came, it subsides. He is on the verge of asking why, without the courtesy of an explanation, should he? Instead, resigned to the pull of a Bihar, he says, yes, he will come if it is necessary, he will come right away. Instantly Cassie retorts, "I have to go now, but I will arrange for you to be picked up at the airport. Just call to let me know when your flight is arriving."

The Birds

When Kay and Harry talk on the telephone later that day, she tells him that she wishes she had accepted his offer to spend the night at his house. He understands that this is not because she should not have driven impaired. He finds himself answering, in response to her admission, that there has been an emergency back home on the island, requiring him to return for a few days. As if her confession entitles her, she wants to know the details of the emergency. He mumbles that an old friend is gravely ill, says that the family has asked him to return. Although he has already arranged with a worker to care for the birds, Kay insists on keeping them herself and on driving him to the airport.

On the way Kay is silent, her face draining of color as Harry is obliged to explain further his relationship to this friend, the woman who had visited him in the summer, and to whose side he is so suddenly rushing. Harry suspects that Kay is congratulating herself on her astuteness in refusing his offer to spend the night at his house.

Curbside on the departure level, he can think of nothing appropriate to say. He leans his body toward her and embraces her briefly, but Kay holds herself stiffly. No words pass between them. He busies himself arranging his luggage on his shoulder, taking his ticket from his jacket inner pocket. Picking up his other bag, he turns and walks slowly toward the terminal.

II

A Story

Guanagaspar. Long ago.

Once a week, the central plains of Guanagaspar, commonly known as Central, used to be supplied with fresh seafood by an old fellow of African origin. Mako the fisherman sold from the back of a pickup truck. After doing this work for over twenty years, Old Man Mako's body began to wear out. Although he continued to fish, he passed his selling route to a young man named Seudath, who was of the Indian race. This fellow, as unlikely as it might have seemed, had, from the time he was a child, been like a son to the old black fisherman.

This Indian named Seudath, carrying a lidded wooden crate half filled with ice, half filled with carite, snapper, and shrimp, topped off with a weigh scale and a once-white canvas bag of weights, got a ride, his bicycle strapped atop, in a public transport jitney into Central. On the outskirts he would disembark, untie the bicycle, strap the crate to the handlebar, and bump his way along the winding dirt roads of the Central plains. Once the first of the line of barrack houses came into sight, he would begin squeezing the spongy salmon-colored rubber ball of his well-polished brass horn. Riding on a dirt road built up high, rice paddies on either side and cane fields on the outskirts, he hooted that horn as if clearing a path through chaotic traffic. In truth, all that darted off to make way for him were swarms of lazy dragonflies and stands, thick as Central's ajoupa mud walls, of hovering mosquitoes. He would honk all the way, a thin sound like a donkey wheezing from the brass horn. He would take his hand off the rubber ball and grasp the handlebars intermittently in order to balance himself, fishy-smelling meltwater dripping the entire way. So doing, he gave the residents of Central enough time to fetch a plate, basin, sheets of paper, and to run outside to catch him and his fish before he passed them by. Central was good business for him. The only fish available to the people were the tilapia and the cascadura, which proliferated in the freshwater dams used to flood the rice fields in the dry season. Tilapia and cascadura were good-tasting but, in comparison to the robustness of fish from the sea, seemed bland.

And that was how the Indian named Seudath and Dolly's worlds collided. When they first saw each other, Dolly wasn't yet fourteen. She thought him to be unlike any Indian she knew. He wasn't like her brother, who was serious and officious. He didn't possess the pious calm or dignity of her father. He was brazen more like black people, she would tell her son with delight and pride; he was brazen, for so, the way he looked you straight in your face, in your eyes when he was talking to you. Brazenness was a sign, she had always heard, of craziness or don't-careness, and an attribute of black people, not of Indian people, who were more careful about how they appeared to others. The unusual Indian fellow rode his bicycle with studied recklessness, swerving it from side to side, his legs splayed wide, honking that brass horn and grinning like a grouper. He was unabashed, asking people—people too withdrawn and suspicious of outsiders to answer—how life was treating them, how they were planning to cook his fish, to recommend a bush cure for this or that ailment. He had the ability to get them to stand up in the hot sun and chat long after they had bought his fish. He laughed and joked forthrightly with women, who came to like him once they put to rest their initial suspicion that he was after more than their

fish money. His shirt, unbuttoned to his waist, exposed a remark-
ably muscled chest and gave the older women something to whisper and joke about lewdly among themselves.

He could not have been more unlike the Indian men of
Central. Central men worked either in the rice fields or on sugarcane plantations or with the roadworks department of the government, cutlass-brushing the edges of the dirt roads and keeping
bush around drains cropped to lower the risk of malaria. With
the low wages they were paid—and they were paid by the task—
they had to work as hard as the water buffalo they kept in mud
ponds behind their barracks houses. They were serious, quiet
men who became brazen, or laughed and raised their voices, only
at the end of the workday, when they headed straight for the rum
shop or congregated under someone's house, where they drank
pineapple babash to excess. Then more than a few of them could
be counted on to exhibit everything from their bare bellies to
their frightening belligerence. The same ones often became violent, ready to stick-fight with real or imaginary foes, or to fistfight
in the privacy of their thin-walled homes.

But this Seudath fellow seemed different.

On hearing the hooting of the fisherman's horn, Dolly's
mother, busy dropping chickpea flour balls into a pot of bubbling oil in the kitchen shed at the back of their house, handed
her the big enamel basin and sent her out to buy four slices of
snapper and a fish head. Dolly was not in the habit of looking directly into the eyes of a man, not even her father's or her brother's,
but once she caught a glimpse of the fisherman's eyes—the ocean
deep and wide with foreign shores swimming in them—she
couldn't help but stare. She became uncomfortable when he
asked her name. If a decent man wanted to know, he wouldn't
have been so crazy or rude as to directly ask a young woman her
name. He would have sent someone of the same standing as her
parents, perhaps the pundit's wife, to inquire it of them—if he

was good and decent, that is, and only, too, if he had some in-
tentions. She thought and thought and concluded that perhaps
she should ignore him. But she was also not in the habit of being
insolent—to anyone, regardless of station. She chose to mumble,
"Dolly," but he heard it. Uncomfortable that she had responded,
she didn't look at him again but kept her eyes on the wheels of
his bicycle. He gave her the snapper slices and the head. As she
walked away without looking back, he rearranged the box of
scales, weights, fish, and ice, climbed on, and rode off. He got
about ten yards away, turned, and called out, "I name Seudath."
He saw her lose her balance on the two steps to the house,
and he grinned. When he returned to his seaside village of
Raleigh, he immediately set out to look for a good piece of
land. When he found what he was looking for, he began clearing it of the hardy old guava trees that grew wild. He brush-
cut a path he named Timbano Trace and began constructing a
one-room dwelling.

Dolly not-yet-St. George was living in her parents' portion of
the barracks that once housed the workers for the sugar estate
not far away in Central Guanagaspar. There was no moon.

    She waited until she heard the deep unconscious breathing of
every person in the house: her parents, sister, brother, and that of
the families who lived on either side of their boxlike homes. She
waited longer, until not even the snorting and braying of the quar-
relsome mule and the water buffalo leashed behind the barracks
line stirred. Then she crept out of the box and, once outside,
traveled stooped along a bed of bitter-smelling marigolds. She
looked back at the barracks. No lamps in any of the long line of
side-by-side dwellings were being lit. She reached the end of the
line and pelted down a slope in the direction of the tamarind
tree, not considering that mapipire or coral snakes might be
underfoot. She stopped by the tree. He was there; she could

smell him. He had a particular scent. This Indian who was coming to meet her by the tamarind tree almost every other night
smelled of sea salt, wet sand, seaside smoke, and ash from the
incineration of discarded newspapers and fish parts. For a young
girl who had never seen the sea, such a smell, such a man, was
excitement.

One particular night when the air was still and humid and yellow, flamelike flashes of fireflies darting about in patterns that
seemed choreographed, Seudath, her seaside Indian with a
Christian last name, St. George, who came twice a week to see
her, touched her in ways that made her body quiver, her heart
quicken.

In the rice paddies all around them, frogs belted out rasping
swamp songs. Seudath bent his head and smelled at the back of
her neck the aromatic wood fire and incense from her family's
evening prayers. He touched her ears with his lips and uttered
one word, "Tonight," which in his excitement was rendered thick
and coarse like a frog's gasp. He cleared his throat and repeated
it more clearly, adding, "Let me take you tonight, nuh?"

She said nothing.

He continued, "I will make you my *dulahin* if anything happen. I promise. Let me do it, nuh? I want to take you tonight."

It didn't take her mother a month to know. Her mother hit
her over the head with a pot spoon, screamed, pulled her own
hair and Dolly's in rage. Dolly's brother ran out of the house on
hearing what shame had befallen the family, and from the yard,
in front of neighbors he ripped up a prayer flagpole with which
he threatened to beat his sister. When Dolly's mother threw
herself in a screaming frenzy on the hard clay ground in front of
him, pleading with him not to hit his sister, and held on to his
trouser legs so that he was able to make only small steps as he
either dragged her along with him or was tripped by her, he

dropped the stick, and in a voice hoarse from screaming, he threatened to douse Dolly later that same day with kerosene for the scandal that would be a handle to the family name forever. After a shower, a meal, and an offering to one of his gods, he decided instead of the dousing to oversee banishing her forever from Central. He sent a message to the fisherman from Raleigh to come and fetch the girl he had destroyed, but not to show his face near the house.

On the day of the banishment, a handful of people congregated near, but not in front of, the house on the pretense of merely going for a stroll. They watched Dolly walk away empty-handed from her parents' house, looking back at her brother, who was the only one standing like a bull ready to charge, and she pleaded in vain with her eyes. The strange more-African-than-Indian Indian in the jitney was waiting at the far end of the line down which he usually rode his bicycle. When they saw him alight and run toward Dolly, everyone started shouting obscenities at him. They all picked up rocks and ran toward Seudath and Dolly, pelting them.

Tante Eugenie, wife of Raleigh's most elderly fisherman, the African Mako, lived down by the coconut tree whose trunk was shaped like a Z. She knew everything and everybody, and everybody knew her, and she had taken care of Seudath St. George from the day he was found, a little child abandoned in the fishing village. He hadn't been at the one-room dwelling with Dolly twenty minutes when Tante Eugenie came shouting out to him, telling him to bring his woman out into the sunshine to meet Tante Eugenie. She didn't come with her arms swinging. She carried her pipe in one hand and in the other a basket woven from vetivier, filled with live crabs whose claws were tied with reeds, edoes, plantain, and green bananas gathered from the land around her house a few minutes' walk away. She settled herself onto the lower board of the front steps, shoving her bare foot into the hot dry sand and wriggling her toes about, sifting the sand through them. She put an arm around Dolly's shoulders and took some long quiet drags on her pipe. She felt the fear and aloneness, the sadness, of the young girl who was likely not going to see her family again. Ahead, the sea sprawled on end-lessly. There was no horizon that day, just a haze where sea and sky became one.

Tante Eugenie told Dolly things about Seudath. He was the only Indian in all the fishing village of Raleigh. He grew up there with everybody, but mainly Tante Eugenie and Uncle Mako, tak-ing care of him.

Tante Eugenie told Dolly that when Seudath was found, they asked him his name. He stopped crying long enough to say in between heaving sobs, "I name Seudath."

Some weeks later, Dolly and her Indian from by the sea were married in a seaside church in Raleigh, in the western parish of St. George.

One of the first things Tante Eugenie warned Dolly was that the wife of a fisherman and the wife of a policeman had much in common, the worst of which was that once their husbands left for work, nobody knew if they would be seen again. Dolly took that warning to heart and cherished her Seudath day and night, dreading the day she was sure her sweet and strange Indian wouldn't return.

Early one morning before the sun was up, mere weeks be-fore their child was born, Seudath went out in a pirogue with two other men. Dolly didn't go out with him that morning like she usually did, carrying a salt-fish-and-bake breakfast and a bottle of tea in a cloth sack for him. She was in her last month of pregnancy. She hadn't slept that night. Her feet were swol-len, her back hurt, she was unbearably big, heavy, and hot, so hot she couldn't breathe all night long. Come morning Seudath could see her discomfort. He told her not to come, and when she didn't protest, he knew she really couldn't. He kissed her bulging belly, and even though he had work to get to, he took the time, all of a couple of minutes, to make the gesture of squeezing one of her swollen feet and assuring her that it wasn't going to be long before she had her body back to herself again. He remained quiet until she had drifted off to sleep. She didn't even hear when he opened the door, or when he pushed it back in behind him.

The wife of one of the men had gone down to the water carrying salt-fish cakes and tea she had made for them that morning. She remembers the sun just breaking the horizon. She recalls watching the three men set the net out quietly and neatly over the sand, unfolding and unknotting, and she watched them walk into the water, leap out over the first small waves, grabbing the side of the pirogue and hoisting themselves in. She knew it was Dolly's husband, by his distinguishing red jersey, who was pulling the cord on the engine many times before it would catch and hold, its slow chug, an emission of blue smoke trailing behind them. But a few minutes later, while she could still see them, and though they were still in hearing distance, the sound of the engine seemed to have died out. She heard it start up and die out several times, then it took again and was steady, and so she walked back up the beach slowly, listening as long as she could hear.

It took three sets of wave patterns—first two or three small waves coming blithely ashore, rolling back out to accumulate as the next larger one, then a lull as they all gathered in a swell towering high over the horizon line, blocking any view she might have had of the boat, then tumbling and breaking with a thunderous crash, a hard, swift roll high up the beach, spreading out so unexpectedly warm all around her feet that it startled her—before she heard that familiar slow chug, the sound of the engine at work. It became gradually faster until it was a full, steady drone taking a good half hour, perhaps more, she said, to fade into the distance. Only after they were but a speck seen in between the rise and fall of the ocean's waves did she go back into her house. That was the last of them.

A few hours later, sky and sea turned shades of gray, and in moments, some parts even black. It was full of tides, lines of ripples, the language of the ocean that fishermen and their families know. The sea chopped and boomed. Waves formed far, far out, and at their fullest, they stretched up like ravenous mouths opening wide. They brutally dissected one another, ran against one another. Ones racing backward slammed into others that were pelting forward, and each wave that shattered rolled high up the beach, scattering chip-chip, pebbles, sea cockroaches, and starfish, spitting fringes of dense, ocher-colored froth laced with seaweed, tangled lengths of fishing lines, bits of old net, and cork floaters. Air that blew in from across the ocean was heavy with the scent of things from the ocean's bed ripped up and churned. Tante Eugenie had sniffed that particular odor early and came immediately to keep a silent watch with Dolly. They went down by the water's edge and watched. Dolly, cradling her belly, rubbing the top as if to soothe the baby growing inside her, stared, her eyes wide and blank. The baby in her belly reached and grabbed some part of her inner anatomy, and she thought then that if she herself were to step into the water, it might pull them both far, far in. She retreated up the beach some paces. A strong wind rolled in from the ocean, bringing with it that smell again. That night the sea calmed. For three days Dolly, accompanied by Tante Eugenie, kept watch on the beach. The sea remained tranquil, barely a wave forming, the water's surface undulating like a sheet of clear cellophane in a light wind. Nights there was the usual soft, benevolent drizzle of rain. Days the sky was cyan in parts, cerulean and sapphire elsewhere, but always shades of blue, and the sun yellowing the sand didn't leave anything alone. The beach glistened. The water close to the shore was clearer than glass; pebbles, shells, fine sand magnified and danced, and farther out to the horizon, it was virtuous. Whitecaps like rows of white roses, bunches of white chrysanthemums, burst, showed off, then frayed, blending into the ocean again. The air had the guileless scent of sun and salt. Coconut trees, brilliant yellow, their trunks white like the sand, fanned the beach, and the fishing pirogues lined up, posing as if nothing had happened, as if awaiting the arrival anytime soon of a photographer from town, or abroad, or an oil painter. It would have been inconceivable to someone passing by on the main road, watching the picturesque seaside village, the ground under the coconut trees covered in orange crocuses waving at them, inviting them even, that tragedy had befallen Raleigh. On the evening of the third day, the sea still close-lipped and innocent-looking, Dolly reluctantly made her way back into her house and wrapped herself in white.

First a big piece of the net, full of seaweed, washed up somewhere along the coastline. Then boards from the pirogue, one piece with the boat's name, *St. Peter,* partially visible. One of the men's jerseys, but not the red one she was hoping and not hoping for. A few days later, more flotsam and jetsam of a nighttime high tide. A month or so beyond that time, the engine was discovered a few miles up the shore, but no bodies were ever recovered.

Dolly would eventually remarry, but how could it be the same?

HUSTLING TO
CATCH TAXI

No matter how the child jostled against his mother's body as she ran breathless down Timbano Trace, he refused to awaken. He was heavy, and sweat streamed down Dolly's face. If she missed the six o'clock taxi, it would be an hour before the next one passed. By then traffic would have piled up. She would end up being over an hour late.

She made haste, and with each breath the odor of the sea: crab, fish bones, seaweed, and chip-chip made her skin crawl. The sand was damp, too; it must have rained, there must have been a storm last night. The smell told her that the sea had pitched back up some of what it had lassoed yesterday or even years back. It had crossed her mind when she first awakened to run down to the water and check if the sea had decided to return any of her belongings. But years of doing just this had taught her that the sea had secrets it held on to and would not give up for any amount of pleading or promises.

It must have been an offshore storm. An offshore storm with the audacity to make shore people sick with its sea-bottom foulness.

It was the cock in the yard clucking, clearing its throat, flapping about like stale news in wind, that woke her. She thought something was meddling with it. Whether it was a dog come to steal the hen's eggs freshly laid under the house, or a man prowling about in the yard, it was she who had to fend for herself and the boy. So she got out of bed and peeped through a gap in the boards. Nothing. She nudged the lopsided window open for a better view. The sea air was damp, clinging to her skin. It was just the cock out there. She recognized it strutting and dancing and prancing. Suddenly eight, nine, ten of them spread throughout the area, made ruckus enough to rouse even the dead, be they on land or tangled up in the bottom of the ocean. Lately she'd had to shoo the one that was hers off the crown of the pawpaw tree. Such an old, heavy bird in such a young and tender tree. It would have brought down the tree if she had not put a stop to it. If her son had not been so attached to that particular bird—and why it was so, she could not understand—she would have wrung its neck and stewed it a long time ago. Clucking about and waking her up like that.

Hustle-hustle: she mustn't miss the taxi.

God, her child had grown, overnight it seemed. Five years she had been carrying him like this, at this time of the morning when he remained asleep on her shoulder, to catch the ride into town. How heavy he had become, too heavy to be carrying so.

The Problem of Traveling in
a Taxi with Black People

Before taxis serviced the link road that connected up the south coast's seaside villages, Raleigh being one of them, Dolly St. George hardly set foot beyond the walking distance between her house and Tante Eugenie's. Raleigh people seldom traveled beyond the village. When they did, it was to obtain one kind of license or another from a government office in the capital city of Gloria, a birth certificate or death certificate, or to go to the hospital in Marion to visit an ailing relative or friend or to see a doctor themselves. If they'd had cause to travel, they would have gone the old way: hired horse cart, mule cart, or donkey cart. After the service became regular in the area, the Indian man from the village farther south, who used to give rides in his donkey cart for a few pence, painted a sign on the wood frame of his cart: Narine Donkey Service. For Hire. Combative Rates, Frenly Driver. Fresh Air & Seenic Route. Garanteed. He and his donkey used to be regularly spotted transporting someone or something in the cart, but he had become scarce these days.

Dolly St. George was among the first to take the opportunity to travel the hour and half—on a good day, that is, twice that and more, when the swamp flooded Link Road—into Marion to look for work. On the day she first took a taxi, she was one of two passengers in the car licensed to carry five. People from the area preferred to wait to hear if the vehicle really was able to make it all the way into the town and back safely. That trip was an investment: a shilling, which was a shilling more than she truly could spare. But thankfully, on that first day looking, she found the washing and ironing job to which she was traveling now.

The driver, Mr. Walter, didn't grip the steering wheel as tightly as he had the first few times she rode in his car. The first day he picked her up, he was as hesitant as she. When she saw him, a black man driving, a man whose ancestors were brought from Africa, she had a moment of uncertainty, and it was only the prospect of work in Marion that made her, a lone Indian woman from the predominantly Negro village of Raleigh, get into the motor car with three black men. Let them run their mouths, she thought. She had a baby to mind; had any of them offered to clothe and feed him?

Mr. Walter, for his part, was surprised to find a woman waiting for him, flagging him down, as he approached Timbano Trace. She was alone that first time, having left the baby with Tante Eugenie. Walter got out of the driver's seat, came around to her, and said, "Mornin,' madam." She didn't like him calling her madam. She wondered what he meant by that. She wasn't any madam. She set her face sternly and waited for him to open the door. He stood looking down Timbano Trace. He turned back to the car, took out a handkerchief from his pants pocket, and wiped the rear window. She still waited for him to open the door. The other two passengers, the two men who were also black-skinned, like Mr. Walter, had stayed in the car, but they were also curiously looking down Timbano Trace. Finally the driver stopped polishing his vehicle, looked all around, and said, "It have somebody else coming?" She shook her head. He raised his eyes and said, "You alone?" She said nothing and looked at the door handle. He said, "Marion?" She nodded. He said, "One shilling, return. If you have it. But you could owe me." She turned her back to him and discreetly withdrew from her bodice a handkerchief that had been tucked in the crease of her bosom. She unwrapped it and, turning again to face him, held out a shilling. He took it from her, yet he laughed and said, "I trust you, you know." Her face burned with shame for traveling in this new manner: by herself, with strangers, with men, ones of African descent at that. She wondered if, in so doing, she had encouraged him to be fresh with her. He opened the door. She backed herself onto the hard-wood seat and sat down, reluctant to draw her sandy shoes into the clean interior. Mr. Walter mumbled to her not to worry, but he waited happily as she dusted off the sole of each shoe. Once she was safely in, he shut the door. Dolly stayed close to the door so as not to end up too near the other passengers. Mr. Walter said nothing more to her until he left her at the petrol station just outside Marion, but she had caught him watching her in the rearview mirror. When she got out, he addressed her, "Re-turn trip from here, two o'clock. Sharp." For a good while, on subsequent trips, he said little more to her than "Mornin'" and "Afternoon."

THE MAN FAST FOR SO

Only when the taxi had left behind the seaside village of Raleigh did the child open his eyes. They passed fields of cane. A man flagged them, but there was no room, and he was left in a trail of dust and blue smoke of engine oil to wait the hour until another taxi came along. Mr. Walter had to swerve and hug his side of the road when a car approached and passed down the middle of the unpaved road. Mr. Walter surprised himself and everyone with a string of curses, but still he waved to the other driver as the cars passed. Mr. Walter's passengers, including Dolly and her son, turned back to watch the other motorcar vanish down the road.

The child scratched sand-fly bites on the back of his hand. She held his hand tightly to stop him from turning new ones into fierce watery eruptions. He complained that he was hot, and in a whisper asked her to roll her window down a little more. She sucked her teeth, ignored him. He sucked his teeth in response and sighed resignedly. Wearily, she unzipped the vinyl bag she carried. The smell of freshly fried dough and melted cheese rose out of the bag. The passenger next to her shifted to get a view. Dolly took out the brown paper containing the thin triangle of roti stuffed with cheese and shut the bag quickly. The boy nibbled at the buttery section of the flat bread, pushed it back at her, barely touched. Under the arch of the bridge, he pressed his face against the window to watch the mesmerizing passage of wood, iron railings, and wires, and through them snippets of the unfathomable black water. She caught his hand in hers just as he was about to reach for the window's handle. Wrestling it out of hers, he whined in a whisper, "I not turning it down, Ma. Don't hold my hand so. You hurting me."

She rested her head back and closed her eyes.

On opening her eyes, she noticed Mr. Walter watching her in the rearview mirror yet again. What wrong with that damn good-for-nothing man? What he still watching so? she asked herself.

Mr. Walter, as if in response, threw his arm over the seat and turned back to face her, a move that caused the other passengers to gasp and, in varying words and expressions, demand that he keep his eyes on the road.

"I was there when they find him, you know."

Dolly's face drained; she didn't know the body had been found. She put her hand to her mouth. The other passengers became stonily silent.

"What you mean, when they find him?" she whispered.

One passenger leaned forward and looked directly at Dolly, anticipating her reaction to Mr. Walter's response.

Mr. Walter, realizing his words had been mistaken, spoke up rather quickly and loudly. "No, no, no. I don't mean his body. His body never surface, ain't so? No, girl, I mean I was there when they find him, a little boy bawling his eyes out on the steps of the dry-goods parlor."

Dolly didn't know whether to be relieved or angry. Her child was busy looking out the window. But she knew well enough that he heard everything, even if he might have appeared involved elsewhere.

"Two, three days so we wait for news that a child gone missing from some other village. But no such news. Then, you know, the old people, Mako and his lady—ent you know them? They say leave the child with them, that it is God who send this little boy for them to keep as their own. A Indian child they bring up, like if he is one of we. And you know, in time he come true-true like one of we!"

He don't have no sense? she asks herself, talking so in front of the child? He driving motorcar and still he stupid so?

"But you know, he was a pretty child. Fair-fair, like Indians from town. Poor thing. He didn't know where he was from or who drop him on the parlor steps. All he know was his name. It was Seudath, not so? But everybody call him Indian. All of we used to play cricket with him. Not just Mako and the lady. He grow up to be a nice fella." Pointing to her son he added, "The child look like him for so."

She turned to look through the window. Why he shaming her so, in front of her child, and in front of people she don't know, she wonders. In a car full of black people who bound to say how Indians does throw-way their own, easy so.

In any case, she did not believe Mr. Walter. Everyone liked saying that they were there when the abandoned Indian boy was found outside Raleigh's only shop. She wanted to tell him to mind his own business, but if he in truth did play cricket with her husband, for the sake of his memory, she would not be rude.

First stop on the edge of Marion was for petrol at a station owned by an Indian man. Initially Dolly was shy to be seen by the man and his workers, all of whom were Indian, in the car otherwise full of black people. On the second trip there, one of the attendants, sitting idle atop an overturned wooden soft-drink crate, picking his teeth with a toothpick, winked at her, removed the pick, puckered his lips, sent a kiss in her direction, and then resumed cleaning his teeth. She sucked her teeth long and hard before turning away from him. But all day long, if the truth be known, she remembered the freshness of the idle attendant with a degree of pleasure, imagining herself as he might have seen her: hair long and thick, black and wavy, her skin almost as dark as a person of African origin, reddened by Raleigh's sun, sea, and wind, her nose and lips unusually slim for an Indian's. When her husband had brought her to Raleigh, Tante Eugenie, taking her pipe out of her mouth long enough to greet her, held her face in her hands, lifted it to the sun, and studying it, said, "Well, Indian couldn't do better. You is the prettiest Indian woman I ever see. How much children you planning for? Don't waste them good looks, you hear? That is all God in heaven does bless human being with looks for, you know."

Dolly took the attendant's attention to mean that caring for a child by herself, doing hard work to make a living, and living for a handful of years without any man in her life had not hurt her appeal. But still, since then, whenever they arrived at the station, she would lean her head against the backrest, close her eyes, and pretend to be fast asleep. If she had not done so, she surely would have noticed that the man was no longer around. If she were to have inquired, a most unlikely thing for her to do, she would have found out that the owner, who did not miss a thing on the grounds of his station, had seen his worker's freshness that day and promptly terminated his employment.

The strong odor as the car's tank was refueled, and the honking of car horns on the busy street, jolted the child. While his mother pretended to sleep, he sat upright expectantly. From Saturdays past, this smell and the sudden busyness had come to signal that they were mere minutes from the center of town, from Ashton Road, from Mrs. Sangha's large spacious house, from what he most looked forward to from one Saturday to the next: an entire day of play with Mrs. Sangha's daughter.

A Woman in
a Bustling Town

Even in the modern and bustling town of Marion, where certain Guanagasparians of Hindu Indian descent migrated when they left estates in the interior of the island, the day may well have begun with a washing of the body and a pooja. From the moment Mrs. Sangha awoke, however, before she applied the copper-handled hibiscus twig dipped in baking soda to her teeth, she went into the living room and switched on the Zenith radio her husband had brought home the week after they married. The radio remained on until last thing at night. To whomever else was in the house, it might have been little more than an audible backdrop to the cleaning and cooking going on. But not to her.

Sometimes she awoke early, after a fitful night of bad dreams and spurts of sitting up with worry caused by some aspect of the previous night's news; the dire direction in which the world seemed to be careening filled her with concern for all humankind and for the future of her daughter and herself.

She would be up so early that when she turned on the radio, prerecorded music played as the station workers were still miles away, only just getting into buses and taxis heading for the station house in the capital. While she awaited the first live broadcast of the day, she would open a tin of New Brunswick sardines and mash the contents with half a tomato and a hard-boiled egg.

Bringing her plate and cup of sweet Ceylon tea with her, she would draw a chair close to the big radio box in the drawing room, and there she would sit listening until her daughter awoke. She would be in time to hear the anthem "God Save the Queen," followed by Guanagaspar's anthem. For these, the official opening of the day, she would stand at attention, one hand lightly touching the edge of the piece of furniture through which the music flowed, the other palm flat upon her breast.

Early morning and then again last thing in the evening, the BBC delivered to the island, via the airwaves, its ten-minute program of news and views of the world. Although the local news might have remained the same throughout the day, Mrs. Sangha would not, as long as she was in the house, miss its hourly broadcast.

At ten A.M. on the dot, an appalling dirge threw the house into moments of mourning. Mrs. Sangha would stand in the doorway demanding silence as she listened to the announcement of the previous day's deaths throughout the island. With one hand pressed to her lips, she grieved immediately for the deceased and shook her head in sympathy for the list of bereaved: beloved wife of so-and-so, father of so-and-so, and so-and-so. Brother of this one, uncle of that one. Friend of so-and-so.

She listened to radio plays, comedy programs, and even the sports news, to the cricket scores at twenty after noon, and to commentary on the test matches played in the Caribbean, South Africa, India, and in the British Isles. She forever spoke of the excitement she felt as she sat all by herself and listened to live commentary as Augustus Martin ran for Guanagaspar in the Berlin Olympics. He had been expected to outrace all other contenders, so his name and the fact that he was from the island of Guanagaspar were invoked on the air time and again. She had the feeling, whenever she heard his and the island's name, that she had become a relevant part of the big world. She held herself proudly on those occasions, as she had the feeling that the world had overnight come to know of her personally. Even though Augustus Martin did not finish the race, having pulled a muscle mere seconds into it, she felt that he had won for the island something bigger than a medal: a place for them on the map of the world.

Her little daughter would, on the other hand, sleep through any radio program, including the one with the audience that cackled loud and long every few minutes on Saturday mornings. Even her mother's laughter at the ventriloquist and his sassy dummy would not awaken her.

But the sound of Dolly and her son's voices, the moment they arrived, was enough to get her up.

The girl waddled sleepily, thumb in mouth, to the kitchen.

"How much times I tell you don't come out here barefoot, child. You want to catch cold? You see how this child like to play? Soon as she hear you come, she wake up." Her mother lifted her off the cool linoleum floor and wrapped her arms around her tightly. The girl rested her head on her mother's shoulder, her face in her mother's neck. The boy, in blue shirt tucked inside khaki short pants, the typical schoolboy's attire that Mrs. Sangha had acquired secondhand from a neighbor for him, leaned against his mother and concentrated on picking at the scab of a sand-fly bite on his knuckles.

"Trouble abroad again, girl. Bad, bad trouble. I can't believe what I hear on the Zenith this morning," Mrs. Sangha addressed Dolly grimly. Every week Mrs. Sangha gave Dolly a highlight or two of the events going on in some country or the other, some country previously unknown to her and always too far away for Dolly to be interested in. These last few weeks, "abroad" was always a place called Europe—too big, too far away, and too everything for Dolly to even have a picture of it in her mind. And these days it was too full of turmoil. The recent news troubled Mrs. Sangha deeply, but all Dolly knew of Europe was that it was a too-distant land full of people who were supposed to be very important but who they were and why they were so important, she had never understood.

"BBC play right on the air, for the whole world to hear, what they call 'live broadcast.' A reporter was in a farmhouse in Spain, and you could hear bombs—yes, you could hear them falling as if you were there yourself. They were falling while the commentator was shouting above it for the whole world to hear."

"Eh-eh. But why he so stupid? He wasn't 'fraid one fall on his head?"

"He is a news reporter. That is what they do. And thank God for people like him, otherwise we wouldn't know what-so going on in these places. God spare his life, yes."

"So what the bombs was about?"

"Is that stupid man again. The one from Germany. Chancellor, they call him. He self had a hand in ordering aeroplanes to fly over a little village in Spain, not much bigger than Marion, you know, and bomb down the village flat, flat. The man is uncivilized, I tell you."

Mrs. Sangha cupped her face in her hands. Dolly saw that she had been crying and was afraid she might start up again. "He pick a market day when it had plenty, plenty people in the village. Man sick, in truth, yes, Dolly. To just go and kill people so? They better watch out over there, yes, before that madman get too big for his britches. And you know they say he is a small man, short-short and ugly. Anyway, I glad too bad we living on an island unto ourselves, yes."

"And I just hear, too, that creek flooding now-now. All you come in time, girl. Not even a Bihar car can pass on it now." Mrs. Sangha laughed halfheartedly at her own joke and pressed her daughter's head against her shoulder, rubbing the little child's back. Dolly was glad for the change of topic.

"You want to pee-pee, baby? Come change clothes and brush teeth. Mammy will make cocoa for the two of you, and then you can play all you want. That is all the two of you good for is play, play, play. You mustn't come out barefoot again, you hear? Dolly, Boss bring some shirts for you to wash. Starch them good, eh?"

Dolly nodded. She didn't, of course, say what was on her mind: why the woman he shack up with don't wash and iron his shirts for him? Why you does send food for him lunchtime and wash clothes for him? She sleeping with him, why she don't look after him? You might as well tell him to bring her clothes and all her children clothes for you—well, not for you, but for me—to wash, too.

Alone in the kitchen with her son, a children's choir on the radio performing "On Yonder Shivering Hills the Holly and the Snow" concealed Dolly's voice as she admonished him, "Sit right here. Don't go in behind them, you hear. Nobody invite you, so you stay right where you is and wait for me. I going to change mih clothes. And don't forget yuh manners. What you say if somebody ask you if you want something?"

"Yes, please."

"And if you don't want what they have to give you?"

"No, please."

"No, thanks. And if and when they give you something?"

"Thanks, please."

"Thanks. Thanks, Mrs. Sangha. You hear? And you don't have to take any and everything she offer you, you hear? Behave yourself proper till I come back."

The girl and the boy who was her age sat next to each other on the couch—at least they were on the easier-to-clean pink vinyl and chrome couch and not on the more formal red velvet one— in the drawing room. The girl had learned to read simple words and numbers at the elementary school she attended on weekday mornings. One of several of her large picture books, some with a few words, several with torn pages, lay on the couch between them. They looked at the pictures and invented stories. The girl fingered a word, uttered it one syllable at a time. He concentrated, tried to remember its length, shape, and sound. The girl glanced about the room. No one else was with them. She tore the page slowly, so as not to make a noise. She was attempting to tear out a single letter from the words grouped on the page, but she did not yet have the dexterity required for so specific a task. She tried another page. This time she succeeded in tearing out the letter H for the word "he." She placed it on the couch between them. She tore another. The letter E. She tried to wrap the two letters into a neat package, but the paper was too small, her fingers unskilled. She told the boy to open his mouth. To stick out his tongue. She placed the two letters on his tongue and ordered him to swallow. He tried, but the paper had stuck to his tongue. He removed the two wet letters, rolled them between his fingers, put them back in his mouth, and quickly swallowed hard, his eyes closed tightly. She handed him a cup half full of orange juice. He drank and gulped as if taking a tablet that would teach him to read.

Dolly, uncomfortable with her son's ease in that big house, left the washing to come up and find him sitting on the couch. But his feet—never mind they were bare—were marked up, unsightly, they had purple patches from insect bites. Her jaw tightened as she quarreled to herself: What he have them drawn up so, right on top the seat for? Is vinyl couch he sitting on, is true, but if he don't know better, I do. She would rather he didn't even sit on the couch, vinyl or no vinyl.

To her mind, he had no right to even enter the drawing room at all. She herself didn't like going farther into the house than the kitchen. She hastened over to him, admonished him in a low urgent voice, pulled his feet off, rearranged his body as if it had no will of its own, his feet sticking over the edge into the air.

Mrs. Sangha came into the drawing room. "Dolly, leave the boy alone, na. Big events unfolding in the world, and you have time to worry about manners? He is only a child. He have more than enough time later for behaving himself."

Dolly's face stung with the contradiction. How would the children know that Mrs. Sangha was only joking with her? But she stood back, expressionless, wondering what events outside of Guanagaspar could be more important than bringing up her son properly. The boy, wide-eyed and made self-conscious, drew his feet up again, grabbed the toes of one foot, and pulled at the scab of a healing sore. Dolly yanked his feet back out. Mrs. Sangha sighed dramatically and said, "Dolly, girl, he is just a child, and that is just a couch."

Back downstairs, Dolly scrubbed the clothes against the corrugated concrete harder than necessary and fretted: That child of mine getting to be too easy in this house, and Mrs. Sangha too indulgent; is not right that she contradicting me so in front of children.

Sweating from her inexpressible anger and frustration, Dolly scrubbed harder and faster.

A thumping came from upstairs. She remained still and listened. A tinny, quivering note on the shiny black upright piano in the drawing room was being continuously thumped. She rushed up the stairs, her hands and arms wet, a clump of soapsuds dangling off an elbow. Thank God he was sitting on the floor, making scribbles that only he could decipher on a pad of blank paper. The girl was kneeling on the piano stool. She had added several notes, using the flat of her palm pressed down hard, one hand holding down the other. When she saw Dolly, she lifted her hands and banged discordantly. "I making music."

She sat down on the stool as part of her motion to slide off it. She ran to Dolly and, taking her by the hand, led her to the kitchen. "I want juice. Give me some juice, please."

Dolly eyed a jug of water in the refrigerator. A glass of it would cool her down good. With one or two ice cubes crackling and splitting in it. But her child was comfortable enough for the two of them in that house. She was not about to take liberties. She would satisfy herself with water from the stand pipe in the backyard, though she could taste its metal flavor just thinking about it.

Stupid Games

There was that time when the girl swirled around the kitchen table to the tune of a piece of Indian music from the *Desi Radio Hour*. She jutted a hip in the air in little staccato thrusts while she swivelled on one foot, one arm held high, rotating the wrist. Dolly's son was twirling around the table, too. From downstairs she heard his laughter, crazy-crazy, no shame whatsoever. Dolly rushed up, intending to take him back down with her. Downstairs, where he belonged.

Weak and giggling, their eyes watering, noses running, they crumpled in a heap on top of each other, rolling about on the ground and carrying on much too loudly for her liking. She was about to be sharp, ready to put a good slap on him, to separate him and the girl once and for all, to take him downstairs with her where he ought to sit quietly and wait while she worked her fingers to bone. Only, Mrs. Sangha was leaning against the door-jamb, her hand barring her laughter one minute, and the next prompting her daughter and the boy by clapping to the beat of the music. They squealed and pretended to be imitating the high-pitched instruments and the voice of the singer.

But Dolly felt that the child had gone too far, was out of control, behaving like that in her employer's drawing room. Mrs. Sangha continued to prompt them.

"Let me see you do it again. Come on, do it with your hand in the air. Put your hand up in the air, boy, like how she doing. Come, come, show him how to do it, child, show him. Yes, that's right, that's right."

And then, there was that stupid game of teatime. "Teatime, my foot," Dolly muttered under her breath, "people in Raleigh don't have tea or time for teatime."

Narine Sangha, returning from one of his regular visits abroad, presented his daughter one Sunday afternoon with the largest toy tea set ever seen in Guanagaspar: tiny blue-lipped white porcelain plates, cups, saucers, and table dishes, each item decorated with a single painted bunch of wispy red and yellow chrysanthemum flowers. There was a white enamel refrigerator that opened to show tiny and perfectly rendered milk bottles and plastic bunches of carrots and grapes and apples, a stove, and a sink mounted on a cupboard with doors and drawers. Part of the ritual of the game was the washing of the wares. They dragged an upholstered dressing-table stool to the bathroom sink, clogged the drain with its rubber stopper, and filled it with water, dropping in the bar of hand soap. They tipped the kitchen set out of the round milk-chocolate tin in which it was stored. Cups and saucers, plates and bowls, pots and pans and cutlery that, before sliding into the water, make a tinny clinking ruckus that pleased them. They quietly splashed water, made a game of trying to catch the large slippery bar of soap in their tiny hands. Using one of the toy utensils, a slotted spoon, they blew bubbles, too dense and ponderous to rise into the air. There on the spoon, the bubble expanded, wobbled, and slid off messily onto the floor. They were drenched, their fingers wrinkled and gray.

Dolly and Mrs. Sangha, realizing that the children were suspiciously quiet, came upon them and the mess they had made. Dolly took them away from the sink, rinsed and rubbed dry the tiny dishes and cutlery. She changed her son's clothing; Mrs. Sangha, her daughter's. They sent the children to the platform at the top of the front stairs to resume another phase of the game.

The girl officiously sent her little friend away with instructions to return for tea and cake at four o'clock—which time it would be whenever she determined it. By herself, she performed all the tea-making actions exactly as she had observed her mother doing. She had a child's table, chair, and rocking chair that her father had had constructed for her by a local furniture maker, and those she arranged for the visit. She set the table using one of her father's monogrammed handkerchiefs for a tablecloth. For napkins, she folded sheets of paper torn from a notepad taken from her father's dresser drawer. She put out a little saucer with three cashew nuts taken from the kitchen pantry, and another with sultanas and red and green candied cherries found there also. In the meantime, in the yard, the boy picked flowers that Mrs. Sangha tied in a bunch for him with a piece of kitchen string to make a bouquet. She tied also a handkerchief around his neck, and wearing one of Mr. Sangha's hats, which engulfed his entire head and had to be prompted back constantly, he awaited an indication from the girl that it was four o'clock and all right to knock on the door. He glanced back occasionally at his imagined horse, parked on the road in front of the house. He didn't too much like this part of the tea-time visitor game, because she, as the hostess, was the one who served the tea and put out the cakes, and she wouldn't let him help her with anything. When he tried to talk, deepening his voice and talking about his day rounding up cattle, pitching and pulling up tents, hunting buffalo, and looking out for Indians, she became impatient, saying that he must be quiet while she poured tea. When he raised the imaginary mug of steaming tea to his parched lips, she stopped him, insisting that it was too hot, that he must let it cool, and she blew on it for him. When he reached for a cashew, she became furious, saying that if he ate the food, there would be none left for the game, and none for the other guests who were to arrive shortly. He didn't like that other guests would arrive. He would have preferred to be the only one invited.

Up the Horizon,
Down the Horizon

Dolly realized that all she had heard from upstairs lately was the distant drone of the radio. Mrs. Audry Talbot—who every day gave advice on everything: home remedies, dealing with willful children, force-ripening plums, killing a live chicken and plucking it, coping gracefully with untidy house-guests, buying presents for servants, for your doctor and dentist, and even on weaning pups—spoke today with a guest about roasting a duck in the Chinese manner. The volume on the radio was high, so that Mrs. Sangha, wherever she was, would hear the programs. Mrs. Sangha was not far, however. She leaned against the doorjamb between the kitchen and the dining room. A kitchen towel hung around her neck.

Dolly asked for the children. Mrs. Sangha was too busy listening to the program. She nodded in agreement with Mrs. Talbot and Mrs. Talbot's guest about the quantity of anise to be used in the seasoning. Dolly wiped her hands on her apron and hesitantly went through the house. She came upon the children in Mrs. Sangha's bedroom and watched them from the doorway. They were standing atop the piano stool, which they had dragged in from the drawing room, peering into the top drawer of a tall dresser. The girl was whispering to the boy that the contents of the drawer belonged to her father. There was a stout blue bottle with a dented silver cap. The bottle was oily. A length of thread and a strand of black hair clung to the oily surface. There was a crumpled silver-colored tube of medicine, an eyedropper with a black rubber cap on one end, a greasy tortoiseshell comb that had short black hairs and matted gray dust wound about its teeth, a silver U-shaped tongue scraper, and several loose pennies. The girl knew which ones were from the U.K. and that a particular one was from someplace called Canada. There was a heavy gold-plated lighter and a number of brass keys, each a different size and shape. There was a big corroded iron one. The children tried each key in the keyhole of the drawer. None worked. There was an empty silver cigarette holder with NRS etched in curly script, a stamp from the U.S.A. that was stuck to one of the drawer's side panels. The boy tried to slip his nail under an edge of the stamp. The sound of his fingernail scraping the wood panel was all he was able to accomplish. The girl pushed his hand away from the stamp, telling him, "No, don't do that. You will tear it." There was a sticky blue jar, the lid of which they managed to unscrew. A faint smell of camphor and eucalyptus escaped. The girl put her forefinger in the jar and scooped up some of the ointment. She put it to the boy's nose.

Dolly watched them, wondering what they might find, and wondering if Mrs. Sangha knew they were in her room, meddling in her husband's dresser. She wondered if it had ever occurred to her son to ask the girl where her father was. When he picked up the lighter and attempted to open it, Dolly rushed to him, grabbed both his hands, and yanked him off the stool. She slapped him sharply on both hands. She hit him again, twice on his bottom. The little girl scrambled off the stool and screamed, "Ma, Ma. Quick. Dolly beating him."

Dolly snapped at her, "You, hush your mouth. He have no right in here." She turned to her son. "What you doing in this room and in that drawer? And who tell you you could drag that stool in here? You can't see it will scratch up the floor? What trouble is this? You can't mind your own business? Look, child, I leave you home next week, yes." She knew that she could not leave him back in Raleigh.

Mrs. Sangha rushed in, tea towel in hand. The boy, who had not shed a tear as yet, set his face up to cry when he saw her. His mother raised her hand to him. "Look, don't start up with that stupidness now, you hear me?" He looked at Mrs. Sangha, who looked back, the corners of her mouth drawn in pity. He watched her, his mouth taking on the downward turn of hers, and squeezed his eyes hard. She reached for him, and the moment he was in her arms, the tears and the heaving sobbing began. Mrs. Sangha chuckled, pleased that she had such a predictable effect on him. He pressed his face in her shoulder. Dolly glared at Mrs. Sangha. Mrs. Sangha patted and rubbed his back, rocked her body side to side. Dolly reached for him, but Mrs. Sangha pivoted swiftly on both feet, turned her back to Dolly, and wrapped her arms around the boy tightly. She laughed at Dolly and said, "But like you don't have enough clothes to wash or what? Why you running up here every few minutes so? Leave the children alone. They doing nothing wrong. They break anything? I have one eye on them. If they was doing wrong, I would have stopped them long ago. What? You think I can't mind child?"

Dolly felt her cheeks redden and her lips thicken with rage she could not, in her position as servant, express. She wanted to grab her child out of her employer's arms, to scream "Put down mih child," but she needed this job.

Mrs. Sangha kept her back rigidly turned to Dolly. She did not want to see Dolly's face set up. She rocked the boy, still rubbing his back. Then she set him down, took his hand and her daughter's, and led them out of the room. Dolly, near tears of fury but determined not to let them fall, watched the three of them. Her son didn't even turn back to look at her. He went so easily with Mrs. Sangha. Dolly shook her head as if trying to dislodge a strange confusion there: anger as tight as a fist for her employer, and for both Mrs. Sangha and her son, simultaneous compassion. Mrs. Sangha sent her home with so much she herself

could not afford to provide him with. Like the clothes he wore
even now. She treated Dolly and the boy like relations, poor ones
perhaps, but nevertheless like family rather than servants. And
no matter how good Tante Eugenie and Uncle Mako were to
Dolly and her son, they were different. Regardless of the mind
those two old people paid them, the fact that they were of African descent loomed large in Dolly's mind. They looked different, they had different ways, different values. Dolly didn't want
her child to grow up boldface, boldface, like Uncle Mako and
the other black-skinned men in the village. Or growing up to be
a fisherman; when they were not catching fish, they were standing up on the beach idle so, listening for drums and voices calling them from across the sea. They gathered on the beach as if
they were a council with authority, pointing up the horizon and
down the horizon, arguing with one another. One saying, "It over
there," the other saying, "No, no. Is over there. You don't see
how the coconut does come in a stream traveling from that direction, man? You have to follow that stream if you want to go
home." When all she ever heard was pounding waves and thunder, they mouthed nonsense all day long about how one of these
good days they would follow sounds beckoning them, all the way
back to their homeland. She saw how the boy, when he was with
Uncle Mako, watched wide-eyed when they jumped up and
danced on the beach, shouting that the day, praise the Lord!
would certainly come when they would see land in the distance,
and that land would either be heaven or the home from which
their ancestors had been taken, and to which they themselves
would, praise the Lord, return. Even her Indian used to talk so,
and she never understood what he meant. He had become so
much like them that he had forgotten his own history. She didn't
want her child dreaming of places that didn't exist. If she'd had
her way, they would have left that place in two twos. But to go
where? Not across any sea, but to the town, to Marion, right here,

and she would live in and work for Mrs. Sangha as she saved her money to send her son to a town school. She and Mrs. Sangha were Indians and Indians alike. Their circumstances were different, it was true, but their ancestors had all landed up in Guanagaspar the same way, by boat from India and as indentured servants. Mrs. Sangha's family came as indentured servants, and it was only chance that had led them down different paths. Mrs. Sangha was a madam and Dolly was a servant, and the boy would have to learn that difference, too.

Dolly knew also that the same child who would not now come to her would expect her to go outside with him in the coming night to look up at the black sky and tell him, as she had done from the time he was born, which constellation was which, and which star which. Can Mrs. Sangha do that? she mockingly thought. He would, on the coconut-fiber mattress behind the sugar-sack curtain dividing the house into two rooms, lie close against her. He would fall asleep, as usual, as she rubbed his back and mumbled songs to him, songs she barely remembered from her mother—whom she hardly thought of anymore, having not seen her since she and her son had banished Dolly. She knew, come tomorrow, weather permitting, the child would sit on her lap on a fallen coconut tree on the beach and ask her to tell him over and over the same stories, stories about his father, stories Mrs. Sangha could not have known.

Dolly retreated downstairs. There, she let herself go, and tears came steadily, like rainy-season rain. Tante Eugenie had asked her countless times to let her keep the child on Saturdays. But Tante Eugenie and Uncle Mako were old now. Minding child was full-time work. What if they turned their backs on him and next thing you knew he was out on the beach, or worse, running into the sea? Uncle Mako had his eyes on that horizon half the day, mumbling his nonsense about how he was sure he had family over there, how he was neglecting his great-grandparents across the

water—an old man like that expecting to have grandparents—
how they must be wondering about him, and how he would surely
meet them one day soon. What if he decided to take the boy with
him? All the foolishness he did, showing the child things to
frighten him. Like the magic he did with his finger, making the
forefinger disappear and telling the child it got cut off. Besides,
if Uncle Mako was not frightening or filling the boy's head with
ideas about seeing what lay out there on the other side of the
water, the other fishermen were always collecting in his yard,
drinking, cussing, talking all kinds of adult business without care
for which child might have been listening.

There was nobody else to leave him with. Besides, if indeed
there had been somebody, she wondered if she could, in all hon-
esty, let him out of her sight for a whole day. Tears ran down her
cheeks, searched out the corners of her mouth. She opened her
mouth and licked in the comforting saltiness. She scrubbed clothing so forcefully, so fitfully, against the concrete that her fingers
and knuckles reddened and bruised.

FELLAS LIKE WE

In the days when the house belonged to Narine Sangha's nana and nani, it had been little more than a barracks-like box sitting atop wood posts. Over the course of three generations, walls had been put up to make extra rooms and other walls taken down to enlarge others. The house was raised; the original packed dirt underneath was paved and enclosed on two sides by lattice woodwork. Unadorned pillars that once had been purely functional were embellished. The original four wood ones at the back were replaced with straightforward concrete ones. And the newer section of the house sported custom-made molded concrete ones with opulent bellies and Corinthian-like crowns. Stairways that connected upstairs and downstairs were erected, a concrete one with wrought-iron banisters at the front, and a plain one of wood at the back. A portion of the downstairs area was walled off in the course of time to make servants' quarters and to enclose a laundry area. A verandah with arched framing eventually wrapped around the house. Decorative vines grew on the latticework, and potted bread-and-butter begonias lined the banister of the verandah.

Narine Sangha, although he had not lived in the house for almost four years, employed a man twice a week to upkeep the garden and the house. As long as the children remained within the view of this man they called the yardman, they were permitted to play downstairs on the paved area, where its spaciousness was interrupted only by the tall supporting pillars. They played hide-and-seek behind the pillars and behind the curtains of sheets and towels that hung from the drying lines. They were allowed outside in the yard also, but only at the front of the house, where they would play among clumps of trimmed and trained shrubs, trees, and flowering plants. At the back, the yard was undeveloped, the bushes there tended only with an occasional swipe of a cutlass, to keep them short enough to discourage snakes, and it was because of the possibility of snakes, scorpions, and other biting and stinging insects and larger fauna that had never been named that the children were not to play there. They took to heart the gardener's threat to chop their feet with his cutlass if they disobeyed him.

He allowed them to think they helped him by letting them drop seedlings of flowering plants into beds of rich black manure. The children would pull up weeds for no longer than just a few minutes, but to them, in the hot sun, it would seem as if they had been out in the yard with the gardener all day, and so they would boast of their labor to Mrs. Sangha and to Dolly, wiping their brows and necks of imaginary perspiration. With a tin watering can belonging to the girl, they watered plants but mostly themselves. Quickly they tired of chores and resorted to digging holes into which they poured can after can of water with an aim only they know. They picked periwinkles and strung them on lengths of thread. One day the gardener caught the boy struggling to get one of these garlands over the girl's long, frizzy hair, with the aim of hanging it around her neck.

"Ey, boy. What is this? Wedding? You taking dulahin so young, boy?" he teased. Once the girl had run off upstairs for one of her frequent visits to her mother, he called the boy into the shed that housed the garden supplies under the back stairway and seized the chance to more quietly advise, "You and she different, boy. That is Narine Sangha daughter. You and me is yard-boy material. She is the bossman daughter. Oil and water. Never the two shall mix. You too young to know what I saying. But I saying it anyway. She will grow up pretty. You so young, and already you have taste. But girls like she does only make fellas like we cry. Hear what I telling you!"

The boy stared into the dark shed, mesmerized by the variety of spades, the coil of hose, the concrete-crusted wheelbarrow, clay pots, saucers, and cans of paint. But he was thinking about what the yardman had just said to him. It sounded like a stern warning. It sounded like the man was saying something unkind about his friend. He did not understand, and he did not like this man who was not always allowed to enter Mrs. Sangha's house saying bad things about his little friend. In any case, why would a child make a big man cry?

The gardener approached him. "You daydreaming, boy? Awright. Come. You going to plant something in this yard. This little number here is a Norfolk pine. I'll dig the hole for you, and you can put it in. One day when you is a big man, you will pass this tree. By then it will be fully grown, and you will be glad of what I tell you when you was a child."

The child patted the earth around the pine while the gardener held it steady. He stood up. He stared at the gardener. So many letters of the alphabet swallowed, there must be words by now inside of him. Finally they came. "Uncle Mako say big people don't cry. If you cry, you is a baby. And you mustn't say bad things about people. And I don't cry."

The gardener set his face in a look of shock, shook his head in mock disbelief, then laughed. "Awright, awright, big boy. You answering back, eh! Well, you get me. You get me there, in truth!"

ART MY ARSE

Their house was small. High-tide nights when, in darkness and quiet, the roaring ocean would seem to be upon them. The house itself, though, lifted a yard off the sand by nine stumps of shaved teak, three sets of three, had never so much as swayed in any of the storms that frequented this unprotected archipelago strewn to one side of the Caribbean Sea. It was but a room, well built, and thanks to Seudath her Indian, it was hers.

One Saturday evening, tired and looking forward to a restful evening—she had in mind a dip in the ocean—Dolly returned with her son to find her house unrecognizable. Except for the placement of the outhouse, the cooking lean-to, and the pawpaw tree with the cock sprawled off in it, she might as well have gotten out of the taxi at the wrong trace. The house ahead, her house, had been—well, she didn't know what to say it had been. Its walls were a garish mishmash of color and pattern. It had been attacked. Attacked by the man known, by reputation only until this day, as the wallpaperer. Her son was too short to see what over the bushes had made her shriek, but when she broke into a run toward the house, he followed right behind. This man, not a resident of Raleigh, had heard about the foreign art of decorating walls with patterned paper. He had decided to become a wallpaperer. Finding jobs hard to come by, the art as yet little known, little desired, in Guanagaspar, he took it upon himself to give gifts of his services as a form of advertising. Dolly had heard about him but had not seen evidence of his skills anywhere, and had only, along with other beach gossips, laughed at the idea of his outrageousness. Suddenly two walls of her own house had been papered with pictures and articles from newspapers and foreign magazines.

She was stomping and cursing, pelting her own house with stones from the yard. Same time, some people who been walking along the beach heard her above the roar of the ocean. Coming up the shore, they saw the startling cacophony of color jumping out of the greenery and clashing with the blue sky. They came running to the front of the house along the path that connected to the beach.

They stood, watched, walked around, inspected, and gasped.

"Oh God, the wallpaperer reach Raleigh. Miss Dolly house get attack!"

"And he calling this art? This is a art?"

"It colorful."

"Ey, all you. You lucky it ent your house. If it was your house, you wouldn't be talking free so, na."

"But what wrong with this fella, in truth?"

"Let he come near my house, I go catch him and buss his arse. Art my arse!"

Dolly sank on her knees and regarded the handiwork. "He trying to make a fool of me? He don't see I is a hardworking woman? And them useless birds can't even keep away a vandal?"

Tante Eugenie huffed her way down the path and went directly to Dolly to throw her arms around her and console her. "And yes, you right, you working hard for so, and this worthless fellow, worthless-worthless, come and deface your house."

Those in the yard made a quick decision: they ran to the back of the house, where they broke off thick lengths of guava trunks, dispersing, promising Dolly to catch the "asstist," as they dubbed him, and to bury him alive right there and then.

The boy didn't understand why the new look of the house was so troubling to everyone else. In some places the concoction

of found, weather-beaten wood boards on the house overlapped
for no reason besides lack of carpentry expertise on the part
of his father. To his mind, the work of the wallpaperer had
transformed the structure into something to walk around and
admire. Inside and outside had, up until this morning, flowed
easily through the unmatched planked walls of this house, but
the wallpapering, he saw, had sealed the gaps between the
warped boards. He stood not three feet high, his hands on his
hips, mannish, his mother would say, and contemplated the new
look of his house. True, from inside there wouldn't be the view
of coconut trees and the ocean, or the sandy yard all the way past
the cooking shed. During the days when the windows would be
shut against heat and sandstorms, he wouldn't be able to peep
through the cracks and watch his hen and her chicks, or see the
pigeon pea boundary and the outhouse beyond. But to him, the
side of his house, previously bleached dry and gray by the sun,
worn thin by rain and sea breeze, was now decorated. It was
pretty. He hoped Mrs. Sangha and her daughter would have the
chance to see it. He waited until his mother went inside the
house, accompanied by Tante Eugenie, as Dolly was afraid of what
might be found there, too. Then he went around to one of the
walled sides. The cock came fluttering down noisily from the
pawpaw tree, falling with a clumsy thump onto the dry ground.
It fluffed its feathers and strutted alongside the boy, as if it, too,
were surveying and approving. The child stooped to stroke the
coarse, oily back feathers of the bird. He stood up and went closer
so that he could see the pictures on the paper covering the side
of the house. He was rather pleased that he recognized a number of words plastered on his house. He found the words "at,"
"a," "the," "this," "man," and "he." He looked long and long-
ingly at the shapes of thousand of others, could almost taste them,
feel them fully formed in his belly.

Dreaming and Then
Waking Up

Although there was an adequate fish market downtown, a visit to the open-air one in Raleigh involved for Mrs. Sangha an outing. She knew better than to imagine an outing for its own sake, so she made the excuse that she wanted to buy fish, fish so fresh that it was still dreaming. So fresh that even after it had been stuffed and baked, shredded morsels of it slid down her throat, revealing to her news of far shores visited that very day before it had landed in a fisherman's net. The children laughed when she talked that way. Hoping to be contradicted, her daughter would plead, "Fish can't dream, Mammy. Not so? Mammy, tell me for true: fish can talk to you?" But Dolly wondered if it could have been this kind of chatter that drove Mr. Sangha to take up elsewhere.

She hurried Dolly to finish the day's work; rather than wait in the stifling four o'clock heat for a taxi, they might as well take a ride in the car. She called out to her neighbor from her bedroom window, asking that neighbor to call out to his neighbor, and that one to the next until eight houses down, contact was made with the chauffeur who worked on call for Narine Sangha.

Mrs. Sangha, and Dolly in a freshly pressed dress, sat in the backseat of the car. Between them sat the girl, nervous about making her first trip to an open-air fish market. She asked her mother and Dolly all kinds of questions, expressing her desire to do this and to do that, to go for a ride in a boat, to buy baby fish that they could keep in a bowl. Dolly's son, in the low front seat with the chauffeur, could hardly have seen out the front window or even through the one at his side. This was, however, better than sitting on his mother's lap, as he would have done had they taken their ride home as usual in Mr. Walter's taxi. Tired from all the play of the day, rocked by the motion of the car, he nodded off to sleep even before they made it out of the town. He slept through the landscape he had been so eager to see earlier that morning. On that hot afternoon, the girl, too, leaning back against her mother, fell asleep, both children awakening only when the car halted at the fish market.

The chauffeur, who was of African descent, opened the door for Mrs. Sangha. The air was hot, salty, and rich with the stink of incinerating fish entrails. At one end of the market, a fire burned in a half barrel fueled by old newspaper, entrails, and the rubbish of the fishermen, sending a plume of dark gray smoke into the air. Flies hovered in the heat, flying so slowly that one saw each individual beat of their wings. Dressed in his white shirt, black tie, and black pants, the chauffeur looked at the fishermen and village people, mostly of the same race as he, with disdain. He kept his distance by the car.

Uncle Mako watched Dolly and her employer from his stall. Dolly waved to him. He nodded to her. The boy was ready to go off and play with his friends, but the girl, less brave than when her journey had begun, stayed close to her mother, watching these strange village men. "Mammy, let's go back in the car," she whispered. Her mother knew well enough what disturbed her. "Behave yourself. This is Dolly's village. I want to buy fish, and is these people who catch and sell fish. You see those children over there? They his age. They his friends. Go and say hello. But don't go far, eh, and don't get yourself dirty."

Closer to the car were a few tables with handicrafts. Behind one a man carved figurines out of teak. Flecks of the wood he chipped caught in the netting of his marino vest and were trapped in the tight curls of his hair. On the table he displayed pieces

that were as small as a pendant and others that were a good two
feet or so high. He had worked the same two faces, one a man's,
the other a woman's, both in profile, several times. The lips of
the figures were broad, the men's puckered and the women's
pouting and fleshy. From the necks of some of the larger rendi-
tions of women hung rows of loose wood rings, and all the tor-
sos bore the same long drooping breasts with protruding, ruffled
nipples. Mrs. Sangha, brushing at stubborn apathetic flies that
alighted on her lips and eyelashes, came nearer to admire the
man's work. How did he get the loose, seamless rings around
the women's necks? she wondered. Mrs. Sangha marveled at how
he had managed to render the earlobes so pendulous that the
wood looked as if it might swing any moment. She wondered
aloud if she had any presents to give. The carver, who was sitting, watching, this woman who came in a car driven by a black-
skinned chauffeur, and stroking layers of wood away from what
would be a woman's cheek, recognized the decision-making in
her face. He knew better than to expect a sale, but still, he
stopped his chip-chip-chipping and stood up. He consented
to hold up one of the larger carvings of a woman. Lobes of dangling breasts with rippled nipples met Mrs. Sangha at eye level.
She thanked him, quickly declined, and turned away. Why, if he
was going to be so bold as to portray naked ladies, did he make
their breasts so old-looking? she wondered, and consoled herself that at least these were not images of Indian women baring
their breasts. He resumed his carving. A shell-jewelry vendor
picked up his guava staff from which necklaces hung and began
to follow Mrs. Sangha. "Madam, madam," he called. The little
girl was attracted by the colored strings threaded with the fanci-
ful shells. Dolly's face was set tight. She didn't want to be embarrassed by these people. Dolly called the children to stay close
to her. She walked ahead of Mrs. Sangha, toward Uncle Mako.
"Madam, wear this, and Boss will see you anew. Take one home,

na," insisted the vendor. Uncle Mako, fanning the air with a dried leafy branch of a lime tree, told the jewelry vendor to leave madam alone. The man sucked his teeth but retreated.

When Dolly introduced Uncle Mako to Mrs. Sangha as "Madam," he said, "I know. Everybody does call me Mako. Is time you come. So long we hear plenty about you from Dolly and mih boy. She is like my daughter, you know, and he, well, he is like my grandchild, too. Thank you for being so good to them."

Dolly blushed, and the boy, still beside Mrs. Sangha and his mother, tiptoed and pointed with pride to a heap of brightly colored footballers. "Uncle Mako, you ketch footballers today. Give me one." His mother snapped sharply that he was not to play with them, they would dirty his hands. Uncle Mako came around to their side of the table. Indicating that his shirt was too dirty, he instructed Dolly to lift up the little girl so that she could better see the table of fish. Dolly lifted her, but the child was clearly hesitant and kept herself pressed hard against Dolly's body. Uncle Mako pulled two limp blue-and-yellow-striped footballers from the top of the pile and showed them to the girl. She was afraid of the black man's closeness, yet he made her feel important. The boy watched with pride as Uncle Mako stroked the fish and told the girl those were for her. She raised her eyebrows and smiled in disbelief. She asked her mother if she could really have them. When Mrs. Sangha asked how much they were, Uncle Mako answered he didn't charge people who couldn't see above the table. He scaled and gutted the footballers and wrapped them in a sheet of newspaper, and told the child that when she returned home, she had to make sure to season them properly. He spoke to her as if she really could season the fish herself, and she nodded somberly, listening with all her strength as he said, "With a pinch of thyme, some slice onions, and plenty, plenty salt, for saltwater fish need a goodly amount of salt, and"——he rubbed his hands together——"then you drag them in a plate that have

flour in it, and then, just so, you fry them up. Quick-quick, because you don't want them to burn and get black, black like this
skin on my body." He laughed, and the girl, still lifted in Dolly's
arms, giggled. He was pleased with himself that he was able to
make the child relax, so he added, "Them does eat good. I promise you that. Come back again, and I will keep more for you,
because once you taste footballer, you can't stop wanting more."

While Dolly and Mrs. Sangha attended to their business, some
of the young boys who spent their spare time milling about their
heroes, the fishermen of the village, called out to Dolly's son,
"Ey! We catch plenty fish today, boy. If you had stayed with us,
you would of catch some, too. Lil ones. Small so, like mih finger. You want to see them? They was trap in the nets. We free
them; we put them in a pail of water. Bring the girl, na. She have
a name? Look them in that pail." The boy was in his world now,
able to show it off to his friend from town. The girl, less hesitant, followed him behind the stalls. They treaded carefully
around a mound of shucked oyster shells, over uneven cracked
slabs of concrete laid haphazardly atop beach sand. The girl's
mother realized the most that might happen to her was fish-
smelling water or fish blood might be splashed on her clothing.
Both women kept their eyes on the children, though they could
not hear what transpired between them and the others. As the
two children stooped to look at five gasping baby fish, by this
time flailing on their sides in the pail of murky salt water, one of
the boys, hardly a year older than Dolly's son, asked him con-
spiratorially if the girl would one day be his dulahin. He did not
know what that was, but he decided that if she was going to be
someone's dulahin, she would be his. Yes, she would be one day
be his dulahin.

Before answering, however, he looked to where Mrs. Sangha
and his mother stood. He remembered the gardener referring
to the girl, telling him, "You and she different, boy," and the boy

blurted out, braver than when he was in town. "She is Narine Sangha daughter." The older boy, not satisfied, rephrased his question, asking if it was she whom he would marry. He had to wait to get married, he whispered back, he had to wait until he became a big man.

Heading back to the car, his mother was given a fish wrapped in a sheet of newspaper from the fishermen who regularly supplied her free of charge. One of the older men grabbed him from behind and threw him high in the air, catching and hugging him to his chest. The boy tried in vain to pull away from the man, who smelled of stale fish blood. Amid his struggling and screaming to be let down, the man said loudly enough for everyone to hear, "Ey, boy. So this is yuh girlfriend?"

Instantly Dolly spun around and snapped at the man who had asked the question. The boy noted that Mrs. Sangha had, the moment the question was asked, walked straight ahead to the car, silent.

His mother was quarreling. "Charlie! What wrong with you? Have some respect, na. Put mih child down and stop talking stupidness so. You ent got no sense, man?"

It was that word, "girlfriend," he realized, that had caused this outburst. He wondered if to be a girlfriend and dulahin were alike and if these were bad things.

Uncle Mako called out to Charlie, shook his head at him, and Charlie, in a show of bravado, threw the boy once more into the air, then set him down as he play-argued with Uncle Mako, attempting to cover his blunder.

The boy, trying to brush the scent of fish off his clothing, thought hard. Yes, she was a girl. And yes, she was his friend. She must be a girlfriend. The word seemed to mean something bad. He did not want anyone to say unkind things about his friend. He wanted to cry. Aware that she was being discussed, the girl held her body stiffly, self-consciously, her eyes blank and wide. Protectively, he took her hand and walked quickly with her, following Mrs. Sangha to the car. When the men whistled and shouted out, "Eh-eh, eh-eh, but look at the big man, na, holding his madam hand, oui, papa!," he dropped her hand as if it had burned him. He bit his lower lip and attempted to get in the backseat with Mrs. Sangha, the girl, and his mother. The two women pushed him out of the backseat and told him to sit in front with the chauffeur. In the car, the girl asked her mother what the men had meant. When Mrs. Sangha answered curtly that it didn't concern her, that it was big-people talk, the boy felt as if he himself had encouraged something dirty and very bad to take place.

Before that moment, the majority of the boy's waking moments used to be full of imagined activities with his little friend, the girl at Mrs. Sangha's house. In his day-and nighttime dreams, she and he were constant companions. Without any comprehension, from that moment on he had the discomfiture of being aware of something but not knowing exactly what that something was. Yes, she definitely was his girlfriend, he thought defiantly, even if he didn't know what that meant, and even if this was a bad thing. He, too, was silent, wanting to cry, but too frightened to do so, and wondering what it meant to be a big man, words he had used earlier without understanding their meaning.

The chauffeur took them, the car leaden with silence, to the trail that led to the partially wallpapered house. As he and Dolly got out of the car, the girl announced she needed to do a pee-pee. She didn't want to go on the side of the road, as her mother suggested, or behind the hibiscus shrub a few yards away. She needed a real toilet. Mrs. Sangha asked Dolly if she would let the child use the toilet. Dolly was about to explain that theirs was not what the child would consider a real toilet. Mrs. Sangha stopped her, laughed, said of course she knew that, but what to do? The drive back to Marion was too long for her to wait.

Besides, it would be a new, interesting experience. Today was full of new experiences for all of them. Let her learn something else new, Mrs. Sangha said with conviction and determination.

They left the car and chauffeur on the side road: the sand trail directly to the house was too narrow and strewn with fallen coconut trees and had dips big enough to swallow a car whole. When the girl saw the house, she slowed down and pulled her mother's arm, wanting to whisper in her mother's ear. Her mother said to her aloud, "That is where Miss Dolly lives."

The boy was uncomfortable. He walked far behind the other three, deep in thought.

Misangha's house, he was thinking, had two toilets, both of which were on the inside of the house. The bowls were made of cold, shiny white porcelain. Each had a tank full of water situated high above its bowl. To clean out the bowl after using it, there was a shiny brass chain to pull. Water would rush out of the walls of the porcelain and rise high up the side of the bowl, then be sucked back, everything disappearing down the drain. The boy had discovered both rooms on the same day, and he paid them several visits, forcing himself to urinate each time so that there was reason to step up on the footstool, placed there for the girl, and pull the chain.

He had an urge to tell his mother that rather than taking the girl to the outhouse, she could bring her the enamel chamber pot stored under the dressing table. But he hesitated, unsure of the wisdom of that. Even though his mother washed it daily, its odor remained sharp, like newly turned worm-ridden dirt.

Dolly fetched a sheet of newspaper from the house. From the backyard where he waited anxiously, the boy heard the girl's inquiring voice and her mother answering, but the content of their talk was inaudible. When they returned to the house, they washed their hands from a bucket of water kept for that purpose at the bottom of the flight of uneven stairs. The boy noticed

with relief and pride the milk cans lining the steps, painted fire-
truck red and full of lush bread and butter begonias.

Mrs. Sangha stood erect, her back to the house. Conducting
sea air toward her nostrils with her hands, she lifted her chest to
the sky and filled her lungs. She was in no hurry to leave.

Dolly asked, her hesitation registered in the dip of her
voice, if Mrs. Sangha would take some tea before the trip back
to Marion. Before Mrs. Sangha had a chance to respond, her
daughter piped up that she would like a soft drink, please, and
so they cautiously ascended the precarious stairs to the house,
Mrs. Sangha gripping her daughter's hand.

Mrs. Sangha sat on the bench at the table, both of which, like
the house itself, had been crudely banged together, the table
covered with a piece of medium-gauge plastic that had a design of bright red and yellow flowers. Dolly leaned, pushed open
the lopsided window, and reached far out of it. From an enamel
basin on a shelf outside the house, she ladled water onto her
hands. She scrubbed her hands clean and returned to the table,
which she busied herself rearranging. She pushed the pitch-oil
lamp, a bowl, a bag of flour, and a bottle with brown sugar against
the wall, out of the way. With a wet cloth and a wide arch, she
wiped the plastic covering, swiftly scooping away two queues of
ants, one heading toward the sugar bottle, the other away from
it. Before long, she and Mrs. Sangha were engrossed in talk about
people in Raleigh and about people in Marion. They did not
mention the incident at the fish market.

The boy stood in the doorway at the top of the stairs and
saw the interior of his house. He would have preferred if they
were all outside in the sandy, breezy yard. He wanted to go, unnoticed, over to the stitched-together flour sack that hung on a
rope dividing his house into two rooms, to pull it taut, so that
the thin and torn coconut-fiber mattress that lay directly on the
floor, and the dressing table—two orange crates side by side,

covered with a printed cotton sheet—were hidden from view. He hoped the girl and her mother would not look upward; there was no fine ceiling over their heads, only the raw galvanize of the roof, parts of which billowed a little with each passing breeze.

His mother opened the two bottles of soft drinks kept especially in case of visitors and divided them between two enamel mugs and one of the two glasses she had taken from the single shelf in the room. She took out six biscuits from a tin on the shelf and put them on a saucer on the table. A fly immediately appeared and hovered above the plate. He moved closer to the table.

His eye intently tracing the movements of the fly, he whispered, "Mammy, it have a fly."

"So, brush it away, child," she answered.

He lifted his hand and flogged the air once, but he did not want to bring attention to the fly in his house. He did not simply want to keep the fly away from the biscuits and the soft drinks. He wanted it to disappear altogether from his house.

Usually he enjoyed those biscuits. They stuck to the roof of his mouth. His mother bought them from the roadside shopkeeper by the half dozen especially because he often asked for them. But today he was aware that they did not have the flavored jamlike centers like the ones Misangha gave him sometimes when he was at her house. The girl took no more than a sip of her carbonated drink—there being no refrigeration in Raleigh—served without ice. She shook her head with surprise at the spitting bubbles and gaseousness bursting in her mouth. Her eyes watered, and she abandoned the room-temperature drink.

Dolly removed a plate covering a bucket that rested on a smaller table behind her. With the remaining glass, she scooped a drink of water for herself. Finally she slumped into the straight-back chair across the table from Mrs. Sangha.

The wind whistled noisily through the remaining spaces in the walls, a draft cut through the boards.

Suddenly Mrs. Sangha said to her daughter, "Darling, you want to go . . ." and his heart ceased beating when he thought they were about to leave. But she finished her sentence: ". . . outside and play a little bit? It have chickens outside. Son, take she outside and show she the yard. It good for her to see new things."

Outside, the girl was fascinated with everything. She wanted to run after the chickens in the yard, but the ground was too uneven, and the chickens were running, flying, squawking raucously, and pooping in fear. Unable to catch them, she flayed her hands about her head and shooed them instead.

At the side of the house, there was a lean-to of corrugated iron that rested on pillars shaved down smooth out of the coarse trunks of guava trees. On the inside of the lean-to, a mound of piled-high rocks encircled a pit. A blackened pitch-oil can was on the ground. The girl climbed the mound. She wanted to pick sticks out of the pit with which to stir the charred coal and bed of ashes on its bottom. He knew better than to play at his mother's stove. The girl stared at the unusual stove for a long time, and he became aware of the aroma of burned coal emanating from it. She asked what the pitch-oil can in the pit was for. He shrugged, unable to say that was what his mother cooked in. She asked if the man who sold fish was his father. He said no, he was just a man who sold fish. She was pensive and then answered that he was a nice man. She wanted to go back to the latrine, but this time with him. As mesmerized as he was with her porcelain and chain and that flushing, so was she with his dark outdoor room. She wanted to go see the bench with the hole, to know what was in the hole, did the hole go all the way out to the sea, if you shone a light down there would you see the ocean, the sky, boats, birds, and trees, how did you flush it after you used it. He had never before so acutely smelled the latrine and the area around it. She insisted that snakes must surely live in it.

Inside, the two women spoke differently than when they were in Mrs. Sangha's house, more like friends than like employer and employee.

"Dolly girl, how you make out by yourself, eh? Look at all I have, and you know, with Boss not there in the house, is like I have nothing, save for this child. If it wasn't for this child, I have nothing, nothing, nothing. You know that?"

Dolly smiled wearily but said nothing, and Mrs. Sangha continued.

"No man in the house to take care of and protect this little child. Sometimes, but only sometimes, I feel so bad that Boss keeping a woman, you know. And though no one says anything, I know everybody knows, and of course people will talk, but they would not do it to my face. You can count on people to talk behind your back, yes."

She thought of something, laughed, and decided she may as well say what had come to her mind. "Well, is it she or is it me he is keeping?"

Dolly not wanting to bad-talk the source of her income, said only, "Well, no need to feel bad. Everybody, every family, have something hiding under they bed." She glanced at her son and said, "Even me. But at least I don't have no society to worry about."

Dolly was ready to tell Mrs. Sangha her own story, about how she met Seudath, and about how he built this house for them before he even asked her to marry him. About her family running her out of Central upon learning that she was pregnant. She wanted to tell her employer everything suddenly.

"Well, when you living in society, you have no business of your own. Everybody does mind everybody business."

When Mrs. Sangha paid no notice to Dolly's comment about herself, Dolly, glad that she hadn't carried on, got up to look for the children. She saw them walking from the latrine. Her son looked very serious. He held Mrs. Sangha's daughter's hand and was leading her back to the house.

For his part, he felt more confident, more capable, than ever before, protecting her like a big man from the uneven ground around his house, from the dangers of the outdoor stove, from the ocean in the distance, and from snakes in the bushes and possibly even in the latrine.

Once the children returned, Mrs. Sangha changed the subject. "At least you have a son. At least he will be there to look after you when you are old and can't work."

Dolly smoothed the tablecloth with her palm, thought better of refilling Mrs. Sangha's cup. She pulled the boy to her and hugged him.

"Look after me? With this one is more like I will be looking after him for the rest of my life." The child made a halfhearted attempt to escape her loving grip. She kissed him on his head and added, "I do good for and by myself. I don't need a soul. Man is trouble."

At Home and Abroad

Mrs. Sangha sipped tea while she waited. She gripped the railing on the top landing of the back stairs with one hand and leaned forward to get a better view of her daughter in the yard. The child had awakened early this morning in response to her too-urgent embrace. When she opened her eyes, put her arms around her mother's neck, and returned the hug, Mrs. Sangha felt safe and, even though it was a child's embrace, comforted.

These days regular radio programming had been preempted. There were hardly any variety programs, no comedy hour, and no tips from Mrs. Talbot. It was all-day analyses and updates about events overseas, broadcast by somber English men who carried on nasally with high-pitched voices. Included in news items more often lately were snippets of frenzied speeches delivered in the even higher-pitched tone and strange German language of a man who, to judge from his actions as detailed in the news bulletins, had gone quite mad. This man seemed to be gaining ground, albeit with unconscionable force, in his desire to rule over all of Europe. There were other speeches, too, slowly, carefully articulated pronouncements and denouncements by the newly elected prime minister of the home country. Most disturbingly, there had been reports from battlegrounds. In them one heard gunfire, bombs exploding, and planes flying overhead. This morning the volume on the radio was turned up loud so that Mrs. Sangha could hear it clearly from the back stairs. For several minutes a piece of piano music by an English composer had been on the air. It had been written after the

Great War, and the broadcaster described it as a relentless, rapid-fire ripping up of notes, an expression of the triumph of the ordinary British citizen, of good, that is, over the evil winds that blew in from foreign shores. Although she tried to feel the triumph and the good, and to hear the suppression of evil as the announcer had directed, Mrs. Sangha, unaware of the frenzy that had been whipped up in her by the morning's news, heard the piece as little more than a cacophonous interruption from the dire news of the world.

Her child walked in the yard at the back of the house, looking for early-morning butterflies among the dewy flowers and shrubs. If anything were to happen to that child, what would I do? she asked herself. What if, one day, one sunny-sunny day, the child, innocent as ever, were walking in the yard, just like she was doing now, or she were playing with her friends in the school yard, and something were to fall out of the sky and hit the child, obliterate her, poof! Just like that, what would she do? How would she ever cope after something like that? She looked up, half hoping and half terrified that she might spot something menacing in the sky.

The child glanced expectantly every few minutes toward the back gate. Finally Dolly and her son arrived. Dolly was surprised to find Mrs. Sangha dressed up so early in the morning, in one of her going-out dresses, stockings, shoes, and all, as if she were going to see a sick person in the hospital, or to the doctor. She noticed, too, her employer's face was drawn. The unusual loudness of the radio, the somber music, further put her on guard. Something must have happened, someone must have died, and that was why she was there on the back steps dressed up like that. Dolly mounted the stairs hesitantly, wondering what would be required of her on this day. Mrs. Sangha paid scant attention to the boy she so liked indulging. Seeing the girl in the yard, he was about to run down the stairs to her. Dolly plucked him back by the collar of his shirt and coaxed a greeting out of him. With his eyes shyly downcast and a grin on his face, he mumbled, "Mornin', Misangha," to which she distractedly replied only, "Mornin', son." The boy turned instantly and pelted back down the stairs so carelessly that Dolly shrieked. He laughed, shouting back at her, "I can fly like corbeau, Mammy!"

Commiserating with Dolly for the briefest moment, Mrs. Sangha shook her head, then began a somber address. "Trouble, Dolly. Trouble itself."

The boy called up, announcing to the two women, as naturally as if it were his right, that he was taking the hose out from the garden shed and, together with the girl, was going to water the plants. Dolly warned him to mind himself. Mrs. Sangha told him he could water the plants later; for now she wanted them both to come upstairs. Upstairs, she sent them out to the verandah to play. She told them sternly not to leave the verandah, to stay where she was able to see them. She put her arm around Dolly's back, her hand clutching Dolly's far shoulder. She was stern: "Come with me.

"The man and his country gone mad. I knew it was bound to happen. The whole world gone mad."

Dolly waited to hear more. Finally she asked, "You going out?"

"No, child, today is not a day to go out. I want to hear what is going on abroad."

"Oh. I was wondering because you dress up. Somebody coming?"

"War is coming."

She saw Mrs. Sangha was truly troubled. She wanted to ask, "You dress up because it have war in another country?" but remained quiet. There must be something she was really not understanding about the world, she conceded, the world, people, and places that the poor lady worried so much about.

"Bring a chair, Dolly," Mrs. Sangha ordered. "Bring a chair. Keep me company."

Mrs. Sangha faced the Zenith, stared at it as if expecting the man whose voice was being transmitted to uncurl himself and step right out into her drawing room. She pulled one of the upholstered armchairs up to it and sat stiffly. Dolly, perplexed, and feeling uncomfortable with Mrs. Sangha's sudden closeness, brought in a kitchen chair.

Some time ago, the previous year, Mrs. Sangha had pulled up a chair and stayed by the Zenith listening for long hours. It was the time when the king of England had abdicated his throne because he had fallen in love with a woman of lesser breeding from another country. Not only was she a commoner, Mrs. Sangha often said, adding with distress—and what, too, seemed like pride and hope—she was also a foreigner and a divorced woman. Dolly remembered Mrs. Sangha looking both worried and pleased, saying things like "Well, Dolly girl, is proof that in the end, and deep in the heart, everybody same-same. Ent so?" Then, changing her mind, she would add, "Well, is not like she was a commoner like everyday commoners. She blood wasn't blue, but she had some pedigree, and they say she had a sizable dowrie. Hmmm. In the end nobody same, yes!"

Dolly still, to this day, didn't understand what all the fuss was about. All she knew was that her life and the lives of people in Raleigh were not changed one little bit by the abdication or the marriage of this king to that woman, who wasn't in the end common at all. So why it was news? She couldn't understand.

A jingle advertising Magic baking powder played. It was a familiar tune, to which Dolly tapped her fingers against the chair. The announcer with the hard-to-understand British accent returned to deliver a lengthy analysis of events in Europe. Dolly stared at the pearlescent pink vase that held a bunch of plastic zinnias and sat on a doily atop the radio. She wondered if she would get all the ironing done in time to catch Mr. Walter's four o'clock ride back to Raleigh. She hadn't realized that the analysis had ended until Mrs. Sangha arose and turned the volume down. Mrs. Sangha explained to Dolly as if she knew that Dolly had not been listening.

"Is war," she uttered gravely. She had expected her announcement to affect Dolly, but Dolly remained unmoved. Mrs. Sangha pleaded, "He killing, killing, killing, Dolly. Everywhere he go, he murdering people because of their looks and beliefs. He rounding up people and snuffing out their lives, poof, just so, like if they are not human beings—who is the one who is not a human being? Tell me. Tell me, na, I want to know. Hundreds of them he killing at a time. More than that. Thousands. I mean, I can't even imagine. If my body was stronger, Dolly, I would be ready to form an army and go after him, you know. I myself. Is like a force equal to his that is rising inside me. I don't know what to do."

Dolly was about to get up, but Mrs. Sangha began again. "Guanagaspar not involved ... *yet,*" she said emphatically, "but watch! You will see, Dolly. Trouble 'round the corner."

Dolly thought back to the taxi ride that morning into Marion. Nobody in the car had mentioned anything about war. She hadn't seen any soldiers, and nobody was fighting in the street. She looked at her employer, imagining her as a minister in the government of Guanagaspar. She imagined her with a dish or a tea towel in one hand, waving it as she spoke up from her seat in parliament—though what she herself ever truly dried or dusted, Dolly wondered. She just couldn't fathom why this woman whose husband had taken up elsewhere was so busy-busy every day paying attention to what was going on in parts of a world she had never seen.

Mrs. Sangha cupped her grim face in her hands and shook her head. She wore the same expression, Dolly recalled, as on that Saturday five years back when a kidnapped twenty-month-old baby belonging to some Lindbergh man from abroad had been found in a wood in America, bludgeoned to death. She was all-day-worried, as if she were close-close family to the Lindbergh man and his wife. The two children had been sleeping on a blanket on the verandah floor. Mrs. Sangha had gone over to them, lay down on the blanket, and hugged each, one at a time, tightly.

Let the white men come, Dolly thought. They would surely buy coconuts and oysters and local handmade toys—bright paper windmills and whistles made from coconut fronds—straw mats, hats, and shell work made by the people in the School for the Blind. Yes, they would make a woman's life, here and there, happy for a day, and miserable for life. They would father a good few children. But, too, they would walk the beaches and buy sugar cake and sour plum from the vendors. They would put a little much-needed money into people's hands. Then, when they were ready to go back where they came from, they would take pictures of everything to show their family and friends. They would take pictures of the fishermen, the shop vendors in the towns, the sea-urchin divers, and the cane farmers. They would tell everybody up there how nice Guanagaspar was. Wasn't Mrs. Sangha always listening for a mention of Guanagaspar on the BBC commentary program? She might finally get it. One of them might give a speech on radio about how the sun shone every day, even in the rainy season; about how Guanagaspar people were friendly and ready to invite "foreign" into their homes for a bowl of pig souse and a shot of local rum or a glass of fresh coconut water. Even if the commentator were to say that Guanagaspar was a hole not worth coming to visit, Mrs. Sangha would be happy to hear the name of her island mentioned from so far away, especially by a man with a British accent.

Dolly wanted to get on with her ironing. Mrs. Sangha, in her opinion, listened to too much radio. Mrs. Sangha began again, as if explaining to someone who did not have an inkling. Most foodstuffs and clothing in Guanagaspar, she said, were imported. Tea, baking powder, canned salmon and tuna, flour, biscuits.

But what stupidness Mrs. Sangha talking? Dolly wondered. Canned salmon and tuna? They were living on an island; anybody could go and catch their own fresh salmon, or buy it from the men in Raleigh or the fish vendors in Marion.

Mrs. Sangha was listing off the things she liked to buy as presents: satin and lace panties, hand soaps, gold bracelets, and toys for children. If war landed up in Guanagaspar, all of these items would be scarce, and when and if you did manage to find them, they would be dear for so. If this madness carried on into the Christmas season, how would she make the fruitcake that all her family expected her to make for them? Mrs. Sangha was saying that she would disappoint a lot of people if she couldn't get the red and green candied cherries and the plump golden sultanas. Unseen by Mrs. Sangha, Dolly had raised her eyebrows. Let them learn to make and eat guava cheese and coconut sugar cake like Raleigh people, she thought. Mrs. Sangha muttered that she should go and buy up cases of canned food and nonperishables— oatmeal and flour—this week self, before the shortages began. That way if, or rather, *when* things did get bad, she would parcel out goods for the less fortunate.

She shifted in her seat and looked directly in Dolly's eyes. People from here could get carted off to fight in Europe, she pronounced, and Dolly wondered if Mrs. Sangha expected or even wished to be one. She told Dolly she had met Miss Fatty from two streets away the day before, and Miss Fatty told her that her sister's husband, a clerk in the town hall, had information that the island was soon to be used as a naval base for this war. The British lent it to the Americans, Mrs. Sangha said. Dolly pursed her lips, stopping herself from asking, "Lent it? Like is a shilling?," but checked herself.

On the radio a woman's voice declared a certain imported body powder for babies to be superior to all others. This advertisement was followed by the return of the announcer's somber voice. Mrs. Sangha turned up the volume, held her hand up for silence, although she was the only one in the room who had been speaking. She rested a firm hand on Dolly's knee and whispered, "Look, girl, don't worry about no ironing today, na. I frighten-frighten. Stay up here. Stay until the news finish." When a local announcer interrupted the report in midsentence to inform listeners that an emergency announcement was to be made within minutes by Guanagaspar's minister for national security, Mrs. Sangha clutched Dolly's knee. She drew a handkerchief from the cleavage of her brassiere, patted her forehead, her lips. Several pieces of solemn music followed. Mrs. Sangha and Dolly waited. Mrs. Sangha looked out to the verandah, to the children there. She whispered, "They so innocent. God, spare them harm, I beg you, Lord Jesus." The announcer returned and introduced the minister, who, in a lengthy speech, confirmed that the island would temporarily be, from that day forward, in the service of other governments and countries for as long as the war should last.

When a gloomy march began, Dolly rose up without any protest from Mrs. Sangha. She went to the verandah, looked out onto the street. She looked up into the sky. It was a clear, bright blue sunny sky. Seagulls circled lazily. A carib grackle made a beeline for somewhere it alone knew. All appeared as usual. She listened for gunfire, low-flying airplanes, bombs, soldiers' feet thumping through the streets, drums and cymbals, and the huffing, puffing twists and turns of bagpipe notes she knew from parades. All she heard were the sounds of municipal workers sweeping the street, two young men chatting and laughing loudly as they sauntered down the road, and the children on the verandah. She tried the front door. Locked. She couldn't see what there was to be worked up about.

Wartime Worries

Saturday after Saturday, Mrs. Sangha worried about this invisible war. She would have been happy for Dolly's company as she listened to the radio, but Dolly, seeing dirty clothing piled up, would make her way downstairs as tactfully as she could and begin her work. Returning home in the taxi one day, she saw an unusual jeep painted with splotches of brown, ocher, and various shades of green. The low, wide jeep with over-size tires would have been an attraction on its own. But the moment the passengers in the taxi saw that the jeep, open at the back, was chock-full of white-skinned men, obviously soldiers, dressed in uniforms colored exactly like the vehicle, conversation came to a sudden halt. The men on the jeep, their helmets pulled low on their heads and their rifles with unsheathed bayonets slung on their shoulders, chatted among themselves and laughed, seemingly un-aware of the motorists, bicyclists, and pedestrians who had slowed to watch them. Mr. Walter broke the shocked silence, reporting that along his route, he had seen other jeeps transporting soldiers. He had heard that restaurants and bars in town were being fre-quented by these white soldiers, who dressed to go to these places exactly as they had just witnessed, guns and all.

Remembering Mrs. Sangha's fears about food shortages, Dolly said aloud, "As long as the sun does shine and rain does fall, as long as it have fish and shrimp in the sea, crab on the beach, coconut, mango, and lime on the tree, rice in Central, cock and hen in the yard, a cow in the area, and provisions in the ground, I can't see what it have so to worry about. I ent got no oven to bake cake. If flour get hold up, what that have to do with me? I never yet hear of pitch-oil-can sponge cake. You?" It was the most she had ever said in the taxi, the most by far. After she spoke, there was a silence as stunned as when the jeep had been sighted. Then everyone in the taxi, encouraged by her forthrightness and disregard for the symbol of war, started to talk at once. There was a general disdain for the presence of foreign soldiers on their soil, and for the idea that this foreign war was any of their business. The boy was proud of his mother, surprised by that side of her he had never before seen or heard. There was, at the same time, much high-pitched excitement, for they'd had the courage, the proud audacity, to criticize and dismiss what they had seen with their own eyes.

It didn't matter to Dolly as much as to Mrs. Sangha, who wasn't able to bake as much as she had in the past, that flour was already being rationed, that you had to stand in a line outside the shop and wait sometimes for a good hour before you could even step foot inside. The sight of jeeps and white-skinned soldiers from time to time never became entirely ordinary but was soon commonplace enough that citizens of Guanagaspar stopped being afraid or too reverential in their presence.

As always, on Saturday night back in his mother's house, the boy was already looking forward to next week's visit to the Sanghas' house. Friday night, come bedtime, sleep was slow to come. He would be so excited that he would be restless in the bed, thinking and planning what games he and his friend might play, what books they would read, what butterflies he hoped to catch, which plants would be blooming in the yard, what clothing and sweet food his mother's employer would send home with him and his mother. Mrs. Sangha sent less lately than she used to, but he always came home with something, no matter how small.

Lately he listened intently to the night. He knew better than to meddle in big people's conversation, but he wasn't deaf to

Mrs. Sangha's noise about the war, or to the contents of the turned-up radio. He would lie staring at the ceiling of the house with his eyes forced wide open, not entirely sure on moonless nights whether they were indeed open. When his mother's breathing told him that she was asleep, he would feel alone and frightened, as if the burden of protecting his home fell on him and depended on his wakefulness. He was sure he could hear far-off bombs and airplanes. He clutched in a tight knot at his neck the cotton cloth that protected him from mosquitoes and listened hard against the wind in the trees and the crashing of ocean waves. He listened so hard that his eardrums stung and his head throbbed, and that throbbing sound blocked out all others. He would, several times, scrunch his eyes shut, then release them open again, checking that he was able to see in the black room. He expected each time that the red jumble of starlights and pinpoints that blossomed and crowded out his vision would give way to the face of a strange uniformed man or group of men who would speak with him in gruff sounds, snapping words and commands that he would not understand. Although he knew nothing of where Germany or Japan might be, he knew the Germans and the Japanese to be conquerors. He pictured them alighting one by one out of the ocean's froth, their boats unseen, scrambling up the beach, beating through crocus and guava patch in the darkness of night. The invaders, German and Japanese alike, he imagined as tall skinny white men who looked not unlike the Americans on his island. Rustling trees sounded to him at times like men speaking strange sounds—sounds he was sure were either the German or the Japanese language. He needed to be able to decipher and distinguish wind crawling through trees, and waves exploding in the sea, from German and Japanese invaders. He imagined that he would be the men's first contact, their first prisoners, Raleigh their first stop on the trek to conquer the island.

The all-night staccato chirping of cicadas and the drone of the sea would measure the night's slow passing. A dreaming cow, mule, or goat might cry out, startling him and slicing apart the darkness, giving shape briefly to the village. As he lay next to his mother, his mind would eventually slow down, and her deep breathing and slight snoring would grow louder than his thoughts, louder than the sounds of bombs and low-flying airplanes and men speaking in strange languages outside. He would slide into a dreamy state and then under into sleep.

After staying awake for so long, he would not hear his cock or the area cocks crowing as dawn came, and he would resist his mother nudging him awake in the morning. She would stroke his face, push the hair from his forehead, and call his name softly. Sometimes she would resort to saying playfully, "You don't want to go by your girlfriend today?" and this would surely draw him from his sleep. He would immediately awaken, a smile on his face. "I don't have a girlfriend. Today is Saturday?"

THE PROTECTOR

They had traveled hardly any distance in the taxi, yet there was traffic backed up, and the normal speed had been reduced to a crawl. Mr. Walter opened his car door, got out, and announced that he could see cars lower down turning around, and white-skinned soldiers directing the traffic to turn back. Dolly sat up abruptly. She muttered, "Eheh, don't tell me war arrive." Mr. Walter said that the road was caked with tracks of unusual oversize wheels. The passengers in the car stiffened. They became quiet. The woman on the far side of the backseat pulled out a rosary from her purse, and though she remained quiet, she fingered the rosary, every few seconds clutching and massaging one of its beads, and then seconds later, the next one. Mr. Walter carried on at crawl pace down the road until the car approached one of the soldiers, who directed him to turn around and go back the way he had come. The passengers shrank into their seats as they watched the soldier. His face was that of a young man, his body fit, his hair yellow and cut close to his head.

Mr. Walter leaned his body against the door and stuck his head out of the window. In an unusually formal manner, he addressed the American soldier. "Good morning, sir. What's the matter? If you don't mind me asking?"

"Bridge construction. Carry on, now. Steady, don't hold up the traffic."

"How long it will take to complete, sir?" His persistence and politeness surprised his passengers.

"A day or two." The soldier clapped his hands to hurry them on, but Mr. Walter had another query.

"What happen? The old one collapse or what?" This sudden confidence relaxed the passengers.

The soldier didn't answer; he clapped his hands more impatiently and said, "Move it. You're holding up the traffic, sir."

Mr. Walter hesitated. He beamed. These white men were not at all like the ones from the mother country. He had heard so, in truth, and now he was seeing it for himself. They did their job, but they were respectful, calling him "sir" and speaking with him like a person and not a taxi driver. He was happy that he, too, had called the soldier "sir." Mutual respect. They were behaving like civilized people, living and working together, even in wartime.

As Mr. Walter completed the U-turn, the passengers looked back down the road. They saw tractors being driven by white-skinned soldiers, and more of them digging up the road, some working away in the ditches that had been made.

Mr. Water had obeyed, but as he drove along in the opposite direction, his spirits were buoyed by having dared to ask a question, to ask it of a soldier, and a white-skinned one at that, and to have been addressed with a great measure of respect. He had to take a route into the town that would practically circumnavigate the cane fields, bypass the town, and come around to enter it from the east. All the talk in the taxi was of the foreign soldiers who were in their country, of their generosity in doing manual labor, building bridges and roads, the kind of work only idlers and alcoholics or gamblers took to make quick money once in a while.

By the time they reached Marion, it was the middle of a blistering day, and they were perspiring. Even with downturned windows, the car was rank with the odor of skin overheating and the perfumed soap that Dolly and one man in the car wore. When they stopped to fill up with petrol, it was almost noon. They reached the Sanghas' house almost four hours later than usual.

Although she had experienced Mrs. Sangha's leniency and kindness time and again, Dolly was taken aback to find her wor-

ried more about her and her son's welfare, that they might be
hungry and thirsty, than that she was late. She knew Mrs. Sangha
was interested in the war abroad, and Dolly was excited to be the
one bearing news for a change. She told Mrs. Sangha about the bridge
and how she herself had seen with her own eyes how the white soldiers were doing dirty street work that you couldn't get even
Guanagaspar men in desperate need of work to do. Mrs. Sangha
treated Dolly as if she had come from a long and arduous journey bearing long-awaited, life-giving news. When Mrs. Sangha
dragged out a chair for her, coaxed her to sit, and poured a glass
of ice water for her, Dolly, enjoying the respect and attention,
carried on. She reported what Mr. Walter had said and embellished everything, said that soldiers were filling up the restaurants in town, bringing trade to the town, which was to prosper
from the abundance of Yankee money. She had never said the
word "Yankee" before. She liked the authority it imparted to her.
She offered her opinions. She was impressed, she said, by the
good work these soldiers were doing, that they were not sitting
around idly waiting to be sent off to where the war was actually
being fought in another country, that they were building up rather
than destroying a country.

Mrs. Sangha didn't immediately tell Dolly that what she had
just described seemed to be bad news. Later that day she wondered aloud if all the repairing and widening of bridges and roads
and building of highways all over the country was not an indication that war was at the doorstep of the island. But Dolly wasn't
able to see what one set of events might have to do with the other.

At the end of the day, Dolly put on a freshly pressed dress,
and pinned her long hair in a bun. Mrs. Sangha and her daughter stayed at the top of the stairs as Dolly descended with her
son to leave for Raleigh. She hadn't made it halfway down when
a man's shrill voice boomed from out of nowhere, crackling in
the hot and hazy Saturday air.

"Attention. Attention."

They all froze, their eyes widened. Dolly and the boy turned and rushed back up the stairs into the house, and Mrs. Sangha locked the door behind them. The boy went to his little friend and slipped his hand into hers. She curled her fingers around it. Mrs. Sangha came up behind them and pulled both against her. She stood still, listening. Dolly went to the window and peeped from the side of it, afraid for the first time. Amid the crackle of a PA system, the voice of the man announced again, "Attention, attention." The sound had gotten considerably closer.

As the words were continuously repeated, they recognized it as the accent of a Guanagasparian man. Relieved but still perturbed, the four of them ran to the verandah to see what was happening. A car with a public address system mounted on its hood was crawling down the street and was almost in the front of the house. There was a man sitting in the front seat next to the driver, speaking into a microphone, and his voice boomed out of the large silver horn on the roof. He was calling the people of the neighborhood to listen to his address. Dolly and Mrs. Sangha could see people coming out of their houses and gathering on their verandahs, some even coming down to the roadside. Mrs. Sangha hushed the two children as they whined to be lifted so that they could see better over the high verandah banister. She rested a hand on Dolly's shoulder.

The car came to a halt, and the man with the microphone stepped out onto the road and began to read aloud from a script he held in his hands.

"Ladies and gentlemen. Your attention, please. This is a message from the minister of national security."

There was crackling and a long pause.

"I repeat: this is a message from the minister of national security. Please do not panic. Remain calm and listen carefully. Our country is presently in a state of emergency."

Mrs. Sangha became frightened, but at the same time she seemed to have a sense of satisfaction. She said as if to herself, "If anything happen to any one of us, it will be our fault self. The signs have all been there, but not a soul wanted to believe that such a thing could happen to us, like if we immune. They think this is paradise and that God live on paradise. But where God reside, so does the devil also reside."

"A state of emergency has been declared. From this moment on, be advised that for your own safety, no more than two people will be permitted to gather on the streets in daylight. Be further advised, no one will be permitted on the streets from sundown to sunup until further notice. If you have no urgent business outside of your house, please remain indoors during the day. In the event of an attack on our island by foreign aggressors, a siren will sound. During the nighttime, if you hear the siren, turn off all lights and take cover on the ground floor of your house or under a heavy table. No candles or flashlights are to be used. All vehicular traffic is suspended from this moment on until further notice."

Dolly looked at Mrs. Sangha with disbelief. What were they to do? How were they to get back to Raleigh? Mrs. Sangha read the unspoken questions on her face and said quietly, "Don't panic. Everything will be all right." She pressed her finger to her lips, telling Dolly to be quiet so that she could hear what else the man had to say.

"There is no radio service at the present time. You will be updated regularly by this public address system. I repeat, a state of emergency has been declared. Thank you."

The driver got back in his car, and the car rolled away.

For some seconds everyone stayed right where they had congregated. An airplane flying low was heard approaching but not seen. In a flash, everyone disappeared into his or her home, and people who were far from their own homes ran into houses that were nearby. Doors and windows were being closed. You could hear the banging shut of wood shutters right along the street. The sound of the airplane faded and was not heard again.

Five minutes later, the voice of the messenger, faint in the distance, could be heard delivering the same message elsewhere.

Mrs. Sangha went around the house drawing the curtains, shutting and locking the two doors between the rest of the house and the verandah, and as she did so, she spoke to Dolly.

"Well, you have to stay here tonight. You can't get home." There was a look of worry on Dolly's face, and on Mrs. Sangha's a look of "Well, I told you so, I kept telling you that it was serious," but all she said was "That is just the way it is, and there is nothing to do about it."

Mrs. Sangha's daughter had become serious, staying very close to the boy. He, too, had become worried but was breathless with the excitement of war and danger. It meant that as the only male in the house, he had to assume some posture of confidence and courage. Mrs. Sangha began to plan where Dolly and her son would pass the night. There was a servant's room downstairs, but she had not for a long time had a live-in servant, and though the room had a bed in it, it had been used mostly for storage and had, for as long as Dolly worked there, been locked with a key.

"The room downstairs have few boxes on top the mattress, and it have some furniture in there, too. I will come down with you and unlock it. We will have to move everything outside the door. You can stay in this house as long as you want. I will make sure the four of us are as safe as safe in times like these can be. I sure the room will be dusty-dusty, but we will clean it good. Is a long time now nobody gone in there. I myself will give it a good wiping." She turned to the boy. "You be a good boy and give it a proper sweeping. You and your mother will sleep there. You will be safe in this house. Go out in the backyard and take some cuttings from the hibiscus tree to make toothbrush, and I will give you baking soda. And Dolly, go and take a towel from the linen cupboard. It don't have water down there, so you can use the bathroom upstairs in the back room. Let us go down now, before it gets too dark and we can't use lights. You will come upstairs after and eat dinner with me."

When Dolly saw the state of the room, her heart sank. Even Mrs. Sangha, who had gone down to unlock the room for Dolly, hadn't realized how unpleasant it had become. There were cobwebs and spiders in the corners of the room. A thick albino lizard with half its tail missing lay in the far corner of the room. It rose up on its front legs and seemed to collapse again from its own weight. Dolly and Mrs. Sangha stepped back out of the room quickly. If there was a bed in there, it was buried under boxes of paper from Mr. Sangha's business, and under boxes of Christmas decorations, old clothing, and whatnot, so you couldn't even see it. Dolly kept her tiny house spotless—she didn't have that many things, certainly nothing to store, nothing to save for any reason—and didn't like the idea of sleeping in such a dusty space. Then Dolly remembered there was a night watchman who walked around the house. She apologized to Mrs. Sangha and asked if she and her son could please sleep upstairs, even the floor in the kitchen would be good, because she was more afraid of a prowling night watchman than of this war that people kept making a fuss about but of which she hadn't seen any concrete evidence. Mrs. Sangha felt ashamed for suggesting they stay downstairs.

That night Mrs. Sangha was happy for the company. It was strange to her not to have the radio on. She went to it and hesitantly turned it on, as if she might be punished by a shock from it, or an admonishment from a voice in it. There was only static, a wheezing and a high-pitched unmusical whistling. She sighed and turned it off. She got out candles in case of electricity blackouts, for it seemed logical to her that war and blackouts went hand in hand—she enjoyed the surmising and preparations—and she prepared the candles using the wax that dripped off a lit candle to cement stubs to saucers. She took down two dusty pitch-oil lamps from on a cupboard in the kitchen and washed and dried the glass shades. Dolly had never seen Mrs. Sangha so quiet, so busy and brisk in her movements. The four of them ate dinner in the kitchen. There was not much talking. The quiet was almost exciting, as if they were all waiting for something to happen. The boy watched Mrs. Sangha and his friend as they ate their dinner, sitting more upright at the table than he and his mother normally would. He followed Mrs. Sangha's manner, but his mother leaned over her food as usual, her head bent toward her plate, never taking her eyes off the food. She did not use the spoon at the side of her plate. With the fingers of one hand, she pushed and pulled the food into a small mound, then, as she had been accustomed ever since she was a child, she balanced a mound on the upturned tips of her fingers and scooped it into her mouth. How he wished she would use the spoon this one time at least. However, Mrs. Sangha and the girl didn't seem to notice. After dinner he helped to clear away the plates from the table. His mother washed the dirty wares and put away the leftover food.

The girl left the kitchen for a wash and to get dressed for bed. Her mother made her wear a new dressing gown, taken from a drawer of new underwear and pajamas in the spare bedroom's armoire. The boy washed himself and put on a crisp new pair of brown-and-cream pin-striped pajamas with drawstring pants that Mrs. Sangha kept wrapped in tissue paper in a gift box in the same drawer. That night, taking advantage of Dolly's presence, Mrs. Sangha got her to prepare the night watchman's cocoa and his slices of bread, but when they were ready, she herself called out to him. By the time Dolly had washed herself and pulled on a yellow cotton nightgown that Mrs. Sangha had given her, Mrs. Sangha had opened out the hideaway bed next to the piano and had already begun to prepare it. From the top shelves of the wardrobe in the spare room, she took out several blankets, too hot for use on that tropical island. She spread them on the hideaway mattress to soften it, as she said that she could feel the springs in it. She topped them with one of her good sheets. She finished the bed with a flowered top sheet and a heavy straw pillow in a case that matched the top sheet. It had to be admitted that even though she sometimes didn't seem to understand anything about village life or poor people, and she paid far too much attention to events abroad, Mrs. Sangha was a very giving woman. But tonight there was an unusual urgency and determination about her actions. She was like a soldier of high rank; it was as if she understood it to be her duty to take care not only of her daughter but of her servant and the boy, and even of the watchman, for in a way, they were all her responsibility. They were all hers. It was, therefore, up to her to protect them from that great unknown called war.

The children went into the front room that was reserved for guests and lay on the bed there, reading, telling each other stories. Mrs. Sangha went out to the verandah, checked to make sure that the door leading from it to the front stairs and front garden was locked. She sat in Mr. Sangha's rocking chair in the dark. Dolly could hear the rocking chair making its rhythmic uneven lurch forward and lunge backward. She took a kitchen stool out to the verandah and waited for Mrs. Sangha to invite her to sit. They kept each other company long into the night, both waiting for the frightful wail of a siren. When nothing happened, Mrs. Sangha sighed with relief, disappointment, and tiredness. She and Dolly decided it was time to go to their beds.

No sound came from the children, and when the two women went to check on them, they found them fast asleep. When Mrs. Sangha tried to awaken her daughter, intending to usher her into her own bed, the girl fussed so much that she left her there. The boy remained sleeping through it all.

They left the children undisturbed in the front room. Dolly was expecting Mrs. Sangha to leave her to turn off the lights, but she encouraged Dolly to go to bed first. She knelt beside the bed and pulled the top sheet over Dolly's shoulder, up against her neck. Placing her hand firmly on the top sheet, she squeezed Dolly's shoulder and told her to sleep well, that everything was going to be all right. Even though the sheets smelled strongly of the camphor and sea grass, the bed was softer than any Dolly had slept in before.

Mrs. Sangha stood up and went to the radio. Not being able to listen to it had a strange effect on her. She felt unusually alone. She stood watching the box. A realization caused her to hug herself as if she had become cold. She was feeling the pain of Narine Sangha's absence. He and the radio were very much connected to each other in her mind and heart. She seemed to know where he was and what he was taking part in when she heard the voices of people in the radio, learned of events occurring here and abroad. All her listening was listening out for him and preparing for his eventual return. With the radio turned off, it was as if her tie to him had been cut.

In the dark Dolly asked, "You thinking something, Madam?"

"It strange. Four people in the house and a watchman outside. And yet the house feeling more lonesome than usual. That is all. Sleep good," she whispered as she left the room.

Mrs. Sangha lay awake well into the night, staring up at the dark ceiling. She listened for airplanes in the sky. There were none. For soldiers in the street. Only a drunkard disobeying the curfew could be heard singing as he made his way home or someplace else. She pursed her lips. Such a person should be in his house protecting his family. The boards of the house contracted and expanded as they usually did day and night, but in the quiet of the night, the creaking noises were noticeable. She listened to make sure that was all that was happening, the house and the boards breathing by themselves. There was no one, she was certain, walking about the house. When the tree outside of her bedroom window dipped in the wind and scraped the wall of the house, she held her breath and listened. It was only the tree stroking the house as it usually did when there was a wind. She was proud, knowing that she had, by herself, the capacity and ability to look after a household during a time of international crisis. But there was sadness in that pride, too. She hoped that wherever Narine Sangha was, whatever he was doing that night, that he, too, would be safe from the war.

Dawn

The sun's warm hand brushed Mrs. Sangha's body, and she awoke. She marveled that, in spite of the state the world was in, the sun still rose and shone, warm as ever on one's body, and birds quarreled and quipped as usual in the tree outside her window. The swishing of the brooms of the municipal Sunday street-cleaning crew pushing debris down the drainage canals at the sides of the road reassured her that at least the world of Marion was still in good order. She lay still, watching the sun stroll the length of her body and up the wall. The redness of first light gradually gave way to yellow that burned the room.

Dolly, in the cooler drawing room outside, began to stir. Together they would prepare a breakfast for themselves and the children, and for the watchman, who customarily ate before leaving the property. Mrs. Sangha wondered what a day of war in the world would require of them. She thought about what she might wear that would gesture to everyone else on her street that she was ready to do whatever was asked of her. She would make the children dress properly, too, and she would comb her daughter's long hair into two tight braids. She would put ribbons on the ends, not bright colorful ones but brown ones, the new brown velvet ones stashed away for special occasions in a drawer of the armoire. But she was jolted out of these musings by the outside front-door lock being rattled and prodded and turned.

Dolly, being closer, had heard it, too, and had jumped up and wrapped the top sheet around her body. Through the sheer lace curtains veiling the glass pane of an interior doorway, she saw

someone at the outside door attempting to open it. Mrs. Sangha
hustled, but quietly, into the drawing room, pulling a dressing
gown around her. She pressed a finger to her lips. She tiptoed
to the door that led to the verandah. Peering through the slightly
parted curtain of the inside door, Mrs. Sangha watched the
doorhandle turn. She guessed, hoped, and feared all at once who
it might be. She spun around and looked at Dolly, panicked.
Before either of them could do anything, the front door opened.
The scent of oak moss and lavender wafted into the house. Mrs.
Sangha gasped and then began fixing her hair. She whispered
urgently, "It's Boss. Shhh, go back in the bed. He come back
home. In the hour of need, he come back here." She had to repeat *"Go back in the bed"* sharply before Dolly did as she was told.

Mrs. Sangha made her way swiftly back into her bed—their
bed—and, holding her breath, she closed her eyes, pretending
to be asleep. She tried to still her body, heaving with anticipation,
tried to listen above the pounding in her temples. She identified the sounds of him walking around the L-shaped verandah
to the door that opened onto the pantry. His keys rattled as he
unlocked that door. He walked a few paces and stopped. She
imagined he was looking around, but at what she couldn't tell.
The spicy cologne he wore had made its way throughout the
house. His footsteps advanced and stopped. He was at the doorway of the drawing room. He retreated. Of course he would have
seen someone in the sofa bed, but he would not have known who
it was, as Dolly covered her face from his view. Mrs. Sangha heard
him move into the kitchen area. Either he had lightened his footsteps or the linoleum in the kitchen had softened them. She heard
the refrigerator door open. A cupboard opened and closed. After
a few seconds the refrigerator door was shut. He walked to the
end of the narrow kitchen. The slight clink suggested to her that
he had placed a glass in the sink. He moved from the kitchen to
the large open back room that served as an at-home office for

him. His chair squealed along the floor as he dragged it away from the desk. Mrs. Sangha wondered if Patsy, the cleaning woman, had dusted his chair and the table that past week. The chair creaked as he sat in it. He stayed there for about five minutes. She couldn't hear a sound, couldn't tell what he was doing. Then the chair creaked again as he released it of his weight. He was at the door of the bedroom he used to share with her. He pushed it open and entered. He stood in the entrance of the room for a moment, oak and lavender boldly announcing him, surrounding him, guarding him. Then he entered the bathroom. Mrs. Sangha heard him lift up the lid and the seat of the toilet. She heard his pee hit the porcelain side first and then its long stream frothing the water in the bowl. He pulled the chain, and the toilet flushed noisily. With such a racket, if she didn't stir, he would know that she was pretending, so, making a little production of it, she turned, yawned, stretched, and then opened her eyes and faced him. He was undressing, removing his suspenders and pulling his shirt out of his pants, unbuttoning it, doing all of this as if it were usual and quite expected. She did not know if he would come into the bed and lie next to her. Should she get up? she wondered. And if she were to remain and he were to lie there, how should she position herself? How could she even breathe calmly? And that lavender and oak moss. He wore it whenever he came to the house. She had not given it to him and didn't imagine him buying it for himself. To her, its scent was that of aloofness, of the distance that separated them. It underlined her own bittersweet independence.

Mrs. Sangha thought better of making a fuss. All she said was "You had no trouble traveling on the road?"

"The driver didn't use lights. He coast the whole way. Where daughter?"

Several answers flashed thorough her mind in an instant, along with the consequences of each. Mrs. Sangha felt herself neglectful,

leaving her daughter to sleep in another room without her. She
didn't want to say that she was in the same room with the washer-
ironer's son. She hurriedly got out of bed and said, "I'll bring
her."

Narine Sangha moved toward the door that led down the hall
to the other bedroom and said, "She in the front room? Why
she not in here sleeping with you?" He sucked his teeth and
continued, "Never mind. I will go and wake her myself."

Mrs. Sangha tried to go before him, but he touched her shoulder in a firm gesture of holding her back and said, "I wouldn't
wake her for long; I only want to say 'morning.' Get some tea
for me." Then he said, "Who is that in the drawing room?"

Mrs. Sangha stood where she was and whispered, "In the
drawing room? Dolly."

She knew he wouldn't know who Dolly was, but thinking of
the boy in the bed as the washer-ironer's son, she couldn't bring
herself to identify Dolly further.

"Dolly? Who is Dolly?"

She had no choice. "The ironer."

He nodded. Lavender and oak moss trailed him as he carried on down the hallway to the front room. She suspected that
she wasn't going to be getting him any tea right away.

Narine Sangha stood at the door of the room. The strong scent
had awakened the boy. He opened his eyes. Or rather, one could
well say that morning the boy's eyes were opened.

He saw a man, a fair-skinned Indian man, standing in the
doorway watching him. He knew instinctively who the man wearing a white merino vest and knee-length underpants was. He tried
to sit up, but he was unable, as if his frame had been transformed
into jelly. The man's shoulders, the defined muscles of his chest,
his thickset body frightened the child. The man came nearer to
the bed. He stopped. He leaned his body to get a better look at

the two children. He had a high forehead, curly black hair, a shiny thick black mustache. Although the man used a low voice, the boy heard the words squeezed through his clenched teeth: "What the *arse* is this?" The man kneed the mattress at the foot of the bed hard, and like a wind, he turned briskly out of the room.

Were it not for the powerful perfume that had invaded the boy's head and chest, he might have said that he was unable to breathe. It was as if a baker's sack of flour had been dropped on his meager child's chest. All the muscles in his body tingled and tickled, weakening him. He tried to budge his legs, to wiggle his toes, but his muscles seemed paralyzed.

He was a child then, and what could he have known? But instinctively he understood something. Raleigh men, the men he knew best, were wiry and muscular, and they wore merinos that were stretched, ripped, full of holes through which they might in jest slip an arm and wear it like a fake sling. He was used to them smelling like the sweat of toiling, of engine oil, of sea entrails, their bodies hard and damp against him when they squeezed him affectionately or hoisted him in the air. He felt intuitively that this short, fair-skinned, muscled, perfume-scented man might more easily hit him than attempt to throw him playfully in the air.

The man reentered the room like an even more forceful wind. Mrs. Sangha followed in his wake. When he saw her, the feeling of paralysis eased, and the boy sat up quickly. Narine Sangha grabbed his daughter's arm roughly. She was jolted upright. "Daddy!" she said sleepily. He hoisted her roughly off, positioned himself behind her, and swiftly ushered her out of the room. The boy wanted to call out after her, to call out to his mother, even to shout at the man, perhaps to tell him not to push the little girl like that, to be gentle. But no words would form in his mouth. He looked at Mrs. Sangha pleadingly, but she didn't protest the man's actions. Rather, she took the boy's hand and pulled him out of the bed onto his feet. The boy asked what was happening. Mrs. Sangha whispered to him to be quiet, to get dressed. Dolly came in and quickly finished dressing him, as if he were unable to do it himself. He asked her if that man was Narine Sangha. Dolly snapped under her breath for him to hush up, to mind his own business. The boy expected to see the girl once he was in the drawing room. Dolly, her face red and bloated with anger, held his hand tightly, and from where they were, he turned and twisted his head and body looking for his friend, but she did not come out to see him. He sensed that he should not protest.

Mrs. Sangha was silent. She looked worried. Although he had seen this worried look several times before, and heard his mother say that if there wasn't something to worry about, Mrs. Sangha would worry about that, he had never seen the stoniness that hardened her mouth. She whispered something to Dolly, barely moving her mouth. Dolly pushed the child ahead of her, holding his shoulders, steering him toward the front steps. Mrs. Sangha told them to wait out there. She ran into the house and came back almost immediately with a half-loaf of bread and an entire package of cheese and a knife. She shoved those and a bundle of crumpled paper in Dolly's hands. Dolly opened her hand to look at the crumpled bundle, several dollar notes, and her face broke, ready to cry. As directed by Mrs. Sangha, they got into Narine Sangha's car, and the chauffeur drove in the low dawn light, without use of the car's headlamps, all the way out of Marion.

By the time they were in the country, the curfew was lifting. Dolly looked out the window the whole time, with one arm around the boy's shoulders. They passed a few cars, a man with a donkey, a bullock cart, and a handful of people making their way to work. Dolly kept her face turned so that the child couldn't see her tears, but he knew he was crying, as she kept daubing her eyes with a cloth she had taken from her bag. She broke off a slice of bread and, still not watching him, handed it to him. He had never seen his mother like this and was too upset, too frightened, to eat. Although he knew, he asked why she was crying. She pulled him against her and told him to try and sleep.

Visitors Bearing Truths

It had been several months since the boy last saw his little friend from Marion. His mother knew they were coming. All he knew, though, was that they were having visitors. She hadn't told him who they would be. She washed him and told him to wear something clean and proper. When he insisted on knowing who the visitors were, she said only, "Visitors. Why you have to know everything? If I tell you, it wouldn't be no surprise. You don't want a surprise?"

The girl and her mother arrived, driven by one of Narine Sangha's chauffeurs on the pretext that they were going to the fish market. Mrs. Sangha, huffing up the sandy path, saw the boy in the yard and rushed to hug him. She held his face in both her hands and kissed his cheek. He wished his mother had told him in advance. He looked at the sand, afraid to meet Mrs. Sangha's eyes, lest she see that his had filled with tears.

"I miss those eyes, boy. Why you crying, darling? You not happy to see us?" Mrs. Sangha said with unabashed emotion. She hugged Dolly.

The girl wouldn't look at him. She looked in the direction of the ocean, at the ground, at her feet, at nothing in particular. She seemed taller, thinner. She kept a hand on her mother's elbow as they walked to the house. When they got to the steps, he pulled her by the hand and asked her to stay in the yard with him. She said it was too hot outside. She pulled her hand out of his and followed her mother and Dolly up the stairs. He followed uneasily. Her mother occupied one of Dolly's two straight-backed wood chairs; the girl stood, leaning against her mother's body.

Dolly looked genuinely happy to see Mrs. Sangha, and seemed not to hold any grudges against her. The boy asked the girl if she wanted to go down to the beach. She looked directly at him, silent. Then she shook her head and stared at the ground again. He asked if she wanted to see the chickens in the avocado tree, or perhaps the four baby chicks in the crawl space under the house, or, better than that, if she wanted to crawl under the house and take fresh eggs from the hen's hiding places. She turned away entirely, whispered something in her mother's ear. Her mother said out loud, "You asking for him all the time, and now you here only a few minutes and you ready to go home?" He had never seen the girl look so before. She pouted, her face turned red, her eyes filled with tears. She whispered again in her mother's ear. Her mother said rather sharply, "We will go in a little while. I want to see Miss Dolly for a little bit. Now stay quiet."

The boy told his mother he was going outside to play, and was surprised by the weakness of own voice. The yard that day seemed to smell more strongly than he ever remembered, of chicken mess and coal ash. He could have choked on the stench that had never been apparent before. He left the yard and ambled down in the direction of the sea. He broke into a run along the sandy path crisscrossed with sea-grape vines to the beach.

He sat heavily on a fallen coconut tree trunk amid the tidal-line debris, a blue bottle cap, a shriveled mango seed, sand-smoothed chips of green and brown glass. Despite the breeze blowing in off the water and lashing his body, the high sun burned his skin, and the sand scorched the soles of his feet. The wind stung his eyes and caused them to water. He dug his toes into the sand, flicking up clumps of the colder damp sand from beneath the surface. He looked back toward the house and saw a tiny weather-worn shack that had a tilt he had not previously noticed. Even though it would have been impossible, with that strong breeze and aromas coming from the ocean, he felt as though the odors of the yard were trapped in his nostrils and chest.

From that distance he could see that the galvanized roof, curled at the corners, was rusted. He had become so used to the wallpaperer's handiwork that he had stopped noticing it. Now he saw that most of the pages had been peeled by the wind; some flapped about noisily; some he himself had ripped off in moments of idleness. And exposed behind the wallpaperer's work was the blandness of weather-bleached boards. The house looked like someone else's foolishly decorated shack. He felt weak and ill in that hot sun. Looking at his thin, bare legs in his khaki short pants, he noticed that his skin, as deep purple as that of a caymit fruit, was dry. He thought of Narine Sangha's light-colored skin. His own always seemed to be covered in a gray film.

It was as if hours had passed before his mother came looking for him. She found him kneeling on the sand, trying to shove the tree trunk one way and, failing that, leaning his back against it, his knees raised, heels dug in the sand, trying to force it backward. With the wind rushing into the trees at the shoreline, the crashing waves behind him, the confusion broiling in his head, he didn't hear her shouting.

"But what wrong with you, child?" She grabbed him by one arm and yanked him upright. He began to kick the trunk over and over with one foot and then the next.

"What stupidness is this, child? You gone mad or what? You don't have no manners?

"What you leave the house so for? Shut up your mouth now-now, or I will give you something to cry for in truth. You too old to be crying over this kind of stupidness. Behaving like this over nothing. You hear me? Nothing!"

She tried to contain his flailing arm, the knot of his small fist. Finally she grabbed him under his arms from behind and tried to pull him backward to the house. He dug his heels into the powdery sand and was dragged. By the time they reached the house, his rage was spent. She spun him around to face her and, kneeling on the sand in front of the house, she pushed his face into her shoulder, pressing his head hard against her. She rocked him from side to side and whispered, "Shhh, shhh, shhh, shhh. I know, my baby. Don't cry. You hear? Listen to me, son. Let me explain something to you. They not our friends. Maybe I myself mislead you." She felt him try to pull away from her, but she held on to him tightly and spoke. "When we used to go by them, it was no social occasion. I work for them, and I used to take you to work with me. They wasn't our friends, you hear me? You must remember that. They different, son, but they not better than you or me." She was speaking to him softly, almost cooing to him. He understood nothing of her words, yet the bitterness in them was clear. "All of we cross Black Water, some-times six and sometimes seven months side by side in the same stinking boat, to come here. Same-same. All of we. One set leaving something unsavory behind, another set looking for a fresh start. How, child, how out of those beginnings some end up higher than others and some end up lower, tell me this? Well, God alone know. We come here same time, same boat, same handling. They not better than we, and *that* you should remember."

The boy had by this time relaxed. She cupped his head in her hands and lifted his face to hers. He let her direct him, but he refused to look into her eyes.

"Where the cock gone, my child? You see it today? Come, my baby, I will mix up the corn. Come and feed them. Is strange, eh, how they does only eat when is you feeding them."

Years passed before he saw her again.

Meeting Ends

Dolly didn't want anybody in Raleigh to know she was unemployed. She didn't look for work to replace her lost job in Marion or anywhere else. She decided that with a little imagination and a little hard work, which she might as well do for herself rather than for someone else, the bush and sea of Raleigh would provide her and her son with their modest needs.

Saturdays, to make sure the boy didn't take off down the path to the beach where he might be seen and so expose her situation, she put him to work around the house. Before the day got too hot, when the pigeon-pea shrubs were laden, she would send him to fill a paper bag. When the guava came in, the branches of the trees would droop to the ground with the extra weight. One, passing some distance from a patch, would be drenched in the fragrance of ripening, bursting, and fallen rotting fruit. There were always more than enough guavas in back of the house for his mother's needs, even when he devoured a good share right there in the guava patch.

Soup can by soup can, he would twice daily ferry water from the barrel at the side of the house to the front steps, where he would soak the sun-baked dirt of the red-painted tin cans in which sun-colored marigolds thrived. He would sweep the yard with the cocyea broom. At the end of the day he would go under the house. The chickens would strut expectantly around him, and eventually, after enjoying their display of dependence, he would scatter corn kernels, cooked rice, and bread crumbs. The cock would proprietiously flutter up onto his lap. It would never settle down but would press and transfer its weight from one foot to the next, stooping low and then stretching up. He liked the attention it paid him.

Inside the house, he picked rice or sorted the good peas from the ones with worms, shelled them, and chopped the guavas in little pieces, flicking away the worm-ridden bits with the tip of the knife. When he sat doing these chores with Dolly in the room, both of them quiet, he would miss hearing music or Mrs. Audry Talbot's voice. He even missed hearing the somber death news and news of Mrs. Sangha's war, which for him and his mother might just as well have ended when they left Marion on that terrible day when Narine Sangha tore apart all that was good and secure in the boy's world.

At the end of the day, he was usually so tired he would go behind the curtain to the coconut-fiber mattress there. He would fall asleep the moment his little body hit the mattress. Sunday morning he would awaken long after his mother, to the aroma of guava, cloves, and sugar bubbling on the stove. And Sunday midday she and he would walk the beach selling the aromatic guava cheese, a penny for a square inch.

Several Saturdays of not going to Marion passed without incident. Then Tante Eugenie, walking down the beach in front of the house, noticed a flicker of movement in the yard. She hustled up the path, a washed-up bottle picked hastily off the beach in her hand in case she needed a missile for protection, to make sure the house was safe from burglars or wallpaperers. To her consternation, she found Dolly under the pawpaw tree, cursing and jabbing away at its lopsided crown with a cobweb broom in an attempt to dislodge the cock.

She heard Dolly mutter, "So much hen in the yard, and this good-for-nothing cock does just sit idle-idle up in the tree so." She jabbed at the cock furiously and shouted, "Get down here, you little so-and-so. I will make curry out of you so fast if you don't put yourself to work, you hear. Come down!"

Tante Eugenie didn't wait for an explanation. "But what is this? I hearing all kind of things, and I telling people to stop their idle talk, that if you get fire I would be the first to know. So, is true? Why you not in Marion now? They fire you, child?"

"Get fire? Who say I get fire? I leave. Let people talk. They could say they fire me all they want."

"I hear the children was in the same bed, and that Sangha fire you for that."

"Fire me? He wish! Because he name Narine Sangha, he think he have license to keep woman left, right, and center? Listen, what harm it have in two children, little so, sleeping in the same bed? Is only a nasty, worthless mind what would see sin in that. And where you getting your news from these days? Who minding my business? Tell them to come talk to me in my face. If you see how bad he treat my child, and what good he think he do to his own child, eh? You mad to think I going back there. Nobody fire me, you hear? It is *I* who fire the job."

As Uncle Mako's age advanced, he complained that fishing the way he knew it, men waking so early that even cocks were still sleeping, pushing pirogues and rowboats into the water by the light of the moon, setting nets by hand, pulling them in the long, slow arduous way, was a dying profession. He would point in disgust to a distant group of youngsters banging on oil cans, on hubcaps, and on bottles with old enamel spoons, dancing, singing, drinking, and smoking, and he would growl, "That is not what our people, African people, would a want for us. Them children shaming us. They ain't got no dreams. You are not African, child, but you living among us. You want to get like them? Eh? Look at them! Shameful-shameful."

To Dolly, he said it was time the child stopped sticking up behind his mother's back, doing woman-work. Shelling peas wasn't man-work. He said that God showed He knew best when

He brought Dolly and the boy back from Marion; in Marion the boy's head was bound to swim with ideas that would cause him confusion and discontent later. The child was getting too accustomed to sticking up so close to a big shot's daughter, and this was only going to cause him a lot of hurt. Better he learn to be content in Raleigh. The boy was old enough, he said, to learn a trade, and the best trade for a fellow in Raleigh, despite everything, was a fishing-related trade. The first thing he taught the boy was to mend a net.

As he and the boy worked the green net cord, heavy in the boy's easily bruised hands, Uncle Mako would babble on about a family waiting for him across the sea. When Tante Eugenie was far enough away, for she'd had enough of his daydreaming and prattling about faraway family, he pointed his finger here and there toward where a country called Africa might or might not be. He told the boy that Africa was really the home of his ancestors, from where he was taken against his will, but the boy couldn't understand this. It was a story Uncle Mako himself could not make sense of, let alone explain to a little boy. He said only that he planned one day to return there. If he was careless and Tante Eugenie heard him talk this way, she would suck her teeth, shake her finger, and bellow.

"Ey, old man, keep up with the times, na, man. What family you have over there, pray tell? We ent going 'there,' you hear? Them days dead and gone. Them people 'there,' you making up stories about them in your head; you think they even have time for we? They bound to laugh at you in your face, old man." And they would start a fight about a country over there, or over this way where there was a hint of coloring on the horizon. The little boy would squint at the horizon, willing to see anything faint that might suggest Uncle Mako was right.

The Man from
the Gas Station

Even while smoking a cigarette, Abrahim the barber could, in five minutes or less, trim a boy's entire head of hair. The boy had already had his turn with Abrahim, but trim-time was an event beyond the cut itself. The crowd that gathered and stayed was an opportunity for the nuts seller, the penny-ice man, the fudge seller, and the whappie trickster not to miss. So the boy stayed and listened to the flip and slap of cards on the trickster's folding table, the cussing as money was more often lost than won, the talk and laughter, heckling, badmouthing, and boasting of those who had already been trimmed and those awaiting their turn. Abrahim's younger customers, too green in the ways of the world, were exposed to conversations they didn't always comprehend. They laughed or nodded gravely whenever any of the older people did.

The boy happened to glance toward his house to see a man in a suit, hat in hand, standing among the orange crocus watching his house. He stood up as the man approached the front stairs. The boy could see that he was calling out, but if the excitement on the beach hadn't drowned his voice, the wind coming in from the ocean would have whipped it away.

The boy left the beach and hurried, avoiding shards of broken shell and bottle, over the patch of flowering sea grape vines that wound about the shores at this time of year.

The man had reached the entrance to the house before the boy could get to him and was rapping on the wood frame with his knuckles. The boy knew his mother was in the backyard hanging out her washing on the hibiscus shrubs to dry. She wouldn't have heard him. When the boy was close enough he called out to the man.

"Mister, you want something?"

The man turned to regard the boy. He looked down toward the beach from where the boy had come. He saw the crowd of people. "Something happen?"

"No. Abrahim the barber giving trim. Is a trim you want?" Even as the child asked, he knew that was not what the man had come for: in this hot sun, he was wearing a brown suit, a white shirt, and a tie. He was not from around there. Cut hair caught in the fibers of his shirt had made him itchy. Suddenly pricked, he tugged at his shirt, twitched his shoulders.

"No. I come for something else. You just had a trim?"

The child ran his hands on his all but shaved head, his scalp feeling hot and prickly in the sun, strangely naked and cold in the breeze, and he nodded.

The man had a paper in his hand. He looked at it. "I don't know if I have the right address. I am looking for one Miss Dolly St. George. Timbano Trace. She living here?" He daubed his face with a large white handkerchief.

"Yes. Wait, please. She in the back. I'll get she. Who to say come?"

"Uhm. She don't know me by name. Anyway, is Persad. Bhatt Persad. You the son?"

"Eh-heh. Wait here."

Dolly undid the red band of cloth that she usually tied like a turban around her head when she was out in the yard working, shook it vigorously, and wound it back on her head. She sucked her teeth, irritated at being disturbed from her work, and said, "Persad. I don't know any Persad. What he want with me, pray?" She looked at her son and shook her head in a mixture of pity and disgust. "Why Abrahim does always cut your hair so short, boy? That ent no trim. That is a shave.

"Who is this Persad, I wonder? Come with me. I don't need no trouble now, you know." She fixed her dress, and they went around to the front.

The man had taken a seat on the front step. He got up when he saw them. "Miss St. George?"

"Well, I was married once. But that is all right. What it is you come about?"

"I got your name from Walter, the taxi driver you used to ride with. I didn't see you for a long time, and I asked him what happen to you and the boy."

Dolly started to frown. He was never a passenger in the car, so how and where had he seen her and the child? And what business did he have asking about her? From his polite manner, the way he spoke, and his dress, he looked more like someone the Sanghas might know. He was a short, balding man, an Indian man with a mustache and gold that flashed from the back and front of his mouth when he spoke. He wore spectacles. Dolly looked at her son. He shrugged.

When Dolly didn't respond, the man continued. "Walter told me you not working in town now. I was wondering if you are working at another job."

Dolly didn't immediately respond. She didn't want to give this stranger any information about herself, but she also didn't want to be impertinent to a man of his apparent standing by asking him what business it was to him. "You have a job for me?"

"You are not working?"

"I might be looking for something to do."

The child remembered having seen the man, and he blurted it out: "You is the man from the gas station."

Dolly looked at the boy quizzically. He held her hand and said, "Ent you remember Mr. Walter used to stop when we reach

Marion to get gasoline?" He pointed to the man and whispered up to her, "He used to be in the station, in the building—behind the counter."

The man heard him. Smiling, he said, "You remember. That is my station. I am the proprietor. I used to see you every Saturday morning."

Now that she knew more, Dolly was less apprehensive. So that she might offer the visitor a soft drink, she sent the boy five minutes up the beach to get a glass of ice from the iceman, the only person in Raleigh to own a freezer, though it was rusted from the salt air and hummed loudly. The boy pulled off his hair-covered shirt and raced back up the beach. When he returned, Dolly was sitting at the kitchen table waiting. The visitor had already gone.

"He want a full-time. I tell him I can't take full-time because I can't leave you day in, day out. He ask if you not going to school. I tell him hardly any children in Raleigh go to school, but you know how to read. He say bring you and he will get a school for you, and I will start work same time the school start, and finish up in time to fetch you by the time school bell ring for the day."

The boy's heart pounded with fear and excitement. "Where, Mammy?"

"In Marion."

Marion. Certainly that would mean they would see Mrs. Sangha and her daughter again. What would Mrs. Sangha say if she knew he was attending school. School! That frightened and appealed to him at the same time. The suggestion alone, that he, son of Dolly the servant, a boy from Raleigh, was being considered, being given the opportunity, to attend school—regardless of his mother's intention—made him feel different. A sweat broke above his upper lip. He spoke as calmly as he could. "What you say, Mammy?"

"School? Well, everybody want for they child to get education. I suppose I ordinary, too. You don't want to go to school?"

He was overcome by an overwhelming desire to attend a school, an activity he had never before thought about. In his mind, an image of Narine Sangha appeared and, almost immediately, vanished. No formed thought accompanied the image of Narine Sangha, but for a brief moment the boy imagined he could smell the cologne. He was simultaneously terrified and delighted. He held his breath, afraid to utter a word, terrified his mother would not accept the man's offer.

Thinking his silence meant that he was uninterested, she said with exasperation, "All you children in this village don't know what is good for you, yes. This place going to get swallow up one day"—he thought then she meant by the sea—"and all of we with it. Listen, forget about Raleigh, you hear. All Raleigh is good for is fishing, and you ent stepping foot in any boat as long as I have a say in your life. The only thing left save for idleness in Raleigh is to drive taxi, and even so the taxi will never be your own, you will always be a driver for Bihar company. You want to be a taxi man? Is true I didn't think about all this before, but I get a glimpse of my son teaching in a elementary school. My son, a teacher! Or even set up behind a table writing letters for people who can't read or write themselves. Is not like we suffering, but education is a kind of freedom, child."

It was too much for him to imagine, but he could tell she was already seeing the future and they were about to head for it.

The school term, something he had never considered before, was to begin in three weeks' time.

A Bustling Town

First week he had neither uniform nor books. His mother, having long been out of work and therefore short of money, couldn't easily have afforded even a pencil. However, Saturday, when they caught Mr. Walter's taxi to Marion, they did not get out at the gas station, as they had done during the previous weekdays. They carried on in the taxi to the heart of the town and got out on a corner of the busiest commercial street.

If there had been a war in the world, there were few signs of it in Marion. The narrow street was lined by tiny dark shops packed with goods. The stores had their names painted on them in large block printing, some in scrolled letters that were harder to read. J. J. RAM AND SON HARDWARE STORE, PATEL DRY GOODS, THE AMERICAN SHOE AND HANDBAG STORE, BISSEY BOOKS AND OFFICE SUPPLIES. The stores must have felt some competition from the vendors hawking just outside their doors; a store clerk stood in each doorway greeting passersby, inviting them to enter and browse. The trays perched on the vendors' laps were bright groupings of items arranged by color and size. There were orderly rows of bicycle bells, back scratchers, sandals, embroidered handkerchiefs from China, and from the other islands, potpourris of vetivier and lavender for placing among clothing in dressers. These particular scents excited the boy and provoked a longing in him. They were the same smells he remembered from the drawers of Mrs. Sangha's front room armoire, the scent of her linen, and of the pajamas he wore that unforgettable night passed in her house. There were playing cards, key rings, mirrors, handwritten song sheets, glass bangles, wood combs. There were spools

of gift-wrapping ribbon, wood swizzle sticks, sticks of cocoa, pen-
cils, socks, incense, windup tin toys, handmade windmills on
sticks, nail clippers, and penknives. A tray of china ornaments
—chickens, dogs, and horses of several different breeds—
caught his attention. He pulled down on his mother's hand.
They stopped and watched. The vendor picked out a slim, shiny
brown and white horse and held it, tiny in the palm of his large
coarse hand. He adjusted his hand so that the sun caught the
ornament's iridescent glaze. He said, "Imported. From China.
Good price. Shilling for one, shilling and a half for two. For a
nice mother, I offering a little break, but for today only: two
for the price of one. Pick what you like, boy." The boy didn't
answer. His mother did: "It nice, but we don't have no place
to put it." She pulled him along. He trailed a step behind her,
thinking of the minute and perfect details of the horse's mane
and tail. He wondered how he might earn a shilling, but lately
they had no time back in Raleigh, nor his mother any more need
to make and sell the guava cheese, or for him to do chores for
Uncle Mako that might bring him a few pennies here and there,
a shilling over time. He shrugged and caught up with his mother's
pace.

The noise of traffic (a clear sign of the availability once more
of car petrol) and of people chanting the attributes and prices
of their goods, greeting one another, haggling (some on the verge,
it would seem, of fighting), and the heat of the inland town were
dizzying. Food vendors lined the street. The nutman with six
different kinds of nuts, all hot and packaged in brown paper
cones, sang out, "Hot nuts, nuts hot, hot-hot." The skinny barra
and channa lady was so busy serving a long line of customers (impatient in the hot sun) that she never lifted her eyes from the
basins of curried channa and barra to look at the customers
who were putting their money on a tray and taking their own
change from the same tray. And there was the anchar man and

the salt-prune man and past them, a row of baked-goods vendors all selling the same goods—currant rolls, coconut cakes,
sweet bread, and more. The scent of car exhaust mixed with the
smells of oil used in frying, of cardamom, vanilla, coconut,
roasted peanuts, and sesame seed. A shaved-ice man was there,
melted ice wetting the ground all around his bicycle that doubled
as transportation and vending stall. And sitting on low benches,
the Indian ladies held on their laps wood trays containing colorful Indian sweets arranged by color—pinks, yellows, blues,
whites. The child eyed these goods. His mouth watered, his fingers dangled only inches away from the trays. His mother held
his hand and walked swiftly to Rahim School Supplies. She followed a salesclerk to where the school's uniform was shelved.
Dolly pulled a shirt from a pile, opened it, and held it up against
her son's chest. She held a pair of the short pants up to the air.
She marched her son to the cubicle that had been curtained off
to make a child's dressing room.

The boy tugged at her. "I don't want to try them on. Why I
have to try them, Mammy?"

She said, "Don't talk back, child, put them on, let me see."

When he had the right fit, she made a pile of two of everything, picked up the lot, and marched to the cashier. To his
wide-eyed surprise, his mother had enough bills rolled up and
concealed in the cleavage of her brassiere. After that transaction,
she counted out the remainder of the money and announced that
they were able to go to the bookstore. He thought of the little
china horse and wondered if there might be enough money left
to go back after, but he also felt shy to ask again after she had
already turned it down. The school uniform store and the bookstore were right next to each other, and although they appeared
to be different stores, there was a narrow and lopsided doorway
at the back that connected one with the other. There Dolly purchased two copybooks, a pencil, a ruler, a sharpener, an eraser,

a textbook for comprehension and writing, and one for sums. It was a typically hot Guanagasparian type of dry-season day, but he was sweating more than usual, frightened that she was spending all her hard-earned money on him. He couldn't help wondering where she had been keeping so much money. As the cashier was writing up the bill, he pulled her aside and whispered in her ear.

"Mammy, you don't have to buy everything one time. How we will eat? How we will catch taxi if you use up so much money now-now?" She, too, was sweating. With the paper on which the school had written down the child's needs, she fanned herself. Breathless, she told him the money was extra. Mr. Persad had given her that money, on top of her regular pay, so that she could buy whatever he needed for school.

He had indeed wanted to attend to school. Yet he felt confused. Before catching a taxi back to Raleigh, his mother bought a barra and channa for him. He halfheartedly took a bite of it, wrapped it back in its greasy brown paper, and held on to it until they arrived back home.

Bettering One's Self:
A Motive for All Reasons

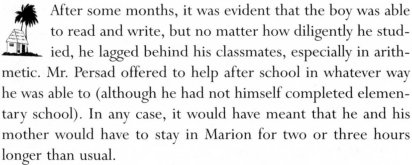 After some months, it was evident that the boy was able to read and write, but no matter how diligently he studied, he lagged behind his classmates, especially in arithmetic. Mr. Persad offered to help after school in whatever way he was able to (although he had not himself completed elementary school). In any case, it would have meant that he and his mother would have to stay in Marion for two or three hours longer than usual.

Mr. Persad persisted. He suggested that they leave Raleigh and move into his house, where he would employ Dolly as a full-time servant. The boy told his mother that he was from Raleigh, that it was his birthplace, that his friends were all there, and that Tante Eugenie and Uncle Mako were there, and Uncle Mako needed him. She marched up to him, her raised hand ready to hit him when he said outright that Mr. Persad was not his father and not her husband. She would not speak with him for what seemed like an interminable amount of time. He was sullen for days. Her lips remained pursed also, for days. Finally she spoke, calm but firm. She was disappointed and ashamed, she said, that her own son could be so ungrateful for a chance to better himself, and that since it was not his fault, as he was too young to know better, she had decided he would have no say in the matter; she knew what was best.

Dolly went to speak with Tante Eugenie about the move to Marion. Tante Eugenie answered first that if Dolly and her son

were to leave Raleigh, it would be as if she and Mako were losing their own child and grandchild, but they would survive. She
sighed and said that their people were survivors by nature. Then
she advised Dolly to tell Mr. Persad she wouldn't go and live in
his house with him just like that. She said, "Say no, and see
what he will do next."

So Dolly did just that. In response, Mr. Persad asked her to
marry him. Tante Eugenie said, "You see? You have to use your
head with these men. Don't let them get away easy-easy so."

After Dolly and Bhatt Persad were married in the Canadian
Friends Presbyterian Church, she and the boy (he anxious yet
excited at once) moved, all their possessions, including a cage
crammed with four chickens and the cock, packed tightly in
Mr. Persad's car.

The Days of the Week
in a Town

There was always something going on in the street directly in front of Mr. Persad's house. The Americans maintained a base on the island. On their days off, soldiers in uniform swept into Marion. The townspeople were often awakened by their aggressive singing, shouting, and laughter as jeeploads of them sped by, uninhibited by the lateness of night.

Myriad odors wafted into the house in Marion: petrol from the station next door, effluvia from the gutters on either side of the street. The latter had to be cleaned daily by the city public works crew; otherwise the surface, made slick and shiny overnight, trembled with mosquito larva. Cars and trucks burned dirty oil, and their exhaust hung heavily in the air. Dolly had to dust and sweep twice daily. She could be heard uttering under her breath that even Raleigh's sand had never invaded her house in such a manner. The boy enjoyed reminding her that the bedsheets there got so sandy, even as they slept, that she used to have to shake them out regularly, sometimes awakening even in the middle of the night to give them a proper brushing.

It didn't take long for the boy to forget, however. He quickly became accustomed to the cacophony of a city. Soon enough, he would tell time by the city's rumblings. Mondays, the Syrian cloth seller called at each and every house without fail. Tuesdays, eight P.M., the bells of the Good Shepherd Evangelical Society clanged out an hour's worth of hymns. Wednesdays, the manure man rolled his loaded odorous truck slowly through the residential quarters of the town. At precisely the same time every Thursday afternoon, the knife sharpener passed in front of Mr. Persad's house. Fridays, the fisherman's jitney rumbled noisily down the street. It was five A.M. when the imam's call to prayer rose from the turret of the mosque, four P.M. when the nutman's rubber-ball horn wheezed by, and it was six-thirty P.M. sharp when melismatic outpourings rang from the Indian cinema down the road.

Naming

If he were asked, he would say he had no memory of his mother and Mr. Persad calling each other by name. In truth, if Mr. Persad wanted Dolly, he would look for her for as long as it took without ever uttering her name. On finding her, he would simply begin talking.

"I was looking for you," he might say, to which she might as gently answer, "Well, I was right here." It was the most natural thing.

She did the same. Initiating communication with him, she would utter, as if it were his name, "Ehem ..." and he would look up in acknowledgment. Speaking of her to the boy, he would say "your mammy." She and the boy spoke of him as "Mr. Persad." This was how the boy addressed him when he was speaking directly with him; in the most muted voice he could manage, he would try, at once, to be neither heard nor impertinent. Mr. Persad called him "son," but he never referred to him as "my son."

The boy didn't have much of a sense of his mother and Mr. Persad's relationship as a married couple. They had separate bedrooms. He never caught Mr. Persad going into hers and knew her to enter Mr. Persad's only when he was not in it, to clean it or to look after his clothing. And yet to his mind, neither of them seemed dissatisfied or wanting.

Once, through his bedroom window, the boy heard them out in the backyard talking. He peeped out to see them walking in the yard, side by side, stopping to examine a rusted bit of the wire netting on the chicken coop. They were discussing things that needed to be done in the yard. His mother wondered if tomato

plants would survive in such soilless gravel. Mr. Persad pointed to
something in the hills behind the house. He and Dolly stood close
to each other, watching whatever it was. He walked over to a clump
of milk tins in which anthurium lilies were planted. He picked one
up, inspected it. She bent over the ones on the ground and broke
off browned, dead leaves. The boy believed he heard his name mentioned, but he couldn't really be sure. He returned to his homework, comforted by the notion that he had been mentioned,
thinking that all in all, his mother might be happy.

In preparation for the upcoming common entrance exam,
Mr. Persad paid for extra lessons. He hired a man who ran a taxi
to meet the boy at the end of each school day and take him directly to a Mr. Joseph's house, a two-story concrete structure
through which no air seemed to circulate. In a room that faced an
unkempt road ridden with potholes, the boy and three others took
two-hour lessons in spelling, comprehension, arithmetic, and the
geography and history of the world. On any given day, Mr. Joseph,
who smelled of sewing machine oil, leaned out of the window no
less than five times to plead for peace and quiet from less ambitious
boys prancing around the potholes in a raucous game of cricket
or football. Mr. Joseph's boys sat on low elementary-school-type
benches on either side of a long low table. Various words and images: flowers, body parts, airplanes, and bombs, to name a few, were
etched on the surface of the table, the groves filled in with years
of grime that a protractor point could, with some determination,
dislodge. There were, here and there, hearts through which Cupid's
arrows were drawn. Each heart and arrow was flanked by a girl's
name on one side and a boy's on the other. Once, when the boy
arrived first, and Mr. Joseph could be heard brushing his teeth,
hacking and expelling phlegm in an adjoining room, he dug the
point of his compass into the soft flesh of the desk and drew a
heart. He wrote no name but etched an image of a rose within the
heart.

The Gift of Eggs

Dolly returned from market one day with news: she had met Mrs. Sangha. Mrs. Sangha, well aware of her previous servant's new station in life, asked how she was adapting, and as if to acknowledge the change, although she suggested no particular date, she said that Dolly must come to the house for tea. Dolly told her son that she had asked Mrs. Sangha if Boss was still home or if he went back to the other lady. The boy thought it brazen of her, was shocked that they could have such easy, matter-of-fact conversation and be light or irreverent about it all. Mr. Sangha was at present abroad, but not for business. He just liked it there; now that the war was over, there was a lot of excitement, even in the queues that still existed for food and clothing. Although one could see hardship in the faces of people, one saw in them hope and determination, too. People who, during the war, were jobless were able to work clearing the streets of the rubble of bombed buildings. Wherever one looked, new buildings were going up, each and every one an architectural wonder. Narine Sangha wanted to be in that great country to witness the changes taking place. Mrs. Sangha told Dolly all of this, describing everything as if she herself had been there in the great country, witness to the changes taking place. Dolly asked Mrs. Sangha if "the woman" went with him. Mrs. Sangha didn't know. Eventually, with a hint of fatigue in her voice, Mrs. Sangha admitted: who knew, maybe the woman did go; it was reasonable to assume so, as that woman was young enough to do that sort of thing. Besides, she added, who would look after her daughter if she went traipsing around the world?

As if in passing, Dolly told her son that Mrs. Sangha had asked about him. She wanted to know how he was doing in school, if he was able to catch up. Dolly said, again as if in passing, that Mrs. Sangha had mentioned that during the holidays, the girl went with her father on an airplane. He took her to the island of Trinidad for a vacation. The boy was surprised. When they were living in Raleigh, his own mother would not have considered allowing him to take a ride in Uncle Mako's boat, even if they were to have remained within her range of vision. If he had ever gone out on a boat even meters off the coast of Raleigh, he at least might have been able to say that he, too, had once stepped off the island of Guanagaspar.

Following Dolly's encounter with Mrs. Sangha, she became contemplative. She would begin to do some ordinary daily house task, then, in the middle of it, would stop. She would think a while. Then she would call Rodney, Mr. Persad's yard boy. He would answer, "Yes, Madam?" She would purse her lips as if to say, "That's right. That's what I am to you." She would get him to complete the task she had started.

Rather than go down to the backyard to catch, kill, and pluck a fowl for dinner, she would awkwardly order Rodney to do it. She would stand right behind him, watching every move he made, correcting him, telling him how to do it her way. So for a while, it was Rodney who washed the dishes, cleaned the windows and mirrors, squeezed oranges for juice, swept the house, dusted, and mopped, whereas, up until a short while before, she had done it all with studied gratitude for Mr. Persad's kindnesses. Before long Rodney could be found sitting on the back stairs hemming Mr. Persad's trousers, at the kitchen table, a mess of cut flowers, bush bugs, and ladybugs crawling on the table, tiny fluorescent-green grasshoppers caught in the curled hairs of his dark brown arms as he trimmed leaves and stems and arranged the lot in a vase. Dolly ordered and watched more and more, and became easier in this new role by the minute. She had become an employer.

One day she sent Rodney down with a bowl to collect eggs from the chickens in the backyard. She carefully washed and patted the eggs dry herself. She arranged them in a green translucent glass bowl, covered the bowl with a fresh kitchen cloth, and handed it to her son. She told him to carry them, a little present for Mrs. Sangha, a mile's walk from where they lived in Marion. Even though a very long period of time had passed since his encounter with Narine Sangha, the boy was not ready to reenter that house. He said, trying to sound more uninterested in the excursion than insolent, "Why you don't send Rodney with them?"

Dolly sucked her teeth loudly. "Look, child, where you learning to talk back so? You feel you could talk to me so now you living in town? You not too big for me to lay mih hand on you, you hear? I ask you to do one thing for me and you can't do it?"

How could he tell her that they didn't live like town people; the yard outside with chickens strutting around and fouling it up smelled like a backward country yard, not like a town yard. He wanted to say that he did not want to make deliveries like a grocery-store errand boy. He wanted to suggest that she bake a cake with the eggs and send the cake, not eggs from the chickens they still kept. But he could not insult her. He was silent.

"Child, you going to let those people curb your movements in the world? We living in town now, and I don't work for nobody no more. I, Dolly Persad, have servant—manservant, to boot—now. And if that is not enough, nobody better than me or my son."

Dolly Persad. The boy wondered if that meant he, too, had become a Persad.

She softened, lowered her voice. "Remember this. How much times I must tell you? But you can't get it through your thick head.

They family come here, to this part of the world, same as mine, you hear? Same as Mr. Persad family. Better than we, my foot!" By now the boy had come to know his mother's rant. He tapped his foot on the floor and rolled his eyes. "You feeling impatient with me? Well, I will say it again and again, until I feel you hear me good." She glared at him and spoke deliberately, as if intending to imprint her words for good this time. "They cross them terrible waters—let me tell you—in the same stinking boats. All of we lie down side by side, catch head lice, cough, and cold, chew betel leaf together, and spit blood. They enter this country through the same procedures. They did have to line up for placement, answer the same questions, and do daily hard labor under estate boss and the hot sun in cane field. Everybody get treat the same way. Everybody had was to line up for pay and for handouts, one and all. And no matter how some rise, how some fall, or how some stay put, all of we—Mr. Persad family, my family, your father family, Mrs. Sangha family, and Narine Sangha family—and by that I mean people who have their eyes in the back of their heads always facing abroad, as if abroad even noticing us here on this island, and people who can't take their eyes off from the one spot where they feet planted—all, one and all, stem from the same tide. And it had a time every one of us was servant. You hear me? But child, I didn't pick up myself and move all the way to Marion just for style. What I do, I do for you. And I don't want you kneeling down before nobody but God, you hear me? And when was the last time you do that in any case, eh? Take the eggs, and go and ring they bell! I have enough to give, and so I will give. Don't look frighten-frighten so. Freshen up your face and go. Now for now, not later. Don't waste no more time thinking in your backyard ways. You attending school, just like town children."

He went briskly down to the shower stall. He scrubbed his arms, elbows, knees, and feet with a chip of pumice stone, washed his ears with a wash rag, inside, outside, and behind.

Mrs. Sangha had never seen him wear long pants. They would make him look more solemn, older, more like a town boy, he thought. Before the mirror in his mother's room, he parted his hair and sleeked it down with a little hair grease. It had grown out and was being cut by a barber in the town, not shaved like Abrahim used to do to everyone in Raleigh, but in the popular fashion for boys of his age. By the time he was ready to leave, he was sweating from all the fussing and nervousness. He walked in the heat, conscious of being a person, of having some sense of stylishness, to the house at the corner of Beau Moreau Street and Ashton Road.

At the gate he couldn't help himself: he hesitated. A jumbled mantra began to play softly in his head. *All of we, one and all. Same tide. Better than me, my foot! You attending school. You attending school.* He grabbed hold of the iron bell that hung from the wrought-iron gate and shook it vigorously. Mrs. Sangha came out onto the verandah. When she saw him, she called out, "Is you Harry, boy? Eheh, wait one minute. I sending Patsy to open the gate for you. But look at him, na, in long pants and thing. You get big, boy."

He tried to be serious, but he broke into a smile, and every particle of his body knew happiness.

Patsy let him in. Even though Mrs. Sangha did not pull him to her like she used to, he didn't mind, for he was a big boy now. Still, when she put a hand on his shoulder and ushered him into the house, he caught the familiar scent of her skin, her body soap, and the washing detergent in her clothing. He handed her the bowl and said, "Mammy send these."

She said, "You mammy never forget me." She picked an egg, held it up, turning it in the light. "But the chicks laying nice eggs. Look, Patsy. Save these for tomorrow breakfast. Feel them: good weight, nice size, better than the ones from Hing Wan shop."

She turned with the bowl and walked swiftly to the kitchen. Dolly's son stood there until Patsy, standing behind him, poked him in his back to move on. As they went through the house to the back where the kitchen was, he hoped to see his friend, but the house, looking smaller than he remembered it, with unfamiliar curtains, was quiet. There was no sign of her.

Mrs. Sangha seemed genuinely happy to see him. She turned and looked at him from his head to his feet while they walked. "You get so good-looking, boy."

He remembered how indulgent she used to be with him. In the kitchen she put both hands on his shoulders. "Look how nice you dress up. Mammy tell me you going to school."

His response came only as a whisper. "Yes. I going to Canadian Friends."

"Yes, yes. I know. You sitting exams same time. You liking school?"

She didn't say same time as whom. He could hardly breathe, wanting not merely a veiled reference to her but to know where she was. He wouldn't ask. Without offering, Mrs. Sangha poured a glass of lime juice from a jug in the refrigerator, then set it and a coconut drop on a saucer on the small kitchen table. She pulled out a bench for him to sit. She sat on the chair opposite him. She pointed to the drop. "Patsy bake today. You remember how you used to like Patsy coconut drops? Good thing you come today. You can eat one fresh."

He continued to wonder about the girl, why she hadn't come out to greet him. Perhaps her father, Narine Sangha, was still abroad, and perhaps she was with him. He was afraid to lift the glass to his mouth, sure that in his mixture of happiness to see Mrs. Sangha, and nervousness about seeing—and also not seeing—the girl, that he might drop it, or might bang it hard against his teeth, causing it or his teeth to break. He was sure that if he picked up the drop, it would crumble to bits between his fingers and make a mess on Mrs. Sangha's spotless linoleum floor.

Patsy had leaned back against the counter. Her arms were folded as she regarded the boy, the son of a onetime fellow maid. He picked up the drop and put it to his mouth. The scents of vanilla and coconut flavorings that Patsy used in all her sweets were achingly familiar. But when he took a bite of it, he felt dizzy and found that in an instant his appetite had vanished. He fidgeted. It was unbearable not knowing where the girl was. He knew it would be improper to ask.

Just when he thought, But I am no longer her maid's son. Look how nicely she is treating me. Surely I will be allowed to ask for my friend, there was a thumping of feet ascending the back steps.

Mrs. Sangha said, almost in a whisper, to Patsy, "Boss." And she jumped up, whipping the plate with the boy's barely touched coconut drop and the glass of untouched juice away from the table and into the sink. He instinctively stood up, backed away from the bench and the table.

Boss appeared at the kitchen door and said, "I sent Munir to pick up daughter from lessons. It is twelve o'clock. What is for lunch?" He saw the boy and stopped. The haunting sensation of a sack of flour weighing down upon his chest returned, and the boy's breath was momentarily arrested. His face burned, and his upper lip broke into a sweat. Even so, he knew now that his friend had not come out to see him not because she was avoiding him but because she was not in the house; she had gone for lessons, perhaps she was studying for the exams. He was dizzy.

"Who is this?"

Mrs. Sangha did not answer. In fear, he almost said his name out loud, but Patsy, seeing his lips part, burst in, "The egg boy. He come to bring eggs."

Mr. Sangha turned and walked away. He had not remembered the boy, which was not surprising, as it had been some years since the boy was last in the house. Mrs. Sangha's shoulders had stooped, and one hand lay flat on her chest, as if to quiet her heaving. Patsy had put her hand on the boy's shoulder and begun to show him the way out when Mr. Sangha shouted, "I have some shoes need cleaning. Let him clean them and give him a shilling. What is for lunch? I am hungry."

Mrs. Sangha shouted, "Patsy making lunch now. It almost ready. Five minutes." She shooed them out of the house, telling Patsy, "I will warm up the roti, take him down and hurry back up." Then she whispered to the boy, "Go now. I will tell him you had to go. Rose gone to swimming lessons. When she come back, I will tell her you was here. Tell your Mammy thanks for the eggs. And you—"

She laid the palm of her hand on his cheek. "I happy to see you. Go now." News of Rose emboldened him; he wanted to know more about her swimming lessons. No particular question, however, would form in his mind. In any case, it was too late: Mrs. Sangha had already hurried away.

When he got down to the padlocked gate, which Patsy unlocked with a key from her apron pocket, she whispered with exasperation, "It not easy to ascend in this place, eh, boy? Once a servant son, always a servant son." The boy turned to look at her. She watched his face redden. She said, "At least you have good looks, and you going to school. Put crack in the mold, child. Go your way and crack mold, you hear?" And she pushed him out, locking the gate behind him.

PASSING

Sunday morning Mr. Persad went down to the gas station to begin the day's work. As usual, first thing after opening the door and pulling up the venetian blind, he picked up and looked at the front page of the newspaper. This day's paper, he quickly realized from its headlines, contained long-awaited important news. He removed his glasses, wiped them, and put them on again. He then flipped anxiously to the appropriate page. Suddenly he stood up. There it was. He fingered and read one single line over and over. When he could believe his eyes, he folded the paper neatly and held it against his chest. Then, as calmly as he might, he swung the minute hand of the WE WILL REOPEN AT cardboard clock on the door of the office to twenty past the hour. He locked the door and went quickly back to his house. Dolly in the kitchen, surprised by his return, asked, "What happen?"

By way of telling her to wait, he said only, "Just now," and carried on through the house.

The boy was awake, but it being a Sunday morning, he lay idly in his bed. Mr. Persad knocked on his door, calling him out to the kitchen.

Dolly stood close to her son as he hesitantly opened the paper to the results of the national exam. Mr. Persad sat and watched. Dolly crowded over his shoulder as he ran a forefinger swiftly down the columns of names. It took him a while to figure out how the paper had ordered the results: name of the area in which the exam had been sat, then by gender, and then alphabetically by surname. South, southwest. Canadian Friends Presbyterian. Boys. And there it was—unbelievably—St. George. There was only one St. George, and it was his name printed right there in the country's national newspaper. And, even more unbelievably, next to his name was that of the school of his first choice. He turned and wrapped his arms around his mother's waist. She cupped his face in her hands and kissed his forehead once.

Mr. Persad said, "So you passed, boy. Good. Very good." He looked at his watch. It was almost twenty past the hour. He got up and turned to go down the back stairs, to return to the gas station.

Dolly said rather loudly, "Ehem . . ."

Mr. Persad turned as if his name had been said.

"Well, he pass. Is true. But is you . . . is you what . . ."

She wasn't able to say exactly what it was Mr. Persad had done. The boy understood her intention, though, and went over to Mr. Persad. He put both hands on his stepfather's shoulders and pressed his body awkwardly against him. As he patted the child's back, Mr. Persad, as if responding to an uttered appreciation, said, "You welcome, boy. You did very good, son, very good. You must be proud of yourself, you hear? You have a future ahead of you."

The boy pored over page after page of children's names. His voice trembling and deep with excitement, he called out to his mother, "Ma, Look. Sangha. Look it here. Mrs. Sangha daughter pass, too. She pass for the convent."

Days later he said to his mother, "Mammy, you see Mrs. Sangha yet?"

"Mrs. Sangha? Why I would see she? What you mean?"

"I mean since our names make the paper."

Dolly knew what her son was thinking. She replied tersely, "No. Where I will see she?"

"Well, we could go and see them. Everybody telling us congratulations, so I was thinking we should go and tell them congratulations, too."

"Who is everybody? Mrs. Sangha come to tell us congratulations?"

He sulked. It was true, he knew, but he hadn't thought about
it that way. It hadn't occurred to him that Mrs. Sangha might
have brought or sent a message of congratulations to him or to
his mother. When, after weeks had passed, there was still no acknowledgment from Ashton Street that he and the girl he still
considered to be the best friend he ever had were now to be in
high school at the same time, he felt the sting in his face like a
slap on his cheek, that old bitterness again. This time, however,
he was deeply grateful his mother hadn't gone to see them when
he wanted her to.

Awakening to Dreams

Supposedly he was studying a biology assignment in his bedroom, the door to which was closed. His source of light was a bare bulb that swung with the slightest breeze by a cord from the center of the ceiling. He lay dressed in a thin, worn merino vest and equally thin and worn cotton short pants on his bed. One leg was propped at the ankle atop the knee of the other, which he had drawn up. His book rested open and facedown on his chest. He was daydreaming. Every few minutes a mosquito buzzed near his head. He would slap the area when he felt the prick of one feeding on his neck or arms, or the frantic wriggling of one trapped in the net of thick and curly hairs that had sprouted on his lower legs. He was thinking about a particular scene from a movie that he and three of his classmates had skipped school several times to see in a nearby cinema.

In the scene he was reliving, a man who has long been in love with a woman who scorns him finds himself alone for the first time with her. They are having a vibrant quarrel where, face-to-face, noses almost touching, he accuses her of being spoiled and childish, while she demands in a high-pitched voice that he not speak to a woman of her standing so insolently. "I shall not stand for this. Stop it at once," she says, staring at him unflinchingly. He then grips her by both shoulders, so firmly that she gasps, but she makes no attempt to get away from him. He says she has a heart of stone and doesn't know what it is to be loved or to love. She stares up into his face, and her eyes flicker as she looks at his lips. How tightly the man holds her, one arm around her waist, pulling her hard into him. The boy imagined he was the man on the screen. The woman's back is arched as she keeps her head away with enough distance to be able to see his eyes and mouth. His other arm, splayed against her upper back, allows her to lean that far back. They are about to kiss. The boy and his friends had gone to see the movie so many times solely for that moment, the moment of their first kiss. The way the man grips her waist tighter, presses her upper back toward him in such a forceful, swift manner that her head whips back and then forward, her mouth perfectly hitting his, hard. With a forefinger, the boy stroked himself.

Suddenly there was a light tap on his door. He jumped up, breathless. His mother. Without entering, she called his name. He turned his back to the door, fixed his shorts, and began to pull on over them the pair of long pants that were thrown on the foot of the bed. She softly called out to him to come, to sit with them awhile. "He" wanted to talk to him, she said. He pulled on a shirt, pressed his hand against his penis, and waited for the blood flooding his brain to subside, his heart to still, before opening the door.

Mr. Persad sat at one end of the verandah on a bentwood and cane rocking chair, she at the other in a vinyl armchair, both shadowed in the soft edges of orange flare extending this far from a streetlamp. The boy stood awkwardly in the doorway. The tip of a mosquito-repellent coil glowed in a corner of the verandah. A steady, slim stream of dense white smoke rose and swirled lazily in the air, spiraled in the space between the three of them, then dissipated into the hot, still night. The porch, though open, smelled heavily of it, yet Dolly and Mr. Persad still slapped at their arms, their faces, and waved their hands about their heads.

"You studying?"

"Mammy say you want me."

"Sit down." Mr. Persad gestured with an open palm to the only other chair on the verandah. The boy nodded and sat in the slatted folding wood chair, the kind sold by pavement vendors in the town center.

Mr. Persad looked out over the wood railing into the impenetrable blackness beyond the light of the streetlamp. As he rocked, there was a rhythmic squeak of dry wood arching against dry wood. When his mother wasn't swiping at the buzzing sounds about her ears, or brushing her skin, she would rest her arms on the shiny curl of metal and padded-vinyl arm of the chair. Her fingers made no sound as she tapped the metal in time to the beat of Mr. Persad's rocking chair. The boy perched on the edge of his chair, waiting. The smoke stung his eyes. He leaned forward, rested his elbows on his knees, and looked at the dark floor.

Finally Mr. Persad spoke. "So, son, next term you choosing subjects for your finals. Not so?"

The boy nodded.

"You have plans for your future, son?"

Plans? Future? Wasn't is as simple as choosing whichever subjects he happened to get the highest grades in? Where could this conversation be headed? he wondered.

"Well, you decide to go into science or the classics?" When the boy was not forthcoming with a response, Mr. Persad asked, "Or you thinking about business?" and without waiting carried on, "Because, you know, I hoping you will take up business. Who else will run all of this?" He indicated with one hand the gas station on the other side of the house, but the gesture made "all of this" appear to be a vast empire, which it was not. The boy thought of the word "heir" and suppressed the urge to grin. The boy's mind skipped to Bihar and Busby, two classmates who were inseparable. This was how the two of them went through their lives, their futures known, mapped out, and secure. They were born with paid passages on ships captained by their surname and headed unequivocally for success.

Perhaps if his own father were alive, he might have assumed that he would become a fisherman, too, or taken up boat building, and seeing that generation after generation moved townward, he might have followed suit and set up a fish market right there in Marion. But the way things had turned out, his mother coming to Marion and marrying this man who had no obligation to him, he had simply supposed he might finish school as best as he was able and get a job as an elementary school teacher, perhaps as a clerk in a store or in a government office, or even as manpower in a construction company.

Reaction from the boy was slow. From the way his mother looked at him, he knew that she was anxious for him to show some interest, to be grateful. Several times over the course of their life in Bhatt Persad's house, he did get the impression his mother was with this man for his benefit. This was one of them.

Mr. Persad waited as long as he could and then unfurled his plans for his future and the boy's.

"You know, it's twenty-one years now I am living here. Twenty-one years, same house, same station. I see this town grow up around me." He paused and rocked and seemed to be reflecting on this fact. "What brought me here was the motorcar, you know. Not many people had cars in those days, but of course those who had, needed petrol to run the cars. There were no petrol stations then. Well, not like we know them today, you know." He said this, his eyes wide open, baring a grin as if he himself were responsible for the development of the gas station. "The car came from an American company. They had set up an office in Trinidad that was to serve the whole Caribbean. All that was here in Guanagaspar was a showroom in Gloria, nothing more than a shoe-box-size office with a picture of the car pin up behind the salesman's desk, and a brochure about it. You signed up, you made your down payment there, and you waited. Then the vehicle arrived via ship three to six months later. But gasoline to run the car was hard to come by. Only one place sold it: you had to go all the way to the docks outside of Gloria. Sometimes the trip to buy gas was enough to cause you to run out of gas! You see, people were afraid that petrol stations right in town were an invitation to hooligans to burn down the entire town in one big"—he made a gesture of an explosion with his hands—"poof!" Dolly pursed her lips and nodded as if in agreement with the people. "And so you can see the problem. If you ran out of gas outside of Gloria, it was headache to find a way to send to the docks for just enough gas so that you could put a little in the tank and make your way back to fill up the rest later. Well, more and more people wanted cars, but it was only the people in the capital who could maintain one. The car company in America and a petrol company over there decided to set up some fellows in business on the outside of the towns. To make a long story short, at that time I was doing manual work in a sugar factory. Well, one day as I was leaving the factory compound, a stranger outside the gate approached me. He asked if he could talk to me a minute. He was a red-skinned man, but he had on nice clean clothes, and he was polite enough. So, I asked myself what harm could there be if I were to spare him a minute or two? He walked with me and we talked a little. He asked how long I worked in the factory, if I was married, and all kinds of other questions. He even asked if I had car. Well, by this time I could tell he was either a real salesman about to try and sell something, or he was a smart man. But I had no money for him to take advantage of me for, so I wasn't too worried. Eventually he asked if I ever had a dream to be my own boss and to be free of money problems. Well, I burst out laughing, but that didn't slow him down. He continued walking with me, telling me how easy that dream was to come true. He was, in fact, working for the very company that made dreams come true. The company was looking for people with ambition, and he said that I looked like a man with ambition. He told me that if I was interested and showed potential, the company would teach me everything. For free. Eventually I would have my own business that I could name after myself, and in no time I would be my own man. They would give me a crash course in keeping books and dealing with customers, all for free. He said they weren't taking any and everybody, ordinarily you had to apply and you had to have certain qualifications. I told the man I had no qualifications, but he told me he had already summed me up and could see I was a very good candidate. So basically he sweet-talked me, and the impressionable young fellow I was, I decided to go to the short-term office that they had set up especially for recruiting, and to apply—without even knowing what exactly I was applying for, except that it was to be my own boss. I found out only then that it was to rent-to-own a gas station. You know, whenever I think back on it, I always realize that all that separates me from this life I living now and continuing on in the sugar factory—maybe one day rising to foreman or driving one of the trucks—was a chance meeting with that fellow outside the factory grounds. Well, I got the job and the station same day. They had to build the station, but in two weeks' time, I was a businessman with a gas station. This same one. Look at that, eh? One day I was a hand in a factory, and next day I was operating a gas station on the way to owning it. You can never really know who somebody was; by that I mean what position they used to occupy, or who they are currently, or who that somebody may one day become, what clout he might one day have. Best, then, to treat everybody the same, not so? Anyhow, it was the first station this side, you know, and that year Marion had five cars. One year later, it had over two hundred motorcars in Marion."

Dolly seemed familiar with the story. The boy had had no idea that this man in whose house he lived had once been an estate hand.

Mr. Persad continued, "So I see the town grow up to be what it is today. Now there are more cars in Marion than there are gas stations to supply gas. You see how this place have line-up Friday night and Sunday morning? Anyway, the thing is, businesses—be they gasoline or house construction or lumberyards or clothing stores—here in Marion and in the rest of the country, they getting bigger and broader, and I am wondering what is Bhatt Persad doing? Well, Bhatt Persad has been thinking. I have been thinking I need to begin to grow with the town. Expansion, that is what it is, you know. I am thinking about expanding, buying another gas station. It have need in this place for more. Need, in truth. Well, I want to purchase another two. One on the other side of Marion and the other along the highway."

Dolly, as surprised as her son, gasped. She said unusually loudly, "Eh?" He looked at her, grinning, and then said that one happened to be for sale right now. She said, "But what you need more than one station for? One is a livelihood, two is headache, and three is . . . three is . . ." She wouldn't finish her thought. She sucked her teeth.

He said right then, very quickly, that he was only thinking about it. She said, "Well, he will choose business, but one station is business enough." Mr. Persad looked at the boy and nodded as if in agreement. His mother got up and went inside. Mr. Persad said to the boy in an excited but low voice, "Later. We'll talk later. Man-to-man. You better go and hit those books hard, boy!"

Feeling taller than he was, the boy walked into the house, strangely aligned with his stepfather, dizzy from the ease with which he found he could betray his mother.

How to Grow a Fire

Mr. Persad did not miss any opportunity when he and the boy were alone. The once-reserved man walked urgently around his property with an arm around the boy's shoulder, ushering him here and there to see and to learn. His attention and trust made the boy feel older than he was. Mr. Persad showed his books to the boy to prove that he had the money and collateral to buy at least the two stations he had his eyes on.

Mr. Persad had a little car that he seldom drove himself, hiring instead one of the younger attendants to take him or Dolly wherever it was they needed to be. One evening, citing the urge to eat blood pudding and fresh hops bread, he told the boy to accompany him. Uncharacteristically, he drove to the most reputable seller of blood pudding, whose business was housed a fair distance by car on the other side of Marion. But rather than returning home directly after purchasing the heavy steaming coils of aromatic pudding and a quart of yeasty rolls, he took the boy on a drive. He wanted to show him something, he said. They drove up a road that zigzagged across the face of a hill. It took them into a hillside residential area. The houses on the side of this terraced hill were large and extravagantly built, with gardens that had been landscaped and were enclosed by high fences. The stillness in the area was underlined only by the twitter of birds. Every house had an unobstructed view of the town far below and the ocean in the distance. They came to a piece of land that had yet to be built on. Here Mr. Persad stopped the car. They got out to admire the view. The houses were sprawling and were designed, it seemed, to hide away the interiors, unlike the houses of the town that had welcoming verandahs, and windows and doors that in the daytime were left wide open to the eyes of passersby. Unlike the wood houses of the town, these were constructed of steel, stone, and concrete. The fanciest house the boy had seen until these was that of the Sanghas. Mr. Persad clasped his hands behind his head and arched his back for a stretch. The boy was uneasy. He wondered if he was about to be told that Mr. Persad had purchased the property in front of which they stood. This was not an area where he would feel comfortable, would know how to carry himself. His mother would be angry, he thought. Mr. Persad put his arm around the boy's shoulder.

The way things were going in Marion, he said, it was not good enough these days to simply make a living. A businessman, he said, must nowadays drive a nice car. He gestured to the car behind them and said, "Not that anything is wrong with this car, you know, it is good enough for me, but a real businessman should have a brighter, bigger one. A bigger engine, you understand?

"And he must live in a house in an area like this, with a view of the sea. The kind of house and home he can invite customers and fellow businessmen to. You know, a nice wife who can cook, make a nice party, and make people feel comfortable. Could fix up flowers in a vase nice and set a table pretty-pretty."

Dolly Persad did not fit this image of the "nice" wife. Her son wondered with dread if she was what this man who had married her really wanted for himself. But Mr. Persad soon clarified without prompting.

"But I self, I never wanted to be involved in all this, you know. This is not for me. I never had desire nor fire to mix in society and that sort of thing. But today things are different, and today a *real* businessman must be able to do these kinds of things. You see, my fire was small.

"But you, you must have the means to send your wife into town to buy nice things for herself and for yourself. Nice clothes, nice shoes, a little perfume from abroad once in a while. Not so, child? You must be able not only to afford but also to choose nice pretty jewelry, nice earrings and bangles, bring these things home for your wife and daughters without them having to ask you for them. You see? You have to have a little style, taste. That is the kind of thing you can learn if you want to, you know. Some people are born into circumstances where they grow up with these things and with opportunities in their midst. But I don't believe anybody is born with style. Style, a person can learn, you learn best when you are young. So I would say, above all, son, to be a real businessman nowadays, you have to be able to go abroad and see how they do things abroad."

The boy could wait no longer. He asked Mr. Persad if he was planning to leave where they lived. Mr. Persad said he was set in his ways, and the house they lived in was good enough for them. He wouldn't be comfortable in a house that had a room for every occasion, but that *he,* the boy, was from a different generation, and when he took over the gas stations—as if he already had more than the one next to the house—he hoped that the boy would live in a place like this, with a big garden landscaped by a professional who had vision, and a house that was designed by a reputable architect with vision, too, and built by a big-time contractor who knew materials and could install modern plumbing and other conveniences.

"You mustn't live in a box," he said, "not one of those make-do things put up by a fellow who has no idea about convenience or comfort, nothing more than how to bang two pieces of wood together. You know, they see no value, no function in prettiness. But prettiness is not slackness, it is a way to call and honor God. God willing, I and your mother will live to see you settled in a nice place, eh?" His arm still around the boy's back, he directed him back to the car, which now smelled of yeast and hot bread.

Back home, the boy saw their house differently. He realized that although he and his mother had bettered their circumstances through the move to Marion, everything was relative. In the eyes of the owners of the houses they had just seen, she and he were probably only a little better off than when they lived in Raleigh.

THEATER

Looking up from some simple accounting, the boy saw the Sangha car being refueled by one of the attendants. He leaped off the stool and pressed his face against a pane of glass that allowed those in the office to observe what was going on outside but not the other way around. Mr. Sangha was in the front seat with the chauffeur. The boy rushed out to the ground and loudly, officiously shouted out to Gordon, the attendant who had been sitting idly on an overturned oil drum. "Ey, Gordon. You don't have nothing better to do or what?" He shouted so loudly that Andrew, the other attendant, was himself startled. The boy saw in his peripheral vision, as he made sure not to look directly at the occupants, that those in the car had heard and had turned to see what was happening.

"Get off that drum, man. You can't see it have vehicle here. Get over there and clean the windshield, man. What you think you getting pay for? Check the tires. Check the oil."

Gordon jumped up and headed to the car. He began to say, "Yes, boss. Sorry. I was just—"

"You was just what! I don't want to hear what you was just. Get some life in you."

The blood in his body was racing, his heart beating wildly with the excitement of being able to exercise his position in front of this particular customer whom he made sure not to look at directly.

He stayed in their view, walking around the station, propitiously checking on the eaves of the office building and pretending to write in a little book pulled out of his pocket, until their car moved off and disappeared out of view.

To his horror, when he went back into the office, he realized that Mr. Persad had been watching him from the little window.

Mr. Persad very quietly said, "Why you were so hard on Gordon?"

"Well, he was just sitting idle, doing nothing."

"Yes. But why you chose to talk to him like that in front of your mother's former employer? You see what I am asking you?"

The boy's face stung with embarrassment and shame. He said nothing.

"Imagine somebody treating you like that. How you would feel? Being a boss does not make you more worthwhile man than your workers, you hear? Without them, how you will carry on your business by yourself? We need each other, boy. Most times it is only luck and chance that separates us, one from the other, village and town people, rich and poor, the customer, the gas-station owner and the gas-station attendant, you know. How you can be so sure that one day you will not have to ask Gordon for something only he can give you? We don't know the twists and turns of the world. I myself was once a factory worker. You must take it easy with people. Even dogs don't respond to being shouted at. They only get frightened." He told the boy to go for a walk and to think hard about why he spoke to Gordon that way.

After the station closed and he and Mr. Persad had gone back up to the house, although the boy was reluctant, he thought it best to apologize at once to Mr. Persad for his attitude toward Gordon, and in so doing to put it all behind them. Mr. Persad simply said, "It's all right. As long as you learn something." Without dwelling on it, he changed the subject. "You see today's newspapers? I want to know what time is low tide. I thinking about taking a drive to the sea. You feel to eat roast corn?" The boy had gotten to know his stepfather well enough to realize that changing the subject was his way of forgiving and sparing him further shame.

PARTIES

 Evenings, after dinner and before settling into homework, the boy would sit on the verandah with the man
he more often than not thought of now as his father.

On one occasion Mr. Persad began—after a long silence and
the rhythmic pensive rocking that had become like an overture
to Dolly and the boy—"Not so the Bihar boy in your class?"

The boy, expecting something but not this, sat upright and
nodded.

"You know, in the early days, when I bought the gas station,
the chamber of commerce used to have a lot of parties. Well,
the time I am about to relate to you, the party was held in the
home of one of its members. I had to take a taxi . . . yes, I had a
gas station, but even then I had no car. So I took a taxi to the
house. Soon as I arrived at the gate to the house, I ready to back
out of there. You never see men dress up so! I was the only one
with shoes that had the sole worn thin. Lots of women, and all
of them looking so tidy and pretty and everything looking very
dear.

"One of them was Bihar. The taxi people. What is the name
of the boy in your class?"

"Shem." The boy could but whisper the name. He was aware
that the Bihar family and the Sangha family were well acquainted,
and now that Mr. Sangha was living at home again, it seemed,
from classroom chatter he overheard, that the families visited
each other's houses regularly. Somehow it had become known
that his mother once worked for Mrs. Sangha, and he was uncomfortable in the Bihar boy's presence.

Mr. Persad hadn't heard what he said, and he had to repeat Shem's name.

"He is the only boy. He have sisters, but it is he who will inherit his father's business, you know. A lot of properties and businesses. The whole taxi service. Now, if we can get the account for gas for the taxi service, we would be in big business, eh? So, he and you might be doing business together, and I was thinking one day you might have to entertain him in your home. It is never too early to start preparing yourself."

Everyone in school knew that Shem didn't want to be a businessman. He was always making fun of business families, as if he were different, saying that he was going to study law when he finished school.

The boy wanted to tell Mr. Persad about a party Shem's parents had thrown for him that year to celebrate his seventeenth birthday. Two boys from the class had been invited. The school day after, they bragged incessantly that they had drunk champagne to toast Shem's birthday. It later became known that it was not champagne at all that they drank, but a new carbonated drink, a bubbly apple-flavored drink the color of champagne that was being advertised as the champagne of soft drinks. According to them, however, they got falling-down drunk from that one glass. That was good champagne, they said again and again, as if they were regular drinkers. The boy wondered what Mr. Persad would have thought about that.

Listening to the wishes of Mr. Persad, knowing he was placing them in the wrong basket, the boy was reminded of a time not long before, which, ever since, had caused him no small measure of grief.

It had been talked about in school that Mr. and Mrs. Sangha were having a party for their daughter's sixteenth birthday. It was to be at the prestigious All India Members Only Club of which her father was treasurer. Shem's family had already received their invitation, which Shem was using as a bookmark in one of his class texts. The boy went home from school every day until the day before the event, expecting to learn from his mother that his family—his mother, businessman Bhatt Persad, and himself—had received an invitation. When none came on that second-to-last day, he decided to take the situation into his own hands. Even as he took the circuitous walking route home from school that passed the Sanghas' house, he did not have a plan. When their house was in view, he paused, watched, and tried to find some reason to enter the yard. He looked to see if there might have been a delivery of the evening newspaper tucked in the wrought-iron fronds of the gate or thrown on the front steps that he could retrieve and take up to the door. There was none. Perhaps a window that had blown open and was not latched. This was a vain wish; there had not been any such obliging wind. But he couldn't have hoped for more than what presented itself like a blessing. When he was close enough, he noticed that a large clay pot that had been on the front verandah lay on the paved yard below, shattered, the bread-and-butter begonia it had contained still looking fresh and salvageable. He felt he had chanced upon a truly urgent situation, not a contrived or convenient reason to call out to the Sanghas, but something he could not in good conscience ignore. He unlatched the front gate. The pine tree he had so long ago planted was almost his height. He ran up the stairs, calling out not to the young lady he thought of as his friend but to Mrs. Sangha. A servant he did not recognize peeped around a wall and disappeared. Mrs. Sangha came out with a dish towel in her hand. She saw him, and the moment of silence between that time and when she said, "Eh-eh, child? What you doing here? I wasn't expecting you," seemed an eternity.

He lied that he was walking home with a friend from school who lived nearby when, as he was passing the house, he saw the fallen begonia. She looked at the place on the verandah wall where the plant would have been. It missing indeed, she quickly glanced over the wall. She shouted out to the woman who had looked out before, saying, "Joyce, the cat was in the house again. Come quick. It knock over a plant again. Come and clean it up. Leave what you doing. Now-now."

Perhaps the boy could have left then, having accomplished that task, but he stayed. He thought about offering to clean it up, but he couldn't bear to be put to work in that house, and he also didn't want to lose the opportunity to chat with Mrs. Sangha. He waited while she seemed preoccupied with Joyce's cleaning. Then she said, "Well, you really growing up, yes, child. How is Mammy?"

He said his mother was fine and that, well, it was true, he was indeed getting older. After all, he was sixteen that year. She seemed oblivious to his opening and said distractedly that, well, everything and everybody was changing. He pointed to the pine and said, "The Christmas tree looking nice," hoping to engage her in a familiarity. She said, "Yes. That is a Norfolk pine. First time you seeing that tree?" He was shocked that she had forgotten it was he who had planted it. He did not remind her. She said nothing more, and in the silence the boy felt, strangely, shame for her, that she, too, had changed. All at once she looked unfamiliar. He would not be invited to the party. In a voice that of its own accord had become coarse and had dropped in volume and enthusiasm, he muttered that he had better get home before it got any later. He ran down the stairs and as fast as he could away from the house.

That night he did not eat his dinner. He suffered bouts of fever, nausea, and profuse sweating. His mother wanted to send for a doctor. He begged her not to send for anyone, assured her that he would be well by the following morning, and only then, if he was not, should she call for the doctor. He remained curled up in his bed under several cotton blankets, crying when he was alone, and praying that Mrs. Sangha would forget that he had gone to her house. He begged God to keep him from being, at that very moment, the topic of conversation and jokes between Mrs. Sangha and her daughter. That he would not be talked about at the party among the children or the adults. That Shem Bihar and Paul Busby would not hear about the visit he had made on the day before the party—to which he remained uninvited.

For weeks he expected his mother to say questioningly, surely with rage, that she had heard he went to the Sanghas' house the day before the birthday party. He fell into a depression that threatened, in the face of Mr. Persad's current conversation, to engulf him again.

THE PASSING ON OF
A SMALL FIRE

Mr. Persad had made his decision. He would buy at least one more station. It was time to tell Dolly. As he contemplated how to make his announcement, he watched her and played with a slice of bread she had warmed and buttered for him. He thought that she was, indeed, a businessman's wife. When he told her that after all these years of being in business, because of her support he had finally developed courage, her response surprised and hurt him a little. She pursed her lips, got up, and busied herself at the sink immediately, uttering only, "Hm." She sent up a pout that lasted a week. When he wasn't around to hear but her son was, she ranted and wouldn't stop. She couldn't understand why this man should want more than the one gas station at the foot of the hill in Marion. Her son recognized in the purchase of another property the opportunity to rise in the eyes of all the Sanghas, Bihars, and Busbys of the island. He did his best to impart his enthusiasm to his mother. If he might have explained this keenness, she didn't give him the chance.

She turned on him and asked, "Why? What making you say so? Since when you interested in gas station? Your head too full of wanting to show off, yes. Is not business you interested in one bit. It is that Sangha family that have you stupid-stupid. And another thing, when will you learn, child, that it is not the girl you interested in but her father and that boy in your class who like to taunt you so? If I really believe you so interested in business for business self, I would pay you some mind, but what you know? Eh?"

At first some semblance of truth in her words slapped him in his face harder than if she had employed a pot spoon. But he convinced himself that his mother had truly misunderstood him, and she had even misunderstood Mr. Persad.

For a good while after, the house felt heavy. Mr. Persad spent more time down the hill in the station. And the boy, feeling insulted and misunderstood by the one person he felt knew him best, sulked and at the same time made determinations to show that he was as capable as anyone else of being business-minded and competent. His mother muttered about the house, using any opportunity even if it wasn't warranted, to state that she wasn't no big shot and didn't want people mentioning her name behind her back, saying she or her son came to Marion to climb ladder.

Then suddenly, the day before Mr. Persad was to close the deal on the first of two stations he had bid on, he suffered a heart attack. In the hospital he suffered two more, one after the other, in quick succession. It was a miracle, the doctors said, that he had not succumbed to them.

When Mr. Persad returned home, he was too weak to go down to the station. After school the boy went directly there. He took cash, did his homework at the desk in the office. His mother surprised him; she knew how to use the cash register and to make simple entries in the station's journal. Somehow, over time, she had learned the basics of the business. Her pouting had come to a halt. On the contrary, she took charge of the overall running of the station and with an acumen her son had never witnessed. His well-meaning compliments offended her. To them she retorted gruffly that she was not stupid, she just had not had any opportunities before. Thinking back, the boy realized that he had often seen her and Mr. Persad bent over the business log-books, and he had heard Mr. Persad mumble things to her about

the figures, but he hadn't understood what attention she was paying, or that Mr. Persad might have been instructing her, or that
she was even capable.

Mr. Persad arose to a quiet house in the mornings; he would be
on the verandah in his pajamas, rocking in his chair, while Dolly
his wife already would have gone down to begin work. She did
everything there was to do in running such a business, and left
only the accounting for her son to check and finalize at the end
of the day, before bringing the books up to the house for her
husband to check. They fell into a comfortable pattern where,
after work and before dinner, she and the boy would sit with him
and together discuss what had taken place down the hill that day,
what went well, who did what, and who was not working up to
standard. What products needed to be ordered, what deliveries
came in, what cash came in, and what went out. Mr. Persad was
pleased to find that besides the products he normally sold in the
shop—engine oils, batteries, jacks for changing tires, cigarettes,
and cigarette lighters—Dolly had taken it in her own hands to
bring in a small assortment of chocolate bars, bottles of soda
water, packages of nuts, and assorted scents of car fresheners in
the form of ornaments that were meant to be hung from rearview mirrors. Mr. Persad began to relax when he realized that
the woman he had married and her son were able to run his business as well as he. She and Mr. Persad seemed to grow closer.
On a few occasions the boy was present when she rubbed
Mr. Persad's head with Limacol, and several times he came upon
her sitting quietly in the chair beside his bed as he lay sleeping.

As if to remind them, and to keep his spirits high, Mr. Persad
spoke urgently and incessantly of his plans to expand once he
was strong enough to meet with a lawyer and his bank manager.
They conferred about the boy going abroad to study business at
university right after the final school exams.

The boy lay awake after the lights in the house and in most of Marion had been turned off, when everything was still and quiet, and only the moon slid in and out of clouds across the frame of his window. He remembered the words of Mrs. Sangha's servant, Patsy: "Once a servant son, always a servant son."

His entrance into the last year of high school coincided with an unpleasant turn of circumstances: Mr. Persad developed complications and was hospitalized. Schooling suffered as the boy worried about Mr. Persad and about his mother being left alone yet again by a husband. As Mr. Persad became weaker, the boy tried to encourage his mother to hurry the purchase of that second station so Mr. Persad might feel that he had realized his dream, but she was ever more decidedly against such expansion.

And then, the week before the exams began, Mr. Persad passed away. The boy knew in his heart that he could not leave his mother. He would not go abroad to study business, or anything else, for that matter.

For the Sake of Business

Guanagaspar. Not as long ago.

By the time Harry St. George was in his early twenties, most of the men he knew from his high school days were either married or engaged to be married. Dolly Persad worried about her son, saying that he was wasting away the productive years of his life on the gas station and on her. Every few days, when they sat in the choking twirl of smoke from the mosquito coil on the verandah, she would ask, as if for the first time ever, if he had met anyone in particular. Harry would laugh and tell his mother that every day he was meeting new people. Irritated by such a response, she would lecture him about getting old alone. He would answer that as long as he had her, he was happy. "Well, I am not company for a young man, besides, I not going to always be here. I ent no spring chicken no more," she would say, pleased that he still cherished her company. He would answer, "But I thought only the good die young," which would cause her to become pensive once she'd had a good laugh over such irreverence.

One day she came home from a visit to the town center, announcing that they had a boarder coming to live with them. Why she had decided to take on a boarder, God alone knew; they certainly did not need extra income, as the gas station kept them comfortable. This boarder-to-be was a schoolteacher from the capital of Gloria who had recently gotten a job teaching in the city of Marion. Dolly had a builder fix up a room downstairs, and on the first day of the following month, a woman boarder arrived to live with them. She moved in upstairs, into what had just before then been Harry's room, and Harry was displaced to the room below.

One Saturday evening Harry was heading out from his downstairs room on the way to the cinema. The woman was leaning on the banister of the verandah, looking out pensively. It was the first time he had seen her without a book or students' papers in her hands. They greeted each other, saying a formal good evening. Then, to his surprise, she asked if he was going for a walk. He answered that he was going to the pictures. She asked what he was going to see and announced that she had not been to a cinema in years. After that comment, it was only natural that he would invite her to accompany him. He saw the corner of his mother's bedroom window curtain fall, and realized that she had been listening. Dolly came out onto the verandah with the woman, whose name was Cynthia. She asked if they would be home for supper. Before he could answer, Cynthia said, "Why we don't go and eat barbecue chicken and chips after the pictures?" His mother piped in, "Yes, go and enjoy yourself, children. You young yet. What you want to come back here for? To sit down and do *what* with an old lady like me? To hear what hurting and what not hurting today? If you don't go quick-quick, I will come, too, you know."

That was their first date, so to speak.

Harry found himself distracted by his proximity to Cynthia in the dark movie theater. She wore a scent that wafted through the air and made people turn to watch her. Each time she spoke to him in the theater, she leaned close, and the warmth of her breath, the heat of her face near his, the flicker of her lips in his ears made him to want to kiss her even while she was speaking. Then, on the back stairs before saying good night, he kissed her on the mouth, a kiss that she returned only fleetingly.

Subsequently they went out almost every evening—to buy corn, to eat chicken and chips, to see the sun set, to get Chinese food, and when next they went to the cinema, they bought tickets for one of the private boxes at the back of the theater. Two months later, Cynthia and Harry married.

Without notice, Cynthia gave up her job as a teacher, and decided on her own to relieve Dolly from work in the gas station by going to work there with Harry. For a while he walked around in dazed happiness, awed that he, a boy from Raleigh whose mother was once a washer-ironer-servant, was now the owner of a gas station and a married man. He thought often of his stepfather's counseling and felt that he was well on his way to fulfilling the dreams that Mr. Persad had set out for him. Without his mother's or Cynthia's knowledge, he had begun making plans to buy, for the time being, one more gas station.

Soon enough, Cynthia began making her own suggestions about the business. She talked about diversifying, about carrying candies, toiletries, hardware. At first Dolly was amused, pleased even. But then, more and more, Cynthia seemed to want to take charge. Then Dolly grew concerned. She said nothing, but as the business's principal proprietress, she kept her eyes wide open.

Almost every day Cynthia sent Harry off the premises to check out other companies' products—to the printers to make business cards and receipt books, to the sign painter's house to commission one thing after another. There was always, it seemed, something for him to do away from the property.

Eventually Cynthia began to do the books. Harry worried she wouldn't do a proper job, so every evening he studied the day's entries. To his delight, she slipped not once in her bookkeeping. Soon she suggested that she could do the banking, too. He and his mother grew to be impressed with her sense of duty and commitment, and Dolly gladly relaxed her wariness. Harry regarded them, his mother, his wife, and himself, as if from a distance—they had become a business family, indeed.

But there soon came a time when Cynthia whispered in his ear no more. He would hold her hand as they lay side by side in bed at night, though she no longer wrapped her fingers around his. She would, rather, move her hand away to scratch some part of her body or fix her hair. She stopped looking at him when they spoke. Harry noticed but said nothing.

One day Dolly, as if in passing, asked Harry if he hadn't found it odd that Cynthia sent him off the premises rather often. Harry demanded to know exactly what his mother might be insinuating, for whenever Cynthia sent him off, it was to do station work. She only wanted him to be more aware, she answered, that the business was his—he shouldn't permit anyone, not even his wife and, she added hesitantly, not even his mother—to run his business so freely. Harry retorted gruffly: he and his wife were doing a very good job taking care of things. Dolly was undaunted. She suggested—merely suggested, she assured him—that he return to the station unexpectedly sometime, just to make sure things were running smoothly, that one could never be too sure, and that since it was still a new marriage, one could easily say that it was common sense to make a little check. Maybe nothing would come of it, she said, adding, "Who knows?" in the most benevolent manner she could muster.

Harry gave Cynthia three days' notice that he would be going to the capital city of Gloria on the pretext that he needed to speak with a banker about some financing for expansion of the business, and since there would be documents to be signed by a lawyer, and letters of reference to be signed by this one and that, the day would be lost to Gloria—not to expect him back for lunch. That day he went to a tailor in the High Street of Marion to be measured for a suit. He returned an hour and a half later, unannounced, to find a man in the office with Cynthia. The man was sitting behind the office desk, and Cynthia was sitting on the desktop facing him. They were in the midst of some conversation that had them both laughing uncontrollably. When Harry entered, the man jumped up from behind the desk. Cynthia turned around calmly. Seeing Harry, she slid off the desk, and with remnants of her laughter still in the smile on her face and in her voice, she introduced the man as her cousin from uptown. Harry shook the man's hand and said he had returned, as the car seemed to be giving a little trouble. He excused himself, saying he was going up the hill for lunch.

Harry let a few days pass before, on the pretext of conducting that unaccomplished business in Gloria, he left the property again. Instead of leaving the city, he parked his car a few streets away and made his way by foot back to the house, whose front entrance was not easily seen from the station's office. He stole upstairs to his mother's bedroom and, from behind the curtain, his mother now peering from behind his shoulder, he waited and watched.

The man showed up soon enough, and he and Cynthia left the property on foot. Harry followed them from a distance. They went to the same cinema he had taken her to. He waited until they had entered the darkened theater, then he bought a ticket and entered. He saw Cynthia, ushered by the man, slip into one of the private boxes.

Harry did not stay in the theater. He returned to the station, gathered up the accounting books, the ledger, and a box of loose receipts, invoices, canceled checks, and took them directly to his accountant to have them sorted and his books balanced. He returned to the office, where he waited for Cynthia and her so-called cousin, but she came back alone. Harry decided to wait until he had heard back from the accountant before confronting her.

That evening after the station closed, enraged by the prospect of anarchy brewing in his house, Harry got in his car and, after several years' absence, drove to Raleigh, directly to the location of the house he and his mother used to live in. The land where the house should have been had been encroached on by wild, tangled shrubbery. There was no longer a house there. The lopsided concrete front stairs were all that was left of it. He could still sit on it, he thought, and walked slowly to the strangely shrunken area. Suddenly a man rose sleepily from behind the stub of stairway. Seeing Harry, the man, pulling himself up with some difficulty, roared fiercely. Harry backed off. Once up, the man wielded a guava stick in one hand and a tin can in the other and chased Harry. A good distance from the place that was once his and his mother's, he whipped off his clothes and hung them over the fallen trunk of a coconut tree, after which he walked into the sea. Waist-high, he stood in thick brown foam, waves rising, crashing and pelting toward him. The sand shifted rapidly under his feet and threatened his balance. Snakelike and trembling, lines of current wrapped about his feet like a lasso.

Once the evening sun and the cool winds off the water had dried him, leaving an oily residue of salt grains on his skin, he dressed and went to the house of Uncle Mako and Tante Eugenie. Tante Eugenie was in the house alone. She immediately placed the coarse heavy palms of her hands on Harry's cheeks. She looked in his eyes and clicked her teeth. Her breath smelled of tobacco. She said, "Is good to see you, child. What happen, something troubling you? If so, you came to the right place. The old man outside. Where your mammy?" She did not move about with her former characteristic briskness. She had gotten wider in her waist and had developed a forward bend. Uncle Mako, fit and strong as ever, sat with Harry outside by the fire that burned in the oil drum to keep sand flies and mosquitoes at bay. Uncle Mako clutched one of Harry's hands in his. Harry regretted not visiting them sooner. Tante Eugenie returned with three enamel plates of fried carite and bake.

Her mouth full of fish, shooting fish bones like arrows between her teeth, she told Harry of her own aches and pains, all the medicines the doctor had prescribed for her and which bush medicine she found to work better than the doctor's pills. She complained that Uncle Mako still took his rowboat out every morning, God willing, still looking for the African shoreline, and how she worried that at his age, he might catch a heart attack and drop dead with all that heavy rowing in the middle of the sea, just like that. She reminded Harry about some of the people of Raleigh. The wood-carver of African faces had become successful, a supplier of carvings made out of the local Mora tree to a tourist shop at the airport and to a boutique located in one of the big hotels in the capital. He had done so well, Tante Eugenie and Uncle Mako boasted, that he had pulled down his wood house and put up a two-story one constructed of concrete bricks on the same plot. That carver had died only three months ago. Harry asked about Walter the taxi driver and learned that he had become a big shot. Mr. Walter had had a son. This son emigrated to New York City in the United States of America, where he had become a district attorney. Several years ago he sponsored Mr. Walter's emigration, and as far as Tante Eugenie knew, Mr. Walter was still in that big city, living with the son and the son's family and running three taxis, all of which he owned but none of which he drove.

Tante Eugenie stood up to take the empty enamel plates to the water barrel behind the house. She told Harry, "Talk to the old man. Tell him everything on your mind, child. What else he there for?"

Harry rose, went over to the rowboat. He lifted a paddle out of the boat, and knowing well that Uncle Mako had carved and polished it, he admired it. Leaning against the boat, he shoved the blade of the paddle into the sand and ran his hand down the gleaming shaft as he related much of what was on his mind. Uncle Mako stared at the horizon, and Harry wondered if he was listening, if, above the sound of the ocean and the wind, he was hearing anything; or if, as he used to do in the past, he was scanning the distance for his piece of Africa. Harry carried on talking, for it was a relief to speak out this misfortune even if his words were being snatched away by the sea breeze. Uncle Mako remained vacantly looking out to sea. When Harry shifted, about to get up, Uncle Mako turned to him. Harry must put his foot down, he said, he must not permit the woman to stay under his roof another day. He said he called Cynthia a woman because, as bad as she was, until Harry did something about it, she was still Harry's wife. He ranted that if Harry had not been married to her, he would have lashed her with every cuss word he knew, up and down her back. He didn't like to think of anyone taking advantage of a boy who was like his own grandson and a woman who was like his own daughter. Harry was taken aback.

Uncle Mako continued to give his advice. If Harry found money missing, he should not go to the police. Count it as a loss. But no matter what, he must not wait a day longer—for in every thief, there is a murderer slumbering. Harry must throw her out come morning. Then he turned to the ocean and complained about town girls, about how these girls nowadays were getting too much education, and said Harry should have come back and married a simple girl from the village. "A good lashing once, just once and watch," he said, his hand raised and forefinger pointing to the sky, "she wouldn't try one bit of nonsense again." Despite the gravity of the conversation, Harry smiled; he knew of Uncle Mako's exaggerations and could not imagine that Uncle Mako or anyone else ever would have dared laid a hand on Tante Eugenie. Uncle Mako added, as if by the way and for good measure, that he knew all along Harry would never consider taking a girl from Raleigh, that he and Tante Eugenie knew he would do like his father, who, even after having lived all his life in Raleigh among the people of African descent, still went far inland to find himself one of his own kind. He said Harry's father was lucky because the woman he met, Dolly, was a good woman, but they all knew she was never at home in Raleigh. Harry understood that Uncle Mako was taking the opportunity to tell him he and Tante Eugenie felt abandoned by him and his mother. He sat outside with Uncle Mako awhile longer in silence until Tante Eugenie, from the doorway of the house, shouted their names above the seaside sounds. Inside, she had laid a table with three glasses and a bottle of pineapple babash.

Harry did not return to his home in Marion until past midnight. Cynthia put on a good display of being worried and angry that he had left without her knowing and that he had returned so late and so drunk. She said he was, after all, a man like all others. He surprised even himself when he told her to hush her mouth before she regretted that he had returned at all. The following morning Harry showered, ate something his mother had prepared, and at nine left the house again, telling only his mother where he was going.

At the accountant's office, Harry learned that from the time Cynthia had started doing the banking, up until the week Dolly had alerted her son, over eight hundred dollars had gone missing. There was a personal canceled check made out by Cynthia to Mervyn Gopeesingh, her man friend.

Harry searched and found Mervyn Gopeesingh's name in the telephone book. He wrote down the address and telephone number on a piece of paper and pocketed it.

Harsh words had hardly ever passed between him and his mother. But now he stood in the kitchen quarreling with her; it was she who had taken in a boarder whom she knew nothing about, and it was she who should deal with the mess at hand. Harry went to the station to use the telephone there. On his way back to the house, he heard Cynthia screaming at his mother, calling her a liar and a user. He had had enough. He rushed to the room. He stood by the door and told Cynthia to pack her clothes. She opened her mouth to say something to him, but he stopped her by waving the check stub at her while saying that Mervyn Gopeesingh was on his way there, he would meet her at the corner, outside the property. She was about to grab the stub from him, but he pulled it out of her reach and told her that if she didn't go easily, he would use it to land her and her Mr. Gopeesingh in jail for the rest of their lives. She started crying and begging forgiveness, and to Harry's great surprise, his mother marched farther into the room, pulled out a suitcase from under the bed, and threw it open on the bed. Dolly herself began pulling out all the clothing from the dresser, all her cosmetics, her shoes from under the bed, and a nightgown that was hanging behind the door. She pushed it all haphazardly into the suitcase, shut it, and threw it into the yard. She went behind Cynthia, who had covered her face with her hands and was sobbing, and shoved her right out of the yard and into the street.

Harry picked up the suitcase and pushed it hard against her. Dolly had gone back into the house; Harry told Cynthia she was heartless, treating a good woman like his mother the way she had. She had no gratitude, no pride. To his surprise, a shoe came flying over his head and hit Cynthia on her shoulder, and then another shoe went flying to the far side of the street, and another nightgown came floating over the fence and landed beside them. Dolly had final words, too. From the yard she shouted out, with no care for the ears of bypassers, "Listen, you! You get far-far-far from

Marion. You hear? And don't come near this town or anywhere near my son again. Otherwise I will make stew out of you and your name. And tell that good-for-nothing wretch you had boldface to bring on my property I will put him in jail if he set foot near these premises again. You hear? Now get away from here. Gone! Harry, get back in here. What more you have to say to she? You don't owe her nothing, you hear? Come in the yard now!"

Out of Ashes
Comes a Fire

Harry was sipping black tea in the kitchen, preparing to head to the newly purchased station on the far side of the town. Dolly sat at the table with her son, as she always did regardless of how she was feeling, dressed in a worn nightgown and a pink pair of bedroom slippers he had given her several Christmases ago. The radio played low from the drawing room. She was awaiting the death news, for at her age, she expected to hear of the death of people she knew, if not personally, at least by rumor. When the dirge came on, she got up and weakly stood at the entrance to the drawing room. When Harry heard the first name mentioned, which sounded like Sangha, he snapped, "Who?"

His mother, too, had started. She pressed a finger to her mouth to silence him. He stood up and listened. Wife of Mr. Narine Sangha, beloved mother of Mrs. Rose Bihar, mother-in-law of attorney general Mr. Shem Bihar. And then the details of the funeral. "But eh-eh," Dolly said, looking at her son, the tips of three fingers of the hand that had silenced him now lightly pressing against her lips. She nodded as if news she was expecting any day had at last arrived.

"I didn't know she was sick," said Harry. Dolly moved her hand from her lips and gestured without speaking that she didn't know of any illness, either. She went to Harry and rested her hand on his shoulder, a gesture that caused his eyes to swell with tears. But before he could react, reach for her hand, she skirted around, picked up his cup and saucer, and took them to the sink.

She stood at the counter for a while, staring out the window to the trees that had grown so fully that they blocked the view of the valley behind.

Harry sat at his desk that day thinking of Mrs. Sangha's daughter. Countless people would be gathering around her. But none of them were likely to have shared early memories of her mother as intimately as he once had. Not even her husband. He was sure of this and was gripped by the unshakable notion that he was the only one who knew the depth of her sorrow, who could comfort her, in this moment. Her husband had not been with her in her early childhood like he had, could not have known the smell or coolness of Mrs. Sangha's skin like he did. Several times he took his jacket off the hook on the wall behind him. Several times he picked up the car keys. But each time he was halted by insecurities; he became unsure which house it was he should visit in order to pay his respects. He became paralyzed with questions like where would Rose Sangha—or rather, Rose Bihar—be? At her father's house, comforting him, or at her own house, being comforted by her husband? It had been some years since his and Shem's paths had crossed. The last time had been before Shem was appointed attorney general, when he was dabbling aimlessly in politics, the year he spoke with everyone, it was said.

"Ey, man. St. George! It's been a while, man, been a while. Times treating you good, man?"

Harry had stood by Shem's car as an attendant cleaned the windshield. He replied reluctantly, "Can't complain."

Shem quipped good-naturedly, "Can't complain? What you mean, you can't complain? You putting on a little paunch there, man. I can see you living up the good life in Marion. Is how heart problems does start, you know. We need to keep healthy! In this country of ours, we want strong, healthy citizens, you know!"

The need to attend the funeral the following day became dizzyingly urgent. Dolly, having begun to suffer with aches and pains in the joints and muscles of her aging body, had not been out of her house in several weeks. Still, Harry expected she would somehow mine the will to attend the funeral. When she told him that she felt it would be too taxing on her own health, he realized his expectation was selfish.

He arrived a half hour before the memorial was to begin at the church where Mrs. Sangha was a devoted member. Even so, he got no farther than the opposite sidewalk, well at the end of the block with the church. "Standing room only, man! You can't get no farther than here. Well-known family, in truth!" a man advised as proudly as if it were an event he had personally organized. The crowd, sweating in the angled heat of the evening sun, had spilled onto the lawn of the churchyard and into the street in front, blocking it from traffic entirely. Once the ceremony was under way, the street was shrouded in silence broken occasionally by an evening flock of lilting parrots flying and squawking high overhead. Still, from where Harry stood, the words of the speakers were indistinguishable. He left before the service ended and went briskly on his own to the cemetery.

He took his place near the freshly dug hole. The air smelled of the candle wax that ran down the sides of stone markers and cement plinths, and of the newly turned earth. A group of men solemnly passed around a bottle of rum, each taking several turns toasting Mrs. Sangha's life and her journey onward. Their toasts acclaimed that she was a good woman, yes, a good woman. Harry moved a few paces away from them and thought of Mrs. Sangha, his dear Mrs. Sangha who had, on their last encounter when he was still in high school, betrayed him. She would soon turn to dust.

The hearse, shrouded by wreaths, rolled in through the cemetery gates and behind it a black Buick. Any sounds either vehicle might have made along the gravel path were muted by the shuffle of the hundreds of feet that slowly followed. The men and women behind Harry began their unabashed display of grieving. Harry walked hurriedly away from them toward the gate.

In the past few years, his and Rose's paths had seldom crossed. He'd had a few fleeting glimpses of her as the car in which she was being driven by her chauffeur sped past his, but if she saw and recognized him, she had not made any attempt, except once, to acknowledge him. That once, when she herself was driving her husband's car, which was well known about town, they stopped opposite each other at a major road. To his surprise, she smiled and waved to him.

He was anxious now. He didn't at first expect that there would be the chance to speak with her longer than to express his and his mother's condolences, yet he was overcome with the desire to be seen, to be recognized, by her.

When the hearse came to a halt, the mourners in the procession filed in, scattered, and regrouped around the grave site. A young man opened one of the back doors of the car, and an aged Narine Sangha alighted, followed by his daughter, whose head was covered with a black mantilla. Through the crowd, Harry caught a glimpse of Rose. He turned his body this way and that and slid through the crowd.

Shem Bihar, who seemed to have been at the head of the walking mourners, approached his father-in-law and his wife. Together they walked to the back of the hearse. The door was opened, and the pallbearers took their place to slide out the lacquered brown coffin. Rose faced her husband, buried her face in his chest. A low wailing ran through the crowd. The coffin was positioned on the bier and the crowd became silent. The ceremony to commit Mrs. Sangha to the earth began. A wail of anguish hushed the crowd, and then the words "Mummy, no, no, no! Oh God, don't go" rang out. Harry stood three people deep away from Rose. He heard her moaning, saw her pound her fists against her husband's chest. Shem, bewildered, struggled to restrain her against him.

The grave diggers lost no time. The thunder of dirt falling on the wood lasted but seconds, then the rhythmic scrape and slide of shovels, the dull thud of dirt on dirt. Rose stopped screaming but wailed softly into her husband's chest. She seemed to lose her strength and was about to collapse. Shem cupped his wife's face in his hands sharply, lifted it toward his, and spoke directly to her. She moved away from his chest, seemed to compose herself, and, standing on her own, covered her face with both hands. Once the dirt had taken on the mounded shape, the crowd began to disperse. Shem left Rose and moved away to attend to a query from one of the grave diggers. It was then that Harry moved over to her. Her head hung down as, under the mantilla, she wiped her nose with a handkerchief. He had not been so close to her since they were children. He tapped her arm, the gesture awkward. She did not respond but seemed to pull her shoulders together, to crouch in toward herself more. In the midst of all the people waiting to speak with her, of all that commotion, he stepped closer and called her: "Rose." Her head remained down, and she kept the kerchief to her nose. He spoke that one word again: "Rose?"

This time she lifted her head and to Harry's utter surprise, she came toward him. Trembling, he reached for both her hands. The mantilla parted slightly and a wet though soft cheek pressed against his. As sudden as she had done so, it was over. She pulled back, but for the briefest moment—so brief that no one else would likely have noticed—her weight seemed to come to rest against Harry. Something had dripped on the breast of his thin white cotton shirt. Startled, he looked to see a gray wet dash and realized that his shirt had caught her tears. He could hardly breathe. He wanted to reach under the veil and wipe the tears

on her cheeks with his hand. In that moment he didn't give a
care in the world, even if it would have been entirely evident,
that he was Mrs. Sangha's long-ago servant's son. It was he who
was permitted to catch a little of the weight of Rose Bihar, Narine
Sangha's daughter, Shem Bihar's wife.

She stood in front of him. He looked directly at her, nowhere else. He was able to draw a curtain around her and him
and shut out everyone in the cemetery, including her father and
her husband. Narine Sangha never would have recognized him,
but Harry knew and didn't really care in that moment that
Shem Bihar would.

It had taken all his strength when Rose touched her cheek
to his not to wrap his arms around her. She looked directly at
him and said weakly, "Thanks for coming. How is your mummy?"

Harry closed his eyes and nodded, unable to utter any words.
His gratitude to her for recognizing him so intimately ran deep
and raw. He was light-headed. She whispered, "Come home and
visit sometime. You know where I live? When you have time?"
Before another word could be exchanged, a woman came and
threw her arms around Rose and began to cry loudly. Rose looked
at Harry over the woman's imposed shoulder, and he nodded
again.

THE EGGMAN

Two weeks after Mrs. Sangha's funeral, Harry went down to the coop with a small basin. He reached in and offered his knuckles to the birds, none of which could take the place of the old cock which had long ago died. He filled the basin with twelve of their large brown eggs and returned to the house.

In the kitchen he washed each one free of feather bits, traces of afterbirth, and dried bird feces. His mother said nothing, but her tightly folded arms, intermittent forced expulsions of breath, and intent gaze spoke loudly. Harry ignored her.

When he was leaving the house, she shoved a wet washcloth at him and gruffly said, "Here. Wipe the bird shit off your shoes before you go making double donkey of yourself, child." Harry looked toward the ceiling and, trying not to smile, shook his head with feigned disbelief. She said, "Eh-eh! What? What is that? Shaking your head? Harry, she is a married woman, you hear? You better study your head good before you bring down yourself—and me—you hear? A married woman! You playing with fire, child. Fire. Hm! I don't know what nonsense is this."

It would be the first time that he would pay a visit to the Bihar house. Years after her marriage, he still called her—in his mind—Rose *Sangha.*

They had married three months after Rose's graduation from high school. Shem was already attending university abroad, and had returned home especially, the gossip section of Guanagaspar's only newspaper reported, to be married. Dolly and Harry had received an invitation to the wedding.

The day before the wedding, leaving home before dawn, returning after dark, Dolly went to the Sangha house, albeit purse-lipped and stoic. She showed up among those who would help with the preparations, that is, the poorer friends and unfashionable family members from the outlying country areas. She and these people helped with the inch-by-inch cleaning of the house and yard and with the outdoor coal-fire cookery of food in large vats.

But on the day of the wedding, which she knew her son had no intention of attending, Dolly asked Harry to drive her to Raleigh to see Tante Eugenie and Uncle Mako.

Once there, a sea bath, a cleansing in salt water, seemed to Harry an antidote to an insalubrious day. But Dolly caught a fit as he headed in his bathing trunks toward the water. She bawled fiercely that it was in that hour, and that hour exactly, of his deep despair at Rose's marriage, when, if it were his fate—like it had been his father's—to die by drowning, the sea was bound to snatch him from her. She didn't have to plead with him. The day had already worn him weak. He went and lay on his back on the hot sand, with a newspaper covering his face.

A photo of them, Shem in an embroidered kurta, a bejeweled turban on his head, and Rose in a sari, the two of them smiling at each other as awkwardly as newlyweds, appeared on the front page of the following day's paper. The day after that, a photo of them was in the section titled "Talk of the Town." He wore a suit, she a blouse, a narrow skirt, and a pillbox hat. They were heading that day, the paper said, back to the U.K. so that Shem could finish his studies. He would graduate with a bachelor of law degree in less than three years, at which time he would be called to the bar. The paper predicted that with his good looks and breeding, he might have a future in politics, like his great-grandfather had had as minister of transport.

Once the couple had returned from abroad, the daily papers were never, to this date, without a photograph of Shem, and often of them both at some official or private function.

Harry's thoughts of and feelings toward Rose, given their futility, had over the course of years gradually slipped—not away entirely but to the back of his mind. The news on the radio of Mrs. Sangha's death was a poker that stoked old embers. Then seeing her. Every minute since was spent, once more, thinking of her: the way she had all but embraced him, and so publicly. The memory of the sensation of that sudden dampness on his shirt spread fire through his body.

It was no doubt the basin of eggs he held as he stood outside the gate. The young girl jumping rope on the concrete paving of the garage could have been Rose as a child. A boy, with the forward-facing, flared ears of his father and the chubbiness that Indian families admire in boy children, looked from around a doorway that entered onto the garage. He said, "Just now," and disappeared again. Harry heard him shout, "Mummy, a man selling eggs by the back gate."

Harry waited, watching the girl. She seemed oblivious. After about five minutes, Harry called out and asked her name. Not looking at him, she said, "My name is Cassie. You selling eggs?"

Harry asked her to run inside and tell her mother Harry had come. She went to the door, but without entering the house, she shouted, "Mummy." She did not wait for an answer. She shouted again, this time louder, "Mummy!" And yet again. She doubled over as if to expel the most forceful voice she had and she screamed, "Muhhhmy!" This time he heard a voice from inside the house but could not make out the words. Cassie shouted out, "Well, I was calling you, and you wouldn't answer." He heard Rose ask,

"Well, what is it?" Cassie said, "It's the Eggman. His name is Harry. Mummy, can I have something to eat?"

Her mother looked around from the doorway. Seeing Harry, she laughed and said, "And I was wondering who is the Eggman!" She apologized for not coming out sooner, said she had been speaking on the telephone with her husband. His work took him daily to the capital, Gloria. He worked such long hours, and so hard, she said. He was busy with a case against a group of black students from the University of the West Indies, the Guanagaspar campus, who had burned down the university chancellor's house. The chancellor was a white-skinned man from the U.K., and they felt that the position should belong to a man born on the island who happened to be black-skinned and had many more letters of learning after his name than had the U.K. chancellor. Harry was well aware of the incident. It had been much publicized in the daily paper, but it was not the only eruption on the island. There was, in general, noticeable discontent brewing in pockets in the north of the island. The Indian population had halted their lavish displays of wealth, no longer allowing photographs of them at private or public functions. The people of African heritage had begun to hold public forums and street-corner meetings where they preached and ranted to ever-increasing crowds about slavery days being over, about a back-to-Africa movement, and about not replacing one form of oppression with another—the new one being an Indian-run government. Perhaps, thought Harry, Uncle Mako wasn't as idle-minded as he and his mother thought. But the north was the north and the south was the south, and in the south, far from the seat of government, life was sleepier, as usual. It was a delicate situation for Shem, Rose told Harry.

But Harry had become distracted; he had imagined them sitting in her living room or on the porch, her offering him a cup of tea, a glass of water, a piece of sponge cake, and he kept expecting they would move from the gate to the inside of the house.

She folded her hands on top of the gate's wide ledge, leaned against it. She said few people her age had known her mother as well or as long as he had. She said her mother always thought highly of him and wondered aloud not long before she died why his marriage hadn't worked out and if he would marry again. She thanked him for the eggs and told him he should come again when she had more time to chat, but she didn't indicate when that might be.

Harry visited her—not more than once every few months in the years since her mother died—bearing the basin full of eggs each time. Shem was publicly hailed, and by the Indian business and religious communities in particular, for putting behind bars several of the dissidents and two high-profile trade union leaders, all of whom were black, and whom he managed to convict for inciting social disobedience. Every day Shem was mentioned and quoted in the newspapers or on the television news hour. They said it was because of him that the country was settling back into its peaceful ways. Harry's mother said, "If they don't kill him first, he will run for prime minister one day, mark my word."

Much public attention was paid to Rose as well. She was written about often in the women's section of the paper as the prime example for all women of the Caribbean. The food and leisure editor interviewed her about housekeeping. The article included recipes of dishes it was said she cooked herself, even though the family employed a cook. It said that in spite of her money and her position as the A.G.'s wife, she was down-to-earth and wore no airs, traits most noticeable in her casual and gentle manner of speaking. On the occasion of being named woman of the year, it was written that other women should strive to be like her: a mother whose children came first and who stood behind her husband, no matter what. That article joked that Caribbean husbands were not the easiest men for wives to put up with, even when that husband was the attorney general, yet Rose Bihar had never been heard to contradict, even in jest, her husband. The paper said that there were two arenas where she upstaged him: those of beauty and charm, and that if she were to run for the symbolic office of president, she would win solely on those two counts.

Harry, on a visit to her, mentioned the articles. She said she didn't care for the publicity and everybody knowing her every move, but Shem liked that kind of thing, and he liked it when the papers paid her all that attention. She said, "When you are in the public eye, you can't stop people from writing all kinds of things. Even when they say it is about you, you don't recognize yourself in their stories."

Over the course of the time during which Harry visited Shem Bihar's outstanding wife, improvements noticeable from the outside had been done to the house. When Rose got a car of her own, the garage was widened to include it. The hedge around the house was pulled up, and a high stone fence that blocked the view of the house was erected. Then a section of the fence came down to make way for the construction of a swimming pool, Shem's birthday present to her—an extravagance, she said to Harry, apologetically, for she was the only one in the family who would make use of it. The mere mention of her birthday had Harry wondering if she had ever found out about his attempt to get invited to her sixteenth birthday party.

Each time he visited, he was announced by the servant or one or both of the children, who seemed to grow in huge spurts, as the Eggman. Each time but the last, Rose and he stood, like that first time, at the gate. Her strange combination of distance and warmth remained the same. Sometimes they were out there for half an hour, and once for almost an hour. Although he never asked, she told him each time about her father. He had been moved to an apartment in a costly private-care facility for older infirm people. It had become fashionable, if not altogether acceptable, for society Indians to leave the care of their infirm parents to strangers in private-care homes. Rose told Harry that "they" had sold the house on the corner of Beau Moreau and Ashton streets. The family had recently started going to the Bihar beach house on the east coast regularly. She still enjoyed swimming, enjoyed that more than anything, and as neither Shem nor the children much liked being in the water, it was time she had to herself. She showed surprise and even disappointment, Harry liked to think, that he, born by the sea, had never learned to swim. She told him inconsequential things about the children, things they did that made her laugh, things about them that caused her worry. How the boy was not as bright as she would have hoped. That he didn't show an interest in anything worthwhile as far as they could see. Not science or reading or even sports. That the girl was just like her father, strong-willed and bright, maybe even too much so for a girl. There were, too, many long silences between them out by the gate. At first they were awkward, but soon enough the quiet was full and calming.

On his last visit, several years since Mrs. Sangha had died, he did make it beyond the gate. It was just past the lunch hour, and her children, now in the final stages of secondary schooling, were at school. Shem was at his office in Gloria. Her live-in servant had the day off. Harry called at the gate, cradling in his hands a brown bag of eggs. Rose opened the back door a crack. Seeing him, she went out and drew open the heavy gate, inviting him into the kitchen. Although she had not been expecting any visitor that day, her lips were colored with shiny burnt-orange lipstick, and her eyes were outlined in black kohl. Harry sat at the table and watched her bustle about the kitchen. He had, come to think of it, never seen her, as an adult, without lipstick or eyeliner, even when he arrived unexpectedly and she came to meet him outside at the gate. At the stove, she set the kettle on a burner, turned on the ignition switch, and bent to see if the flame had come up. She took a round coconut bake out of the oven, where it was stored in a bright yellow kitchen cloth, cut a wedge from the bake, sliced it, and, using her fingers, packed it with layers of already cut cheese. She did all of this quietly. She knew he was watching. He could tell from the way she moved— everything she did, she angled herself so that he saw her face. He was not shy to watch keenly, for each minuscule motion she made seemed considered and significant. He relished being in this interior world of hers.

She set a place mat before him, stopped close enough and long enough beside him to arrange the knife and fork on the mat. He had to stop himself from reaching around her waist, standing up, and holding her against him. Such closeness and attention on that single and particular occasion when, inviting him into her privacy, no one else around—surely she, too, had hoped that he would hold her. But he did not. In that moment of possibility, he had glimpsed his own dignity and was satisfied to have been finally afforded a recognition.

They sat across from each other. She poured them both cups of tea, and they sat in silence, except for when he told her the bake was delicious. She didn't respond. He sipped his tea slowly, and when it was finished, with more confidence than he had previously known, he slid his chair back. It grazed, a screeching sound against the terrazzo floor that underscored the complicity of their time together. She remained seated, her eyes set on the plate from which he had just eaten. He wiped his mouth on the napkin and got up. He moved toward the door that led to the garage. She did not get up or look at him. He turned sharply to face her, a question brimming in his mouth. He opened his mouth, ready to demand an answer of her, and just as urgently as it came, it evaporated. It began with "why," but no words would follow. The question burned like a fire in his chest. Even if he could have framed it, there would have been, and he knew it well, no answer to the question. He wanted to beg it of her, but in truth, it was a question for Narine Sangha. For Mrs. Sangha. For his mother. None of whom, in any case, would have had the answer. He uttered with a marked note of uncertainty that he'd come again, and he left.

Compelled by the same urgency as the question that would not form, he did return, three days later, at the same time. But the servant came to the door. She said, "Oh, you is the Eggman! Just now." She went back into the house and returned to say that Madam was sleeping. She held her hands out for the eggs, but he had brought none.

The Hardest Goodbye

Dolly Persad passed away during the early days of a period dubbed in a calypso by the Mighty Engineer "The Days of Guanagasping." Long-standing racial tensions between blacks and whites, and blacks and Indians, were erupting on a daily basis across the island. Backyard grumblings gave way to organized mobilization when the son of the minister of housing and works, driving in a drunken state after a party, hit and killed a black woman in an impoverished neighborhood at the heart of the capital city. Although his car was witnessed flying recklessly down the middle of a narrow unlit road, the young man (whose prominent family of white English descent had fingers deep in the sugar and sea-urchin industries, and in towel manufacturing) was charged only with driving a vehicle while intoxicated, and with public mischief. The judge (a man of Indian origin) reprimanded the dead woman for being out in the middle of the road late at night in clothing that did not make her more visible, and the minister's son's license was suspended for a month. The black population of Guanagaspar had endured enough. For them the incident was bigger than itself. It was about the history of their forced displacement. It was about racial, social, and economic injustices. It was, for many in the country, an ending and also a beginning.

Crowds of protesters, the vast majority of whom were of African origin, gathered daily in front of the government house, bearing placards and banners, banging insistently on tin cans and discarded hubcaps. On the streets in downtown Marion, Indians and blacks no longer blocked the pavement while standing to chat and joke with each other. There was such apprehension in the air that in general, people, regardless of race or other background, did not have the inclination to linger amicably.

During those endless days and nights of simmering discontent, Harry thought often of Uncle Mako. Uncle Mako was not, after all, a mere dreamer.

Harry had gotten in the habit of remaining upstairs during the night, in case his mother needed anything, not going down to his room until she herself had slept. She seemed to manage sleep later and later with each passing night.

It was almost ten o'clock. The animated sounds of demonstrators chanting antigovernment slogans in the square outside of the town hall wafted in and out of the neighborhood on the crest of the night breezes. Harry sat at the kitchen table, the newspaper spread on it. He had become accustomed to the noise of the late-night meetings. He struggled to remain awake. Surely his mother would be asleep by this time, he thought, and he tiptoed to the door of her bedroom. She was awake. She said she had been calling him, but her voice was too weak to compete with that of the protestors, so he had not heard her. With the frail gesture of wriggled fingers, she offered him her hand. It was cold. She was tired, she whispered. Her breathing seemed labored. When he said he would quickly go down to the station to call the doctor, she shook her head and asked him not to leave her side. A finality in her voice, her knowing nod, he understood. Although he had anticipated this moment, he was unprepared. His neck tightened. He kissed her forehead. His tears wet her face. He heard her weakening voice utter, "Don't cry, my baby. You are a good boy. I was lucky." He gripped her hand tightly. He pressed his lips against the back of her hand and hoped that in the fierceness of that gesture, she would know all that he was incapable of verbalizing. She pulled him closer to whisper in his ear that he should turn off the lights now and leave her, let her try and sleep. He let go of her slowly, backing away from her with the unfathomable awareness that he was already alone.

When he looked in on her again, her eyes were closed. He went slowly to her and touched her hand. It was cold, as he had feared.

Mako the African

The country was indeed gasping. Unionized sugar workers and elementary, primary, and high school teachers,
most of whom were of African origin, were regularly on
the march. Every few months there was a union-organized na-
tionwide strike. Kidnappings had become commonplace. Mur-
ders, as asides to robberies, too. The white-skinned people were
terrified to show their faces and seemed to have disappeared from
the streets. They were, in fact, departing the country in droves.

Unlike the Africans, who had been brought to the islands
against their will and enslaved, the Indians had come as indentured laborers, armed with the promise, the guarantee even, of
a return trip to India, or, if they chose, after the completion of
their indentureship, a parcel of land, gratis. Still, a century and
more later, they bowed before the white-skinned British, yet lorded
superiority over those of African descent. Suddenly the Indian
population was terrified. Younger nationalistic Guanagasparian
Indians, infuriated by the divide of Africans and Indians and therefore of the country they knew as their one and only home, fanned
the fires of protest. Pandemonium threatened to drown the little
island.

Harry sensed that it was as dangerous not to take a side as it
was to take one. The very day the rumor of an army-led coup
spread, grocery shops emptied of food and fuel. Harry hurried,
along with almost everyone who owned an unprotected yard,
to the hardware store to buy wire fencing. With his workers,
he frantically fenced off the station at the foot of the house,
then boarded the windows and the glass-paned front door of

the house. They then hopped in the truck with the remaining fencing, intending to reach the station on the other side. The town was jammed with car and truck traffic. Nothing budged for hours. Tempers began to flare. Harry and the workers abandoned the truck with all the goods on it and made their way back between vehicles amid the honking of horns and pounding of fists on car roofs. Nothing happened that night, but there was a frightening stillness about the town. Occasionally a dog howled, and one waited fearing that it might have been at a band of arsonists entering the town. In one day, four businesses owned by Indians in downtown Marion went up in flames. Harry, although anxious about being an Indian and a businessman, risked the drive into the capital. He passed by the American embassy first and then by the Canadian High Commission. Fingering in his pocket the ten-dollar note needed to pay for a visa, he joined the shorter queue at the gates of the Canadian High Commission.

Harry took a loss on the value of the house, and one could say, for what pittance he sold them, he gave the two gas stations away.

Before leaving, Harry took his mother's cremated ashes to the banks of the sea just around the bend from Muldoon Bridge. He beat his way through the tall rozay bush until he found a high point from which he cast her ashes into the tumultuous waters where the sea and river met. He sat on the bank for almost an hour, recalling much that his mother had done. In this moment of letting go of her, it seemed to him that everything she had ever done was indeed for him.

From there he continued his journey to the village of Raleigh. He took with him his immigration papers and the stamp of his visa to show to Uncle Mako and Tante Eugenie, as if he held in his hand a school report card. Tante Eugenie held his hand and would barely let go of it. Uncle Mako seemed stronger, happier, too. Tante Eugenie put Uncle Mako's unusual smiling and good-naturedness down to all the noise in the country about Africa, about what was being called black power, and about black beauty. He had started calling her "my beauty," she told Harry. It was clear that this pleased her deeply. She sucked her teeth, talking about all the noise in the country, but she, too, stood taller than he had ever seen her. With their renewed lease on life, he left with the hope of perhaps one day seeing them again.

The day before his departure, he went after a long absence, eggs in hand, to see Rose. The area in which she and her family lived was heavily patrolled by private security outfits. His car that spat and sputtered clearly did not belong in that neighborhood. He was stopped and the vehicle searched by guards who carried guns on their hips. After they found only a flat of eggs on the backseat, he was allowed to continue into the neighborhood. On his arrival at the back gate of the house, a sleepy policeman guarding the house and family of the attorney general stopped him. The man asked Harry what business he had there. Harry told him he was there to see Mrs. Bihar. The man looked at Harry's car. He looked at the flat of eggs. He asked if Harry owned chickens. Harry said yes, but fearing the policeman might take the eggs to deliver them inside himself, he added quickly that he was a friend of Mrs. Bihar. The man looked up at Harry sharply and then grinned as if he understood something. Annoyed with the assumption, Harry sidestepped him and pressed the doorbell.

Rose's daughter, Cassie, untouched by the dramas unfolding in the city below, came to the gate. She said her mother was taking a nap. What different worlds they lived in, mused Harry. She could afford to nap, while he was on the verge of fleeing the island for fear of losing all he owned, including his life.

He handed the girl the eggs and a note on which he had scribbled that he'd gotten his papers and was leaving for Canada the following day. He included his home phone number.

That night Rose telephoned. Shem was in the capital brief-
ing the prime minister and his cabinet, but still she couldn't speak
long, as it was well past the children's dinnertime and Jeevan,
still with homework unfinished, needed her help. But, she said,
she wanted to call before it was too late, to wish him all the best.
She said when he found the time that he should send a note with
his address, adding that if she were ever to come up to Canada,
she would try and look him up. She repeated "if," clarifying further that it was unlikely, since Shem—like her father, if Harry
remembered—preferred taking his holidays in the U.K.

If he had been unsure before, he knew now, in his blood, that
he was doing the right thing: he was, after all, about to step out
from under the cloud of circumstance that seemed to have ruled
his heart and mind for far too long.

III

Returning Arrival

Guanagaspar. Present day.

Heroman, Piyari's brother, leads Harry from the airport terminal to the white Austen in the taxis-only zone. It is not yet ten
o'clock in the morning, but the sun blasts its heat, reproachful
to those who have stayed away from their homeland too long.
On reaching the car, Harry is damp with perspiration.

Heroman throws the luggage on the backseat and hands his
charge an envelope, a letter from Cassie Bihar. He leans back
against the car and cleans his teeth with a reed pulled from a grass
just off the road and watches Harry.

> Dear Harry,
>
> I hope you made the connection in Toronto smoothly
> and that both flights were tolerable. Heroman will take
> you to his house in Central to meet his sister Piyari right
> away. He will let me know where you are staying, and I
> will ring you. Please wait for me to ring. I will call you at
> eight o'clock tonight.
>
> Sincerely,
CB

Harry is perplexed. Why has she not written word of her
mother?

Getting in behind the wheel Heroman says, "My sister waiting for you. They feed you on the plane? She make food. She say her madam used to say how plane food bad for so, so she cook up a little something."

The airport grounds give way to endless fields of sweet-smelling sugarcane. Abruptly the sugarcane fields end and the land spreads out in a prairielike flatness. The land on either side of the divided two-lane road forms a hatchwork of rectangular-shaped rice paddies. Lots of green fluorescence are interspersed with waterlogged lots from which no rice grows, but where broad-leafed water lilies with waving pink flowers flourish. Workers are bent over in the paddies. Harry and Heroman pass communities of no more than four thatch-roofed bungalows that hug the land close to the road. A stubborn cow belonging to one of these communities stands glassy-eyed in the middle of the road unperturbed by the vehicle and the horn's staccato blasts, and Heroman must swerve off the road to avoid it. In a ditch, a buffalo—meager to the bone and covered in dried caking mud—stands statue-like.

They are driving in the middle of the island, at least an hour away from the ocean, yet the brilliant beckoning light, the stifling humidity, and a taste of salt in the air give Harry the keen sense that at any moment, upon rounding a corner or cresting a hill, they will be afforded a glimpse of the Caribbean Sea. The dark skin of the driver of the car in which he travels, of the people they pass, the lanky coconut trees arching here and there to the thin blue sky, the iridescent haze of heat trembling off the spongy asphalt of the road, all have the power of a moon over him, stroking and pulling at the blood in his veins. Now that he is here, there are stops, he decides impetuously that he will make. Once he has seen Rose, he will head straight for the ocean, the tropical ocean that his body is suddenly aching to be submerged in. He will visit Raleigh, too, to see what is left of the plot of land on which he and his mother lived, to see Uncle Mako and Tante Eugenie, and he will go to the house he and his mother lived in in Marion with Bhatt Persad.

The sea is still not visible, yet the air is saturated with its odors. He can smell, almost taste, its washed-up debris. Roadside pedestrians, some transporting pails of water on their head, people sitting in rockers on their front porches, and men riding bicycles, some of whom are barefoot, wave as the Austen passes. A tide of belonging washes over Harry. Elderberry Bay and all that he has accomplished in that part of the world seem in an instant like a dream, a good dream, but very far away.

Soon they arrive in the village where the Bihars' servant, Piyari, and her taxi-driving brother live. A short, dilapidated billboard with a sun-faded painting of a worker wielding a cutlass above a stand of cane announces WELCOME TO THE HEARTLAND OF THE COUNTRY. DRIVE SAFELY.

A dark-skinned, wiry woman runs toward the car, waving. Heroman has barely brought the car to a halt before Piyari opens the passenger door and reaches a hand out to Harry. He gets out of the car. Overcome, she puts her face in her hands and lets out a sob. Heroman shakes his head as if in pity. Salty sweat runs off Harry's furrowed forehead. He is noticeably confused and embarrassed, so Piyari catches herself and directs Heroman to park the car and warm the plate of food she had prepared. She leads Harry into the yard. The property—on which sits a small wooden house not unlike the one he lived in with his mother in Raleigh—is outlined by a hedge of the lush benediction plant. They round the house to the back, to a table and a low bench under a pomerac tree. Not a bird is in sight, not a whistle or chirp can be heard. Harry moves slowly in the heat.

Piyari turns to him. "Miss Cassie didn't tell you nothing in the letter?"

He shakes his head.

"Madam gone, Mr. Harry. Madam ent here no more." She began to cry. "You understand? She gone."

He doesn't understand. He shrugs and frowns. Seeing his confusion, she wrings her hands in frustration. She lets herself bawl. "Madam dead. She dead and gone."

A cow at the far end of the yard stands motionless, a cattle egret perched on its back. A rooster crouches in the cool beneath the wooden stairs of the house. Piyari is telling him something about someone he doesn't know, Harry is thinking. Cautiously he utters, all but inaudibly, "Madam? Who are you talking about?"

"My madam. Mrs. Bihar. He drown she in the sea."

Heroman has brought out a clear glass plate with a triangle of roti and a serving of curried chataigne. Between his sister and the visitor from abroad is a coarse, stunned silence. Awkwardly he cuts through, apologizing for the heat, saying that they had bought an air-conditioning unit from a stranger who came to their door with it in his hand, but it worked for a day and then quit. Harry stares at Heroman, thinking, There has got to be some mistake. She can't be dead. Why didn't Cassie tell me this? I didn't come all this way for that. What does she mean, "he drowned she"?

Piyari's Mouth Runneth

"Oh Lord, Mr. Harry. Where to start from?" Piyari moans. She dips her hand into a pocket of her dress and pulls out a gold-plated chain from which hangs a cross.

"You know, when Madam return back from Canada, she make a trip—she self drive the car—to Raleigh, to buy fish. She come back with a necklace—she say a woman who was like a relative to you give she it. Madam wear that necklace from that day on, and it surprise me, because why a woman in her position would wear plate around her neck? But she wear it, and when Boss ask she what is that around she neck, she say is a good-luck necklace a lady in the market give she as a present. He twist up his face, but he never ask about it again.

"But the morning I want to tell you about, she had removed it. Day before she had went in the sea wearing it, so why, I want to know, that morning she remove it? I ask her. She say how the water was looking real rough and she didn't want to lose it. She tell me keep it safe for her. Well, when the police declare she drown, I go quiet-quiet and I take the chain from the kitchen drawer where I had put it, and I hide it. Why I do that is a mystery, because it have no value to me. I say is God who make me pick it up and hide it away, until I was to meet you."

Harry accepts the chain weakly. His desire to speak with Cassie has weakened. He has the fervent will of the newly bereaved, that the ending of the story he is about to hear will have changed in the telling of it, and there would be no inclusion of a drowning. That, in the telling, a mistake indeed will be seen to have been made.

He listens to Piyari as he fingers the chain. He wants to be taken directly to Raleigh. There seems no reason to linger at this house in the stifling country heat any longer. But Piyari, relentless in her need to impart, continues.

"When you doing this kind of work, you see more than you want to see. I leave the job, you know. I leave before Boss fire me. He know I see everything, because it happen right in front my eyes. But he confident that nobody will ever think to inquire of the servant what she might and might not know. Miss Cassie, like she can't believe what happened. She ask me plenty times what happened. But Mr. Harry, why I will tell she? To spoil the rest of her life? In any case, when you do this kind of work, you are nobody. In a way, nobody see nothing.

In the simmering heat he trembles.

"I work with them nine years, Mr. Harry. But I not going back. Just because a man is attorney general does not mean he is exempt from manlike behavior, or that he is just. He put food on the table and clothes on their back and give Madam monthly house allowance. But that don't mean nothing. It have a woman used to phone the house boldface and ask to speak with Boss. If Madam answer the phone, she would hang up, but if I answer, she would ask for him. You can believe that?

"Now, Miss Cassie independent and strong-willed. She tell Madam: separate for a little while. Let Boss feel what it is to come home to a empty house. But is not a good thing for the attorney general wife to pick up herself and leave her husband. Then, sudden so, Madam start talking all kind of nonsense about how life not worth living, how she repeating her own mother life, that this late in life a person should finally be experiencing a little happiness, not more head- and heartache. Is then Boss decide to take Madam to Canada and leave her with Miss Cassie for a little holiday.

"Now, as I say, Madam didn't spare me details of what went on up there. But you know everything. You was there. I don't have to tell you. When she returned, Madam had changed. She tell me that up there she reacquaint with a childhood friend— that is you—who had immigrated some years before. She say she get a glimpse of herself, and of the happiness she miss out on. She say it was like this man in Canada—you, eh?—she say you see she. Really see she. Not with your eyes, you understand, but with your heart. You see deep inside of she. I never see Madam so bright, so talkative, own-way, and hopeful before.

"Madam say the night you show up at Miss Cassie apartment, you look handsome for so, and that if she had stopped to talk with you in the kitchen, everybody would of see her blushing. She and Boss would of surely had words that night. You see, the two children used to tease her when you used to bring eggs by the back gate, and at first it was a joke in the house. But then Boss find you was coming too often, and he start getting vexed . . ."

The Wine Taster

The beginning of that summer past.

Harry had heard the phone in his house ringing as he was getting out of the truck. Overcome by fatigue, he made no effort to reach it. Later, he lay with his back flat on the rug in the living room, a glass of Scotch perched on his stomach, contemplating the following day's task: reviving a neglected water garden. He drifted off to sleep. When the phone rang again, Harry bolted upright, toppling the unfinished drink. He grunted into the mouthpiece of the receiver. There was for a second no response, and the moment the female voice on the other end said, "Hello? Um, I wonder if I have the right number?" despite the years that had elapsed, her voice was unmistakable. She and Shem, Rose said, were in the city for a few days only. She had gotten his number from directory assistance.

In recent years he had thought of her only occasionally, but he was ready to get into his car instantly. Forget the water garden, he thought, invigorated. He offered to meet them the following day. He would take Rose and Shem—for there would be no chance of leaving Shem behind—to see some of Vancouver's sights, and of course, he would bring them to Elderberry Bay for a drink. They agreed that Rose would telephone him the following morning to arrange a meeting time.

That night Harry hardly slept. He scrubbed the toilet and bathtub, which he had not attended to in some weeks, washed the kitchen floor—and was shocked at how dirty it had become without his notice—and wiped with a wet cloth every horizontal surface in the house. Finally, at about four o'clock, he drifted off to sleep, but he awoke an hour later and rushed outside to prepare for the Bihars' visit. After washing the windows of the front of the house, he tackled the yard. He pruned and deadheaded the rosebushes, weeded and shored up the bed around four yak rhododendrons.

The following morning Rose telephoned him. Unknown to her, plans for the day had been made. A friend of Cassie's was taking them out, and later in the evening Cassie had invited a number of her friends to come to her apartment to meet them. Their day was entirely booked. But they were available the day after, when they would be alone, as Cassie had to work that day. They wanted to do some sightseeing and a bit of shopping, she informed him, and asked if he would have the time to drive them around. The Once a Taxi Driver Club was having their monthly meeting that night. He could ferry Rose and Shem around and still make the meeting, which was in Vancouver. He took Cassie's address and agreed to meet them the next day around noon.

So, his spirits dampened by the change of plans, he set off, exhausted from the lack of sleep and dashed hopes, to the watergarden project, where his employees were already at work. He and one of his workers set off to the hardware and building supply outlet in Squamish. They returned with the truck cab full of sheets of steel netting and lengths of PVC piping. He worked hard and long, as if Shem and Rose would surely visit the site. Were they to see this water garden completed as he—with them in mind—imagined it, a dazzling knit of stepping stones between which mosses sprang, ornamental grasses and lilies on the pond's banks, dashes of dragonfly iridescence above, orange koi brilliance beneath, tadpoles, lemon-yellow frogs grunting on velvety lily pads, were they to see all of this, much more would be revealed to them about him than he would ever speak about himself.

By the end of the day, after many hours of hard work with hardly any breaks, nothing of his skills showed. An untrained eye would see only an unremarkable lined crater off to one end of the yard. Harry returned to Elderberry Bay to have a quiet evening. He would bake a package of chicken legs, infuse the house with the aromas of home cooking, and while the chicken was cooking, he would neaten up the yard, pack a little topsoil around the stand of Alice Artindale delphiniums. A fistful of the tall wands would brighten his staid living room. He would spend the evening with a Scotch on the rocks and a newspaper.

He took the package of legs out of the refrigerator. He held it in his hands. He could think of nothing other than the fact that Shem Bihar and Rose were currently in his country. Rose, a car drive away, not an hour from him, and he was about to cook and eat alone. Just down the road she was, so to speak.

It was true that he had not been invited to Cassie's party. But if he were to show up—well after dinner, of course (he would buy a hamburger and a soft drink from a fast-food restaurant on his way into the city)—his eagerness to welcome them to the city was all that could be inferred, and how could anyone fault him for that? Especially since they had asked him to chauffeur them around the following day.

In no time he was driving to the city, on the backseat of his vehicle a bottle of red wine, recommended by the nice lady at the liquor store for the club meeting.

Cassie called her mother to the door when he arrived. His instinct was to embrace Rose, but she took his hand, and though she held it warmly, she maintained a distance. She had put on a little size around her waist, but her skin was as flawless and her hair as perfectly coiffed as he remembered.

"So, it's true: the cold really preserves people," she said.

Harry, holding on to her hand even as he could feel her already taking it back, retorted hoarsely, "Well, the warm weather doesn't hurt, either. It's been over ten years? And you look not a day different."

She asked if he happened to be in the area. He answered truthfully that he was eager to see her. She turned to look for Shem. Relaying an anecdote rather loudly above the crisp sounds of recorded classical guitar music, his voice was unmistakable. Rose, hesitating noticeably, invited Harry into the apartment. The odor of burned coals and barbecued meat saturated the air. Harry handed her the paper bag with the bottle in it. She asked what it was. When he said it was a bottle of wine, she twisted the paper around the bottle's neck and slid it to the far back of the kitchen counter, well away from where the other drinks were displayed. Although still a beautiful woman who kept herself well groomed and heeled, she seemed more subdued than he had remembered her.

Shem stood to greet Harry, vigorously shaking his hand. He clapped Harry's back and ushered him deeper into the living room. He introduced Harry, explaining their relationship, with equivocation that did not go unnoticed by Harry. "We are from the same town—well, you came to live in my town when you were quite young, eh? And we went to the same high school. Marion is a small city, and in a small place everybody knows everybody. Goodness, man, we even liked the same girl when we were teenagers, not so?" At this Shem thumped Harry's back again and laughed deeply as he repeated, "Not so, man, St. George?" Harry smiled awkwardly and made sure not to look in Rose's direction. Avoiding a request from one of Cassie's friends to tell all, he uttered quietly, "Oh, those were ancient times. With a memory like mine, I would have to make up more than half of what I might tell about those days." He turned back to Shem. "What about Busby? Do you remember him? He had left Guanagaspar right after high school, hadn't he?"

Shem brushed off the question, saying, "Childhood acquaintances. We wrote each other a couple of times, then we lost touch." Shem and Harry avoided mention of their knowledge of each other as adults, Shem preferring to rejoin conversation with Cassie's friends, who were mesmerized by the loquacious and commanding attorney general of the Caribbean island of Guanagaspar.

Cassie apologized to Harry that they had finished eating dinner, but complained that there was still much too much food remaining, enough to feed everyone who lived in her apartment building, she exaggerated, and insisted on preparing a plate for him. Myriad aromas permeated the air, tantalizing him, but not wanting to appear to have invited himself for dinner, he profusely declined.

Rose remained for most of the evening in the kitchen, washing up glasses and wiping counters, shelving dishes from the dishwasher and packing and putting away leftover food. He wanted to go into the kitchen, to uncork the bottle he had brought and at the same time to chat with her, but he suspected his closeness in front of Cassie, her friends, and Shem might make Rose uncomfortable.

Shem had provided the evening's alcohol, rum, whiskey, and a few bottles of wine, sweet German Rieslings that he had been pleased to recognize in a Vancouver liquor store, as they were what was available and considered quality wines at Guanagaspar's high-society gatherings.

Harry went into the kitchen. Neither the bag nor the bottle he brought was on the counter. He asked Rose for it. She said as there was more than enough alcohol for the occasion, she had put it away.

Harry, trying to bridge time and distance, asked if she liked what she had seen of the city so far. He invited her to try and fit time into their tight schedules to see the lovely seaside area where he lived. Their exchange was amicable if not noteworthy, and then she excused herself. She turned off the kitchen light and went down the corridor to the room she and Shem were staying in.

Harry, intrigued by Rose's discomfort, returned to the living room. A long time passed—he heard only snatches of conversation monopolized by Shem, and he laughed when others laughed—and then Rose finally returned and joined them. Cassie got up and went into the kitchen. Within minutes she returned with Harry's opened bottle in her hand. Rose sat up sharply and, looking at the bottle in her daughter's hand uttered loudly, "Um . . ."

What more she was about to say was interrupted by Cassie. "Here's a different wine. You didn't buy this one, Daddy. Let's try it." When her father saw her with a fresh, unfamiliar bottle, he threw back the last drop in his glass and held it out to her for a refill. Rose slumped back in her chair as if defeated. She put her head down and looked at her hands expectantly. Her husband sipped in due course. With his flair for excess, he stopped the conversation with a pronounced "Ahhh!" He held up the glass and asked to see the bottle. He read the label, then asked, "But who brought this?" Harry said nothing. Rose's lips were pursed, her eyes darting about, from Cassie to Shem and back. When Shem said it was a full and flavorful wine, one of the best he had ever tasted, that he would like to get a bottle of that to take back to Guanagaspar with him, Rose spoke up: "Harry brought that one. Perhaps he could take us to buy a few bottles tomorrow."

Shem held the glass up and said, "Well, this place is doing you a lot of good, eh! Here's to you."

At four the following morning Harry awoke, plagued by a replaying of the slights of the past evening that he had at the time chosen to ignore. Anger drew him immediately into wakefulness.

He was resentful toward Rose, was reminded of going to visit her before he left Guanagaspar only to be told by Cassie that she was napping. Incidents from those days he had called ancient suddenly seemed current. But most of all, he was angry with himself for, rushing to a party to which he had clearly not been invited. Had he learned nothing all of his life?

He would meet them at noon, as planned. But he would not lose an entire day's work and income on their account. Birds were awakening in the bushes outside his bedroom window, singing one minute, squabbling the next. As he was unable to return to sleep, before the sun was up, he drove to the water-garden site.

THE EGG JUGGLER

Guanagaspar. Present day.

"Yes, it was hard for her that you show up at Miss Cassie house just so, with no warning. And you right, she was not expecting Harry St. George, the Eggman from home, to know wine from water. She hide away the bottle to spare you the embarrassment. But when Boss take a sip and liked it, she say she wanted to laugh out loud with happiness.

"She say next day when you drive them to do shopping, Boss get discouraged-discouraged. He find everything too dear. He had to count out his money and calculate how much everything cost in Guanagaspar dollars in front you, and when he realize how expensive everything turning out to be, and that in front of you he was having to change his mind about buying this and that, he get vex and start talking rude-rude to her. Then, in a store, he was waiting in the line-up to pay for something, and a white woman step in front him like he didn't even exist. The sales-clerk, like she, too, didn't see Boss, she take the woman goods and money. And Boss say nobody ever treat him so. How up there nobody have a clue who he is, and that get him vex for so. Madam say you pretend you didn't see, but Boss not stupid. He feel you was watching everything. She say Boss make demands to speak to the manager, and when he ask the clerk for the manager, she say is she self who is manager. Up there, his money, by the time he convert it, ten to one, couldn't buy him what all his life he know to be his right. That is why Madam tell you to go and wait for them in a coffee shop while they finish up their shopping. Not so, you had to do that? You see? I tell you, she tell me everything. Madam say she know she was slighting you but she was just doing what she had to do until Boss leave.

"Boss didn't want you to know that she was staying on longer than he. He vex for so, from the start, when he hear that she had telephone you. By the time you show up at Miss Cassie house, they had already had words about you. But she was buying time. Time teach her how to get from Boss what it was she want, in all kinds of ways, without him even noticing. But I think she wait too long in the end."

The Attorney General
of Guanagaspar

That summer past, unfolding.

After the afternoon's shopping adventure, which ended in few purchases, Harry chauffeured them back to Cassie's apartment. Shem had become reticent, acknowledging Rose's attempts to elicit a little humor and politeness with grunts and general unpleasantness. Rose boldly insisted Harry eat something before leaving them. He declined, saying he had an engagement that he was already late for. Shem wanted to know what kind of engagement. Harry hesitated. But then he took perverse delight in answering Shem Bihar forthrightly. He belonged to a wine-tasting club, and the club's monthly tasting was scheduled that night. "Wine tasting!" Shem chuckled. He asked if guests were permitted. Rose laughed and said, "You inviting yourself to a private club? And besides, you want to go and drink tonight? You will get high, and the mood you are in, I can't take any back chat tonight, you know." Shem got serious again and shook his head at her. Harry decided to defy her, only in order to calm him. "It's men only," he offered. "We haven't had a guest before, but these men are my good friends. You'd be welcome, I'm sure."

All in all, Rose seemed pleased that Shem and Harry were going off to do something together. Harry stopped at a liquor store. Shem picked out a costly bottle of Puerto Rican rum. That would be his contribution, he said proudly. Harry reiterated that it was a wine club, they drank only wine at these meetings. Shem asked who these people were. His first friends in Canada, Harry told him, fellows who had come from India, Sri Lanka, Fiji, and two were Indians from East Africa. Shem insisted that Harry stop to get a carton of grapefruit juice, some lemons, and several bottles of soda water. He would make an old-fashioned rum punch that would be better than any wine. "Just you wait and see," he said.

The Once a Taxi Driver members obliged good-humoredly. On Shem's insistence, the bottles of wine remained uncorked. After his second punch, and questions about how they met, what work they did, and more, Shem asked why it was that so many Indians drove cabs in the city. One of them blurted out, as if the question had been much asked of him before and the answer well considered, "Connections."

Shem turned to Harry. "From cabdriver to gardener. You should have stayed in Guanagaspar, boy! At least there you had those two little gas stations. You know, they have been shut down now."

Harry's friend Anil spoke up. "But this man is no ordinary gardener, you know. He has his own business and employs eight men. He has some of the biggest accounts up the coast. Harry, you should take him to see the golf course and your gardens at some of those big houses."

Harry did not correct Anil. He currently employed only five full-time workers, and had long ago given up the golf course. In any case, he was rather pleased that Shem was finding out there was more to him than he knew.

Shem fired a question. "But you are a gardener, aren't you? What does he mean you have employees? In any case, it is gardening that you do, not so?"

Harry said, "I design and execute gardens from scratch. Then, in some cases, I do the maintenance. Well, not me personally, but I have a crew who does that part of the work."

"Design? Well, come now. You would have had to go to school for that, not so? So, you have certification? You see, for my profession, one needs a degree. Papers, articling, credentials. You can't just put up a sign and call yourself attorney general, you know."

Partap raised his eyes and said, "Attorney general? You mean to say we have an attorney general in our midst? From which country did you say you are?"

"I am the attorney general of Guanagaspar," Shem said proudly.

There was silence and then hard, heckling laughter when Partap, assuming a pose of true quizzicality, said, "Where is that?"

Good friends, indeed. But this all seemed foolish and painful to Harry, and it had nothing to do with his quiet, unassuming friends. It had everything to do with Rose, with Shem and with Harry, with Shem's embarrassments earlier that day. Harry said, "Yes. I am a gardener, it is true. And we are all ex–taxi drivers here. Each one of us owns a business now. But nothing was handed down to us. We had to work from the ground up, for everything we have nowadays. But you know, you are right, we will, no matter what else we achieve, always, in the eyes of many, remain taxi drivers. Once a taxi driver, always a taxi driver. Not so, fellows?"

Harry's good friends, recognizing the guest's prickly disposition, aware that a rivalry was taking place and that there was potential for unpleasantness, said almost in unison, "Hear, hear, once a taxi driver, always a taxi driver. Let's drink to that, and to our good guest, the attorney general of Guanagaspar." They raised their glasses in the air, and before Shem could begin again, they dispersed into smaller groups, talking among themselves and ignoring their venerable visitor.

Shem fell asleep in the car on the way back to Cassie's apartment. As he was quite drunk, Harry did not want to simply leave him on the street level and drive away, so he accompanied him to the buzzer. He told Cassie to come and get her father. She and Rose came down. Rose was annoyed and embarrassed. She left it to Cassie to thank Harry. Alone at the curbside, Cassie asked Harry if he was available the following day. He had no interest in wasting more of his time with that man, and not knowing Rose's mind, Harry also did not care to spend more time with her. He would spend the day up at the water garden. He told Cassie he had to work. She said her mother would be disappointed, as she had hoped he would have time to take them to the area where he lived; she wanted to see his house. Cassie said she, too, was free and had been expecting that he would take them up that way. She said her mother would love the greenery, the mountains, the coast. She asked Harry if there were eagles up there at this time of the year. Harry ran his hand through his hair pensively. He smiled at her and said he was his own boss and could put off work for a day. He would return to fetch them before eleven the next morning.

A Show of Hands

 The first time Shem was about to light up inside the car, Cassie snapped, "Dad! Ask first! You're going to smell up the car and all of us!"

Harry stopped so that Shem could enjoy his cigarette at one of the many lookouts along the scenic highway. At the house, when he flicked a smoldering butt on the path that led to the beach, Rose stepped up behind him and quietly picked it up. She disappeared into the house, where she put the butt under running water before disposing of it in the garbage can. She contemplated the flower wands in the vase on the dining table. Outside, she asked Harry if he knew whether or not those flowers in there—delphiniums, he informed her—might grow back home. She was indeed mesmerized by the size of the rhododendron blossoms. She used a pocket camera to take a photograph of Harry standing beside the bush. She took pictures of the mountains backdropping the Sound, of Shem and Cassie with the Sound behind them, and one of Harry in front of the house. She wanted to know how cold the water in the Sound was and if anyone ever swam in it. Before Harry could answer, Shem did. "It must be like ice water, but of course people here would swim in it. They do all kinds of crazy things here, just to say they did them."

Shem asked Harry if he did his own gardening or if he got the workers to do it. Shem said, "But you have all of this and no wife, man? It's time you got married, don't you think? There must be someone we don't know about. Not so?"

Harry was compelled to take them to the water garden. They were uncomfortable traipsing through a private yard until they realized there was no one around, that the owner was away on holiday. Rose paid attention to the variety of roses, to the groupings of colors, and to the juxtaposition of differently textured plants. She sniffed open blooms and pinched old leaves and spent buds from the flowering plants.

Cassie had wandered off, leaving Shem and Harry together.

Shem persisted. "So, the owners tell you what they want, don't they? Do they supervise you?"

Shem walked around surveying the pond, the work mess on the lawn, and at the outside edge of the property, a natural spring that bubbled out of the ground and flowed into a canal. He approached Harry. "But you didn't go to a university and get a degree, did you?"

Back in the car, Shem, sitting in the front passenger seat, was pensive. Harry drove down the main street in Squamish, trying to decide upon a restaurant that might serve Canadian beef, a good steak, as that was what Shem had announced he wanted to eat. Suddenly, Shem perked up and said he had a suggestion. Harry should tap in to the spring and direct it upward, and in so doing create a fountain, or build a wall and let the water from the spring come up behind the wall and cascade down the front, a waterfall! He turned back and said to Rose, "Now, if there were a spring near my property, that is what I would get a contractor to come and put in, not so?" Rose lifted her chin in the air and said, "Uh-hm." Encouraged by her response, Shem asked hadn't Harry thought of that? It seemed so obvious to him.

Cassie spoke out, attempting to sound as if she were teasing her father. "Dad! But why you interrogating him so? Since when do you know anything about landscaping? And how would you like it if we came telling you how to do your work?"

Shem retorted, "I am only trying to understand the difference between a regular gardener, a designer, and a landscapist. It seems like the boundaries blur in this country. But I am sure that up here, a notary public wouldn't offer to defend in a court of law."

In the rearview mirror, Harry noticed Cassie roll her eyes. Rose's teeth were clenched. She had pressed a finger to her lip, indicating to Cassie that she leave the issue alone.

Fortunately, at that point, they were coming upon a spaghetti house advertising on its billboard that it served steak. Harry asked Rose if Italian food was good enough for her. She said, "Oh yes, anything, as long as they also serve steak." Harry said that almost any place in the area would serve steak, so if she preferred something else, they could carry on. Watching Harry in the rearview mirror, she reiterated that as long as there was steak on the menu, they could go there.

A Story of Silver
and a Little Brass

Guanagaspar.

"Madam say when they get back in Cassie's apartment, Boss didn't mention a word to Cassie, but he went in the bedroom and close the door. When she went in to pack his clothes for him, as he was to leave next morning, he tell her how all day everybody was contradicting him and making him feel like he was small and stupid. He tell her how you come up here and just because you could buy house with a view and because you can hire people to do your work, you think you rise up to their level. It didn't please him one bit to be driving in your car all day. He say you don't know your place, that you think money is all a person need to step out from a backward fishing village, and how you playing landscape man but you really nothing more than a yardman. He didn't want you becoming a nuisance, thinking that because you living up there in Canada, you rise up in class. He didn't want you thinking you could telephone or come and meet Madam and take all kind of liberties. Madam say she couldn't wait for Boss to leave. He talk and talk, and she remain quiet and pack his clothes in the suitcase. She went in the bed with him and play she fall asleep straightaway, but soon as she hear him breathe like he sleeping, she open her eyes and all night she lie awake thinking about the flowers you plant and how you take care of that house and yard all by yourself. She say she wonder in truth if you had a madam of your own, hide away somewhere. She picture the mountains across from your house, a little snow on them, and she imagine herself swimming in the water in front your house, and she tell me how she couldn't get it out of her mind how you had asked her if she wanted to eat spaghetti or if she wanted you to look for something else for her to eat.

"When Madam came back here, she was not the same Madam who had left for Canada three months earlier, you know. That place make her strong-willed, and it put ideas in her head. She was brisk, and her voice—you know how she used to be quiet-quiet? Her voice get bright. And almost every day she went to bathe in the swimming pool. She was looking after herself. I don't mean going to the hairdresser and that kind of thing. But rather, she stop eating too much fat and meat and say how she feeling like a young woman again, and how, sudden-sudden so, she want to be fit. She exercise, swim two-three times a day, back and forth in the pool, you see it there, nobody else using it. First few days Madam look like her age was in reverse. A few times after I gone into my room for the evening, I had to go back into the kitchen, as I thought I had forgotten to turn off the radio. It was no radio: it was Madam singing, humming old-time tunes, and even making up her own words and music as she herself sat there doing work that the yardman is supposed to do—polishing the silver and the brass.

"Sometimes I walk out there to find her holding up a piece of silver from on the sideboard, a cake knife, for instance, or from the coffee table down in the front of the house, a crystal ashtray in the palm of her hand. One day I find her taking out her col-lection of expensive coffee cups and teacups that she used to use only when her lady friends used to come for tea, and she take out the little-little spoons to look at them, too. Just sitting, look-ing at all them things. I never see her do that kind of thing be-fore. Those were nights when Boss was out until two-three in the morning, and you didn't know if it was really work he was doing, as he say it was, or if it was galavanting. And galavanting in this place always involve a woman. When I ask Madam what she doing out there late so, she hold up the items to the light as if to see them better, and she say, 'Piyari, these things pretty, and they dear for so, it is true, but they don't talk to me. In my next life, I will have no need for things like these.'

"She was really watching them as if for the last time. And then those same pieces, one by one, started going missing. In a short time, the sideboard and the buffet that had been covered with all kind of stupidness—nice stupidness: silver cigarette box and lighter to match, a crystal bird with a long, long, long neck that Madam used to always tell me to careful with when I dusting, six crystal decanters, two silver fighting cocks, a pewter bud vase, a bone-china bowl with a picture of yellow roses inside it, expensive stupidness, in truth—in a short time so, the buffet top was empty-empty.

"One day I open a drawer in the buffet. The special knife-and-fork set—a kind of set that had knife for regular food, knife for meat, knife for fish, knife for butter, and knife for what else I don't know, and three different kind of spoons, and a fork for this and for that, the set that they use for parties—well, it was gone, the drawer was empty.

"Another time I come outside and see Madam lean over the dining room table, almost lying on top of it, cleaning and shining the top with a cloth and tung oil. She tell me take another cloth and help her. But I stand up right there and I watch her. You know it is I who tell Madam that if Boss don't miss anything else, he was bound to miss the table and the chairs. She come down from the table and say quiet-quiet, 'You right. He might notice, in truth.' Is like she wasn't thinking. It was then that everything start falling apart."

DREAMS

In a hotel room in Marion, Harry paces and waits for Cassie's telephone call. There is no air-conditioning in the room, and the heat has not subsided. The current edition of the *Guanagaspar Times* is folded on the desk. He has not, until now, seen a local paper. The headline is clearly visible. A.G.'S WIFE'S BODY STILL NOT FOUND. The paper's half fold occurs along a photograph, the major part of which is hidden under the paper. He moves the paper so that its writing faces him, but he does not pick it up or turn it over. He stares at the visible part of the photograph that, had he opened it out, would have been close to life-size. All that shows of the photograph is the familiar wavy hair, the hairline, and the forehead. He places his palm, opened flat, on the photograph. He wants to remember the feel of her hair. But the flat surface, the rigidity and coolness of newsprint, and a scent of printer's ink send a tremor through him. His aloneness is acute. Had he ever told his good friend Anil about Rose, he would have telephoned him right away. He couldn't have admitted to Anil, such a devoted husband, father, and grandfather, that he had become intimately involved with a married woman, the wife of the foolish man who had come and brought rum to one of their wine tastings.

Wearing his underpants only, he lies on the bed clutching the gold-plate chain and cross in his fist. From outside of his window, he listens to the idle chatter and unrestrained laughter of three of the hotel workers. He hears water running from the kitchen into an open drain, and the quips of birds fighting for dusk cover on the branches of the flamboyant trees. Cicadas chirp relentlessly. Harry thinks of Kay back in Canada. His home, his business, his meager belongings, his friends are all there, yet that world seems alien to him.

He lifts his hand and dangles the chain over his face, opens his mouth and lets it drop, link by link, onto his tongue. It is cool. He closes his mouth, and profuse quantities of saliva form. The clump of chain shifts and slips toward the back of his throat, and he bolts upright and spits it back into his hand. The momentary choking has caused his eyes to well with tears, and then, as if a dam has been opened, he begins to sob uncontrollably.

Harry replays and replays in his mind Rose's servant's full accounting.

"I start watching, and I watching and watching, and sudden-so I realize that the amount of knickknacks in the house getting smaller and smaller. The yard boy, too, he say every time he clean silver or brass, it was as if he had less and less to clean. A day come it was so noticeable that even Boss, who hardly pay attention to how the house looking, come in the kitchen and in front of me he say to Madam that he find the cabinet with the glass front—where her pretty coffee cups used to be displayed—was looking empty. Madam tell Boss she lend the neighbor the cups for a party.

"Then one day a lady telephoned while Madam was in the bathroom, and Boss answered. The lady tell Boss she hear that he was selling out his silver, and she wanted to come and take a look. Boss march down to the front of the house, and in truth he notice the silver candlesticks and cocks missing, and so he open the buffet drawer and see the silver knife-and-fork set not there. Boss didn't say nothing right away, but he get quiet-quiet. Then the next day I hear Boss and Madam quarreling. A woman from a travel agency had bring a paper with all the flights from Guanagaspar to Canada to Boss office, saying Madam ask her to bring it to the house for her, but as she was passing by Boss office, she decide to drop it off there. Well, how Madam allow that mistake to happen is beyond me. She get too carefree, in truth. So, Boss realize what was going on—he is not attorney general for nothing, you know—and he and Madam had quarrel for so. She say she wanted to go and live with Cassie. He ask her if it had anything to do with you. She start a nervous kind of laughing, asking him if he was going crazy, but not answering direct. In anger, he tell her to leave. 'Leave now, get out my damn house,' he tell her. Well, he didn't exactly tell her. He was shouting, shouting, shouting. Even Boss, who always so concerned about what the neighbors going to think, didn't care at all. He take out a thick-thick bundle of dollar bills from his pocket and throw it at her, shouting that he himself would pay her passage. But when she say all right, she want to leave, he get vex, he start to cry, he beg, he shout, he threaten to take his own life, and Madam say okay, okay, she not going anywhere. But it was out in the open, and the two of them remain sour with each other from then on.

"Well, it was no surprise. Boss start opening drawers and cupboards every day after that to see what was there, and what more, if anything, was missing. One day I hear them fighting in they bedroom, and I get worried. I take a dust cloth and I start wiping out the ornaments on a table in the hallway right outside their door. Boss was shouting. 'You have no shame? He is a gardener. You gone crazy? You need to get your head checked. You want to bring shame on us?' And Madam say calm-calm, 'Shame? Who brought shame on this family? Not you? You are the one who is out almost every night with some woman hanging from your elbow.' And Boss say, 'What about your father? I am no different from him.'

"And, Mr. Harry, now I am coming to the end of my story: you remember when you telephone the house in Marion and I speak with you? I knew it was you. Who else it could be? Same day I travel back to their house by the sea. But, I had to wait until I was alone in the kitchen with Madam. I was sure I had of seen Boss swinging in the hammock in the garden. I decide to take the chance then to tell Madam you call for she. But next thing I know, it was Boss standing up in the doorway, real serious, asking what it is you had of wanted. Madam jump, like she get frighten. He standing there, and still I couldn't believe my eyes. I look out the window again: it was the man who had come to pick coconuts who boldface so take a liberty and lie down in the hammock. Boss, calm-calm, repeat himself. I had to lie, I say you ask for both of them. I tell Boss that you ask me to wish him all the best for the New Year. He say, 'And what message he ask you to give Madam?' Well, is like I get stupid and I didn't know what to say. He come right up to my face and ask me again, but this time he shout at me and like he was ready to hit me. I say, 'Nothing. Nothing. He didn't ask for Madam. He didn't leave no message for she. I telling the truth, Boss.'

"Boss get vex. And by that time I couldn't say I didn't really know if it was you in truth who had called. He slam his hand against the counter and he shout so loud I don't know how the neighbors both sides ent hear him, even above the wind and the waves breaking on the beach.

"'You take me for a damn fool? What message he send for Madam? Tell me now, before I hit you!' Madam tell him to leave me alone. He turn to her and raise his hand like he was going to hit her. She stand up to him. Is like she push out her chest and she tell him, 'You want to hit? Is hit you want to hit? Go ahead, I waiting. Hit!'

"He turn around and walk a few feet back to the dining room. It had a vase, a purple glass vase, on the dining room table. He pick it up and fling it, and it went flying into the wall. Like if his voice catch in a tube, Boss say, 'What the ass is this? You have the servant taking message for you? In my own house all this going on? Look here, you playing with your life if you think you going to make a fool out of me. You want to bring shame on us? You forget who have the police and the law on his side. You wouldn't live a day to shame me, you hear? And that yard boy—no place is far enough for him to hide from the kind of people who loyal to me. Hear me good: I will not let you or him destroy my family name. And you'—it was me he turn to speak to now—'you,' he say, 'pack your bags. I don't want you in this house, you hear? Get your ass out of here, now-now.'

"Boss storm out the house, and next thing I see him through the window, marching over to the hammock—the coconut man had take off when he hear quarreling going on. Boss sit in the hammock for one minute, and then he jump out and turn to face the house. In broad daylight and out in the open so, he bend down and he pick out a coconut, big like a football, from a pile the gardener pick that day, and he pelt that coconut at the house. And you know it shatter one whole set of glass louvres? It was then Madam break. She hold she head and how she bawl. She and me, the two of we, we duck down like we expecting more coconuts to come, this time right through the hole he make, and we run out the back door straight to the servant room outside, and we lock the door and the window, and is there we stay—in that hot-hot room—stoop down behind the door, quiet like cockroach, for a good hour. Is only when we hear Boss car start up and pull out the driveway that we come out again. Boss did not come back that night. But Madam was 'fraid too bad, and she ask me to sleep in the room with she. I lie down on the floor next to she, but neither of us sleep. Every time a car pass, we bolt upright, our eyes big and white in the dark. Next day, by the time the glass company from Gloria came and fix up everything, Boss still hadn't returned. I suppose he had called them from wherever he was.

"Madam carry on, making like she was brave, but I know she was frightened. She eat breakfast, trembling all the while, her eyes darting left and right. But still she went for her morning dip, as usual, but we agree on a signal if Boss return, and from the water she was going to keep her eye on the house for the signal. The signal was that the moment I hear his car pulling in, I was to go in the front yard and stand up by the hammock. But all day we wait so, trying to carry on as if nothing happened. Then that evening he come back around dinnertime. I frighten, as I had not of left the house and the job like he tell me to.

"But me he ignore. I set the table for the two of them, and Madam put out their food. He come and take his plate and he went in the drawing room. He sit in front of the television with his food. I clean up the kitchen, and by the time I turn out the light, he was still sitting there. From the servant room outside, never mind winds and waves and the coconut trees brushing against the roof of the house, I was so frighten that my ears could hear like the ears on the Bionic Man. I listen to the television until he turn it out about three-so in the morning. I get up and look through the open bricks at the top of the wall of my room, to see if the light in their bedroom or bathroom upstairs went on. But it had no lights on. I don't know if he and Madam exchange words that night, but next morning she tell me he never went upstairs. He sleep on the couch downstairs, and in the morning when she come down, he rise and went upstairs.

"Me and Madam make sure not to talk another word about you, and whatever else we talk about, we talk quiet-quiet, so as not to get in his way.

"I see Boss vex before, but even when he take in some drinks, he wasn't a violent man. He was difficult but not violent.

"Anyway, after she eat breakfast, Madam went upstairs and come back down in her bath suit. She had a towel wrap around her waist, and she tell me to curry crab and boil rice for lunch. Is then she take the chain off from around her neck, and she put it in my hand. I say, 'Eh-eh. What make you take off the chain,

Madam?' She tell me, 'The sea rough. Keep it safe. Don't lose it. Remember where you put it.' and she went out the front door, pulling it in behind her. I was making lime juice in the kitchen, and I hear the front door slide open again. I wonder why Madam come back, so I went to see if she forget something. By the time I reach the front door, I see Boss in bath trunks, heading down to the water. Well, my heart stop. In all the years I work for them, I never know Boss to go in the sea. He would wear short pants in the house and on the beach, but not bath trunks. Yes, they have swimming pool in the backyard in the house in Marion, and when friends and family come over, he will go in with them, but he can't swim, and he never put his head under the water. He would walk around in the shallow end of the swimming pool with his sunglasses on, smoking a cigarette, keeping his hand high so the cigarette wouldn't get wet. And every long weekend, regardless of weather, they rush to the coast to stay in their beach house, and still he never go in the sea; the salt does sting his skin and give him a rash. But that day I telling you about was different.

So, I run back in the house frighten for so, and I want to call somebody for help, but I didn't know who to call. If I call police, I would say what? 'Come quick, Boss never go in the water and today he put on his trunks and gone in'? But I should of call, no matter how foolish it would of sound. In any case, I start to tremble. I decide to call Mr. Jeevan, but so many times I dial that boy number for Madam, and suddenly I couldn't remember the number. I try to dial, and it was like my fingers couldn't even go straight in the holes, I was shaking so much. I look out the window and see Boss in the shallow of the sea, and he was walking in deeper. When Boss reach Madam, instead of stopping, he carry on walking. Madam turn to watch him, and then she start hurrying to catch up with him. He take a dive into a wave, and when he come out the other side, he start heading out farther.

"I say to myself maybe Boss was full of remorse about how he treat Madam, not just the day before but all the years they married, and I thought he was—what is the word? Depress— that is how they call it? Well, I feel the man was depress and that he was getting ready to drown himself.

"I start to think about what that would mean. You know, if Boss drown himself, then what? I was thinking, and same time I find myself walking back to the kitchen. I put the jug of lime juice in the refrigerator, and I wipe down the counter so flies wouldn't gather on it. I thinking all the time, wondering if he would really do a thing like that. And then I feel it was probably better to get help than to be sorry. So I run out the back door to see if the gardener was there. He wasn't there, so I run up by the fence to see if I could see anybody. I went quick-quick up the gravel road to the main road, hoping to stop a car. But the main road was quiet. It didn't even have a donkey tie up in sight. I look back toward the house and see the neighbor servant coming through the back door with a basket of clothes in she hand. I start shouting out to her to call police, but the breeze coming up from the sea whip my voice in the other direction. By the time I reach that neighbor yard, somebody was in Madam back-yard, screaming my name. When I turn around, it was Boss. He leave the yard and was running up the gravel road, screaming, 'Oh God, get help, Piyari, get help quickly. Oh God! A riptide. Madam got caught in a riptide. She just went under. She hasn't come back up.'

"Well, I just stop where I was. I couldn't move. I was so sure he was going to drown himself, and he was right in front of me telling me Madam get ketch in riptide. I start to tremble. I want to know how Madam, who always instructing everybody about how to stay calm in a riptide, gone under in it, and not Boss— who can't even stay floating on his back in water. I lower myself until I was sitting on the gravel road. Boss come right up to me and grab me by my shoulders with his two hands. 'Piyari. Get up. Get up, I tell you. Help me, please. Get help!'

"The Coast Guard, the police, the fire brigade, the Boy Scouts who was camping down the road, everybody—one and all—they come. They comb that sea and the river that come out into the sea half a mile away. Night and day they walk the beach. The house was full of people. Family and friends land up here. Mr. Jeevan and his wife. People from government. The head of the Coast Guard. The head of the army. Newspaper people. The assistant attorney general. And the deputy prime minister, too. Boss stay in his bedroom for almost the whole day. He talk only to his son, Mr. Jeevan, and he talk to the chief of police. It was then he call Miss Cassie in Canada. Next day it come out in the papers that the day before Madam drown, she and Boss had domestic quarrel. The papers say how he mash up a window and break a vase. It say that he was remorseful that they had fight because now she gone and he wouldn't ever get a chance to make up with she again. Nobody ask me a thing. It was like I was invisible. And what I would tell them, in any case? That she was planning to leave him and he had of realize that? All I could of say was that I never see Boss wearing bathing trunks by the beach before that morning. But even me—I had of thought he was going to drown himself! I realize it was the attorney general I was dealing with, and I decide that what happen had already happen and that nothing I say now would bring back Madam.

"And this is what I want to tell you, Mr. Harry. From the day she return after that holiday, she was planning, all this time, to leave him. In another month she would of gone to Canada to be with you. She didn't want to tell you anything until she was sure it could of happen."

*   *   *

It is dark. Even though there is wire mesh in the window of his room, mosquitoes have found their way in and hover about his body. It is still too hot, much too much to put on a shirt, and so he uses his arms to brush away the buzzing creatures as they near his head. The number of cicadas chirping has increased. Dance music from a distant source floats in and out of his hearing. Harry rises. The people who were chatting outside his window have left. The city beyond is in darkness. He wonders, had he not made that call to Rose, the one Piyari took, rather had he waited for her to call him would any of this have happened?

No Body

Harry refuses to be put on hold a minute longer. He makes the call, and to his relief, it is Cassie who answers. To offer condolences seems untimely. Cassie sounds exhausted and, to his dismay, distanced.

"What is most unsettling is not having a body to confirm that she is gone. I know my mother had thoughts of leaving my father and moving to Canada. According to him, they quarreled about you. What's going on, Harry?"

He can't help himself: "My God! This is ridiculous. I hadn't spoken with your mother in almost two months."

Cassie unfazed, continues, "When I arrived here and telephoned you back in B.C., I did have the impression you were truly clueless about her whereabouts. But when you agreed to fly here to Guanagaspar, I just kept hoping; I was hoping you would know where she might be. It's a nightmare, there being no body."

He hears Cassie's grief, and the accusation in her voice. He knows it is unwarranted, and yet he feels oddly guilty. After a silence in which it becomes clear that Cassie is crying, he is not surprised when she says in a breaking voice, "The funeral is tomorrow, Harry. I know you have traveled all this way, but it's best if you don't come."

TROPICAL SEA

Piyari attends the funeral service. She travels to Marion by taxi so that Heroman is free to take Harry wherever he might need to go. He asks to be taken to the coast. It is there, where Rose went missing, that he will spend the morning.

The road ascends gradually into forested hills. The air, cooler than in the town, is redolent with the sweet and sour of the tropical forest's constant cycle of decomposition and rebirth.

Here and there, sudden clearings of well-tended lawn punctuate the miles of jungle through which the road to the ocean cuts. In the center of each clearing squats a modest, unpainted wood house. Curtains billow in the open windows and doorways. How many people, presumed missing, might be seeking all manner of refuge in places like these, he wonders. As Heroman drives slowly along the dangerously winding and narrow road, Harry peers into the houses, but not a soul seems to be about.

Heroman points to the sky ahead. A flock of green parrots flaps from one range of forest to another.

As they descend, the verdant lushness recedes. Stretches of dead man's fingers, devil's claw, and cockscomb hug the roadside. Guanaga and cuticut grow high, and pigeon peas are in bloom. Lush bamboo outlines the meandering passage of a river. Every now and then a single towering coconut tree punctuates the landscape. Soon the soil on either side of the road changes entirely from moist black dirt to drier coarse sand out of which lofty coconuts soar. Between their lanky trunks, Harry spots in the distance the powerful breaking waves of the foamy Caribbean Sea. A chill washes over him. As they head toward the seafront roadway, the air turns salty and oily. In no time, he hears the rhythmic crack of the ocean's waves.

Harry asks to be taken to the area where the Bihars have their beach house.

"Oh God, man, I had a feeling you was going to ask me this. What you want to go there for?"

Harry insists on being dropped off, not at the house directly but in its vicinity.

"You know you shouldn't go there. Why you want to go and torture yourself so for? Suppose now she wash up and is you and me who will find she?"

Nevertheless, Heroman drives to an undeveloped lot not far from the Bihars' house. Harry is firm that he needs to be alone and asks Heroman to meet him back in an hour.

He walks uncertainly through the thicket of crocuses, fallen branches, and nuts out onto the open beach. He observes the taut silkiness in the belly of a cresting wave, wondering why some bodies, once snatched by the sea, are thrown back out, and why some are never returned.

At the water's edge, he ambles toward a house he ascertains from Piyari's story to be the Bihars' beach house. The glare coming off the water and the scorched sand is merciless. He becomes uncomfortable, the hair on his body rising and stiffening. A policeman leans against the front wall of the house. Harry remains close to the water, but the man sees Harry looking in his direction and greets him with a nod. Harry returns the gesture and continues walking straight ahead, scanning not the beach or the water but the dark mass of foliage growing beneath the endless thicket of coconut trees. A rustling in the bushes behind him frightens him. He spins around, expectant, the pulse at his temples pounding. It is only a wild and skinny beach dog emerging to pick at scavenger birds' leftover fish parts.

A quick glance toward the house again, and there is the hammock of Piyari's story, still hanging between two coconut trees, the sliding doors to the house, the mound of coconuts, the louvered windows.

His head has become hot. Perspiration runs down his temples. He has brought no drinking water with him, and there is no tap in sight. The other holiday houses are closed up, no caretakers to be seen. Still, he cannot, dares not, approach that house to ask for anything. He removes his shoes and socks and tucks his belongings behind a fallen tree trunk. He rolls the hems of his trousers to midcalf and enters the water. The salt water he splashes against his face and on his head calms him instantly. Beyond the breakers, the water seems serene, almost as still as the water in front of his house in Elderberry Bay.

Rose swimming in the icy waters in front of his house there comes to mind. He recalls watching her, pleased that she was so clearly enjoying herself, and then turning away briefly, only to look back and find that she had disappeared. Then he saw her, a speck walking up the beach toward him. She had seen the small child clinging to an inflatable tire, so she swam down the coast and pulled the girl to shore. She had told Harry then that most drownings occur because of panic. Even in a riptide, she instructed him, a person shouldn't panic. "Stay calm and go with the current. Let it take you where it will," she had informed him, "and if you can just ride it, you will end up in still waters, perhaps a distance away." He wonders where along the coast her body might have drifted. He studies the faint curving coastline toward the north, then turns to regard the southernmost peninsular. Couldn't she have followed her own counsel, let it take her where it would?

He scoops and splashes more water on the top of his head, pats the back of his neck with it. A wave has broken close and is rushing forward. He is suddenly in water up to his knees. He looks behind him. The water has crept all the way up and stopped just before the tree trunk behind which his clothes are stashed. For several long seconds, there is no beach. Just as swiftly, the water retreats and, in rejoining the ocean, tumbles impatiently over new waves already pulsing toward shore. The sand under his feet slides away, and he sinks in deeper. Unsteadily he treads backward until he is in water so shallow that it only swirls about his feet. Silver mud skippers leap over the rippling water, and sea cockroaches nose their bodies vertically into the sand. He squints at the hazy northerly coast again. He turns and faces the peninsula. Around that crooked finger of land is the south coast of the island, uncultivated land, mosquito- and sand-fly-ridden beaches and coves that are accessible from land only by brush-cutting high razor grass and then ascending steep cliffs. There are no major towns down there, only a string of fishing villages. This Harry knows, for Raleigh is one of these villages. So many years later, those villages still remain distanced from the main towns. To get to them from here by car, one must travel all the way back to Marion, then carry on from there on the circuitous Link Road and over the Muldoon Bridge. It is not an area of the country that would likely have changed too much over the years. A body deposited along the south coast by a sea current has a good chance of being caught there and lost forever. He puts his hand in the pocket of his trousers and clutches the chain. He recalls Piyari's words: "Day before she had went in the sea wearing it, so why, I want to know, that morning she remove it?"

The words repeat, mantra-like, in his head. As if whacked on his back with a thick plank of wood he stiffens: what if Rose counted on the chain landing in his hands? He shades his eyes from the glare and squints hard in the direction of the south peninsular. It is a good distance away. Perhaps as far away as Howe Sound's far shore is from his house in Elderberry Bay. She told him, during idle conversation, that if she had to, she could swim that distance. Forced to, she would know how to pace herself.

What if she had put an inordinate amount of faith in Piyari? What if she had hoped that he would return to the island, and that Piyari would reveal to him all that was necessary? And that he would calculate what no one else likely would? Such thinking, he quickly admonishes himself, is foolish dreaming. If she took such a chance, she would have had more faith in him than he has in himself. A bigger wave prepares to break even closer to the shore. Running toward his clothing, he chides himself; such ideas are the dementia of denial. He slips a hand in his pocket again, grasping the chain tightly. Wasn't it too strange a coincidence that she had removed it from around her neck on the very day she disappearred though? He whips up his bundle and races through the trees in search of Heroman.

WHIPLASH

In the Central plains a good many miles away from Marion, Heroman does not drive under the speed limit, yet Harry is irritable, certain that at the current pace, it will be late evening before they arrive back in Marion. At a bend in the road, Heroman swerves to avoid a man foolishly riding a bicycle in their lane, coming toward them. A turquoise-colored box is strapped above the front wheel of the bicycle. FISH is crudely painted in bright red on the front of the box. Harry spins around to look at the man as they pass. Heroman wants to know when, other than this trip to the island, was the last time Harry traveled this route. Harry squeezes his eyes shut, whiplashed by the past: the fish seller on the bicycle calling up the fact that his father, the drowned Seudath St. George, had taken his mother—or had he rescued her, kidnapped her, assisted her in leaving?—away from her family whom she never saw again. He is sure that if he were to utter a single word, he would vomit, his nausea caused by his unbearable impatience with the long ride back to his hotel, by the throbbing hope and improbability of a string of what-ifs, by the narrow winding road, the constant swerving to avoid potholes, bicyclists, pedestrians, and stray dogs or the bloated, putrid carcasses of animals lying on their back.

Shem's words, relayed to him by Piyari, echo in Harry's mind, not in her voice or diction, but in Shem's, as if Harry had heard them pronounced himself: "What the ass is this? You have the servant taking message for you? . . . You forget who have the police and the law on his side . . . That yard boy—no place is far enough for him to hide . . . Hear me good: I will not let you or him destroy my family name."

The threat implied is of concern. Harry thinks of his house and yard in Elderberry Bay. Of Howe Sound, the thick, cool gray mist that hangs at this time of year. The logging road to Carol Lake. Even in this present heat, the glacier there looms brightly in his mind. He thinks of his truck with all his gardening tools. Of the yards he has designed and of clients who held summer garden parties so that they could show off his work and introduce him around. He was indispensable to them. He pictures Anil, Partap, and the Once a Taxi Driver Wine-Tasting fellows. In his mind he sees the winding mountainside road from Elderberry Bay to Squamish, a landscape that is no longer far enough away.

And Kay. Had no call come that early New Year's morning from Cassie, and none again from Rose, what would have transpired between them? They might well have entered into a comfortable companionship. Some form of quiet passion might have developed in him for her. Perhaps a passion akin to the one he felt for Rose.

He knows that he will not return to Elderberry Bay, and succumbs to the pull of the old riptide.

At the end of that interminable drive, Harry, without revealing more than he must, informs Heroman that he will end the rest of his time on the island among friends.

"You still have friends here? You didn't mention them before. I had of planned to drive you into Gloria for the evening. The capital come a real worldly place, yes. It have skyscrapers, buildings six stories tall, you know. And it have two nice shopping malls. They would be closed now, but they light up pretty in the night. And if you see how nice people does dress up in town. Guanagasparian women come nice-nice, too."

Surprised to receive no sign of interest from Harry in tour-
ing the city, Heroman insists, "The capital come a first-class
place, man. A lot of eating places, too. Not just Chinese food,
but it have places you could sit down, and waitress that come
and serve you hamburgers and milk shakes and that kind of thing.
You don't want to drink a coconut or take a oyster cocktail from
the vendors in town? I ready to take you and show you the town
now-now. It will take your mind off things."

Harry can no longer hide his impatience. "I am not here for
much longer. There are people I must look up. Family friends.
Please tell your sister thanks for everything. You were both very
good to me. I will write from Canada."

Still unwilling to so easily release this foreign charge who has
seeds of scandal sprouting about him, Heroman offers to fetch
Harry wherever he is on the day of his return flight and to drive
him to the airport. Harry is firm that friends will look after him
from then on.

Once he is sure that Heroman has driven off and is nowhere
to be seen, Harry checks out of the hotel and walks with his suitcase and shoulder bag to a taxi stand several streets away from
the hotel. There he catches a Link Road taxi and travels, along
with other passengers, in the long rush-hour traffic.

Paying Respects

Muldoon Bridge, ablaze in the golden light of the evening sun, has been widened and is now a four-lane asphalt-paved highway. The river—it, too, shimmering gold, seems narrower than he recalls, and tamer. A log that had been wedged in its center since the days of traveling in Mr. Walter's car, and which trapped debris that washed in from the sea and debris headed down the river toward the sea, is, to his pleasure and at the same time horror, still there. The mangrove, kept under control by the municipality, has been cut back well away from the roadway. Harry is curious about the flooding of the road in high tide, wonders if the new raised bridge and the new walled-off roadway have alleviated this problem; wanting to avoid attention, he does not inquire.

The area where he dispersed his mother's ashes has been altered, too. Where once were bamboo and rozay forests through which one had, in the past, to brush-cut one's way is now a parking lot. Beyond the parking is an area of kept lawn on which several people sit, watching the dying sun set. He had intended that as the taxi passed, he would pay his respects to his mother's memory, but he is caught off-guard by this recreation area with picnic tables and fire pits and seated people. The taxi speeds past before he has the chance to look out to the water's horizon and invoke his mother's name.

He gets out of the taxi at a junction well before Timbano Trace. He waits in the twilight on the roadside, as if expecting someone. Then, when no one is in sight, he slips away, down the dark and narrow path.

He is in too much of a hurry to take the time to try and identify the small plot of land he and his mother lived in. In any case
the steps, which might have revealed the spot, must have—along
with the much-crazed man who once lived in its shadow—
finally succumbed.

He recognizes Tante Eugenie's large and bent frame as she
spreads wet clothing on the tops of the jasmine bushes at the
side of the house. From his approach, he scrutinizes the clothing as best as he can in the low light to see if he might recognize
any of it. She turns and sees him. Although she has thrown her
hands in the air, ready to embrace him, he notices that she is,
oddly, frowning. She limps hurriedly toward him, her mouth set
tight. He is about to speak, but she snaps a finger to her lips.
"Shhh," she cautions urgently.
    Energy instinctively drains from his body. He wants quick
confirmation to the question "Is she here?," but, afraid of any
and all answers, he has lost his breath. He glances side to side,
peering hard into the dark surroundings. Reaching him, Tante
Eugenie throws her arms around him, tightening her grip to still
his tremble. As if someone might be eavesdropping, she whispers, "Why it take you so long to come? We waiting and waiting
for you. Come. You alone?"
    She grips his hand hard and pulls him purposefully around,
past the house down to the beach. She points. Sitting on the sand,
leaning against a log that only somewhat conceals her, is the familiar body. He cups Tante Eugenie's face in his hands and kisses
her on her tobacco-blackened lips. Coarse hairs on her upper
lip prick his face.

She sees him just as he is upon her, and she smiles broadly. "Oh
Lord, Harry. I knew you would figure it out." He is exhausted,
bent by the faith she has in him. Anger that she has caused such

grief with the staging of her drowning grips him, even as he is overwhelmingly relieved, grateful that she is alive. He wants to shove her hard, and at the same time to hold and never let her go. He presses her hand to his mouth, and when she feels the wetness of tears on her hand, she cradles him in her arms. "We don't have too much time, Harry. Everything ready. We were only waiting." Then she laughs and adds, "Well, we were waiting, but more than that, we were hoping." She begins to stand up. He holds her back. "Your face was on the front page of yesterday's paper. It is probably in today's paper, too. Everyone in this country knows you. You are on people's minds right now."

"I know that. I know we can't stay here. Everything is arranged. It is only for you to agree to. I ready for a fresh start."

She puts a hand on his leg and presses it there firmly to quiet him. In this place I am dead, Harry. They had funeral for me today. This is my chance. If they find me now, you know what will happen?"

Rose regards her hand on his leg and takes time to plead, time as if the world had slowed around them and nothing was pressing. "Harry, I want a simple-simple thing—to be able to look at you, to look at those eyes, and talk about all kinds of things, and I want you to look back at me, and talk with me. That is not a lot to want. It is a person's right. To give and get love—not mother-and-child love, but the kind two adults share? You remember how happy I was, swimming in the sea in front of your house? You remember how happy we, you and me, were?"

Plaintively he responds, "But don't you see? We can't even go back there now. I spent yesterday with Piyari. She said enough for me to know that if there is a hint of an idea that you are alive, the first place you will be looked for is Elderberry Bay. That side of the world is out of the question."

"Well, that was clear to me from the start."

She stands up first, covers her head in a scarf, and then tops that with a straw hat. Even so, if it were not immediately evident that she is Rose Bihar, the quality and contemporary pattern of the fabric of the scarf and the stylishness of the hat she wears would have drawn attention had there been anyone else on the beach to notice. She holds out her hand for his and helps him up.

He walks beside her, stunned, back up the beach.

Uncle Mako began making the pirogue safe and seaworthy from the time Rose stepped out of the sea in front of their house several days ago. He has relished abetting in adventure that he had never managed to arrange for himself. If Tante Eugenie had agreed, he confided earlier to Rose, he already would have used the pirogue, and all the hope he could have mustered for himself, and he would have gone in search of Africa. But the way things had been going in the country these days, politically, that is, he had no more need for the pirogue. Here was a woman who was ready, he said to Rose, joking that it was too bad he wasn't a younger man, and nothing was going to stop him from now giving that same pirogue to her and his favorite grandson.

Tante Eugenie is not as happy as she makes them believe she is. She thinks that a man who is used to waiting—if and when the time and the thing he has long been waiting for were to arrive—must use muscles in his brain and heart, muscles so long dormant that they would not easily be found. She frets, albeit quietly. Her Harry St. George is about to get into a boat, to travel open waters with the intention of reaching not Africa but Honduras. A day has not passed that she does not recall some morsel of it: the nights and days keeping watch with Dolly, they and the wives of the other men awaiting the return of Seudath's boat, and then waiting for parts of the boat, of the men's clothing, of their bodies to be washed ashore, if only to confirm and put to rest what they already knew.

For now they remain inside the house, Harry and Rose well away from the window and door, and they eat: fish, string beans, rice, and peas. Uncle Mako jokes with Rose that he and Tante Eugenie are Harry's love counselors. That anytime Harry has a lady-related situation, he lands up there for them to help him out. Tante Eugenie, frying several days' worth of bakes and stuffing them with dried pork hocks, jerk chicken, cheese, and jam fillings, sucks her teeth and asks Uncle Mako if he is trying to cause trouble bringing up Cynthia's memory in front of Rose. To humor Uncle Mako, Rose feigns curiosity and jealousy and says that at least now, out on the quiet sea, she and Harry have lots to talk about. It surprises Harry that they have remembered Cynthia, and by her name, too. Clearly it pleases them to be involved in his life at crucial times. Tante Eugenie's lips are pursed as she makes up packages of food and numbers them, so that they will be consumed according to order of perishability.

When it is dark enough, and likely that the few remaining residents of Raleigh are at least indoors if not asleep, Uncle Mako and Harry, out of the dry sandpit in which it was hidden, pull the boat quietly along wood-plank tracks. Harry climbs in, and Uncle Mako hands him bottles of water that Tante Eugenie has been discreetly filling at the standpipe several days in a row, a car tire, and a thick coil of heavy rope. Harry peers into the cabin, so low that one can enter it only by crouching, to see a mattress, a thin blanket, and next to the mattress, a bundle hidden under a large canvas tarpaulin. Curious, he lifts the tarp to find a bottle of rum and six jelly coconuts, two life jackets, and a pail. A flour sack he opens contains five rolls of toilet paper, a flashlight, a package of candles and matches, and a compass that not only gives north-south-east-west directions but also shows the position of the stars throughout the year. He is speechless; his future has been planned, without his knowledge, to the detail.

Back inside the house, Uncle Mako hands Rose rolled navigation charts. He explains to Harry that Rose, before she "drowned," had made contact with a man who fixed up documents to help people leave the island and enter a foreign country without the intervention of Immigration. Harry has the odd sensation of watching himself descend into a deep whirlpool. He considers Rose. The Rose he once knew and would have done everything for has turned into a confident, take-charge kind of woman. She feels foreign to him. Uncle Mako is telling him that the man has arranged passage for them to Honduras in Central America. The man came to the house some nights ago, Uncle Mako is recounting, and showed Rose how to read the maps using the compass in the day and the sky at night. She should, with maps, compass, and the blessings of a star-studded sky, be able to guide them on the three-day journey to a cove on a small uninhabited island. There they must drop anchor and wait.

Abruptly Uncle Mako jerks his chin in the direction of Rose and interjects proudly, "Don't make joke with this one, you hear, she is a bright-bright lady." Harry remembers his own mother, recalling how quickly and unexpectedly she took up Mr. Persad's business.

On the third day, continues Uncle Mako, weather and God above permitting, a shrimp trawler will meet and deliver them to the mainland. They will get a ride inland.

They sit and wait in awkward quiet until Uncle Mako gets up and says wearily, "Is time." They gather at the pirogue, and Uncle Mako shows Harry how to start up the engine. The four of them shove the laden vessel to the water's edge. Uncle Mako, taking a good look at the sky, declares the weather—from where they stand—to be as good as one might hope for. They help Rose into the boat, and the three of them send it farther into the warm water. While Uncle Mako digs his feet into the sand and grips the boat with all of his strength, which is still considerable for a man of his age, Tante Eugenie holds Harry's face in her wet hands and kisses his lips. He wraps his arms around her and lets go only when she pushes him away, saying with an air of finality that they will not meet again but in heaven. Uncle Mako helps Harry hoist himself into the boat. His fears are all too immediately alerted by the boat lurching from side to side in that section of the sea where incoming and outgoing waves vie with each other. Harry reaches for the engine's cord and pulls until it catches several tries later. The boat swerves erratically from side to side. Rose dares not look at Harry. They are drenched in sea spray even before Harry can aim the boat directly at the breaking waves ahead. When he looks back to wave, Tante Eugenie and Uncle Mako are wading quickly toward the shore. The pirogue leaps over small waves, then medium-sized ones, and as it goes out farther, over larger ones that break just ahead of it, each time it lands with a hard firm slap.

Uncle Mako and Tante Eugenie, gripping each other's hands, stay on the damp nighttime beach well past the time the boat has vanished, waiting until they hear the engine's chug no more.

Air

He is holding her hand and leading her into the bright turquoise sea. The beach is littered with reclining sunbathers. The air sizzles with heat and buoys the wild, carefree sounds of families and friends playing volleyball on one section of the beach, cricket on another. Children in the shallow waters squeal with delight, and seagulls shriek overhead. She follows him easily. They wade into the warm water as far as the breakers, where they are cradled and the water reaches them comfortably at their waist. This far out, the shouting and laughter of people are reassuring. A ribbon of cold water lashes about his loins, but in a flash, it warms. They face each other, holding each other's hands. They are smiling with shyness at their hope that here they are finally free. She slips a hand out of his to lower a shoulder strap of her bathing suit and expose her breast to him. The water weighs on his hand as he tries to lift it so that he might touch her. Suddenly the sky darkens; the water has turned from turquoise to lifeless gray, and when he turns, he sees that a wave in the distance, several times their height, is blocking the light of the sun and is fast approaching them. He turns again, to look for the shore this time, intending to calculate its distance so that he might know whether they ought to swim swiftly to the safety of the shore or, not having enough time to do that, to dive beneath the base of the approaching wall of wave. But he sees instead yet another wave, equally high, coming from the opposite direction, and he realizes that he is unsure which direction the shore lies. It is abundantly clear that the distended bellies of both tidal waves, moving toward each other with equal grace and purpose, will clash at the precise place where she and he stand. He looks at the sky and then at her breast, at the dark purple nipple. He longs to touch it. The two waves, like opposing armies, advance more rapidly. There is time only to tell her to hold on to him, to instruct her to do only as he does. He waits until the uppermost curves of both waves, towering and stretching higher yet, form the two sides of a roof that is closing in above them. He shuts his eyes, tightens his grip on her hand, and draws her under the water to lie on the bottommost layer of the sea. With one hand, he grasps at the coarse, shifting sand, and miraculously he is braced. But the waves seem only to hover, to dance above them, refusing to slam together just yet, and he is running out of breath. She, too, so she tries to pull her hand out of his, intending to swim back to the surface. He suspects, however, that the instant she breaks the surface will be the very one when the waves collide, and they, split apart, will be pulverized.

He holds her tightly there, and interminable minutes later, the ocean begins to heave, to sway back and forth and sideways. He opens his eyes, but in the swirl of sand and salt, he is unable to see her, so he grips her hand, perhaps too tightly, but he will not risk losing hold of her. He opens his mouth to whisper to her, his words pushing through and against the water, telling her to cling to the ground, to lay her stomach flat against it, to press her face to the sand. When he has finished speaking to her, his mouth is full of the taste of salt and the grit of sand, and his eyes sting. He knows beyond any doubt that if she does precisely as he tells her, they will survive. Then there is silence. A cold hard silence, and it all begins. There is a tremendous sway of water, followed by insistent thrusting and pushing. The surges and upheavals threaten to dislodge and rip them off the floor. Long strands of uprooted seaweed wash by them, brush against them, and wrap fronds menacingly about their legs and stomachs, but they concentrate on holding on to the ground, and so manage to remain firmly planted there.

Several minutes pass, and finally the weeds, salt, and sand have settled and the water has stilled about them. Hesitantly they raise themselves and find that the sea is calm again, that the sun shines as brazenly as before, and the sounds of the people continue, as if uninterrupted, and they, he and she, have broken the water's surface.

ACKNOWLEDGMENTS

The writing of this novel occurred in a variety of landscapes. I began working on it in Vancouver. I would like to thank Margaret Watts and Kelsey Gerbrandt for gallivanting with me as I mapped out Harry's adult world in the inspiring terrain of the Sea to Sky Highway.

Acknowledgment is due to the Department of Foreign Affairs and International Trade in Canada and to the Canadian High Commission in Australia for generously affording me the privilege of a residency to work on this book at the Varuna Writers' House in the Blue Mountains.

As part of its Visiting Scholars Program, I worked on the manuscript at Mills College in California and am grateful to Edna Mitchell, then head of the Women's Leadership Institute, for inviting me. I am also happily indebted to Carol Flake, a fellow scholar at Mills College, who exercised leadership in tomfoolery during arduous wine-tasting research conducted in various valleys of California.

The manuscript began to take shape during the year I spent in Edmonton as writer-in-residence at the University of Alberta. I wish to acknowledge Doug Barbour, in charge of the program there, for providing that invaluable space and time. Kris Calhoun and the office staff of the English department made possible and smooth the concentrated effort needed at that stage of the writing.

My dear friends Isabel Hoving, Gamal Abdel-Shehid, Brenda Middagh, Ted Bishop, and my brother-in-law Shekhar Mahabir read various drafts of the manuscript, offering brilliant insights and critiques, and conversation to match about the process and nature of fiction writing. Many thanks to you all.

As the reality of a book finally loomed, my confidence often waned. Aline Brault's encouragingly firm grasp of my intent, coupled with astute readings of the manuscript, reminded me of the how and the what, of my love for language and stories. Her perennial enthusiasm spurred me on to the finish. Deepest thanks, Aline.

I am fortunate to have had this work edited by Grove/Atlantic's Elisabeth Schmitz, who instantly understood and, from start to finish, supported my larger vision. I would also like to thank Morgan Entrekin at Grove/Atlantic, and Ellen Seligman and Jennifer Lambert at McClelland & Stewart.

Finally, a most special and very loud thank-you is due to my trusted agent, Maria Massie of Lippincott Massie McQuilkin.